Mythology

Fascinating Chinese Myths, Legends, Folklore, and History

By Sally Stephens

If you like my book, please leave a review. I would appreciate it. Thank you!

Chinese Mythology

Gods, Goddesses, Monkeys, Eternal Beings, and More

By Sally Stephens

If you like my book, please leave a review. I would appreciate it. Thank you!

Table of Contents

Chapter 1: The Sociology of the Chinese *6*
Chapter 2: Inorganic Environment *9*
Chapter 3: Sociological Environment *11*
Chapter 4: The Government *15*
Chapter 5: Institutions in Society *18*
Chapter 6: Spirits and Habits *24*
Chapter 7: Background of the Mythology *32*
Chapter 8: Several Myths *41*
Chapter 9: The 5 Elements *44*
Chapter 10: More about the Gods of China *48*
Chapter 11: Information about Buddhism in China *61*
Chapter 12: The 3 Pure Ones *64*
Chapter 13: The First Taoist Pope *72*

Chapter 1: The Sociology of the Chinese

In spite of much research and conjecture, the beginning of the Chinese people remains undetermined. We do not know who they were nor whence they came. Such proof as there is points to their immigration from elsewhere; the Chinese themselves have a tradition of a Western beginning. The first picture we have of their actual history shows us, not a people acting just as if long settled in a land which was their home and that of their predecessors, but an alien race combating with wild beasts, clearing dense forests, and driving back the aboriginal occupants.

Setting aside several theories (including the one that the Chinese are autochthonous and their society indigenous) now concerned by the best authorities as untenable, the looks into of sinologists seem to show an origin (1) in early Akkadia; or (2) in Khotan, the Tarim valley (normally what is now referred to as Eastern Turkestan), or the K'un- lun Mountains (concerning which more presently). The 2nd hypothesis may relate only to a layover of longer or much shorter period en route from Akkadia to the supreme settlement in China, particularly since the Khotan society has been revealed to have been imported from the Punjab in the 3rd century B.C. The fact that some bad mistakes have been made relating to the recognitions of early Chinese rulers with Babylonian kings, and of the Chinese po-hsing (Cantonese bak-sing) 'people' with the Bak Sing or Bak tribes, doesn't exclude the possibility of an Akkadian origin. But in either case the immigration into China was most likely gradual, and may have taken the route from Western or Main Asia direct to the banks of the Yellow River, or may potentially have followed that to the south-east through Burma and then to the north-east through what is now China-- the settlement of the latter country having actually thus spread from south-west to north-east, or in a north-easterly direction along the Yangtzŭ River, and so north, instead of, as is normally supposed, from north to south.

Southern Origin Improbable

However this latter path would present tons of difficulties; it would seem to have been put forward simply as ancillary to the theory that the Chinese come from the Indo-Chinese peninsula. This theory is based upon the presumptions that the ancient Chinese ideograms include representations of tropical animals and plants; that the oldest and purest forms of the language are found in the south; and that the Chinese and the Indo-Chinese groups of languages are both tonal. However all of these truths or supposed facts are as quickly or better represented by the supposition that the Chinese shown up from the north or north-west in succeeding waves of migration, the later arrivals pushing the earlier further and further toward the south, so that the oldest and purest types of Chinese would be found just where they are, the tonal languages of the Indo-Chinese peninsula remaining in that case regarded as the languages of the vanguard of the migration. Also, the ideograms referred to represent animals and plants of the temperate zone instead of the tropics, but even if it could be revealed, which it cannot, that these animals and plants now belong specifically to the tropics, that would be no evidence of the tropical beginning of the Chinese, for in the earliest times the environment of North China was much milder than it is now, and animals like tigers and elephants existed in the thick jungles which are later found only in more southern latitudes.

Growth of Races from North to South

The theory of a southern origin (to which an additional serious objection will be stated currently) implies a steady seepage of Chinese immigrants through South or Mid-China (as above suggested) toward the north, but there is little doubt that the movement of the races has been from north to south and not vice versa. In what are now the provinces of Western Kansu and Ssŭch' uan there lived a people associated to the Chinese (as proved by the research study of Indo-Chinese comparative philology) who moved into the present area of Tibet and are known as Tibetans; in what is now the province of Yünnan were the Shan or Ai-lao (modern Laos), who, forced by Mongol intrusions, emigrated to the peninsula in the south and became the Siamese; and in Indo-China, unrelated to the Chinese, were the Annamese, Khmer, Mon, Khasi, Colarains (whose residues are dispersed over the hill tracts of Central India), and other people, extending in prehistoric times into Southern China, but consequently driven back by the growth of the Chinese in that direction.

Arrival of the Chinese in China

Taking into account all the existing proof, the objections to all other theories of the origin of the Chinese appear to be greater than any yet raised to the theory that immigrants from the Tarim valley or beyond (i.e. from Elam or Akkadia, either direct or via Eastern Turkestan) struck the banks of the Yellow River in their eastward journey and followed its course till they reached the localities where we first find them settled, namely, in the region covered by parts of the three modern-day provinces of Shansi, Shensi, and Honan where their frontiers join. They were then (about 2500 or 3000 B.C.) in a reasonably sophisticated state of civilization. The nation east and south of the district was occupied by aboriginal people, with whom the Chinese fought, as they did with the wild animals and the dense vegetation, but with whom they also commingled and intermarried, and among whom they planted groups as centres from which to spread their culture.

The K'un- lun Mountains

With with reference to the K'un- lun Mountains, designated in Chinese mythology as the abode of the gods-- the ancestors of the Chinese race-- it needs to be kept in mind that these are determined not with the range dividing Tibet from Chinese Turkestan, but with the Hindu Kush. That brings us somewhat nearer to Babylon, and the obvious merging of the 2 theories, the Central Asian and the Western Asian, would appear to point to a possible resolution of the problem. Nü Kua, among the alleged creators of human beings, and Nü and Kua, the very first two human entities (according to a variation of the legend), are put in the K'un- lun Mountains. That looks hopeful. Unfortunately, the K'un- lun legend is shown to be of Taoist beginning. K'un- lun is the main mountain of the world, and 3000 miles in height. There is the fountain of immortality, and thence flow the four great rivers of the world. In other words, it is the Sumêru of Hindu folklore transplanted into Chinese legend, and for our present purpose without historic value.

It would take up way too much space to explain of this fascinating problem of the origin of the Chinese and their society, the cultural connexions or similarities of China and Western Asia in pre-Babylonian times, the origin of the two distinct culture-areas so marked throughout the greater part of Chinese history, etc., and it will be sufficient for our present purpose to mention the conclusion to which the evidence points.

Provisionary Conclusion

Pending the discovery of definitive evidence, the following provisional conclusion has much to advise it-- particularly, that the ancestors of the Chinese people came from the west, from Akkadia or Elam, or from Khotan, or (more most likely) from Akkadia or Elam via Khotan, as one wanderer or pastoral tribe or group of nomad or pastoral tribes, or as succeeding waves of immigrants, reached what is now China Appropriate at its north-west corner, settled round the elbow of the Yellow River, spread north-eastward, eastward, and southward, conquering, absorbing, or pushing right before them the aborigines into what is now South and South-west China. These aboriginal races, who represent a wave or waves of neolithic immigrants from Western Asia earlier than the relatively high-headed immigrants into North China (who came about the twenty-fifth or twenty-fourth century B.C.), and who have left so deep an impress on the Japanese, mixed and intermarried with the Chinese in the south, eventually producing the noticable differences, in physical, mental, and psychological qualities, in beliefs, ideas, languages, procedures, and products, from the Northern Chinese which are so obvious at the present day.

Chapter 2: Inorganic Environment

At the beginning of their recognized history the nation occupied by the Chinese was the comparatively little area above pointed out. It was then a tract of an irregular elongate shape, lying between latitude 34 ° and 40 ° N. and longitude 107 ° and 114 ° E. This area round the elbow of the Yellow River had a part of about 50,000 square miles, and was gradually extended to the sea-coast on the north-east as far as longitude 119 °, when its location was about doubled. It had a population of maybe a million, increasing with the growth to 2 million. This may be called infant China. Its duration (the Feudal Duration) was in the 2 thousand years between the twenty-fourth and third centuries B.C. During the first centuries of the Monarchical Duration, which lasted from 221 B.C. to A.D. 1912, it had expanded to the south to such an extent that it included all of the Eighteen Provinces constituting what is called China Proper of modern times, with the exception of a part of the west of Kansu and the greater parts of Ssŭch'uan and Yünnan. At the time of the Manchu conquest at the beginning of the seventeenth century A.D. it embraced all the territory lying between latitude 18 ° and 40 ° N. and longitude 98 ° and 122 ° E. (the Eighteen Provinces or China Correct), with the addition of the huge distant territories of Manchuria, Mongolia, Ili, Koko-nor, Tibet, and Corea, with suzerainty over Burma and Annam-- an area of more than 5,000,000 square miles, consisting of the 2,000,000 square miles covered by the Eighteen Provinces. Usually, this area is mountainous in the west, sloping gradually down toward the sea on the east. It contains 3 chief series of mountains and large alluvial plains in the north, east, and south. 3 great and about thirty large rivers intersect the nation, their numerous tributaries reaching every part of it.

As concerns geological features, the great alluvial plains rest upon granite, brand-new red sandstone, or limestone. In the north is found the peculiar loess formation, having its origin probably in the built up dust of ages blown from the Mongolian plateau. The passage from north to south is generally from the older to the more recent rocks; from east to west a comparable series is found, with some volcanic features in the west and south. Coal and iron are the chief minerals, gold, silver, copper, lead, tin, jade, and so on, being also mined.

The climate of the vast location is not consistent. In the north the winter season is long and rigorous, the summertime hot and dry, with a short rainy season in July and August; in the south the summer season is long, hot, and wet, the winter short. The mean temperature level is 50.3 ° F. and 70 ° F. in the north and south respectively. Typically, the thermometer is low for the latitude, though maybe it is more correct to say that the Gulf Stream raises the temperature level of the west coast of Europe above the average. The mean rainfall in the north is 16, in the south 70 inches, with variations in other parts. Tropical storms blow in the south between July and October.

The wild animals consist of the tiger, panther, leopard, bear, sable, otter, monkey, wolf, fox, twenty-seven or more species of ruminants, and many species of rodents. The rhinoceros, elephant, and tapir still exist in Yünnan. The domestic animals consist of the camel and the water-buffalo. There are about 700 species of birds, and innumerable species of fishes and insects.

Chapter 3: Sociological Environment

On their arrival in what is now called China the Chinese, as already noted, battled with the aboriginal tribes. The latter were gotten rid of, taken in, or driven south with the spread of Chinese rule. The Chinese "chosen the eyes of the land," and consequently the non-Chinese people now live in the unhealthy forests or marshes of the south, or in mountain areas tough of access, some even in trees (a voluntary, not compulsory big promotion), though several, just like the Dog Jung in Fukien, keep settlements like isles amongst the ruling race.

In the 3rd century B.C. started the hostile relations of the Chinese with the northern nomads, which continued throughout the majority of their history. During the very first six centuries A.D. there was intercourse with Rome, Parthia, Turkey, Mesopotamia, Ceylon, India, and Indochina, and in the seventh century with the Arabs. Europe was brought within the sociological environment by Christian tourists. From the tenth to the 13th century the north was occupied by Kitans and Nüchêns, and the entire Empire was under Mongol sway for eighty-eight years in the 13th and fourteenth centuries. Relations of a commercial and spiritual nature were held with neighbours during the following 4 hundred years. Routine diplomatic sexual intercourse with Western countries was developed as a result of a series of wars in the eighteenth and nineteenth centuries. Till recently the country held aloof from alliances and was typically averse to foreign sexual intercourse. From 1537 onward, as a follow up of war or treaty, concessions, settlements, and so on, were gotten by foreign Powers. China has now lost some of her border countries and large adjacent islands, the army and business pressure of Western nations and Japan having actually taken the place of the military pressure of the Tartars already referred to. The great issue for her, a farming nation, is how to find methods and the military spirit to preserve her integrity, the further violation of which could not but be concerned by the student of sociological history as a great tragedy and a world-wide catastrophe.

Physical, Psychological, and Intellectual Characters
The physical characters of the Chinese are too well known to need comprehensive recital. The original immigrants into North China all came from blond races, but the modern Chinese have little left of the immigrant stock. The oblique, almond-shaped eyes, with black iris and the orbits far apart, have a vertical fold of skin over the inner canthus, concealing a part of the iris, a peculiarity identifying the eastern races of Asia from all other families of man. The stature and weight of brain are generally beneath the average. The hair is black, coarse, and round; the beard scanty or missing. The colour of the skin is darker in the south than in the north.

Mentally the Chinese are sober, industrious, of remarkable endurance, grateful, considerate, and ceremonious, with a high sense of mercantile honour, but timorous, vicious, unsympathetic, mendacious, and libidinous.

Intellectually they were till recently, and to a large degree still are, non-progressive, in chains to harmony and system in culture, imitative, unimaginative, torpid, indirect, suspicious, and superstitious.

The character is being customized by intercourse with other tribes of the earth and by the strong force of physical, intellectual, and moral education.

Marital Relationship in Early Times

Certain parts of the marital relationship ceremonial of China as now existing suggest that the original form of marital relationship was by capture-- of which, certainly, there is proof in the classical Book of Odes. But a routine form of marital relationship (in reality an agreement of sale) is revealed to have existed in the earliest historical times. The form was not monogamous, though it appears soon to have assumed that of a qualified monogamy including one spouse and one or more courtesans, the number of the latter being as a rule restricted only by the methods of the husband. The higher the rank the larger was the number of courtesans and handmaids in addition to the marriage partner proper, the palaces of the kings and princes including some hundreds of them. This form it has kept to the present day, though associations now exist for the abolition of concubinage. In early times, along with throughout the whole of Chinese history, concubinage was in fact universal, and there is some evidence also of polyandry (which, however, cannot have prevailed to any great level). The age for marriage was twenty for the man and fifteen for the girl, celibacy after thirty and twenty respectively being formally discouraged. In the province of Shantung it was usual for the wives to be older than their husbands. The mother's and father's consent to the betrothal was sought through the intervention of a matchmaker, the proposal coming from with the parents, and the wishes of the future bride and bridegroom not being considered. The conclusion of the marital relationship was the progress of the bride-to-be from the home of her parents to that of the bridegroom, where after numerous events she and he worshipped his ancestors together, the praise amounting to little bit more than a statement of the union to the ancestral spirits. After a short layover with her spouse the bride-to-be revisited her father and mother, and the marriage was not considered as finally consummated till after this visit had taken place.

The status of women was low, and the power of the spouse great-- so great that he could kill his wife with impunity. Divorce was common, and all in favour of the husband, who, while he could not be separated by her, could put his spouse away for disobedience or perhaps for loquaciousness. A widower remarried immediately, but rejection to remarry by a widow was esteemed an act of chastity. She often mutilated herself or perhaps committed suicide to stop remarriage, and was posthumously honoured for doing so. Being her partner's as much in the Otherworld as in this, remarriage would engage of the character of unchastity and insubordination; the argument, obviously, not using to the case of the spouse, who by remarriage simply adds another member to his clan without infringing on anybody's rights.

Marriage in Monarchical and Republican Periods

The marital system of the early classical times, of which the above were the basics, changed but little bit throughout the long period of monarchical rule lasting from 221 B.C. to A.D. 1912. The principal item, as before, was to protect a successor to sacrifice to the spirits of departed progenitors. Marriage was elective, but old bachelors and old maids were really limited. The courtesans went through the spouse, who was thought about to be the mother of their children in addition to her own. Her status, though, was not considerably superior. Implicit obedience was exacted from her. She could not have property, but could not be hired for prostitution. The latter vice was common, in spite of the early age at which marriage took place and in spite of the system of concubinage-- which is after all but a legalized transfer of prostitutional cohabitation to the domestic circle.

Since the facility of the Republic in 1912 the 'landslide' in the direction of Western progress has had its influence also on the domestic organizations. However while the essentials of the marriage agreement stay virtually the same as before, the most conspicuous changes have been in the accompanying ceremonial-- now in some cases rather foreign, but in a large, maybe the best, number of cases that repellent thing, half foreign, half Chinese; as, for instance, when the procession, otherwise native, includes foreign glass-panelled carriages, or the bridegroom wears a 'bowler' or top-hat with his Chinese dress-- and in the greater freedom permitted to women, who are seen out of doors far more than previously, sit at table with their spouses, attend public functions and suppers, gown mainly in foreign fashion, and play tennis and other games, instead of being detainees of the 'inner apartment or condo' and home drudges bit better than servants.

One unforeseen result of the increased flexibility is definitely impressive, and is one not very likely to have been predicted by the most far-sighted sociologist. A lot of the 'progressive' Chinese, now that it is the fashion for Chinese wives to be seen in public with their spouses, finding the ignorant, gauche, small-footed household drudge unable to take on the smarter foreign-educated wives of their neighbours, have actually repudiated them and taken unto themselves spouses whom they can show in public without 'loss of face'! It is, though, only fair to add that the overall number of these cases, however by no methods inconsiderable, appears to be proportionately small.

Parents and Children

As was the power of the partner over the marriage partner, so was that of the father over his kids. Infanticide (due chiefly to hardship, and varying with it) was frequent, specifically in the case of female children, who were but a little esteemed; the practice dominating extensively in 3 or four provinces, less thoroughly in other ones, and being virtually absent in a large number. Beyond the simple fact that some charges were enacted against it by the Emperor Ch' ien Lung (A.D. 1736-- 96), and that by statute it was a capital offence to murder kids in order to use parts of their bodies for medicine, it was not legally restricted. When the abuse ended up being too scandalous in any district pronouncements condemning it would be released by the local authorities. A man might, by purchase and agreement, adopt an individual as son, daughter, or grandchild, such person acquiring therefore all the rights of a daughter or son. Descent, both of real and personal property, was to all the sons of partners and courtesans as joint heirs, regardless of seniority. Bastards received half shares. Estates were not divisible by the kids throughout the lifetime of their mom and dad or grandparents.

The head of the family being but the life-renter of the family property, bound by set rules, wills were superfluous, and were used only where the customary respect for the parents gave them a voice in arranging the specifics of the succession. For this purpose spoken or written guidelines were typically given.

In the absence of the father, the male relatives of the same surname assumed the protectorship of the young. The protector exercised full authority and took pleasure in the surplus revenues of his ward's estate, but may not alienate the property.

There are many instances in Chinese history of severe devotion of kids to parents taking the form of self-wounding and even of suicide in the hope of curing father's and mother's diseases or saving their lives.

Political History

The country populated by the Chinese on their arrival from the West was, as we saw, the district where the modern-day provinces of Shansi, Shensi, and Honan join. This they extended in an easterly direction to the coasts of the Gulf of Chihli-- a stretch of area about 600 miles long by 300 broad. The population, as already specified, was between one and 2 millions. During the very first two 1,000 years of their recognized history the boundaries of this area were not significantly bigger, but beyond the more or less undefined borderland to the south were chou or people, nuclei of Chinese population, which continually increased in size through conquest of the neighbouring territory. In 221 B.C. all the feudal states into which this territory had been shelled out, and which combated with one another, were subjugated and absorbed by the state of Ch'in, which in that year set up the monarchical form of federal government-- the form which obtained in China for the next twenty-one centuries.

Though the origin of the name 'China' has not yet been finally determined, the best authorities regard it as stemmed from the name of the feudal state of Ch'in.

Under this short-lived dynasty of Ch'in and the famous Han dynasty (221 B.C. to A.D. 221) which followed it, the Empire broadened until it embraced nearly all the territory now known as China Proper (the Eighteen Provinces of Manchu times). To these were added in order between 194 B.C. and A.D. 1414: Corea, Sinkiang (the New Area or Eastern Turkestan), Manchuria, Formosa, Tibet, and Mongolia-- Formosa and Corea being annexed by Japan in 1895 and 1910 respectively. Numerous other extra-China nations and islands, gotten and lost throughout the long course of Chinese history (at one time, from 73 to 48 B.C., "all Asia from Japan to the Caspian Sea was tributary to the Middle Kingdom," i.e. China), it is not necessary to point out here. Throughout the Southern Sung dynasty (1127-- 1280) the Tartars owned the northern half of China, as far down as the Yangtzŭ River, and in the Yüan dynasty (1280-- 1368) they dominated the entire country. During the duration 1644-- 1912 it was in the belongings of the Manchus. At present the five chief component tribes of China are represented in the striped nationwide flag (from the leading downward) by red (Manchus), yellow (Chinese), blue (Mongolians), white (Mohammedans), and black (Tibetans). This flag was adopted on the establishment of the Republic in 1912, and supplanted the triangular Dragon flag previously in use. By this time the population-- which had varied considerably at different periods owing to war, scarcity, and plague-- had increased to about 400,000,000.

Chapter 4: The Government

The general department of the nation was into the King and the People, The former was considered as selected by the will of Heaven and as the moms and dad of the latter. Besides being king, he was also law-giver, commander-in-chief of the armies, high priest, and master of ceremonies. The people were separated into four classes: (1) Shih, Officers (later Scholars), including Ch' ên, Authorities (a few of whom were ennobled), and Shên Shih, Gentry; (2) Nung, Agriculturists; (3) Kung, Artisans; and (4) Shang, Merchants.

For administrative purposes there were at the seat of central government (which, initially at P'ing- yang-- in modern Shansi-- was moved eleven times throughout the Feudal Period, and was finally at Yin) ministers, or ministers and a hierarchy of officials, the country being split into provinces, varying in number from nine in the earliest times to thirty-six under the First Emperor, 221 B.C., and finally twenty-two at the present day. In the beginning these provinces included states, which were models of the central state, the ruler's 'Middle Kingdom.' The provincial administration was in the hands of twelve Pastors or Lord-Lieutenants. They were the chiefs of all the nobles in a province. Civil and army offices were not separated. The feudal lords or princes of states typically lived at the king's court, officers of that court being also sent forth as princes of states. The king was the source of legislation and administered justice. The princes in their several states had the power of rewards and punishments. Profits was stemmed from a tithe on the land, from the income of artisans, merchants, anglers, foresters, and from the homage brought by savage tribes.

The general structure and concepts of the system of administration stayed the same, with few variations, down to the end of the Monarchical Period in 1912. At the end of that period we find the emperor still thought about as of divine descent, still the head of the civil, legislative, army, ecclesiastical, and ritualistic administration, with the nation still divided into the same 4 classes. The chief ministries at the capital, Peking, could most of the times trace their descent from their models of feudal times, and the primary provincial administrative officials-- the Governor-General or Viceroy, governor, provincial treasurer, judge, etc.-- had similarly a pedigree running back to offices then existing-- a continuous duration of adherence to type which is most likely distinct.

Appointment to office was at initially by selection, followed by an evaluation to check efficiency; later was introduced the system of public competitive literary assessments for office, fully organized in the seventeenth century, and eliminated in 1903, when official positions were tossed open to the graduates of colleges established on a contemporary basis.

In 1912, on the defeat of the Manchu monarchy, China became a republic, with an elected President, and a Parliament consisting of a Senate and House of Representatives. The numerous government departments were rearranged on Western lines, and a ton of new workplaces instituted. Approximately the present year the Law of the Constitution, owing to political dissension between the North and the South, has not been put into force.

Laws

Chinese law, like primitive law usually, was not set up so as to make sure justice between man and man; its item was to impose subordination of the ruled to the ruler. The laws were punitive and vindictive rather than reformatory or restorative, criminal rather than civil. Penalties were harsh: branding, cutting off the nose, the legs at the knees, castration, and death, the latter not necessarily, or certainly ordinarily, for taking life. They included in some cases penalty of the family, the clan, and the neighbours of the offender. The lex talionis was in full blast.

However, in spite of the extreme nature of the punishments, possibly adapted, more or less, to a harsh state of society, though the "appropriate end of punishments"-- to "make an end of penalizing"-- was really missed, the Chinese developed a series of exceptional legal codes. This series began with the revision of King Mu's Punishments in 950 B.C., the first routine code being issued in 650 B.C., and ended with the popular Ta Ch'ing lü li (Laws and Statutes of the Great Ch'ing Dynasty), provided in A.D. 1647. Of these codes the great prototype was the Law Traditional prepared by Li K'uei (Li K'uei fa ching), a statesman in the service of the first ruler of the Wei State, in the 4th century B.C. The Ta Ch'ing lü li has been highly praised by proficient judges. Originally it approved only 2 types of penalty, death and flogging, but others were in use, and the barbarous ling ch'ih, 'lingering death' or 'slicing to pieces,' developed about A.D. 1000 and abolished in 1905, was inflicted for high treason, parricide, on women who killed their husbands, and murderers of 3 individuals of one family. In fact, until some first-hand knowledge of Western systems and process was obtained, the vindictive as opposed to the reformatory idea of penalties continued to get in China down to rather recent years, and has not yet totally vanished. Though the crueller kinds of punishment had been legally abolished, they continued to be used in tons of parts. Having actually been joint judge at Chinese trials at which, in spite of my protests, detainees were hung up by their thumbs and made to kneel on chains to extort confession (without which no implicated person could be penalized), I can testify that the real meaning of the "proper end of punishments" ran out participated in the Chinese mind at the close of the monarchical régime than it had 4000 years in the past.

As a result of the reform movement into which China was pushed as an alternative to foreign domination towards the end of the Manchu Period, but mainly owing to the bait held out by Western Powers, that extraterritoriality would be eliminated when China had reformed her judicial system, a brand-new Provisional Criminal Code was published. It replaced death by hanging or strangulation for decapitation, and jail time for various lengths of time for bambooing. It was adopted in large procedure by the Republican régime and is the primary legal instrument in usage at the present time. But close evaluation reveals the fact that it is almost a precise copy of the Japanese penal code, which in turn was modelled upon that of Germany. It is, in fact, a Western code imitated, and as it stands is rather out of harmony with present conditions in China. It will have to be customized and modified to be an ideal, just, and practicable nationwide legal instrument for the Chinese people. Additionally, it is often overridden in a high-handed way by the authorities, who often keep a person acquitted by the

Courts of Justice in custody till they have 'squeezed' him of all they can hope to get out of him. And it is notable that, though arrangement was made in the Draft Code for trial by jury, this arrangement never entered into influence; and the slavish replica of alien approaches is revealed by the strangely enough irregular reason given-- that "the fact that jury trials have been eliminated in Japan is a sign of the inadvisability of transplanting this Western institution into China!"

City government

The central administration being a remote network of officialdom, there was hardly any room for local government apart from it. We find it only in the village elder and those related to him, who took up what federal government was necessary where the jurisdiction of the system of the central administration-- the district magistracy-- stopped, or at least did not issue itself in meddling much.

Chapter 5: Institutions in Society

Armed force System

The peace-loving farming settlers in early China had at first no army. When occasion emerged, all the armers exchanged their ploughshares for swords and bows and arrows and went forth to combat. In the periods between the harvests, when the fields were clear, they held manoeuvres and practised the arts of warfare. The king, who had his Six Armies, under the 6 High Nobles, forming the royal army force, led the troops face to face, accompanied by the spirit-tablets of his forefathers and of the gods of the land and grain. Chariots, drawn by 4 horses and consisting of soldiers armed with spears and javelins and archers, were much in usage. A 1,000 chariots were the regular force. Warriors wore buskins on their legs and were often gagged in order to stop the alarm being provided to the enemy. In action the chariots occupied the center, the bowmen the left, the spearmen the right flank. Elephants were in some cases used in attack. Spy-kites, signal-flags, hook-ladders, horns, cymbals, drums, and beacon-fires were in usage. The ears of the vanquished were brought to the king, quarter being rarely if ever given.

After the establishment of absolute monarchical government standing armies ended up being the rule. Military science was taught, and soldiers often trained for seven years. Chariots with upper floors or spy-towers were used for battling in narrow defiles, and hollow squares were formed of combined chariots, infantry, and dragoons. The weakness of disunion of forces was well understood. In the 6th century A.D. the massed soldiers numbered about a million and a quarter. In A.D. 627 there was an efficient standing army of 900,000 men, the term of service being from the ages of twenty to sixty. Throughout the Mongol dynasty (1280-- 1368) there was a navy of 5000 ships manned by 70,000 trained fighters. The Mongols totally revolutionized methods and enhanced on all the army knowledge of the time. In 1614 the Manchu 'Eight Banners,' composed of Manchus, Mongolians, and Chinese, were instituted. The provincial forces, designated the Army of the Green Standard, were divided into land forces and marine forces, superseded on active duty by 'braves' (yung), or irregulars, enlisted and discharged according to scenarios. After the war with Japan in 1894 reforms were seriously undertaken, with the result that the army has now been modernized in gown, weapons, techniques, etc., and is by no means a negligible quantity on the planet's battling forces. A modern navy is also being obtained by structure and purchase. For a lot of centuries the soldier, being, like the priest, ineffective, was related to with disdain, and now that his indispensableness for defensive purposes is recognized he needs to fight not only any actual opponent who might attack him, but those far subtler forces from over the sea which seem likely to acquire supremacy in his army councils, if not actual control of his whole army system. It is, in my view, the duty of Western countries to take steps before it is too late to prevent this great disaster.

Ecclesiastical Institutions

The dancing and chanting exorcists called wu were the first Chinese priests, with temples consisting of gods worshipped and sacrificed to, but there was no special sacerdotal class. Worship of Paradise could only be performed by the king or emperor. Ecclesiastical and political functions were not entirely separated. The king was pontifex maximus, the nobles, statesmen, and civil and military officers served as priests, the ranks being similar to those of the political hierarchy. Praise took place in the 'Hall of Light,' which was also a palace and audience and council chamber. Sacrifices were offered to Heaven, the hills and rivers, forefathers, and all the spirits. Dancing held a conspicuous spot in worship. Idols are spoken of in the earliest times.

Of course, each faith, as it formed itself out of the original ancestor-worship, had its own spiritual places, functionaries, observances, ritualistic. Hence, at the State praise of Paradise, Nature, and so on, there were the 'Great,' 'Medium,' and 'Inferior' sacrifices, including animals, silk, grain, jade, and so on. Panegyrics were sung, and robes of proper colour worn. In spring, summer season, fall, and winter there were the seasonal sacrifices at the suitable altars. Taoism and Buddhism had their temples, monasteries, priests, sacrifices, and routine; and there were village and wayside temples and shrines to forefathers, the gods of thunder, rain, wind, grain, farming, and many others. Now encouraged, now tolerated, now persecuted, the ecclesiastical personnel and structure of Taoism and Buddhism endured into contemporary times, when we find complete plans of ecclesiastical gradations of rank and authority implanted upon these two priestly hierarchies, and their temples, priests, etc., satisfying typically, with worship of forefathers, State or official (Confucianism) and personal or informal, and the observance of various annual celebrations, like 'All Souls' Day' for roaming and starving ghosts, the spiritual requirements of the people as the 'Three Faiths' (San Chiao). The emperor, as high priest, took the duty for calamities, and so on, making confession to Paradise and hoping that as a punishment the wicked be diverted from the people to his own person. Statesmen, nobles, and authorities discharged, as already kept in mind, priestly functions in connexion with the State faith in addition to their normal duties. As a rule, priests correct, frowned upon as non-producers, were hired from the lower classes, were celibate, unintellectual, idle, and immoral. There was absolutely nothing, even in the fancy ceremonies on unique occasions in the Buddhist temples, which could be likened to what is referred to as 'public worship' and 'common prayer' in the West. Praise had for its sole object either the attainment of some great or the avoidance of some evil.

Normally this represents the state of things under the Republican régime; the chief differences being greater overlook of ecclesiastical matters and the conversion of a great deal of temples into schools.

Professional Institutions

We read of doctors, blind musical artists, poets, instructors, prayer-makers, designers, scribes, painters, diviners, ceremonialists, orators, and other ones throughout the Feudal Duration, These professions were of ecclesiastical beginning, not yet entirely separated from the 'Church,' and both in earlier and later times not always or typically differentiated from one another. Hence the historiographers combined the duties of statesmen, scholars, authors, and generals. The professions of authors and instructors, musicians and poets, were united in someone. And so it continued to the present day. Priests release medical functions, poets still sing their verses. But skilled medical experts, though couple of, are to be found, as well as women physicians; there are veterinary cosmetic surgeons, musicians (mainly belonging to the poorest classes and usually blind), actors, instructors, attorneys, diviners, artists, letter-writers, and lots of others, men of letters being perhaps the most popular and most esteemed.

Accessory Institutions

A system of schools, academies, colleges, and universities gotten in towns, districts, departments, and principalities. The direction was divided into 'Main Learning' and 'Great Learning.' There were unique schools of dancing and music. Libraries and almshouses for old guys are discussed. Associations of academics for literary functions appear to have been many.

Whatever form and direction education might have taken, it became stereotyped at an early age by the roadway to office being made to lead through a knowledge of the classical writings of the age-old sages. It ended up being not only 'the thing' to be well versed in the phrases of Confucius, Mencius; and so on, and to be able to compose great essays on them including not a single mistakenly written character, but worthless for aspirants to office-- who constituted practically the whole of the literary class-- to acquire any other knowledge. So consumed was the national mind by this literary mania that even babies' spines were made to bend so as to produce when adult the 'academic stoop.' And from the simple fact that besides the academic class the remainder of the community included agriculturists, craftsmens, and merchants, whose knowledge was that of their fathers and grandpas, inculcated in the sons and grand sons as it had been in them, showing them how to continue in the exact same groove the calling to which Fate had assigned them, a departure from which would have been thought about 'unfilial'-- unless, naturally (as it extremely rarely did), it went the length of achieving through research study of the classics a location in the main class, and hence shedding eternal lustre on the family-- it will easily be seen that there was absolutely nothing to trigger education to be concerned with any but one or two of the subjects which are included by Western peoples under that classification. It ended up being at an early age, and remained for lots of centuries, a rote-learning of the elementary text-books, followed by a similar acquisition by heart of the texts of the works of Confucius and other classical authors. And so it remained till the abolition, in 1905, of the old competitive evaluation system, and the replacement of all that is included in the term 'modern education' at schools, colleges, and universities all over the nation, in which there is rapidly growing up a force that is regenerating the Chinese people, and will make itself felt throughout the entire world.

It is this keen and shrewd gratitude of the learned, and this desire for knowledge, which, disallowing the catastrophe of foreign domination, will make China, in the truest and best sense of the word, a great country, where, as in the United States of America, the rigid class status and undervaluation, if not disdaining, of knowledge which are showing so dreadful in England and other European countries will be kept away from, and the upper class of learning established in its place.

Besides educational institutions, we find organizations for poor relief, health centers, foundling healthcare facilities, orphan asylums, banking, insurance, and loan associations, visitors' clubs, mercantile corporations, anti-opium societies, co-operative burial societies, along with a lot of others, some mimicked from Western models.

Physical Mutilations

Compared with the practices found to exist among most primitive races, the mutilations the Chinese were in the practice of inflicting were but few. They flattened the skulls of their children by methods of stones, so as to cause them to taper at the top, and we have already seen what they did to their spinal columns; also the mutilations in warfare, and the penalties caused both within and without the law; and how filial kids and loyal spouses mutilated themselves for the sake of their mother and father and to prevent remarriage. Eunuchs, obviously, existed in great numbers. People bit, cut, or marked their arms to pledge oaths. However the practices which are more peculiarly related to the Chinese are the compressing of women's feet and the wearing of the line, misnamed 'pigtail.' The former is known to have been in force about A.D. 934, though it may have been introduced as early as 583. It did not, however, become strongly developed for more than a century. This 'very unpleasant mutilation,' started in infancy, illustrates the tyranny of style, for it is supposed to have arisen in the imitation by the women usually of the small feet of a royal courtesan appreciated by among the emperors from ten to fifteen centuries ago (the books vary regarding his identity). The second was a badge of bondage inflicted by the Manchus on the Chinese when they dominated China at the beginning of the seventeenth century. Discountenanced by governmental orders, both of these practices are now tending toward extinction, however, obviously, compressed feet and 'pigtails' are still to be seen in every town and village. Legally, the line was eliminated when the Chinese rid themselves of the Manchu yoke in 1912.

Funeral Rites

Not comprehending the real nature of death, the Chinese believed it was merely a state of suspended animation, in which the soul had couldn't go back to the body, though it may yet do so, even after long intervals. Subsequently they postponed burial, and fed the dead body, and went on to the house-tops and called aloud to the spirit to return. When at length they were convinced that the absent spirit could not be caused to return to the body, they put the latter in a coffin and buried it-- offering it, however, with all that it had found essential in this life (food, clothes, spouses, servants, and so on), which it would require also in the next (in their view rather a continuation of the present presence than the start of another)-- and, having inducted or persuaded the spirit to get in the 'soul-tablet' which accompanied the funeral procession (which took place the moment the tablet was 'dotted,' i.e. when the character wang, 'prince,' was become chu, 'lord'), carried it back home again, set it up in a shrine in the main hall, and fell down and worshipped it. Hence was the spirit propitiated, and as long as occasional offerings were not ignored the power for evil possessed by it would not be exerted against the making it through inmates of the home, whom it had so thoughtlessly deserted.

The latter grieved by yelling, wailing, marking their feet, and beating their boobs, renouncing (in the earliest times) even their outfits, residence, and valuables to the dead, getting rid of to mourning-sheds of clay, fasting, or eating only rice gruel, sleeping on straw with a clod for a pillow, and speaking only on subjects of death and burial. Office and public duties were resigned, and marital relationship, music, and separation from the clan restricted.

During the lapse of the long ages of monarchical rule funeral service rites became more fancy and splendid, but, though less rigid and ceremonious since the organization of the Republic, they have maintained their important character down to the present day.

Funeral ceremonial was more exacting than that connected with the majority of other observances, including those of marriage. Invitations or alerts were sent to good friends, and after receipt of these fu, on the numerous days selected therein, the visitor was obliged to send presents, just like money, paper horses, servants, and so on, and go and take part the lamentations of the hired mourners and attend at the prayers recited by the priests. Funeral etiquette could not be pu 'd, i.e. made good, if overlooked or disregarded at the right time, as it could in the case of the marriage ritualistic.

Rather than symmetrical public graveyards, as in the West, the Chinese cemeteries belong to the family or clan of the departed, and are normally lovely and serene places planted with trees and surrounded by creative walls enclosing the grave-mounds and huge tablets. The cemeteries themselves are the metonyms of the towns, and the graves of the houses. In the north particularly the tomb is really typically surmounted by a huge marble tortoise bearing the inscribed tablet, or what we call the gravestone, on its back. The tombs of the last 2 lines of emperors, the Ming and the Manchu, are magnificent structures, topped huge areas, and always creatively situated on hillsides facing natural or artificial lakes or seas. Contrary to the practice in Egypt, with the two exceptions above pointed out the dominating dynasties have always damaged the burial places of their predecessors. But for this savage vandalism, China would most likely possess the most spectacular assembly of royal burial places worldwide's records.

Laws of Customs

Throughout the entire course of their existence as a social aggregate the Chinese have pushed ritualistic observances to an extreme limitation. "Events," says the Li chi, the great classic of ceremonial uses, "are the best of all things by which men live." Ranks were distinguished by different headdresses, garments, badges, weapons, writing-tablets, number of attendants, carriages, horses, height of walls, etc. Daily as well as official life was regulated by minute observances. There were written codes embracing practically every attitude and act of inferiors towards superiors, of superiors towards inferiors, and of equates to towards equates to. Visits, types of address, and giving of presents had each their set of solutions, known and observed by each as strictly and regularly as each kid in China learned by heart and repeated aloud the three-word sentences of the elementary Trimetrical Timeless. But while the school text-book was extremely basic, ceremonial observances were exceptionally sophisticated. A Chinese was in this respect as much a slave to the living as in his funeral rites he was a servant to the dead. Only now, in the rush of 'modern-day progress,' is the doffing of the hat replacing the 'kowtow' (k'o-t'ou).

It is in this matter of ceremonial observances that the East and the West have misconstrued one another maybe more than in all other ones. Where rules of etiquette are not only different, but are diametrically opposed, there is every chance for misconception, if not estrangement. The points at problem in such questions as 'kowtowing' to the emperor and the worshipping of ancestors are normally known, but the Westerner, as a rule, is oblivious of the simple fact that if he wishes to conform to Chinese rules when in China (rather than to those Western customs which are in tons of cases regrettably taking their place) he should not, for example, take off his hat when entering a house or a temple, should not shake hands with his host, nor, if he wants to express approval, should he clap his hands. Clapping of hands in China (i.e. non-Europeanized China) is used to repel the sha ch'i, or deathly impact of evil spirits, and to clap the hands at the close of the remarks of a Chinese host (as I have seen prominent, well-meaning, but ill-guided guys of the West do) is comparable to disapproval, if not insult. Had our diplomatists been sociologists instead of only industrial representatives, more than one war may have been avoided.

Practices and Customs

At periods throughout the year the Chinese make holiday. Their public festivals begin with the celebration of the introduction of the new year. They let off innumerable firecrackers, and make much merrymaking in their homes, drinking and feasting, and visiting their good friends for some days. Accounts are squared, homes cleaned, fresh paper 'door-gods' pasted on the front doors, strips of red paper with characters suggesting happiness, wealth, good luck, durability, etc., stuck on the doorposts or the lintel, tables, and so on, covered with red cloth, and flowers and decorations displayed all over. Business is suspended, and the joviality, wearing new clothes, feasting, going to, offerings to gods and ancestors, and idling continue quite regularly during the first half of the very first moon, the getaway ending with the Banquet of Lanterns, which inhabits the last 3 days. It came from the Han dynasty 2000 years ago. Numerous lanterns of all sizes, shapes, colours (except wholly white, or rather undyed material, the colour of mourning), and designs are lit in front of public and private structures, but making use of these was an addition about 800 years later, i.e. about 1200 years ago. Paper dragons, hundreds of yards long, are moved along the streets at a slow pace, supported on the heads of men whose legs only show up, giving the impression of huge snakes winding through the roads.

Of the other primary celebrations, about 8 in number (not counting the celebrations of the 4 times with their equinoxes and solstices), four are specifically interested in the propitiation of the spirits-- particularly, the Earlier Spirit Celebration (fifteenth day of second moon), the Festival of the Tombs (about the 3rd day of the third moon), when graves are put in order and special offerings made to the dead, the Middle Spirit Celebration (fifteenth day of seventh moon), and the Later Spirit Festival (fifteenth day of tenth moon). The Dragon-boat Celebration (fifth day of fifth moon) is said to have stemmed as a celebration of the death of the poet Ch' ü Yüan, who drowned himself in disgust at the main intrigue and corruption of which he was the victim, but the thing is the procuring of adequate rain to make sure a good harvest. It is celebrated by racing with long narrow boats shaped to represent dragons and propelled by scores of rowers, pasting of charms on the doors of houses, and eating a unique kind of rice-cake, with an alcohol as a beverage.

Chapter 6: Spirits and Habits

The Spirit That Clears the Way

The fifteenth day of the eighth moon is the Mid-autumn Celebration, understood by immigrants as All Souls' Day. On this occasion the women praise the moon, offering cakes, fruit, etc. The gateways of Purgatory are opened, and the hungry ghosts troop forth to enjoy themselves for a month on the good things provided for them by the pious. The ninth day of the ninth moon is the Chung Yang Celebration, when every one who possibly can ascends to a high place-- a hill or temple-tower. This inaugurates the kite-flying season and is supposed to promote longevity. During that season, which lasts some months, the Chinese people the sky with dragons, centipedes, frogs, butterflies, and hundreds of other cleverly devised beings, which, by means of basic mechanisms worked by the wind, roll their eyes, make suitable noises, and move their paws, wings, tails, etc., in a most sensible manner. The festival originated in a caution gotten by a scholar called Huan Ching from his master Fei Ch' ang-fang, a local of Ju-nan in Honan, who lived during the Han dynasty, that a terrible calamity was about to happen, and enjoining him to leave with his family to a high place. On his return he found all his domestic animals dead, and was told that they had died rather than himself and his family members. On New Year's Eve (Tuan Nien or Chu Hsi) the Kitchen-god ascends to Heaven to make his yearly report, the wise feasting him with honey and other sticky food right before his departure, so that his lips might be sealed and he be unable to 'let on' too much to the powers that be in the regions above!

Sports and Games

The first sports of the Chinese were festival gatherings for functions of archery, to which had a lot of success exercises partaking of a army character. Searching was a preferred amusement. They played games of computation, chess (or the 'game of war'), shuttlecock with the feet, pitch-pot (tossing arrows from some distance into a narrow-necked jar), and 'horn-goring' (battling on the shoulders of others with horned masks on their heads). Stilts, football, dice-throwing, boat-racing, dog-racing, cock-fighting, kite-flying, along with singing and dancing marionettes, afforded leisure and amusement.

A lot of these games ended up being obsolete in course of time, and brand-new ones were created. At the end of the Monarchical Period, throughout the Manchu dynasty, we find those most in usage to be foot-shuttlecock, lifting of beams headed with heavy stones-- dumb-bells four feet long and weighing thirty or forty pounds-- kite-flying, quail-fighting, cricket-fighting, sending birds after seeds tossed into the air, roaming through fields, playing chess or 'morra,' or gambling with cards, dice, or over the cricket- and quail-fights or seed-catching birds. There were numerous and varied kids's games tending to develop strength, ability, quickness of action, adult impulse, precision, and sagacity. Theatricals were performed by walking performers on stages put up opposite temples, though long-term theatres also existed, female parts until recently being taken by male stars. Peep-shows, magicians, ventriloquists, acrobats, fortune-tellers, and story-tellers kept crowds entertained or interested. Usually, 'young China' of the present day, related to the party of progress, seems to have adopted the majority of the outside but extremely few of the indoor games of Western countries.

Domestic Life

In domestic or personal life, observances at birth, betrothal, and marital relationship were sophisticated, and maintained superstitious aspects. Early rising was general. Shaving of the head and beard, as well as cleansing of the ears and massage, was done by barbers. There were public baths in all cities and towns. Shops were closed at nightfall, and, the streets being till current times ill-lit or dark, guests or their attendants brought lanterns. A lot of homes, except the poorest, had private watchmen. Usually two meals a day were taken. Dinners to good friends were served at inns or dining establishments, accompanied or followed by musical or theatrical performances. The place of honour is specified in Western books on China to be on the left, but the fact is that the place of honour is the one which shows the utmost solicitude for the security of the guest. It is therefore not always one fixed place, but would generally be the one facing the door, so that the visitor might be in a position to see an opponent get in, and take measures appropriately.

Lap-dogs and cage-birds were kept as pets; 'wonks,' the huang kou, or 'yellow dog,' were guards of homes and street scavengers. Aquaria with goldfish were usually to be seen in the houses of the upper and middle classes, the gardens and courtyards of which usually contained rockeries and creative shrubs and flowers.

Hairs were never ever used, and moustaches and beards only after forty, before which age the hair grew, if at all, very scantily. Full, thick beards, as in the West, were practically never ever seen, even on the aged. Snuff-bottles, tobacco-pipes, and fans were brought by both sexes. Nails were used long by members of the literary and leisured classes. Non-Manchu ladies and girls had cramped feet, and both Manchu and Chinese ladies used cosmetics easily.

Industrial Institutions

While the guys addressed farm-work, ladies looked after the mulberry-orchards and silkworms, and did spinning, weaving, and embroidery. This, the primitive department of labour, held throughout, though added to on both sides, so that eventually the men did most of the farming, arts, production, circulation, battling, and so on, and the women, besides the duties above named and some field-labour, mended old clothes, drilled and sharpened needles, pasted tin-foil, made shoes, and gathered and arranged the leaves of the tea-plant. In course of time trades became highly specialized-- their number being legion-- and localized, bankers, for instance, gathering together in Shansi, carpenters in Chi Chou, and porcelain-manufacturers in Jao Chou, in Kiangsi.

Regarding land, it became at an early age the property of the sovereign, who grown it out to his family members or favourites. It was arranged on the ching, or 'well' system-- 8 personal squares round a ninth public square cultivated by the 8 farmer families in common for the advantage of the State. From the starting to the end of the Monarchical Period tenure went on to be of the Crown, land being unallodial, and mainly kept in clans or families, and not entailed, the conditions of period being payment of an annual tax, a fee for alienation, and cash compensation for individual services to the Government, usually incorporated into the direct tax as scutage. Slavery, unidentified in the earliest times, existed as an acknowledged organization throughout the entire of the Monarchical Duration.

Production was chiefly confined to human and animal labour, equipment being only now in use on a large scale. Internal circulation was carried on from numerous centres and at fairs, stores, markets, etc. With few exceptions, the great trade-routes by land and sea have remained the same during the last two 1,000 years. Foreign trade was with Western Asia, Greece, Rome, Carthage, Arabia, and so on, and from the seventeenth century A.D. more normally with European nations. The typical primitive methods of conveyance, like human beings, animals, carts, boats, and so on, were partially displaced by steam-vessels from 1861 onward.

Exchange was affected by barter, cowries of different values being the prototype of coins, which were cast in greater or less amount under each reign. But till within current years there was only one coin, the copper money, in use, bullion and paper notes being the other media of exchange. Silver Mexican dollars and subsidiary coins entered into use with the introduction of foreign commerce. Weights and steps (which normally decreased from north to south), formally set up partly on the decimal system, were discarded by the people in normal business deals for the easier duodecimal neighborhood.

Arts

Searching, fishing, cooking, weaving, coloring, carpentry, metallurgy, glass-, brick-, and paper-making, printing, and book-binding were in a more or less primitive phase, the mechanical arts showing much servile imitation and simpleness in design; but pottery, carving, and lacquer-work were in an extremely high state of development, the articles produced being gone beyond in quality and charm by no other ones worldwide.

Farming and Rearing of Livestock

From the earliest times the greater part of the available land was under growing. Other than when the country has been devastated by war, the Chinese have dedicated close attention to the growing of the dirt continuously for forty centuries. Even the hills are terraced for extra growing room. However, hardship and governmental inaction triggered much to lie idle. There were 2 yearly crops in the north, and 5 in two years in the south. Maybe two-thirds of the population cultivated the dirt. The methods, though, remained primitive; but the great fertility of the ground and the great market of the farmer, with generous but cautious use of fertilizers, made it possible for the vast territory to support an enormous population. Rice, wheat, barley, buckwheat, maize, kaoliang, several millets, and oats were the chief grains cultivated. Beans, peas, oil-bearing seeds (sesame, rape, etc.), fibre-plants (hemp, ramie, jute, cotton, etc.), starch-roots (taros, yams, sweet potatoes, etc.), tobacco, indigo, tea, sugar, fruits, were amongst the more crucial crops produced. Fruit-growing, however, lacked scientific approach. The rotation of crops was not an usual practice, but grafting, pruning, dwarfing, enlarging, selecting, and differing species were well comprehended. Vegetable-culture had reached a high state of perfection, the tiniest spots of land being made to produce perfectly. This is the more creditable inasmuch as a lot of small farmers could not afford to acquire expensive foreign machinery, which, in many cases, would be too large or complicated for their functions.

The principal animals, birds, etc., reared were the pig, ass, horse, mule, cow, sheep, goat, buffalo, yak, fowl, duck, goose, pigeon, silkworm, and bee.

The Ministry of Agriculture and Commerce, the successor to the Board of Agriculture, Produces, and Commerce, set up throughout recent years, is now adapting Western techniques to the growing of the fertile soil of China, and even greater results than in the past may be expected in the future.

Sentiments and Moral Ideas

The Chinese have always shown an eager enjoy the stunning-- in flowers, music, poetry, literature, embroidery, paintings, porcelain. They cultivated decorative plants, practically every house, as we saw, having its garden, big or small, and tables were often embellished with flowers in vases or decorative wire baskets or fruits or sweetmeats. Confucius made music an instrument of federal government. Paper bearing the written character was so appreciated that it might not be thrown on the ground or trodden on. Pleasure was always displayed in beautiful scenery or tales of the wonderful. Commanding or agreeable situations were chosen for temples. But till within the last few years streets and houses were usually unclean, and decency in public frequently absent.

Morality was favoured by public opinion, but in spite of early marital relationships and concubinage there was much laxity. Cruelty both to humans and animals has always been a significant quality in the Chinese character. Savagery in warfare, cannibalism, luxury, drunkenness, and corruption dominated in the earliest times. The mindset towards women was despotic. But moral principles pervaded the classical writings and formed the basis of law. Despite these, the inferior belief of revenge was, as we have seen, authorized and preached as a sacred duty. As a result of the universal yin-yang dualistic doctrines, immorality was leniently concerned. In contemporary times, at least, mercantile honour was high, "a merchant's word is as good as his bond" being truer in China than in many other nations. Intemperance was uncommon. Opium-smoking was much enjoyed till making use of the drug was by force repressed (1906-- 16). Even now much is smuggled into the country, or its development neglected by paid off authorities. Clan quarrels and battles prevailed, vendettas sometimes continuing for generations. Suicide under depressing situations was approved and honoured; it was regularly resorted to under the sting of great oppression. There was a deep respect for parents and superiors. Disregard of the truth, when useful, was universal, and unattended by a sense of pity, even on detection. Thieving was common. The illegal exactions of rulers were difficult. In times of prosperity pride and fulfillment in material matters was not hidden, and was typically short-sighted. Politeness was virtually universal, though said to be often shallow; but gratitude was a marked particular, and was heartfelt. Shared conjugal affection was strong. The love of gaming was universal.

But little has taken place recently to modify the above characters. However the inferior traits are certainly being changed by education and by the formation of societies whose members bind themselves against immorality, concubinage, gaming, drinking, smoking, etc.

Religious Ideas Chinese religion is inherently a mindset towards the spirits or gods with the thing of acquiring a benefit or averting a calamity. We shall handle it more fully in another chapter. Suffice it to say here that it came from ancestor-worship, and that the majority of it remains ancestor-worship to the present day. The State religious belief, which was Confucianism, was ancestor-worship. Taoism, originally an approach, became a worship of spirits-- of the living souls of dead guys supposed to have used up their residence in animals, reptiles, bugs, trees, stones, and so on-- borrowed the cape of religious belief from Buddhism, which eventually outshone it, and deteriorated into a system of exorcism and magic. Buddhism, a faith coming from India, in which Buddha, once a man, is worshipped, in which no beings are known with greater power than can be attained to by man, and according to which at death the soul migrates into anything from a deified human being to an elephant, a bird, a plant, a wall, a broom, or any piece of inorganic matter, was imported all set made into China and took the side of popular superstition and Taoism against the orthodox belief, finding that its power lay in the impact on the popular mind of its doctrine respecting a future state, in contrast to the indifference of Confucianism. Its pleading for empathy and preservation of life met a sobbing need, and but for it the state of things in this respect would be worse than it is.

Religion, apart from ancestor-worship, does not go into largely into Chinese life. There is none of the real 'love of God' found, for instance, in the impassioned as distinguished from the standard Christian. And as ancestor-worship slowly loses its hold and dies out agnosticism will take its spot.

Superstitions A practically unlimited variety of superstitious practices, because of the belief in the great or evil impacts of departed spirits, exists in all parts of China. Days are fortunate or unlucky. Eclipses are because of a dragon attempting to eat the sun or the moon. The rainbow is supposed to be the result of a conference between the impure vapours of the sun and the earth. Amulets are used, and appeals hung up, sprigs of artemisia or of peach-blossom are positioned near beds and over lintels respectively, children and adults are 'locked to life' by means of locks on chains or cords worn round the neck, old brass mirrors are supposed to cure madness, figures of gourds, tigers' claws, or the unicorn are used to guarantee good fortune or ward off sickness, fire, etc., spells of tons of kinds, composed mainly of the written characters for joy and durability, are used, or written on paper, cloth, leaves, and so on, and burned, the ashes being made into a decoction and intoxicated by the young or sick.

Divination by methods of the divining stalks (the divining plant, milfoil or yarrow) and the tortoiseshell has been carried on from time immemorial, but was not originally practiced with the thing of ascertaining future events, but in order to decide doubts, much as lots are drawn or a coin tossed in the West. Fêng-shui, "the art of adapting the residence of the living and the dead so as to co-operate and harmonize with the regional currents of the cosmic breath" a doctrine which had its root in ancestor-worship, has exercised a massive impact on Chinese idea and life from the earliest times, and particularly from those of Chu Hsi and other philosophers of the Sung dynasty.

Knowledge

Having actually kept in mind that Chinese education was primarily literary, and why it was so, it is simple to see that there would be little or no need for the kind of knowledge classified in the West under the head of science. In up until now as any need existed, it did so, at any rate in the beginning, only since it subserved crucial needs. Therefore, astronomy, or more appropriately astrology, was studied in order that the calendar may be controlled, and so the routine of agriculture correctly followed, for on that depended the people's everyday rice, or rather, in the start, the different fruits and types of flesh which constituted their means of sustentation before their now universal food was understood. In philosophy they have had 2 durations of great activity, the very first start with Lao Tzŭ and Confucius in the 6th century B.C. and ending with the Burning of the Books by the First Emperor, Shih Huang Ti, in 213 B.C.; the second beginning with Chou Tzŭ (A.D. 1017-- 73) and ending with Chu Hsi (1130-- 1200). The department of approach in the imperial library consisted of in 190 B.C. 2705 volumes by 137 authors. There can be no doubt that this zeal for the orthodox learning, integrated with the literary test for office, was the reason scientific knowledge was stopped from developing; so much so, that after four thousand or more years of nationwide life we find, throughout the Manchu Duration, which ended the monarchical régime, few of the informed class, giants though they were in knowledge of all departments of their literature and history (the continuity of their traditions laid down in their twenty-four Dynastic Annals has been referred to as among the great wonders of the world), with even the elementary clinical learning of a schoolboy in the West. 'Crude,' 'primitive,' 'average,' 'vague,' 'inaccurate,' 'want of analysis and generalization,' are terms we find applied to their knowledge of such leading sciences as geography, mathematics, chemistry, botany, and geology. Their medicine was much obstructed by superstitious notion, and maybe more so by such beliefs as that the seat of the intelligence is in the stomach, that thoughts follow the heart, that the pit of the stomach is the seat of the breath, that the soul lives in the liver, and so on-- the outcome partially of the idea that dissection of the body would maim it permanently during its presence in the Otherworld. What development was made was due to European instruction; and this again is the causa causans of the great wave of development in clinical and philosophical knowledge which is rolling over the entire country and will have marked effects on the history of the world throughout the coming century.

Language

Initially polysyllabic, the Chinese language later presumed a monosyllabic, separating, uninflected form, grammatical relations being shown by position. From the earliest forms of speech some secondary vernacular languages emerged in different districts, and from these sprang regional dialects, and so on. Tone-distinctions emerged-- i.e. the same words pronounced with a different intonation came to mean different things. Development of these distinctions resulted in carelessness of articulation, and multiplication of what would be homonyms but for these tones. It is inaccurate to assume that the tones were invented to distinguish comparable sounds. So that, at the present day, anybody who says ma will mean either an exclamation, hemp, horse, or curse according to the quality he offers to the sound. The language remains in a primitive state, without inflexion, declension, or distinction of parts of speech. The order in a sentence is: subject, verb, complement direct, enhance indirect. Gender is formed by unique particles; number by prefixing characters, and so on; cases by position or proper prepositions. Adjectives precede nouns; position identifies contrast; and absence of punctuation causes obscurity. The latter is now introduced into a lot of freshly published works. The new education is bringing with it many words and expressions not found in the old literature or dictionaries. Japanese idioms which are now being imported into the language are making it less pure.

The written language, too well known to really need in-depth description, a thing of appeal and a joy for ever to those able to appreciate it, said to have taken initially the form of knotted cables and then of notches on wood (though this was more probably the beginning of numeration than of writing appropriate), took later that of disrespectful outlines of natural items, and then went on to the phonetic system, under which each character is composed of two parts, the radical, showing the meaning, and the phonetic, indicating the sound. They were symbols, non-agglutinative and non-inflexional, and were written in vertical columns, most likely from having in early times been painted or cut on strips of bark.

Achievements of the Chinese

As the result of all this fitful fever during so many centuries, we find that the Chinese, after having actually lived in nests "in order to keep away from the animals," and then in caves, have built themselves houses and palaces which are still made after the pattern of their prototype, with a flat wall behind, the openings in front, the walls put in after the pillars and roof-tree have been repaired, and out-buildings added on as side extensions. The k' ang, or 'stove-bed' (now a platform made of bricks), found all over the northern provinces, was a location dug of the side of the cave, with an opening underneath in which (as now) a fire was lit in winter. Windows and shutters opened upward, being a survival of the mat or shade hung in front of the apertures in the walls of the primitive cave-dwelling. 4 of these structures dealing with each other round a square made the yard, and one or more courtyards made the compound. They have fed themselves on almost every little thing edible to be found on, under, or above land or water, except milk, but live primarily on rice, chicken, fish, vegetables, consisting of garlic, and tea, though at one time they ate flesh and drank wine, sometimes to excess, right before tea was cultivated. They have dressed themselves in skins and feathers, and then in silks and satins, but primarily in cotton, and hardly ever in wool. Under the Manchu régime the kind of dress adopted was that of this horse-riding race, demonstrating the chief attributes of that honorable animal, the broad sleeves representing the hoofs, the queue the mane, etc. This line was formed of the hair growing from the back part of the scalp, the front of which was shaved. Unlike the Egyptians, they did not wear wigs. They have almost always had the decency to wear their coats long, and have despised the Westerner for wearing his too short. They are now paradoxical enough to make the error of adopting the Westerner's costume.

They have made to themselves great canals, bridges, aqueducts, and the longest wall there has ever been on the face of the earth (which could not be seen from the moon, as some sinologists have mistakenly presumed, any more than a hair, however long, could be seen at a short distance of a hundred yards). They have made long and broad roads, but couldn't keep them in repair work throughout the last few centuries, however much zeal, potentially because of commerce on oil- or electricity-driven wheels, is now being shown in this direction. They have built honorary portals to chaste widows, pagodas, and arched bridges of great beauty, not forgetting to surround each city with a high and substantial wall to stay out hostile people. They have made many implements and weapons, from pens and fans and chopsticks to ploughs and carts and ships; from fiery darts, 'flame elephants,' bows and spears, spiked chariots, battering-rams, and hurling-engines to mangonels, trebuchets, matchlocks of wrought iron and plain bore with long barrels resting on a stock, and gingals fourteen feet long resting on a tripod, cuirasses of quilted cotton cloth covered with brass knobs, and helmets of iron or polished steel, sometimes inlaid, with neck- and ear-lappets. And they have been content not to surpass these to any considerable level; but have lately shown a propensity to make the later patterns imported from the West in their own factories.

They have produced among the greatest and most remarkable build-ups of literature the world has ever seen, and the finest porcelain; some music, not very fine; and some magnificent painting, though barely any sculpture, and little architecture that will live.

Chapter 7: Background of the Mythology

Folklore and Intellectual Development

The Manichæst, yin-yang (dualist), idea of presence, to which further recommendation will be made in the next chapter, finds its illustration in the double life, real and fictional, of all the peoples of the earth. They have both real histories and mythological histories. In the preceding chapter I have dealt briefly with the very first-- the life of reality-- in China from the earliest times to the present day; the succeeding chapters are interested in the second-- the life of creativity. A survey of the first was required for a total grasp of the 2nd. The 2 respond upon one another, affecting the nationwide character and through it the history of the world.

Folklore is the science of the unscientific man's clarification of what we call the Otherworld-- itself and its citizens, their mysterious habits and surprising actions both there and here, generally including the creation of the world also. By the Otherworld he does not always mean anything remote or perhaps invisible, though the things he explains would mostly be included by us under those terms. In some countries myths are plentiful, in others limited. Why should this be? Why should some peoples tell a lot of and marvellous tales about their gods and other ones say little about them, though they may say a great deal to them? We remember the 'great' myths of Greece and Scandinavia. Other races are 'poor' in myths. The difference is to be clarified by the psychological characters of the peoples as moulded by their environments and hereditary propensities. The issue is naturally a mental one, for it is, as already kept in mind, in creativity that myths have their root. Now creativity grows with each stage of intellectual progress, for intellectual development indicates increasing representativeness of thought. In the lower phases of human development imagination is weak and ineffective; in the greatest phases it is strong and positive.

The Chinese Intelligence

The Chinese are not unimaginative, but their minds did not go on to the construction of any myths which should be world-great and immortal; and one reason that they did not construct such myths was that their intellectual development was arrested at a relatively early phase. It was jailed since there was not that contact and competitors with other tribes which demands brain-work of an active kind as the option of subjugation, inferiority, or extinction, and because, as we have already seen, the knowledge needed of them was primarily the parrot-like repetition of the old rather than the thinking-out of the new1-- a state of things rendered possible by the seclusion just described. Confucius discountenanced conversation about the super, and just as it is probable that the admonitions of Wên Wang, the virtual creator of the Chou dynasty (1121-- 255 B.C.), against drunkenness, in a time right before tea was understood to them, helped to make the Chinese the sober people that they are, so it is likely-- more than probable-- that this attitude of Confucius may have nipped in the bud much that might have developed an energetic mythology, though for a factor to be mentioned later it might be doubted if he thus deprived the world of any gorgeous and marvellous actual results of the highest flights of poetical creativity. There are times, like those of any great political turmoil, when human nature will assert itself and break through its shackles in spite of all artificial or conventional restraints. Considering the massive impact of Confucianism throughout the latter half of Chinese history-- i.e. the last two 1000 years-- it is unexpected that the Chinese attempted to think of supernatural matters at all, except in the matter of propitiating their dead forefathers. That they did so is evidence not only of humanity's intrinsic propensity to tell stories, but also of the irrepressible strength of sensation which breaks all laws and rules under great stimulus. On the opposing unæsthetic side this might be compared to the feeling which prompts the unpremeditated assassination of a man who is guilty of great oppression, despite the fact that it be certain that in due course he would have met his deserts at the hands of the general public executioner.

The Influence of Faith

Apart from this, the impact of Confucianism would have been even greater than it was, but for the royal partiality periodically revealed for rival teachings, just like Buddhism and Taoism, which tossed their weight on the side of the superhuman, and which sometimes were exalted to such great heights regarding be formally acknowledged as State religious beliefs. These, Buddhism especially, interested the popular imagination and love of the wonderful. Buddhism mentioned the future state and the nature of the gods in no unpredictable tones. It showed men how to reach the one and get to the other. Its founder was virtuous; his commandments pure and life-sustaining. It provided in great part what Confucianism did not have. And, as in the fifth and 6th centuries A.D., when Buddhism and Taoism joined forces and a working union existed between them, they practically excluded for the time all the "chilly development of Confucian classicism."

Other opponents of myth, consisting of a vital thinker of great ability, we will have event to see currently.

History and Myth

The sobriety and precision of Chinese historians is common. I have dilated upon this in another work, and really need include here only what I accidentally omitted there-- a point hitherto unnoticed or at least unremarked-- that the really word for history in Chinese (shih) means impartiality or an unbiased annalist. It has been said that where there is much myth there is little history, and vice versa, and though this may not be universally true, undoubtedly the persistently genuine recording of realities, events, and phrases, even at the danger of loss, yea, and actual death of the historian as the outcome of his refusal to make incorrect entries in his chronicle at the bidding of the emperor (as when it comes to the historiographers of Ch' i in 547 B.C.), suggests a type of mind which would need some very strong stimulus to trigger it to skyrocket very far into the hazy worlds of fanciful creativity.

Chinese Rigidness

A further cause, already hinted at above, for the arrest of intellectual development is to be found in the development of the country in size throughout tons of centuries of isolation from the primary stream of world-civilization, without that increase in heterogeneity which comes from the moulding by forces external to itself. "As iron sharpeneth iron, so a man sharpeneth the countenance of his friend." Consequently we find China what is understood to sociology as an 'aggregate of the very first order,' which during its advancement has parted with its internal life-heat without taking in enough from external sources to enable it to retain the plastic condition required to farther, or at least rapid, development. It is in a state of rigidness, a state recognized and comprehended by the sociologist in his study of the evolution of countries.

The Requirements to Myths

But the mere boost of constructive imagination is not enough to produce myth. If it were, it would be sensible to argue that as intellectual development goes on myths become more numerous, and the greater the development the greater the number of myths. This we do not find. In fact, if constructive imagination went on increasing without the intervention of any further aspect, there need not always be any myth at all. We might almost say that the reverse holds true. We connect myth with primitive folk, not with the best philosophers or the most advanced nations-- not, that is, with the most innovative phases of national development where positive imagination makes the country great and strong. In these phases the philosopher studies or criticizes myth, he does not make it.

In order that there might be myth, three more conditions should be satisfied. There must, as we have seen, be positive imagination, but, nevertheless, there need to not be too much of it. As specified above, mythology, or rather myth, is the unscientific man's clarification. If the useful creativity is so great that it becomes self-critical, if the story-teller doubts his own story, if, in other words, his mind is scientific enough to see that his clarification is no clarification at all, then there can be no myth appropriately so called. As in religious belief, unless the myth-maker believes in his myth with all his heart and soul and strength, and each new disciple, as it is taken care of and grows under his hands throughout the course of years, holds that he must put his shoes from off his feet because the spot whereon he treads is holy ground, the faith will not be propagated, for it will do not have the essential stimulate which alone can make it a living thing.

Stimulus Necessary

The next condition is that there should be a stimulus. It is not ideas, but feelings, which govern the world, and in the history of folklore where sensation is missing we find either weak replica or repeating of the myths of other peoples (though this should not be puzzled with certain aspects which seem to be common to the myths of all races), or mixture, contamination, or "genealogical tree-making," or myths come from by "leisurely, tranquil tradition" and not having the necessary qualities which attract the human soul and make their holders really careful to maintain them amongst their most really loved and valued treasures. But, on the other hand, where sensation is stirred, where the requisite stimulus exists, where the people are in great risk, or attracted by the reward of some out of breath adventure, the contact produces the stimulate of magnificent poetry, the myths have plenty of creative, philosophic, and spiritual suggestiveness, and have abiding relevance and appeal. They are the kids, the poetic fruit, of great labour and serious battles, exposing the most basic forces, hopes, and cravings of the human soul. Nations highly strung, going through difficult emotion, strongly stimulated by constant conflict with other countries, have their creativity stimulated to remarkable poetic creativity. The background of the Danaïds is Egyptian, not Greek, but it was the danger in which the Greeks were put in their wars with the sons of the land of the Pharaohs that stimulated the Greek creativity to the creation of that great myth.

This clarifies why so many of the greatest myths have their staging, not in the nation itself whose valued belongings they are, but where that country is 'playing the great game,' is carrying on wars decisive of significant national events, which excite to the best pitch of enjoyment the feelings both of the contenders and of those who are watching them from their houses. It is by such great events, not by the romance-writer in his tranquil study, that mythology, like literature, is "incisively determined." Imagination, we saw, goes pari passu with intellectual progress, and intellectual progress, in early times, is advanced not so much by the simple contact as by the real dispute of nations. And we see also that myths may, and extremely regularly do, have a character quite different from that of the nation to which they appertain, for environment plays a crucial part both in their beginning and subsequent growth--a reality too obvious to need in-depth elaboration.

Relentless Soul-expression

A third condition is that the kind of creativity need to be consistent through fairly long periods of time, otherwise not only will there be a lack of sufficient sensation or momentum to trigger the myths to be repeated and kept alive and transmitted to posterity, but the inducement to add to them and so allow them to mature and become complete and rounded off and sufficiently attractive to appeal to the human mind in spite of the foreign character they typically bear will be lacking. To put it simply, myths and legends grow. They resemble not so much the narrative of the story-teller or author as a slowly developing art like music, or a body of ideas like viewpoint. They are human and natural, though they reveal the idea not of any one individual mind, but of the folk-soul, exhibiting in poetical form some great psychological or physiographical truth.

The Character of Chinese Myths

The nature of the case therefore forbids us to expect to find the Chinese myths displaying the advanced state and brilliant heterogeneity of those which have become part of the world's permanent literature. We should expect them to be true to type and conditions, as we expect the other ideas of the Chinese to be, and looking for them in the light of the knowledge we shall find them just where we should expect to find them.

The great legends and eddas exalted among the world's literary masterpieces, and forming part of the very life of a large number of its occupants, are missing in China. "The Chinese people," says one well-known sinologist, "are not prone to mythological creation." "He who expects to find in Tibet," says another author, "the poetical appeal of Greek or Germanic folklore will be dissatisfied. There is a striking hardship of imagination in all the myths and legends. A great uniformity pervades them all. Much of their stories, drawn from the sacred texts, are rather puerile and insipid. It might be kept in mind that the Chinese folklore labours under the same flaw." And then there comes the squashing judgment of an over-zealous Christian missionary sinologist: "There is no hierarchy of gods taken in to rule and populate the world they made, no conclave on Mount Olympus, nor judgment of the mortal soul by Osiris, no transfer of human love and hate, enthusiasms and hopes, to the powers above; all here is credited disembodied firms or principles, and their works are represented as carrying on in quiet order. There is no religion [], no imagination; all is impassible, passionless, dull ... It has not, as in Greece and Egypt, been explained in superb poetry, shadowed forth in gorgeous ritual and stunning festivals, represented in beautiful sculptures, nor preserved in faultless, enforcing fanes and temples, filled with ideal productions." Besides being inaccurate as to tons of its supposed truths, this view would certainly be revealed by further research study to be greatly overemphasized.

Periods Fertile in Myths

What we should expect, then, to find from our philosophical study of the Chinese mind as affected by its surroundings would be barrenness of useful imagination, other than when birth was provided to myth through the operation of some external firm. And this we do find. The period of the defeat of the Yin dynasty and the establishment of the great house of Chou in 1122 B.C., or of the Wars of the 3 States, for example, in the 3rd century after Christ, a time of awful anarchy, a medieval age of legendary heroism, sung in a hundred kinds of prose and verse, which has gotten in as reason into one dozen dramas, or the advent of Buddhism, which opened a brand-new world of idea and life to the easy, sober, peace-loving agricultural folk of China, were stimuli not by any methods lacking result. In China there are gods tons of and heroes tons of, and the really fact of the existence of so great a wide range of gods would realistically indicate a wealth of mythological lore inseparable from their apotheosis. You cannot-- and the Chinese cannot-- get behind reason. A man is not made a god without some cause being assigned for so crucial and far-reaching a big step; and in matters of this sort the stated cause is apt to take the form of a narrative more or less wonderful or amazing. These resulting myths might, naturally, be born and grow at a later time than that in which the situations triggering them occurred, but, if so, that simply proves the persistent power of the coming from stimulus. That in China these stories always or often reach the greatest flights of positive creativity is not kept-- the upkeep of that argument would indeed be inconsistent; but even in those countries where the mythological garden has produced some of the finest flowers countless seeds should have been sown which either did not emerge at all or at least couldn't bring forth fruit. And in the world of mythology it is not only those gods who sit in the greatest seats-- developers of the world or heads of great religions-- who dominate mankind; the humbler, however often no less powerful gods or spirits-- those even who run on all fours and live in holes in the ground, or buzz through the air and have their thrones in the shadow of a leaf-- have usually made a much deeper impress on the minds and in the hearts of the people, and through that impress, for good or evil, have, in greater or less degree, customized the life of the visible universe.

Sources of Chinese Myths

" So, if we ask whence comes the heroic and the romantic, which provides the story-teller's stock-in-trade, the answer is easy. The legends and history of early China furnish abundance of material for them. To the Chinese mind their age-old world was crowded with heroes, fairies, and demons, who played their part in the mixed-up drama, and left a name and popularity both amazing and piquant. Each who recognizes with the methods and the language of the people knows that the country is full of typical challenge which poetic names have been given, and with a lot of them there is associated a legend or a misconception. A deep river's canyon is called 'the Blind Man's Pass,' because a strange little rock, looked at from a certain angle, assumes the summary of the human form, and there becomes linked therewith a pleasing story which reaches its climax in the petrifaction of the hero. A mountain's crest shaped like a stroking eagle will from some one have gotten the name of 'Eagle Mountain,' whilst by its side another formed like a couchant lion will have a name to match. There is no absence of poetry amongst the people, and the majority of striking objects claim a poetic name, and not a few of them are related to curious legends. It is, however, to their nationwide history that the story-teller goes for his most fascinating subjects, and as the so-called history of China imperceptibly passes into the famous period, and this again fades into the legendary, and as all this is assuredly really believed by the masses of the people, it is obvious that in the national life of China there is no dearth of heroes whose deeds of expertise will command the rapt attention of the crowds who listen." 2.

The soul in China is all over in evidence, and if myths have "most importantly to do with the life of the soul" it would appear odd that the Chinese, having spiritualized everything from a stone to the sky, have not been creative of myth. Why they have not the foregoing factors to consider show us clearly enough. We must take them and their myths as we find them. Let us, then, note briefly the outcome of their psychological workings as reacted on by their environment.

Stages of Chinese Myths

We cannot recognize the earliest mythology of the Chinese with that of any primitive race. The myths, if any, of their spot of beginning might have faded and been forgotten in their sluggish migration eastward. We cannot say that when they came from the West (which they most likely did) they brought their myths with them, for in spite of certain conjectural derivations from Babylon we do not find them possessed of any which we can determine as imported by them at that time. But research seems to have gone at least as far as this-- specifically, that while we cannot say that Chinese myth was derived from Indian myth, there is great reason to actually believe that Chinese and Indian myth had a typical origin, which was of course beyond China.

To state in detail the various phases through which Chinese myth has passed would involve a technical description foreign to the purpose of a well-known work. It will sufficiently serve our present purpose to outline its most popular features.

In the earliest times there was an 'age of magic' followed by an 'heroic age,' but myths were very rare right before 800 B.C., and what is called primitive mythology is said to have been developed or mimicked from foreign sources after 820 B.C. In the eighth century B.C. myths of an astrological character began to draw in attention. In the age of Lao Tzŭ (604 B.C.), the reputed founder of the Taoist religion, fresh legends appear, though Lao Tzŭ himself, soaked up in the abstract, records none. Neither did Confucius (551-- 479 B.C.) nor Mencius, who lived two a century later, include any legends to history. However in the Duration of the Warring States (500-- 100 B.C.) fresh stimuli and great feeling triggered to mythological creation.

Tso-ch' iu Ming and Lieh Tzŭ

Tso-ch' iu Ming, analyst on Confucius's Annals, often introduced legend into his history. Lieh Tzŭ (5th and fourth centuries B.C.), a metaphysician, is one of the earliest authors who handle myths. He is the first to discuss the story of Hsi Wang Mu, the Western Queen, and from his day onward the fabulists have vied with one another in great descriptions of the wonders of her fairyland. He was the first to point out the islands of the immortals in the ocean, the kingdoms of the overshadows and giants, the fruit of immortality, the fixing of the paradises by Nü Kua Shih with five-coloured stones, and the great tortoise which supports deep space.

The T'ang and Sung Epochs

Religious love started at this time. The T'ang date (A.B. 618-- 907) was one of the resurrection of the arts of peace after a long period of dissension. A purer and more long-lasting form of intellect was slowly conquering the grosser but less solid superstitious notion. Nevertheless the intellectual movement which now manifested itself was not strong enough to dominate against the powers of mythological darkness. It was reserved for the experts of the Sung Period (A.D. 960-- 1280) to execute to triumph a strong and sustained offensive against the spiritualistic fixations which had weighed upon the Chinese mind more or less constantly from the Han Duration (206 B.C.-A.D. 221) onward. The dogma of materialism was specifically cultivated at this time. The battle of sober reason against superstitious notion or creative creation was mainly a battle of Confucianism against Taoism. Though many centuries had expired since the great Master walked the earth, the anti-myth movement of the T'ang and Sung Periods was in reality the long arm and heavy fist of Confucius stressing a truer rationalism than that of his opponents and denouncing the risk of leaving the firm earth to skyrocket into the unknown hazy areas of fantasy. It was Sung scholarship that gave the death-blow to Chinese mythology.

It is unneeded to labour the point farther, because after the Sung date we do not meet with any period of new mythological creation, and its lack can be ascribed to no other cause than its defeat at the hands of the Sung theorists. After their time the tender plant was always in danger of being stunted or killed by the withering blast of philosophical criticism. Anything in the nature of myth ascribable to post-Sung times can at best be concerned only as a late blossom born when summer days are past.

Myths and Doubt

It will bear repetition to say that unless the myth-builder strongly actually believes in his myth, be he the layer of the foundation-stone or one of the raisers of the superstructure, he will hardly make it a living thing. Once he actually believes in reincarnation and the suspension of natural laws, the limitless vistas of space and the unlimited æons of time are opened to him. He can perform wonders which astonish the world. But if he enable his mind to ask, for instance, why it ought to have been essential for Elijah to part the waters of the Jordan with his garment in order that he and Elisha may pass over dryshod, or for Bodhidharma to stand on a reed to cross the great Yangtzŭ River, or for numerous Immortals to rest on 'favourable clouds' to make their journeys through space, he ruins myth-- his kid is stillborn or does not make it through to maturity. Though the growth of viewpoint and decay of superstition might be good for a nation, the process is definitely conducive to the destruction of its myth and much of its poetry. The real mythologist takes myth for myth, participates in its spirit, and enjoys it.

We may hence expect to find in the world of Chinese mythology a large number of little hills instead of several great mountains, but the little hills are great ones after their kind; and the item of the work is to present Chinese myth as it is, not as it may have been had the universe been differently made up. Nevertheless, if, as we may appropriately do, we judge of myth by the beliefs pervading it and the ideals supported and taught by it, we shall find that Chinese myth must be ranked among the best.

Myths and Legends

The general concepts thought about above, while they clarify the paucity of myth in China, clarify also the abundance of legend there. The six hundred years during which the Mongols, Mings, and Manchus sat upon the throne of China are barren of myth, but like all durations of the Chinese nationwide life are fertile in legend. And this chiefly for the reason that myths are more general, nationwide, magnificent, while legends are more regional, individual, human. And since, in China as in other places, the lower classes are as a guideline less educated and more superstitious than the upper classes-- have a certain amount of useful creativity, but insufficient to be self-critical-- legends, declined or perhaps ridiculed by the academic class when their knowledge has become sufficiently clinical, continue to be developed and believed in by the peasant and the occupant in districts far from the madding crowd long after myth, properly so called, has exhaled its last breath.

Cosmogony-p' an Ku and the Creation Myth

The Creator of deep space

The most obvious figure in Chinese cosmogony is P'an Ku. He it was who chiselled the universe out of Turmoil. According to Chinese ideas, he was the progeny of the original dual powers of Nature, the yin and the yang (to be considered presently), which, having in some incomprehensible way produced him, set him the task of giving form to Chaos and "making the heavens and the earth."

Some accounts describe him as the real creator of deep space--" the forefather of Paradise and earth and all that live and relocation and have their being." 'P'an' means 'the shell of an egg,' and 'Ku' 'to protect,' 'strong,' describing P'an Ku being hatched from out of Turmoil and to his settling the plan of the causes to which his beginning was due. The characters themselves might, though, mean nothing more than 'Investigates into antiquity,' though some bolder translators have designated to them the value if not the literal sense of 'aboriginal abyss,' or the Babylonian Tiamat, 'the Deep.'

P'an Ku is imagined as a man of dwarfish stature dressed in bearskin, or simply in leaves or with an apron of leaves. He has 2 horns on his head. In his right hand he holds a hammer and in his left a sculpt (in some cases these are reversed), the only executes he used in carrying out his great task. Other photos show him gone to in his labours by the 4 supernatural creatures-- the unicorn, phoenix, tortoise, and dragon; others again with the sun in one hand and the moon in the other, some of the firstfruits of his stupendous labours. (The reason for these being there will be apparent currently.) His job occupied eighteen 1,000 years, during which he formed the sun, moon, and stars, the heavens and the earth, himself increasing in stature day by day, being day-to-day six feet taller than the day before, until, his labours ended, he died that his works may live. His head ended up being the mountains, his breath the wind and clouds, his voice the thunder, his limbs the 4 quarters of the earth, his blood the rivers, his flesh the soil, his beard the constellations, his skin and hair the herbs and trees, his teeth, bones, and marrow the metals, rocks, and gemstones, his sweat the rain, and the insects sneaking over his body people, who hence had a lowlier origin even than the tears of Khepera in Egyptian cosmology.1.

This account of P'an Ku and his achievements is of Taoist origin. The Buddhists have given a somewhat different account of him, which is a late adjustment from the Taoist myth, and should not be misinterpreted for Buddhist cosmogony correct.2.

The Sun and the Moon.
In some of the images of P'an Ku he is represented, as already kept in mind, as holding the sun in one hand and the moon in the other. Sometimes they are in the form of those bodies, often in the classic character. The legend says that when P'an Ku put things in order in the lower world, he did not put these 2 stars in their correct courses, so they retired into the Han Sea, and the people dwelt in darkness. The Terrestrial Emperor sent out an officer, Terrestrial Time, with orders that they should come forth and take their spots in the heavens and give the world day and night. They refused to obey the order. They were reported to Ju Lai; P'an Ku was called, and, at the magnificent direction of Buddha, wrote the character for 'sun' in his left hand, and that for 'moon' in his right hand; and went to the Han Sea, and extended forth his left hand and called the sun, and then stretched forth his right-hand man and called the moon, at the exact same time repeating a charm fervently seven times; and they forthwith ascended on high, and apart time into day and night.3.

Other legends recount that P'an Ku had the head of a dragon and the body of a serpent; and that by breathing he triggered the wind, by opening his eyes he created day, his voice made the thunder, and so on.

Chapter 8: Several Myths

P'an Ku and Ymer.
Hence, we have the paradises and the earth fashioned by this terrific being in eighteen thousand years. With regard to him we may adapt the Scandinavian ballad:

It was Time's morning.
When P'an Ku lived;
There was no sand, no sea,
Nor cooling billows;

Earth there was none,
No lofty Heaven;
No area of living green;
Only a deep profound.

And it is fascinating to keep in mind, in passing, the similarity between this Chinese artificer of the universe and Ymer, the giant, who discharges the same functions in Scandinavian mythology. Though P'an Ku did not have the exact same type of birth nor meet the violent death of the latter, the results as concerns the beginning of deep space seem to have been pretty much the same.4.

P'an Ku a Late Creation.
But though the Chinese creation myth deals with primeval things it does not itself come from a primitive time. According to some authors whose views are entitled to respect, it was created during the 4th century A.D. by the Taoist recluse, Magistrate Ko Hung, author of the Shên hsien chuan (Bios of the Gods). The stunning person of P'an Ku is said to have been a concession to the well-known dislike of, or inability to understand, the abstract. He was conceived, some Chinese writers say, as the philosophical descriptions of the Universe were too recondite for the common mind to understand. That he did fulfil the purpose of providing the ordinary mind with a fairly quickly comprehensible picture of the creation might be confessed; but, as will presently be seen, it is over-stating the case to say that he was conceived with the set purpose of providing the regular mind with a concrete solution or illustration of the great problem. There is no proof that P'an Ku had existed as a tradition before the time when we meet the written account of him; and, what is more, there is no evidence that there existed any demand on the part of the well-known mind for any such solution or illustration. The normal mind would seem to have been either indifferent to or pleased with the abstruse cosmogonical and cosmological theories of the early sages for 1,000 years. The cosmogonies of the I ching, of Lao Tzŭ, Confucius (such as it was), Kuan Tzŭ, Mencius, Chuang Tzŭ, were impersonal. P'an Ku and his myth should be concerned rather as an accident than as a production arising from any abrupt flow of psychological forces or wind of discontent ruffling the placid Chinese mind. If the Chinese brought with them from Babylon or anywhere else the elements of a cosmogony, whether of a basically abstruse clinical nature or an individual mythological story, it must have

been subsequently forgotten or at least has not made it through in China. But for Ko Hung's eccentricity and his desire to experiment with cinnabar from Cochin-China to find the elixir of life, P'an Ku would probably never ever have been invented, and the Chinese mind would have been content to go on neglecting the issue or would have silently acquiesced in the abstract philosophical explanations of the learned which it did not comprehend. Chinese cosmogony would then have consisted specifically of the recondite impersonal metaphysics which the Chinese mind had captivated or been fed upon for the 9 hundred or more years preceding the development of the P'an Ku myth.

Nü Kua Shih, the Repairer of the Paradises.
It is very true that there exist a couple of other explanations of the origin of things which introduce a personal developer. There is, for instance, the legend-- very first discussed by Lieh Tzŭ (to whom we shall revert later)-- which represents Nü Kua Shih (also called Nü Wa and Nü Hsi), said to have been the sister and heir of Fu Hsi, the mythical sovereign whose reign is credited the years 2953-- 2838 B.C., as having been the developer of humans when the earth initially show upd from Turmoil. She (or he, for the sex appears uncertain), who had the "body of a snake and head of an ox" (or a human head and horns of an ox, according to some authors), "moulded yellow earth and made man." Ssŭ-ma Chêng, of the eighth century A.D., author of the Historical Records and of another work on the three great legendary emperors, Fu Hsi, Shên Nung, and Huang Ti, gives the following account of her: "Fu Hsi was followed by Nü Kua, who like him had the surname Fêng. Nü Kua had the body of a serpent and a human head, with the virtuous endowments of a divine sage. Towards the end of her reign there was among the feudatory princes Kung Kung, whose functions were the administration of penalty. Violent and enthusiastic, he ended up being a rebel, and looked for by the influence of water to get rid of that of wood [under which Nü Kua reigned] He did battle with Chu Jung [said to have been among the ministers of Huang Ti, and later the God of Fire], but was not triumphant; whereupon he struck his head against the Imperfect Mountain, Pu Chou Shan, and brought it down. The pillars of Heaven were broken and the corners of the earth gave way. Hereupon Nü Kua melted stones of the 5 colours to fix the heavens, and cut off the feet of the tortoise to set upright the 4 extremities of the earth.5 Collecting the ashes of reeds she stopped the flooding waters, and therefore saved the land of Chi, Chi Chou [the early seat of the Chinese sovereignty]".

Another account separates the name and makes Nü and Kua brother and sister, defining them as the only 2 people around. At the creation they were positioned at the foot of the K'un- lun Mountains. Then they prayed, saying, "If thou, O God, hast sent us to be man and marriage partner, the smoke of our sacrifice will stay in one place; but if not, it will be scattered." The smoke stayed fixed.

But though Nü Kua is said to have moulded the first man (or the first human entities) out of clay, it is to be noted that, being only the successor of Fu Hsi, long lines of rulers had preceded her of whom no account is given, and also that, as relates to the paradises and the earth at least, she is regarded as the repairer and not the developer of them.

Heaven-deaf (T'ien- lung) and Earth-dumb (Ti-ya), the two attendants of Wên Ch' ang, the God of Literature (see following chapter), have also been drawn into the cosmogonical net. From their union came the paradises and the earth, humanity, and all living things.

These and other brief and unelaborated personal cosmogonies, even if not to be considered spurious replicas, definitely have not become established in the Chinese mind as the clarification of the method which the vast universe became: in this sphere the P'an Ku legend reigns supreme; and, owing to its concrete, quickly apprehensible nature, has probably done so ever since the time of its innovation.

Early Cosmogony Dualistic

The duration before the appearance of the P'an Ku myth may be divided into 2 parts; that from some early unknown date up to about the middle of the Confucian epoch, say 500 B.C., and that from 500 B.C. to A.D. 400. We know that throughout the latter period the minds of Chinese academics were regularly occupied with speculations as to the origin of deep space. Before 500 B.C. we have no documentary remains telling us what the Chinese actually believed about the beginning of things; but it is exceedingly not likely that no theories or speculations at all concerning the beginning of themselves and their environments were formed by this intelligent people during the eighteen centuries or more which preceded the date at which we find the views held by them took into written form. It is safe to presume that the dualism which later occupied their philosophical thoughts to so great a degree as nearly to appear inseparable from them, and worked out so powerful an impact throughout the course of their history, was not only developing itself throughout that long period, but had gradually reached an advanced phase. We might even presume as to say that dualism, or its beginnings, existed in the very earliest times, for the belief in the 2nd self or ghost or double of the dead is in reality absolutely nothing else. And we find it operating with obviously undiminished energy after the Chinese mind had reached its maturity in the Sung dynasty.

The Canon of Changes

The Bible of Chinese dualism is the I ching, the Canon of Modifications (or Permutations). It is kept in great veneration both on account of its antiquity and also just because of the "unfathomable knowledge which is supposed to lie concealed under its mystical symbols." It is positioned initially in the list of the classics, or Holy Books, though it is not the oldest of them. When exactly the work itself on which the subsequent elaborations were founded was made up is not now understood. Its origin is credited to the legendary emperor Fu Hsi (2953-- 2838 B.C.). It does not furnish a cosmogony appropriate, but merely a dualistic system as a description, or attempted explanation, and even maybe only a record, of the constant changes (in contemporary philosophical language the "redistribution of matter and movement") going on everywhere. That clarification or record was used for purposes of divination. This dualistic system, by an easy addition, became a monism, and at the exact same time provided the Chinese with a cosmogony.

Chapter 9: The 5 Elements

The Five Aspects or Forces (wu hsing)-- which, according to the Chinese, are metal, air, fire, water, and wood-- are first discussed in Chinese literature in a chapter of the traditional Book of History.6 They play a very fundamental part in Chinese thought: 'aspects' meaning usually not so much the real compounds as the forces vital to human, life. They have to be seen in passing, because they were associated with the development of the cosmogonical ideas which happened in the eleventh and twelfth centuries A.D.

Monism

As their creativity grew, it was natural that the Chinese should start to ask themselves what, if the yang and the yin by their permutations produced, or gave shape to, all things, was it that produced the yang and the yin. When we see traces of this curious tendency we find ourselves on the borderland of dualism where the transition is happening into the realm of monism. However though there may have been a propensity towards monism in early times, it was only in the Sung dynasty that the philosophers definitely put behind the yang and the yin a Very first Cause-- the Grand Origin, Grand Extreme, Grand Terminus, or Ultimate Ground of Presence.7 They gave to it the name t' ai chi, and represented it by a concrete indication, the symbol of a circle. The complete plan shows the development of the Sixty-four Diagrams (kua) from the t' ai chi through the yang and the yin, the 4, Eight, Sixteen, and Thirty-two Diagrams successively. This conception was the work of the Sung thinker Chou Tun-i (A.D. 1017-- 73), frequently referred to as Chou Tzŭ, and his disciple Chu Hsi (A.D. 1130-- 1200), referred to as Chu Tzŭ or Chu Fu Tzŭ, the popular historian and Confucian analyst-- 2 of the best names in Chinese philosophy. It was at this time that the tide of positive imagination in China, tinged though it always was with classical Confucianism, arose to its greatest height. There is the thinker's seeking for causes. Yet in this matter of the First Cause we identify, in the full flood of Confucianism, the powerful influence of Taoist and Buddhist speculations. It has even been said that the Sung viewpoint, which grew, not from the I ching itself, but from the appendixes to it, is more Taoistic than Confucian. As it was with the P'an Ku legend, so was it with this more philosophical cosmogony. The more fertile Taoist and Buddhist imaginations caused the conservation of what the Confucianists, wondering about the wonderful, would have allowed to die a natural death. It was, after all, the magical foreign aspects which gave indicate-- we may appropriately say settled-- the early dualism by transforming it into monism, carrying philosophical speculation from the Knowable to the Unknowable, and providing the Chinese with their very first scientific theory of the beginning, not of the changes going on in deep space (on which they had already formed their opinions), but of the universe itself.

Chou Tzŭ's "T'ai Chi T' u".

Chou Tun-i, properly apotheosized as 'Prince in the Empire of Reason,' finished and integrated the philosophical world-conception which had hitherto obtained in the Chinese mind. He did not ask his fellow-countrymen to discard any part of what they had long held in high esteem: he raised the old theories from the sphere of science to that of approach by unifying them and bringing them to a focus. And he made this marriage intelligible to the Chinese mind by his well-known T'ai chi t' u, or Diagram of the Great Origin (or Grand Terminus), demonstrating that the Grand Original Cause, itself uncaused, produces the yang and the yin, these the 5 Elements, and so on, through the male and female norms (tao), to the production of all things.

Chu Hsi's Monistic Approach

The works of Chu Hsi, specifically his treatise on The Immaterial Principle [li] and Main Matter [ch' i], leave no doubt regarding the monism of his approach. In this work occurs the passage: "In deep space there exists no main matter lacking the immaterial principle; and no immaterial principle apart from primary matter"; and though the 2 are never ever split up "the immaterial principle [as Chou Tzŭ clarifies] is what is previous to form, while primary matter is what is subsequent to form," the idea being that the two are different symptoms of the same mysterious force from which all things continue.

It is unneeded to follow this philosophy along all the different branches which outgrew it, for we are here concerned only with the seed. We have observed how Chinese dualism ended up being a monism, and how while the monism was established the dualism was retained. It is this mono-dualistic theory, integrating the older and more recent approach, which in China, then as now, makes up the accepted explanation of the origin of things, of deep space itself and all that it consists of.

Lao Tzŭ's "Tao".

There are other cosmogonies in Chinese approach, but they need not apprehend us long. Lao Tzŭ (sixth century B.C.), in his Tao-tê ching, The Canon of Reason and Virtue (in the beginning entitled just Lao Tzŭ), offered to the then existing spread sporadic conceptions of the universe a literary form. His tao, or 'Way,' is the producer of Heaven and earth, it is "the mother of all things." His Way, which was "in the past God," is but a metaphorical expression for the manner in which things came at first into running out the primal nothingness, and how the phenomena of nature continue to go on, "in stillness and tranquility, without striving or sobbing." Lao Tzŭ is hence so far monistic, but he is also mystical, transcendental, even pantheistic. The way that can be walked is not the Immortal Way; the name that can be called is not the Immortal Name. The Unnameable is the originator of Heaven and earth; manifesting itself as the Nameable, it is "the mom of all things." "In Immortal Non-Being I see the Spirituality of Things; in Immortal Being their constraint. Though different under these 2 elements, they are the same in beginning; it is when development occurs that different names have to be used. It is while they are in the condition of sameness that the secret concerning them exists. This secret is certainly the secret of secrets. It is the door of all spirituality."

This tao, indefinable and in its essence unknowable, is "the fountain-head of all entities, and the norm of all actions. But it is not only the developmental principle of the universe; it also appears to be primordial matter: chaotic in its structure, born right before Paradise and earth, soundless, formless, standing alone in its privacy, and not changing, universal in its activity, and unrelaxing, without being exhausted, it is capable of ending up being the mother of the universe." And there we might leave it. There is no scheme of creation, correctly so called. The Unwalkable Way leads us to absolutely nothing farther in the way of a cosmogony.

Confucius's Agnosticism.

Confucius (551-- 479 B.C.) did not throw any light on the problem of origin. He did not speculate on the creation of things nor the end of them. He was not bothered to represent the origin of man, nor did he seek to know about his hereafter. He meddled neither with physics nor metaphysics. There might, he thought, be something on the other side of life, for he confessed the existence of spiritual entities. They had an influence on the living, as they triggered them to clothe themselves in ceremonious dress and take care of the sacrificial events. But we should not trouble ourselves about them, anymore than about supernatural things, or physical prowess, or monstrosities. How can we serve souls while we do not know how to serve guys? We feel the existence of something invisible and mysterious, but its nature and meaning are unfathomable for the human understanding to understand. The safest, certainly the only reasonable, course is that of the agnostic-- to leave alone the unknowable, while acknowledging its existence and its secret, and to try to comprehend knowable phenomena and guide our actions appropriately.

Between the monism of Lao Tzŭ and the positivism of Confucius on the one hand, and the landmark of the Taoistic transcendentalism of Chuang Tzŭ (4th and 3rd centuries B.C.) on the other, we find several "guesses at the riddle of existence" which need to be quickly kept in mind as links in the chain of Chinese speculative thought on this essential topic.

Mo Tzŭ and Creation

In the philosophy of Mo Ti (5th and 4th centuries B.C.), generally called Mo Tzŭ or Mu Tzŭ, the theorist of humanism and utilitarianism, we find the idea of creation. It was, he says, Paradise (which was anthropomorphically related to by him as an individual Supreme Being) who "created the sun, moon, and innumerable stars." His system closely looks like Christianity, but the great power of Confucianism as a weapon wielded against all challengers by its doughty defender Mencius (372-- 289 B.C.) is shown by the complete suppression of the impact of Mo Tzŭism at his hands. He even went so far regarding define Mo Tzŭ and those who thought with him as "wild animals."

Mencius and the First Cause

Mencius himself regarded Heaven as the First Cause, or Cause of Causes, but it was not the same personal Paradise as that of Mo Tzŭ. Nor does he hang any cosmogony upon it. His chief concern was to eulogize the doctrines of the great Confucius, and like him he preferred to let the beginning of the universe take care of itself.

Lieh Tzŭ's Absolute

Lieh Tzŭ (said to have lived in the 5th century B.C.), one of the brightest stars in the Taoist constellation, considered this nameable world as having developed from an unnameable outright being. The development did not happen through the direction of an individual will working out a strategy of creation: "In the beginning there was Turmoil [hun tun] It was a mingled potentiality of Form [hsing], Pneuma [ch'i], and Substance [chih] An Excellent Change [t'ai i] took place in it, and there was a Fantastic Starting [t'ai ch'u] which is the beginning of

Form. The Great Beginning developed a Fantastic Beginning [t'ai shih], which is the beginning of Pneuma. The Great Beginning was followed by the Great Blank [t'ai su], which is the very first development of Substance. Substance, Pneuma, and Form being all developed out of the primitive chaotic mass, this material world as it lies right before us came into existence." And that made it possible for Mayhem to progress was the Solitary Indeterminate (i tu or the tao), which is not created, but is able to produce everlastingly. And being both Singular and Indeterminate it tells us absolutely nothing determinate about itself.

Chuang Tzŭ's Super-tao

Chuang Chou (4th and third centuries B.C.), typically known as Chuang Tzŭ, the most dazzling Taoist of all, maintained with Lao Tzŭ that deep space started from the Anonymous, but it was if possible a more outright and transcendental Anonymous than that of Lao Tzŭ. He dwells on the relativity of knowledge; as when asleep he did not know that he was a guy dreaming that he was a butterfly, so when awake he did not know that he was not a butterfly dreaming that he was a guy.8 However "all is embraced in the eliminating unity of the tao, and the sensible man, entering the world of the Infinite, finds rest therein." And this tao, of which we hear so much in Chinese approach, was right before the Great Ultimate or Grand Terminus (t' ai chi), and "from it came the strange existence of God [ti] It produced Paradise, it produced earth."

Popular Cosmogony still Individual or Dualistic

These and other cosmogonies which the Chinese have devised, though it is required to note their presence to give a just idea of their cosmological speculations, need not, as I said, apprehend us long; and the reason why they need not do so is that, in the matter of cosmogony, the P'an Ku legend and the yin-yang system with its monistic elaboration occupy practically the whole field of the Chinese psychological vision. It is these 2-- the well-known and the clinical-- that we mean when we mention Chinese cosmogony. Though occasionally a stern sectarian might deny that deep space came from one or the other of these two ways, still, the general rule holds great. And I have handled them in this order since, though the P'an Ku legend belongs to the 4th century A.D., the I ching dualism was not, appropriately speaking, a cosmogony till Chou Tun-i made it one by the publication of his T'ai chi t'u in the l lth century A.D. Over the unscientific and the clinical minds of the Chinese these two are critical.

Using the general principles specified in the preceding chapter, we find the same cause which operated to limit the development of folklore in general in China ran also in like way in this specific branch of it. With one exception Chinese cosmogony is non-mythological. The cautious and studiously accurate historians (whose work focused on being ex veritate, 'made of truth'), the sober literature, the huge influence of agnostic, matter-of-fact Confucianism, supported by the heavy Mencian weapons, are unassailable indications of a useful creativity which grew too quickly and became too rapidly scientific to admit of much skyrocketing into the worlds of fantasy. Unaroused by any strong stimulus in their ponderings over the riddle of the universe, the sober, plodding researchers and the calm, truth-loving theorists gained a serene victory over the mythologists.

Chapter 10: More about the Gods of China

The Birth of the Soul

The dualism noted in the last chapter is well highlighted by the Chinese temple. Whether as the outcome of the co-operation of the yin and the yang or of the final dissolution of P'an Ku, people originated. To the primitive mind the body and its shadow, an object and its reflection in water, reality and dream life, sensibility and insensibility (as in fainting, etc.), suggest the idea of another life parallel with this life and of the behaviors of the 'other self' in it. This 'other self,' this spirit, which leaves the body for longer or shorter intervals in dreams, swoons, death, might return or be brought back, and the body restore. Spirits which do not return or are not brought back might cause mischief, either alone, or by entry into another human or animal body and even an inanimate item, and should therefore be propitiated. For this reason worship and deification.

The Populous Otherworld

The Chinese pantheon has slowly ended up being so countless that there is scarcely a being or thing which is not, or has not been at some time or other, propitiated or worshipped. As there are great and evil people in this world, so there are gods and demons in the Otherworld: we find a polytheism restricted only by a polydemonism. The dualistic hierarchy is almost all-embracing. To get a clear idea of the populated Otherworld, of the supernal and infernal hosts and their companies, it needs but to imagine the social structure in its highlights as it existed throughout the majority of Chinese history, and to make sure additions. The social structure consisted of the ruler, his court, his civil, army, and ecclesiastical authorities, and his subjects (classified as Scholars-- authorities and gentry-- Agriculturists, Artisans, and Merchants, in that order).

Praise of Shang Ti

When these passed away, their other selves continued to exist and to hold the same rank in the spirit world as they did in this one. The ti, emperor, ended up being the Shang Ti, Emperor on High, who stay in T'ien, Heaven (initially the great dome).1 And Shang Ti, the Emperor on High, was worshipped by ti, the emperor here below, so as to pacify or please him-- to ensure a continuation of his benevolence on his behalf in the world of spirits. Confusion of ideas and paucity of primitive language result in personification and praise of a thing or being in which a spirit has used up its house in place of or in addition to praise of the spirit itself. Thus Heaven (T'ien) itself came to be personified and worshipped in addition to Shang Ti, the Emperor who had gone to Paradise, and who was considered as the chief ruler in the spiritual world. The worship of Shang Ti was in existence before that of T'ien was introduced. Shang Ti was worshipped by the emperor and his family as their forefather, or the head of the hierarchy of their forefathers. Individuals could not praise Shang Ti, for to do so would indicate a familiarity or a claim of relationship punishable with death. The emperor worshipped his ancestors, the authorities theirs, the people theirs. But, in the exact same way and sense that the people worshipped the emperor in the world, as the 'father' of the nation, namely, by love and obeisance, so also could they in this way and this sense worship Shang Ti. An Englishman may take off his hat as the king passes in the street to his coronation without taking any part in the main service in Westminster Abbey. So the 'praise' of Shang Ti by the people was not done officially or with any unique ritualistic or on repaired State occasions, as when it comes to the worship of Shang Ti by the emperor. This, subject to a credentials to be mentioned later, is actually all that is meant (or should be meant) when it is said that the Chinese worship Shang Ti.

As relates to sacrifices to Shang Ti, these could be offered officially only by the emperor, as High Priest in the world, who was attended or helped in the ceremonies by members of his own family or clan or the appropriate State authorities (often, even in relatively modern times, members of the imperial family or clan). In these main sacrifices, which formed part of the State worship, the people could not take part; nor did they at first offer sacrifices to Shang Ti in their own homes or elsewhere. In what way and to what extent they did so later will be revealed presently.

Worship of T'ien

Owing to T'ien, Paradise, the residence of the spirits, ending up being personified, it became worshipped not only by the emperor, but by the people also. But there was a big difference between these 2 worships, because the emperor performed his praise of Paradise formally at the great altar of the Temple of Heaven at Peking (in early times at the altar in the suburban area of the capital), whereas the people (continuing always to worship their ancestors) worshipped Heaven, when they did so at all-- the tradition being observed by some and not by others, just as in Western nations some people go to church, while other people stay away-- generally at the time of the New Year, in a basic, unceremonious way, by lighting some incense-sticks and waving them towards the sky in the courtyards of their own houses or in the street just outside their doors.

Confusion of Shang Ti and T'ien

The credentials necessary to the above description is that, as time went on and especially since the Sung dynasty (A.D. 960-- 1280), much confusion emerged relating to Shang Ti and T'ien, and thus it happened that the terms ended up being blended and their definitions obscure. This confusion of ideas has prevailed down to the present time. One outcome of this is that the people might often state, when they wave their incense-sticks or light their candles, that their humble sacrifice is made to Shang Ti, whom in reality they have no right either to praise or to use sacrifice to, but whom they may unofficially pay respect and make obeisance to, as they might and did to the emperor behind the high boards on the roadsides which shielded him from their view as he was borne along in his sophisticated procession on the few events when he came forth from the royal city.

Hence we find that, while only the emperor could praise and sacrifice to Shang Ti, and only he could formally worship and sacrifice to T'ien, the people who early personified and worshipped T'ien, as already revealed, came, owing to confusion of the significances of Shang Ti and T'ien, unofficially to 'worship' both, but only in the sense and to the level showed, and to use 'sacrifices' to both, also only in the sense and to the level showed. However for these credentials, the declaration that the Chinese worship and sacrifice to Shang Ti and T'ien would be apt to communicate an incorrect idea.

From this it will appear that Shang Ti, the Supreme Ruler on High, and T'ien, Heaven (later personified), do not mean 'God' in the sense that the word is used in the Christian religion. To state that they do, as so many writers on China have done, without explaining the necessary distinctions, is misguiding. That Chinese religious belief was or is "a monotheistic worship of God" is more disproved by the simple fact that Shang Ti and T'ien do not appear in the list of the popular pantheon at all, though all the other gods are there represented. Neither Shang Ti nor T'ien mean the God of Abraham, Isaac, and Jacob, or the Dad, Son, and Holy Ghost of the New Testament. Did they mean this, the efforts of the Christian missionaries to convert the Chinese would be mostly superfluous. The Christian faith, even the Holy Trinity, is a monotheism. That the Chinese religion (although a summary of extracts from the majority of foreign books on China may point to its being so) is not a monotheism, but a polytheism and even a pantheism (as long as that term is taken in the sense of universal deification and not in that of one spiritual being immanent in all things), the rest of the chapter will abundantly prove.

There have been 3 periods in which gods have been created in abnormally large numbers: that of the legendary emperor Hsien Yüan (2698-- 2598 B.C.), that of Chiang Tzŭ-ya (in the twelfth century B.C.), and that of the very first emperor of the Ming dynasty (in the fourteenth century A.D.).

The Otherworld Similar to this World
The similarity of the Otherworld to this world above alluded to is well revealed by Du Bose in his Dragon, Image, and, Satanic force, from which I estimate the following passages:

" The world of spirits is a specific equivalent of the Chinese Empire, or, as has been mentioned, it is 'China tilled under'; this is the world of light; put out the lights and you have Tartarus. China has eighteen [now twenty-two] provinces, so has Hades; each province has 8 or 9 prefects, or departments; so each province in Hades has 8 or nine departments; every prefect or department averages ten counties, so every department in Hades has 10 counties. In Soochow the Ruler, the provincial Treasurer, the Criminal Judge, the Intendant of Circuit, the Prefect or Departmental Ruler, and the three District Magistrates or County Governors each have temples with their apotheoses in the other world. Not only these, but every yamên secretary, runner, executioner, policeman, and constable has his counterpart in the land of darkness. The market-towns have also mandarins of lower rank in charge, besides a host of revenue collectors, the bureau of federal government works and other departments, with some hundred 1000 officials, who all rank as gods beyond the grave. These divine entities are citizens; the military having a comparable gradation for the armies of Hades, whose captains are gods, and whose battalions are fiends.

" The of this wonderful scheme for the spirits of the dead, having no higher standard, moved to the authorities of that world the etiquette, tastes, and venality of their correlate authorities in the Chinese Federal government, therefore making it needed to use similar ways to appease the one which are found essential to move the other. All the State gods have their assistants, attendants, door-keepers, runners, horses, horsemen, investigators, and executioners, corresponding in every specific to those of Chinese authorities of the same rank." (Pp. 358--359.)

This likeness clarifies also why the hierarchy of entities in the Otherworld concerns itself not only with the affairs of the Otherworld, but with those of this world too. So faithful is the similarity that we find the gods (the term is used in this chapter to consist of goddesses, who are, however, reasonably couple of) subjected to tons of the guidelines and conditions existing on this earth. Not only do they, as already revealed, vary in rank, but they hold levées and audiences and might be promoted for recognized services, just as the Chinese authorities are. They "may arise from a modest position to one near the Pearly Emperor, who provides the reward of merit for ruling well the affairs of guys. The correlative divine entities of the mandarins are only of equivalent rank, yet the fact that they have been apotheosized makes them their superiors and in shape things of worship. Chinese mandarins turn in office, usually every 3 years, and then there is a corresponding change in Hades. The image in the temple remains the same, but the spirit which stays in the clay tabernacle changes, so the idol has a different name, birthday, and tenant. The priests are notified by the Great Wizard of the Dragon Tiger Mountain, but how can the people know gods which are not the same to-day as the other day?"

The gods also enjoy amusements, wed, sin, are punished, die, are resurrected, or die and are changed, or die finally.

The Three Religious beliefs

We have in China the universal praise of ancestors, which constitutes (or did till A.D. 1912) the State religion, typically referred to as Confucianism, and in addition we have the gods of the specific faiths (which also originally took their arise in ancestor-worship), specifically, Buddhism and Taoism. (Other faiths, though endured, are not acknowledged as Chinese faiths.) It is with a short account of this great hierarchy and its folklore that we will now concern ourselves.

Besides the regular ancestor-worship (as distinct from the State praise) the people required to Buddhism and Taoism, which became the well-known religions, and the literati also honoured the gods of these 2 sects. Buddhist deities gradually became installed in Taoist temples, and the Taoist immortals were given seats next to the Buddhas in their sanctuaries. Every one bought from the god who appeared to him the most popular and the most financially rewarding. There even happened unified in the exact same temple and worshipped at the exact same altar the 3 religious creators or figure-heads, Confucius, Buddha, and Lao Tzŭ. The 3 religious beliefs were even considered forming one whole, or at least, though different, as having one and the same object: san êrh i yeh, or han san wei i, "the three are one," or "the 3 join to form one" (a quotation from the phrase T'ai chi han san wei i of Fang Yü-lu: "When they reach the severe the 3 are seen to be one"). In the well-known pictorial depictions of the temple this impartiality is plainly revealed.

The Super-triad

The toleration, fraternity, or co-mixture of the three religions-- ancestor-worship or Confucianism, Chinese Buddhism, and Taoism-- clarifies the substance nature of the triune head of the Chinese pantheon. The numerous deities of Buddhism and Taoism culminate each in a triad of gods (the 3 Precious Ones and the 3 Pure Ones respectively), but the three religions collectively have also a triad compounded of one representative member of each. This general or super-triad is, naturally, made up of Confucius, Lao Tzŭ, and Buddha. This is the officially decreed order, though it is varied occasionally by Buddha being put in the centre (the spot of honour) as an act of ritualistic deference revealed to a 'stranger' or 'guest' from another nation.

Praise of the Living

Right before continuing to think about the gods of China in detail, it is required to note that ancestor-worship, which, as right before specified, is worship of the ghosts of departed persons, who are generally but not inevitably loved ones of the worshipper, has at times a sort of preliminary phase in this world including the worship of living beings. Emperors, viceroys, popular officials, or people cherished for their kind deeds have had altars, temples, and images put up to them, where they are worshipped in the exact same way as those who have already "shuffled off this mortal coil." The most usual cases are maybe those of the worship of living emperors and those in which some high authority who has acquired the gratitude of the people is transferred to another post. The clarification is basic. The 2nd self which exists after death is identical with the second self inhabiting the body throughout life. Therefore it might be propitiated or gratified by sacrifices of food, drink, and so on, or theatricals performed in its honour, and continue its security and good offices even though now far away.

Confucianism

Confucianism (Ju Chiao) is said to be the religious belief of the learned, and the learned were the authorities and the literati or lettered class, which includes academics waiting on posts, those who have couldn't get posts (or, though certified, prefer to live in retirement), and those who have retired from posts. Of this 'religious belief' it has been said:

" The name embraces education, letters, principles, and political viewpoint. Its head was not a religious man, practised couple of spiritual rites, and taught nothing about faith. In its usual acceptation the term Confucianist means 'a gentleman and a academic'; he might praise only once a year, yet he comes from the Church. Unlike its two sisters, it has no priesthood, and fundamentally is not a religion at all; yet with the many rites implanted on the original tree it becomes a religious beliefs, and the one most difficult to handle. Thought about as a Church, the classics are its scriptures, the schools its churches, the teachers its priests, ethics its faith, and the written character, so sacred, its symbol." 3.

Confucius not a God.

It should be noted that Confucius himself is not a god, though he has been and is worshipped (66,000 animals used to be offered to him every year; probably the number is about the same now). Suggestions have been made to make him the God of China and Confucianism the religious belief of China, so that he and his faith would hold the exact same relative positions that Christ and Christianity do in the West. I was present at the prolonged dispute which occurred on this subject in the Chinese Parliament in February 1917, but in spite of tons of long, learned, and significant speeches, primarily by academics of the old school, the movement was not brought. However, the praise accorded to Confucius was and is (other than by 'brand-new' or 'young' China) of so extreme a nature that he might practically be described as the great unapotheosized god of China.4 Some of his portraits even credit him superhuman characteristics. However in spite of all this the simple fact remains that Confucius has not been appointed a god and holds no exequatur entitling him to that rank.

If we explore the reason of this we find that, impressive though it may seem, Confucius is classed by the Chinese not as a god (shên), but as a devil (kuei). A brief historic declaration will make the matter clear.

In the classical Li chi, Book of Ritualistic, we find the categorical task of the worship of certain challenge certain subjective beings: the emperor worshipped Heaven and earth, the feudal princes the mountains and rivers, the officials the hearth, and the literati their ancestors. Heaven, earth, mountains, rivers, and hearth were called shên (gods), and ancestors kuei (demons). This difference is due to Paradise being considered as the god and the people as satanic forces-- the upper is the god, the lower the fiend or devil. Though kuei were generally bad, the term in Chinese consists of both good and evil spirits. In old times those who had by their meritorious virtue while in the world prevented calamities from the people were posthumously worshipped and called gods, but those who were worshipped by their descendants only were called spirits or devils.

In the praise of Confucius by emperors of different dynasties (details of which need not be given here) the greatest titles gave on him were Hsien Shêng, 'Former or Ancestral Saint,' and even Win Hsüan Wang, 'Accomplished and Renowned Prince,' and other ones containing like epithets. When for his image or idol there was (in the eleventh year-- A.D. 1307-- of the reign-period Ta Tê of the Emperor Ch' êng Tsung of the Yüan dynasty) replaced the tablet now seen in the Confucian temples, these were the engravings inscribed on it. In the inscriptions authoritatively put on the tablets the word shên does not take place; in those cases where it does occur it has been placed there (as by the Taoists) unlawfully and without authority by too ardent devotees. Confucius might not be called a shên, since there is no record demonstrating that the great ethical teacher was ever apotheosized, or that any order was considered that the character shên was to be applied to him.

The God of Literature
In addition to the ancestors of whose praise it truly consists, Confucianism has in its temple the specialized gods worshipped by the literati. Naturally the chief of these is Wên Ch' ang, the God of Literature. The account of him (which differs in several particulars in different Chinese works) relates that he was a man of the name of Chang Ya, who was born throughout the T'ang dynasty in the kingdom of Yüeh (modern Chêkiang), and went to live at Tzŭ T'ung in Ssŭch' uan, where his intelligence raised him to the position of President of the Board of Ceremonies. Another account refers to him as Chang Ya Tzŭ, the Soul or Spirit of Tzŭ T'ung, and mentions

that he held office in the Chin dynasty (A.D. 265-- 316), and was killed in a battle. Another again specifies that under the Sung dynasty (A.D. 960-- 1280), in the 3rd year (A.D. 1000) of the reign-period Hsien P'ing of the Emperor Chên Tsung, he repressed the revolt of Wang Chün at Ch' êng Tu in Ssŭch' uan. General Lei Yu-chung triggered to be shot into the besieged town arrows to which notices were attached welcoming the inhabitants to give up. All of a sudden a man installed a ladder, and indicating the rebels cried in a loud voice: "The Spirit of Tzŭ T'ung has sent me to inform you that the town will fall into the hands of the enemy on the twentieth day of the ninth moon, and not a bachelor will get away death." Efforts to strike down this prophet of evil failed, for he had already disappeared. The town was caught on the day suggested. The general, as a reward, caused the temple of Tzŭ T'ung's Spirit to be repaired, and sacrifices offered to it.

The thing of worship nowadays in the temples committed to Wên Ch' ang is Tzŭ T'ung Ti Chün, the God of Tzŭ T'ung. The practical flexibility of dualism allowed Chang to have as many as seventeen reincarnations, which varied over a period of some 3 thousand years.

Different emperors at various times bestowed upon Wên Ch' ang honorific titles, until eventually, in the Yüan, or Mongol, dynasty, in the reign Yen Yu, in A.D. 1314, the title was conferred on him of Supporter of the Yüan Dynasty, Diffuser of Renovating Influences, Ssŭ-lu of Wên Ch' ang, God and Lord. He was therefore apotheosized, and took his spot among the gods of China. By steps couple of or tons of a man in China has typically become a god.

Wên Ch' ang and the Great Bear

Thus we have the God of Literature, Wên Ch' ang Ti Chün, duly set up in the Chinese temple, and sacrifices were offered to him in the schools.

But scholars, specifically those ready to go into for the general public competitive examinations, worshipped as the God of Literature, or as his palace or home (Wên Ch'ang), the star K'uei in the Great Bear, or Dipper, or Bushel-- the latter name stemmed from its resemblance in shape to the measure used by the Chinese and called tou. The term K'uei was more generally applied to the four stars forming the body or square part of the Dipper, the 3 forming the tail or handle being called Shao or Piao. How all this happened is another story.

An expert, as popular for his literary ability as his facial deformities, had been admitted as first academician at the cosmopolitan examinations. It was the habit that the Emperor should give with his own hand a rose of gold to the fortunate prospect. This academic, whose name was Chung K'uei, presented himself according to custom to get the benefit which by right was because of him. At the sight of his repulsive face the Emperor refused the golden rose. In despair the unhappy turned down one went and tossed himself into the sea. At the moment when he was being choked by the waters a mystical fish or monster called ao raised him on its back and brought him to the surface area. K'uei rose to Paradise and became arbiter of the destinies of men of letters. His house was said to be the star K'uei, a name given by the Chinese to the sixteen stars of the constellation or 'estate' of Andromeda and Pisces. The academics quite quickly began to praise K'uei as the God of Literature, and to represent it on a column in the temples. Then sacrifices were offered to it. This star or constellation was considered the palace of the god. The legend generated an expression frequently used in Chinese of one who comes out initially in an evaluation, particularly, tu chan ao t'ou, "to stand alone on the sea-monster's head." It is especially to be kept in mind that though the two K'ueis have the same noise they are represented by different characters, and that the two constellations are not the exact same, but are situated in widely different parts of the heavens.

How then did it happen that experts worshipped the K'uei in the Great Bear as the house of the God of Literature? (It may be said in passing that a literary people could not have chosen a more appropriate palace for this god, since the Great Bear, the 'Chariot of Paradise,' is considered as the centre and governor of the whole universe.) The worship, we saw, was at initially that of the star K'uei, the apotheosized 'homely,' successful, but rejected prospect. As time went on, there was a general demand for a practical, concrete representation of the star-god: a simple character did not please the well-known taste. But it was no simple matter to comply with the need. Ultimately, directed doubtless by the community of pronunciation, they substituted for the star or group of stars K'uei ,5 venerated in old times, a new star or group of stars K'uei , forming the square part of the Bushel, Dipper, or Great Bear. But for this again no bodily image could be found, so the form of the written character itself was taken, and so drawn as to represent a kuei (3) (disembodied spirit, or ghost) with its foot raised, and bearing aloft a tou (4) (bushel-measure). The love was hence lost, for the constellation K'uei (2) was mistaken for K'uei , the correct thing of praise. It was because of this confusion by the academics that the Northern Bushel became worshipped as the God of Literature.

Wên Ch' ang and Tzŭ T'ung

This worship had nothing whatever to do with the Spirit of Tzŭ T'ung, but the Taoists have connected Chang Ya with the constellation in another way by saying that Shang Ti, the Supreme Ruler, turned over Chang Ya's child with the management of the palace of Wên Ch' ang. And experts gradually got the habit of saying that they owed their success to the Spirit of Tzŭ T'ung, which they falsely represented as being an incarnation of the star Wên Ch' ang. This is how Chang Ya came to have the honorific title of Wên Ch' ang, but, as a Chinese author mentions, Chang belonged correctly to Ssŭch' uan, and his worship must be restricted to that province. The literati there venerated him as their master, and as a mark of affection and thankfulness built a temple to him; but in doing so they had no objective of making him the God of Literature. "There being no real connexion between Chang Ya and K'uei, the praise ought to be stopped." The gadget of integrating the personality of the client of literature enthroned among the stars with that of the deified mortal canonized as the Spirit of Tzŭ T'ung was basically a Taoist technique. "The thaumaturgic track record assigned to the Spirit of Chang Ya Tzŭ was confined for centuries to the valleys of Ssŭch' uan, until at some duration antecedent to the reign Yen Yu, in A.D. 1314, a combination was arranged between the functions of the local god and those of the stellar customer of literature. Imperial sanction was acquired for this stroke of priestly shrewd; and notwithstanding demonstrations constantly repeated by orthodox sticklers for precision in the religious canon, the composite divine being has kept his claims undamaged, and an inseparable connexion between the God of Literature created by imperial patent and the spirit lodged amongst the stars of Ursa Major is completely acknowledged in the State ritualistic of the present day." A temple committed to this divinity by the State exists in every city of China, besides other ones put up as personal benefactions or speculations.

Wherever Wên Ch' ang is worshipped there will also be found a different depiction of K'uei Hsing, showing that while the main deity has been enabled to 'obtain magnificence' from the well-known god, and even to assume his personality, the independent existence of the outstanding spirit is nevertheless sedulously preserved. The spot of the latter in the heavens above is usually represented by the lodgment of his idol in an upper floor or tower, known as the K'uei Hsing Ko or K'uei Hsing Lou. Here students worship the customer of their occupation with incense and prayers. Therefore, the old outstanding divinity still largely monopolizes the popular idea of a defender of literature and research study, notwithstanding that the deified recluse of Tzŭ T'ung has been included this capability to the State pantheon for more than five hundred years.

Heaven-deaf and Earth-dumb

The popular likenesss of Wên Ch' ang illustrate the god himself and 4 other figures. The main and biggest is the demure portrait of the god, clothed in blue and holding a sceptre in his left hand. Behind him stand two vibrant attendants. They are the servant and groom who always accompany him on his journeys (on which he rides a white horse). Their names are respectively Hsüan T'ung- tzŭ and Ti-mu, 'Sombre Youth' and 'Earth-mother'; more frequently they are called T'ien- lung, 'Deaf Celestial,' and Ti-ya, 'Mute Terrestrial,' or 'Deaf as Paradise' and 'Mute as Earth.' Therefore, they cannot reveal the secrets of their master's administration as he disperses intellectual gifts, literary ability, etc. Their cosmogonical connexion has already been referred to in a previous chapter.

Picture of K'uei Hsing

In front of Wên Ch' ang, on his left, stands K'uei Hsing. He is represented as of diminutive stature, with the visage of a demon, holding a writing-brush in his right-hand man and a tou in his left, one of his legs kicking up behind-- the figure being undoubtedly planned as an impersonation of the character k' uei .6 He is considered as the supplier of literary degrees, and was invoked above all in order to obtain success at the competitive evaluations. His images and temples are found in all towns. In the temples devoted to Wên Ch' ang there are always 2 secondary altars, one of which is consecrated to his praise.

Mr Redcoat

The other is devoted to Chu I, 'Mr Redcoat.' He and K'uei Hsing are represented as the two inseparable companions of the God of Literature. The legend related of Chu I is as follows:

During the T'ang dynasty, in the reign-period Chien Chung (A.D. 780-- 4) of the Emperor Tê Tsung, the Princess T'ai Yin saw that Lu Ch'i, a native of Hua Chou, had the bones of an Immortal, and wished to marry him.

Ma P' o, her neighbour, introduced him one day into the Crystal Palace for an interview with his future wife. The Princess gave him the choice of 3 careers: to live in the Dragon Prince's Palace, with the guarantee of immortal life, to enjoy immortality among the people on the earth, or to have the honour of becoming a minister of the Empire. Lu Ch' i first answered that he wishes to live in the Crystal Palace. The young lady, overjoyed, said to him: "I am Princess T'ai Yin. I will at once inform Shang Ti, the Supreme Ruler." A minute later the arrival of a celestial messenger was announced. Two officers bearing flags preceded him and conducted him to the foot of the flight of steps. He then presented himself as Chu I, the envoy of Shang Ti.

Addressing himself to Lu Ch' i, he asked: "Do you wish to reside in the Crystal Palace?" The latter did not reply. T'ai Yin advised him to give his answer, but he continued keeping silent. The Princess in despair retired to her apartment or condo, and highlighted 5 pieces of valuable fabric, which she presented to the magnificent envoy, pleading him to have patience a little bit longer and wait for the answer. After a long time, Chu I repeated his question. Then Lu Ch' i in a firm voice answered: "I have consecrated my life to the tough labour of research study, and desire to attain to the self-respect of minister on this earth."

T'ai Yin ordered Ma P' o to perform Lu Ch' i from the palace. From that day his face ended up being transformed: he obtained the lips of a dragon, the head of a panther, the green face of an Immortal, and so on. He took his degree, and was promoted to be Director of the Censorate. The Emperor, valuing the common sense displayed in his advice, selected him a minister of the Empire.

From this legend it would appear that Chu I is the purveyor of main posts; however, in practice, he is more generally considered as the protector of weak candidates, as the God of Good Luck for those who present themselves at the examinations with a somewhat light equipment of literary knowledge. The unique legend associating with this rôle is understood all over in China. It is as follows:

Mr Redcoat nods his Head

An examiner, engaged in remedying the essays of the prospects, after a superficial examination of one of the essays, put it on one side as manifestly inferior, being quite determined not to pass the prospect who had composed it. The essay, moved by some mystical power, was changed in front of his eyes, as though to welcome him to analyze it more diligently. At the exact same time a reverend old man, dressed in a red garment, unexpectedly appeared before him, and by a nod of his head gave him to understand that he ought to pass the essay. The inspector, shocked at the novelty of the event, and strengthened by the approval of his transcendent visitor, admitted the author of the essay to the literary degree.

Chu I, like K'uei Hsing, is invoked by the literati as an effective protector and help to success. When anybody with but a poor chance of passing presents himself at an evaluation, his good friends motivate him by the well-known expression: "Who knows but that Mr Redcoat will nod his head?"

Mr Golden Cuirass

Chu I is sometimes joined by another personage, called Chin Chia, 'Mr Golden Cuirass.' Like K'uei Hsing and Chu I he has charge of the interests of experts, but varies from them in that he holds a flag, which he has only to wave in front of a home for the family inhabiting it to be ensured that among their descendants will be some who will win literary honours and be promoted to high offices under the State.

Though Chin Chia is the protector of experts, he is also the redoubtable avenger of their evil actions: his flag is saluted as a promise, but his sword is the horror of the wicked.

The God of War

Still another client divine being of literature is the God of War. "How," it may be asked, "can so peaceful a people as the Chinese put so tranquil a profession as literature under the patronage of so military a divine being as the God of War?" But that question betrays ignorance of the character of the Chinese Kuan Ti. He is not a harsh tyrant delighting in fight and the slaying of enemies: he is the god who can avert war and protect the people from its horrors.

A youth, whose name was initially Chang-shêng, later changed to Shou-chang, and then to Yün-chang, who was born near Chieh Liang, in Ho Tung (now the town of Chieh Chou in Shansi), and was of an intractable nature, having actually annoyed his father and mother, was shut up in a room from which he escaped by breaking through the window. In one of the neighbouring houses he heard a girl and an old man weeping and regretting. Going to the foot of the wall of the substance, he asked the reason of their sorrow. The old man replied that though his daughter was already engaged, the uncle of the regional authority, smitten by her charm, wished to make her his courtesan. His petitions to the authority had only been declined with curses.

Next to himself with rage, the youth took a sword and went and killed both the official and his uncle. He left through the T'ung Kuan, the pass to Shensi. Having with problem kept away from capture by the barrier officials, he knelt down at the side of a brook to clean his face; when lo! his appearance was entirely changed. His skin tone had ended up being reddish-grey, and he was absolutely unrecognizable. He then presented himself with guarantee before the officers, who asked him his name. "My name is Kuan," he replied. It was by that name that he was afterwards understood.

The Meat-seller's Obstacle

One day he got to Chu-chou, a reliant sub-prefecture of Peking, in Chihli. There Chang Fei, a butcher, who had been selling his meat all the early morning, at midday decreased what stayed into a well, positioned over the mouth of the well a stone weighing twenty-five pounds, and said with a sneer: "If anyone can raise that stone and take my meat, I will make him a present of it!" Kuan Yü, going up to the edge of the well, raised the stone with the exact same ease as he would a tile, took the meat, and left. Chang Fei pursued him, and ultimately the 2 came to blows, but no one dared to separate them. Just then Liu Pei, a hawker of straw shoes, showed up, interposed, and stopped the battle. The community of ideas which they found they possessed quickly triggered a firm friendship between the 3 guys.

The Oath in the Peach-orchard

Another account represents Liu Pei and Chang Fei as having gotten in a village inn to drink white wine, when a guy of massive stature pushing a wheelbarrow stopped at the door to rest. As he seated himself, he hailed the waiter, saying: "Bring me some wine rapidly, since I need to speed up to reach the town to get in the army."

Liu Pei looked at this man, nine feet in height, with a beard 2 feet long. His face was the colour of the fruit of the jujube-tree, and his lips carmine. Eyebrows like sleeping silkworms shaded his phoenix eyes, which were a scarlet red. Horrible undoubtedly was his bearing.

" What is your name?" asked Liu Pei. "My family name is Kuan, my own name is Yü, my surname Yün Chang," he responded. "I am from the Ho Tung country. For the last 5 or 6 years I have been roaming about the world as a fugitive, to get away from my chase afterrs, as I killed a powerful man of my country who was oppressing the poor people. I hear that they are gathering a body of soldiers to crush the brigands, and I should like to join the exploration."

Chang Fêi, also named Chang I Tê, is described as eight feet in height, with round shining eyes in a panther's head, and a pointed chin bristling with a tiger's beard. His voice looked like the rumbling of thunder. His ardour was just like that of a fiery steed. He hailed Cho Chün, where he had some fertile farms, and was a butcher and wine-merchant.

Liu Pei, surnamed Hsüan Tê, otherwise Hsien Chu, was the 3rd member of the group.

The 3 men went to Chang Fei's farm, and on the morrow met together in his peach-orchard, and sealed their friendship with an oath. Having actually procured a black ox and a white horse, with the numerous accessories to a sacrifice, they immolated the victims, burnt the incense of friendship, and after two times prostrating themselves took this oath:

" We 3, Liu Pei, Kuan Yû, and Chang Fei, already unified by mutual friendship, though coming from different clans, now bind ourselves by the union of our hearts, and join our forces in order to help one another in times of risk.

" We wish to pay to the State our financial obligation of faithful residents and give peace to our black-haired compatriots. We do not ask if we were born in the exact same year, the same month, or on the same day, but we desire only that the same year, the exact same month, and the same day may find us united in death. Might Paradise our King and Earth our Queen see clearly our hearts! If any among us violate justice or forget advantages, might Heaven and Man join to punish him!"

The oath having been officially taken, Liu Pei was saluted as senior brother, Kuan Yü as the 2nd, and Chang Fei as the youngest. Their sacrifice to Heaven and earth ended, they killed an ox and served a banquet, to which the soldiers of the district were welcomed to the number of 3 hundred or more. They all drank copiously till they were intoxicated. Liu Pei enrolled the peasants; Chang Fei obtained for them horses and arms; and then they set out to make war on the Yellow Turbans (Huang Chin Tsei). Kuan Yü showed himself worthy of the affection which Liu Pei revealed to him; brave and generous, he never ever turned aside from danger. His fidelity was revealed particularly on one occasion when, having actually been taken detainee by Ts' ao Ts' ao, together with 2 of Liu Pei's wives, and having actually been allocated a typical sleeping-apartment with his fellow-captives, he preserved the girls' reputation and his own credibility by standing all night at the door of the room with a lighted lantern in his hand.

Into details of the numerous exploits of the 3 Sibling of the Peach-orchard we really need not get in here. They are written in full in the book of the Story of the Three Kingdoms, a romance in which every Chinese who can read takes eager delight. Kuan Yü stayed faithful to his oath, despite the fact that lured with a marquisate by the great Ts' ao Ts' ao, but he was at length captured by Sun Ch' üan and put to death (A.D. 219). Long celebrated as the most popular of China's army heroes, he was ennobled in A.D. 1120 as Faithful and Loyal Duke. 8 years later he had given to him by letters patent the still more remarkable title of Splendid Prince and Pacificator. The Emperor Wên (A.D. 1330-- 3) of the Yüan dynasty added the appellation Warrior Prince and Civilizer, and, finally, the Emperor Wan Li of the Ming dynasty, in 1594, gave on him the title of Faithful and Loyal Great Ti, Advocate of Paradise and Protector of the Kingdom. He therefore ended up being a god, a ti, and has since received worship as Kuan Ti or Wu Ti, the God of War. Temples (1600 State temples and countless littler ones) set up in his honour are to be seen in all parts of the nation. He is just one of the most well-known gods of China Throughout the last half-century of the Manchu Period his fame greatly increased. In 1856 he is said to have appeared in the paradises and successfully turned the tide of fight in favour of the Imperialists. His portrait awaits every camping tent, but his worship is not confined to the officials and the army, for tons of trades and occupations have chosen him as a tutelary saint. The sword of the public executioner used to be kept within the precincts of his temple, and after an execution the administering magistrate would stop there to praise for worry the ghost of the criminal may follow him home. He knew that the spirit would not dare to enter Kuan Ti's presence.

Therefore, the Chinese have no less than three gods of literature-- maybe not too many for so literary a people. A fourth, a Taoist god, will be discussed later.

Chapter 11: Information about Buddhism in China

Buddhism and its mythology have formed a fundamental part of Chinese thought for almost 2 1000 years. The faith was given China about A.D. 65, ready-made in its Mahayanistic form, in effect of an imagine the Emperor Ming Ti (A.D. 58-- 76) of the Eastern Han dynasty in or about the year 63; though some knowledge of Buddha and his teachings existed as early as 217 B.C. As Buddha, the chief deity of Buddhism, was a guy and ended up being a god, the religion stemmed, like the others, in ancestor-worship. When a guy passes away, says this faith, his other self comes back in one form or another, "from a clod to a divinity." The way for Buddhism in China was paved by Taoism, and Buddhism reciprocally impacted Taoism by useful development of its doctrines of sanctity and immortalization. Buddhism also, as it has been well put by Dr De Groot,7 "contributed much to the ritualistic accessory of ancestor-worship. Its salvation work on behalf of the dead saved its place in Confucian China; for of Confucianism itself, piety and dedication towardss parents and forefathers, and the promotion of their joy, were the core, and, as a result, their praise with sacrifices and ceremonies was always a spiritual duty." It was hence that it was possible for the gods of Buddhism to be introduced into China and to maintain their unique characters and fulfil their unique functions without being absorbed into or submerged by the existing native religious beliefs. The result was, as we have seen, in the end a partnership instead of a relation of master and servant; and I say 'in the end' because, contrary to common belief, the Chinese have not been tolerant of foreign spiritual faiths, and at different times have maltreated Buddhism as relentlessly as they have other rivals to orthodox Confucianism.

Buddha, the Law, and the Priesthood
At the head of the Buddhist gods in China we find the triad called Buddha, the Law, and the Church, or Priesthood, which are personified as Shih-chia Fo (Shâkya), O-mi-t' o Fo (Amita), and Ju-lai Fo (Tathagata); otherwise Fo Pao, Fa Pao, and Sêng Pao (the San Pao, '3 Precious Ones')--that is, Buddha, the prophet who came into the world to teach the Law, Dharma, the Law Immortal, and Samgha, its mystical body, Priesthood, or Church. Dharma is an entity underived, containing the spiritual aspects and product constituents of the universe. From it the other two evolve: Buddha (Shâkyamuni), the creative energy, Samgha, the totality of existence and of life. To the people these are 3 individual Buddhas, whom they worship without concerning themselves about their origin. To the priests they are just the Buddha, past, present, or future. There are also several other of these groups or triads, ten or more, composed of different divine entities, or often containing a couple of the triad already named. Shâkyamuni heads the list, having a location in at least six.

The legend of the Buddha belongs rather to Indian than to Chinese mythology and is too long to be reproduced here.

The principal gods of Buddhism are Jan-têng Fo, the Light-lamp Buddha, Mi-lo Fo (Maitrêya), the expected Messiah of the Buddhists, O-mi-t' o Fo (Amitabha or Amita), the guide who conducts his followers to the Western Paradise, Yüeh-shih Fo, the Master-physician Buddha, Ta-shih-chih P' u-sa (Mahastama), companion of Amitabha, P' i-lu Fo (Vairotchana), the greatest of the Threefold Embodiments, Kuan Yin, the Goddess of Mercy, Ti-tsang Wang, the God of Hades, Wei-t' o (Vihârapâla), the Dêva protector of the Law of Buddha and Buddhist temples, the Four Diamond Kings of Paradise, and Bodhidharma, the very first of the six Patriarchs of Eastern or Chinese Buddhism.

Diamond Kings of Heaven

On the right and left sides of the entryway hall of Buddhist temples, 2 on each side, are the massive figures of the four great Ssŭ Ta Chin-kang or T'ien- wang, the Diamond Kings of Heaven, protectors or rulers of the continents lying in the direction of the 4 cardinal points from Mount Sumêru, the centre of the world. They are 4 brothers called respectively Mo-li Ch' ing (Pure), or Tsêng Chang, Mo-li Hung (Vast), or Kuang Mu, Mo-li Hai (Sea), or To Wên, and Mo-li Shou (Age), or Ch' ih Kuo. The Chin kuang ming states that they bestow all types of happiness on those who honour the Three Treasures, Buddha, the Law, and the Priesthood. Kings and countries who disregard the Law lose their security. They are defined and represented as follows:

Mo-li Ch' ing, the oldest, is twenty-four feet in height, with a beard the hairs of which are a lot like copper wire. He carries a splendid jade ring and a spear, and always fights on foot. He has also a magic sword, 'Blue Cloud,' on the blade of which are etched the characters Ti, Shui, Huo, Fêng (Earth, Water, Fire, Wind). When brandished, it causes a black wind, which produces tens of countless spears, which pierce the bodies of guys and turn them to dust. The wind is followed by a fire, which fills the air with tens of countless golden fiery serpents. A thick smoke also rises up out of the ground, which blinds and burns guys, none being able to escape.

Mo-li Hung carries in his hand an umbrella, called the Umbrella of Chaos, formed of pearls had of spiritual properties. Opening this wonderful carry out causes the heavens and earth to be covered with thick darkness, and turning it upside down produces storms of wind and thunder and universal earthquakes.

Mo-li Hai holds a four-stringed guitar, the twanging of which transcendently impacts the earth, water, fire, or wind. When it is played all the world listens, and the camps of the enemy take fire.

Mo-li Shou has two whips and a panther-skin bag, the home of an animal resembling a white rat, known as Hua-hu Tiao. When at big this creature presumes the form of a white winged elephant, which feasts on men. He in some cases has also a snake or other man-eating creature, always prepared to obey his behests.

Legend of the Diamond Kings

The legend of the Four Diamond Kings given up the Fêng shên yen i is as follows: At the time of the combination of the Chou dynasty in the twelfth and l lth centuries B.C., Chiang Tzŭ-ya, chief counsellor to Wên Wang, and General Huang Fei-hu were safeguarding the town and mountain of Hsi-ch' i. The supporters of the house of Shang interested the four genii Mo, who lived at Chia-mêng Kuan, praying them to come to their help. They concurred, raised an army of

100,000 celestial soldiers, and traversing towns, fields, and mountains shown up in less than a day at the north gate of Hsi-ch' i, where Mo-li Ch' ing pitched his camp and entrenched his soldiers.

Hearing of this, Huang Fei-hu sped up to warn Chiang Tzŭ-ya of the danger which threatened him. "The four great generals who have just gotten to the north gate," he said, "are marvellously effective genii, professionals in all the mysteries of magic and usage of wonderful charms. It is much to be feared that we shall not have the ability to resist them."

A lot of intense fights occurred. In the beginning these entered favour of the Chin-kang, thanks to their magic weapons and particularly to Mo-li Shou's Hua-hu Tiao, who terrified the opponent by devouring their bravest warriors.

Hua-hu Tiao feasts on Yang Chien

Sadly for the Chin-kang, the brute attacked and swallowed Yang Chien, the nephew of Yü Huang. This genie, on getting in the body of the monster, lease his heart asunder and cut him in two. As he could transform himself at will, he presumed the shape of Hua-hu Tiao, and went off to Mo-li Shou, who unsuspectingly put him back into his bag.

The 4 Kings held a celebration to celebrate their accomplishment, and having drunk copiously gave themselves over to sleep. Throughout the night Yang Chien came out of the bag, with the intention of having himself of the 3 magical weapons of the Chin-kang. But he succeeded only in carrying off the umbrella of Mo-li Hung. In a subsequent engagement No-cha, the child of Vadjrâ-pani, the God of Thunder, broke the jade ring of Mo-li Ch'ing. Bad luck followed misfortune. The Chin-kang, denied of their magic weapons, began to lose heart. To complete their discomfiture, Huang T'ien Hua brought to the attack a matchless magical weapon. This was a spike 7 1/2 inches long, enclosed in a silk sheath, and called 'Heart-piercer.' It projected so strong a ray of light that eyes were blinded by it.

Huang T'ien Hua, hard pressed by Mo-li Ch'ing, drew the mysterious spike from its sheath, and hurled it at his foe. It entered his neck, and with a deep groan the giant fell dead.

Mo-li Hung and Mo-li Hai accelerated to avenge their brother, but ere they could come within striking range of Huang Ti'en Hua his redoubtable spike reached their hearts, and they lay susceptible at his feet.

The one remaining hope for the sole survivor was in Hua-hu Tiao. Mo-li Shou, not understanding that the creature had been killed, put his hand into the bag to pull him out, whereupon Yang Chien, who had returned to the bag, bit his hand off at the wrist, so that there stayed absolutely nothing but a stump of bone.

In this moment of extreme pain Mo-li Shou fell a simple prey to Huang T'ien Hua, the magic spike pierced his heart, and he fell bathed in his blood. Therefore died the last of the Chin-kang.

Chapter 12: The 3 Pure Ones

Turning to the gods of Taoism, we find that the triad or trinity, already noted as forming the head of that hierarchy, consists of three Supreme Gods, each in his own Paradise. These three Heavens, the San Ch' ing, '3 Pure Ones' (this name being also applied to the sovereigns ruling in them), were formed from the three airs, which are neighborhoods of the one prehistoric air.

The very first Paradise is Yü Ch' ing. In it reigns the very first member of the Taoist triad. He populates the Jade Mountain. The entryway to his palace is called the Golden Door. He is the source of all truth, as the sun is the source of all light.

Different authorities give his name in a different way-- Yüan-shih T'ien- tsun, or Lo Ching Hsin, and call him T'ien Pao, 'the Treasure of Heaven,' Some state that the name of the ruler of this very first Heaven is Yü Huang, and in the well-known mind he it is who occupies this supreme position. The 3 Pure Ones are above him in rank, but to him, the Pearly Emperor, is entrusted the superintendence of the world. He has all the power of Paradise and earth in his hands. He is the correlative of Heaven, or rather Heaven itself.

The second Paradise, Shang Ch' ing, is ruled by the second person of the triad, called Ling-pao T'ien- tsun, or Tao Chün. No information is given regarding his origin. He is the custodian of the spiritual books. He has existed from the beginning of the world. He computes time, dividing it into different dates. He occupies the upper pole of the world, and identifies the movements and interaction, or regulates the relations of the yin and the yang, the 2 great concepts of nature.

In the 3rd Heaven, T'ai Ch' ing, the Taoists put Lao Tzŭ, the promulgator of the real teaching drawn up by Ling-pao T'ien- tsun. He is alternatively called Shên Pao, 'the Treasure of the Spirits,' and T'ai- shang Lao-chûn, 'one of the most Distinguished Aged Ruler.' Under different presumed names he has appeared as the instructor of kings and emperors, the reformer of succeeding generations.

This three-storied Taoist Paradise, or three Paradises, is the result of the desire of the Taoists not to be out-rivalled by the Buddhists. For Buddha, the Law, and the Priesthood they substitute the Tao, or Reason, the Classics, and the Priesthood.

As regards the organization of the Taoist Heavens, Yü Huang has on his register the name of 8 hundred Taoist divinities and a plethora of Immortals. These are all split into 3 categories: Saints (Shêng-jên), Heroes (Chên-jên), and Immortals (Hsien-jên), occupying the three Paradises respectively in that order.

The Three Causes

Connected with Taoism, but not specifically associated with that faith, is the praise of the 3 Causes, the deities presiding over 3 departments of physical nature, Heaven, earth, and water.

They are known by numerous classifications: San Kuan, 'the 3 Representatives'; San Yüan, 'the 3 Origins'; San Kuan Ta Ti, 'the 3 Great Emperor Agents'; and T'ai Shang San Kuan, 'the 3 Supreme Agents.' This praise has gone through four chief phases, as follows:

The first comprises Paradise, earth, and water, T'ien, Ti, Shui, the sources of happiness, forgiveness of sins, and deliverance from evil respectively. Each of these is called King-emperor. Their names, written on labels and offered to Heaven (on a mountain), earth (by burial), and water (by immersion), are supposed to treat illness. This idea dates from the Han dynasty, being very first kept in mind about A.D. 172.

The second, San Yüan dating from A.D. 407 under the Wei dynasty, recognized the 3 Representatives with three dates of which they were respectively made the patrons. The year was split into 3 unequal parts: the very first to the seventh moon; the seventh to the tenth; and the tenth to the twelfth. Of these, the fifteenth day of the first, seventh, and tenth moons respectively became the 3 principal dates of these durations. Therefore the Representative of Heaven ended up being the primary client of the first department, honoured on the fifteenth day of the very first moon, and so on.

The 3rd phase, San Kuan, resulted from the very first two being found too complicated for popular favour. The San Kuan were the 3 sons of a man, Ch'ên Tzŭ-ch'un, who was so handsome and intelligent that the 3 daughters of Lung Wang, the Dragon-king, fell for him and went to deal with him. The oldest girl was the mom of the Superior Cause, the second of the Medium Cause, and the 3rd of the Inferior Cause. All these were gifted with superhuman powers. Yüan-shih T'ien-tsun canonized them as the 3 Great Emperor Agents of Heaven, earth, and water, governors of all beings, devils or gods, in the three regions of the universe. As in the first phase, the T'ien Kuan provides joy, the Ti Kuan grants remission of sins, and the Shui Kuan delivers from wicked or misery.

The 4th phase consisted simply in the alternative by the priests for the abstract or time-principles of the three great sovereigns of ancient times, Yao, Shun, and Yü. The literati, happy with the apotheosis of their ancient rulers, accelerated to provide incense to them, and temples, San Yüan Kung, occurred in many parts of the Empire.

A variation of the phase is the canonization, with the title of San Yüan or Three Causes, of Wu-k'o San Chên Chün, 'the 3 Real Sovereigns, Guests of the Kingdom of Wu.' They were 3 Censors who lived in the reign of King Li (Li Wang, 878-- 841 B.C.) of the Chou dynasty. Leaving the service of the Chou on account of Li's dissolute living, they went to reside in Wu, and brought success to that state in its war with the Ch'u State, then went back to their own country, and ended up being pillars of the Chou State under Li's inheritor. They appeared to secure the Emperor Chên Tsung when he was offering the Fêng-shan sacrifices on T'ai Shan in A.D. 1008, on which occasion they were canonized with the titles of Superior, Medium, and Inferior Causes, as previously, conferring upon them the regencies of Heaven, earth, and water respectively.

Yüan-shih T'ien- tsun.

Yüan-shih T'ien- tsun, or the First Cause, the Highest in Paradise, normally put at the head of the Taoist triad, is said never ever to have existed but in the fertile imagination of the Lao Tzŭist sectarians. According to them Yüan-shih T'ien- tsun had neither origin nor master, but is himself the cause of all beings, which is why he is called the First Cause.

As first member of the triad, and sovereign ruler of the First Heaven, Yü Ch' ing, where reign the saints, he is raised in rank above all the other gods. The name appointed to him is Lo Ching Hsin. He was born right before all beginnings; his substance is imperishable; it is formed basically of uncreated air, air a se, invisible and without perceptible limits. Nobody has had the ability to penetrate to the beginnings of his presence. The source of all truth, he at each remodelling of the worlds-- that is, at each new kalpa-- gives out the mystical teaching which confers immortality. All who reach this knowledge get by degrees to life everlasting, become fine-tuned like the spirits, or instantly become Immortals, even while upon earth.

Initially, Yüan-shih T'ien- tsun was not a member of the Taoist triad. He resided above the Three Paradises, above the Three Pure Ones, enduring the destructions and restorations of deep space, as a stationary rock in the midst of a stormy sea. He set the stars moving, and triggered the planets to revolve. The chief of his secret authorities was Tsao Chün, the Kitchen-god, who rendered to him an account of the good and evil deeds of each family. His executive representative was Lei Tsu, the God of Thunder, and his subordinates. The 7 stars of the North Pole were the palace of his ministers, whose offices were on the various sacred mountains. Nowadays, though, Yüan-shih T'ien- tsun is usually neglected for Yü Huang.

An Avatar of P'an Ku.

According to the custom of Chin Hung, the God of T'ai Shan of the fifth generation from P'an Ku, this being, then called Yüan-shih T'ien- wang, was an avatar of P'an Ku. It came about in this smart. In remote ages there lived on the mountains an old man, Yüan-shih T'ien- wang, who used to sit on a rock and preach to the multitude. He mentioned the greatest antiquity as if from individual experience. When Chin Hung asked him where he lived, he just raised his hand toward Heaven, iridescent clouds enveloped his body, and he responded: "Whoso wishes to know where I dwell should rise to impenetrable heights." "But how," said Chin Hung, "was he to be found in this tremendous emptiness?" Two genii, Ch' ih Ching-tzŭ and Huang Lao, then descended on the summit of T'ai Shan and said: "Let us go and visit this Yüan-shih. To do so, we need to cross the limits of the universe and pass beyond the farthest stars." Chin Hung begged them to give him their directions, to which he listened attentively. They then rose the highest of the spiritual peaks, and thence installed into the paradises, calling to him from the misty heights: "If you wish to know the origin of Yüan-shih, you need to pass beyond the confines of Paradise and earth, as he lives beyond the limitations of the worlds. You must ascend and rise till you reach the sphere of nothingness and of being, in the plains of the luminescent shadows."

Having actually reached these ethereal heights, the two genii saw a bright light, and Hsüan-hsüan Shang-jên appeared before them. The two genii acquiesced do him homage and to reveal their appreciation. "You cannot better show your appreciation," he replied, "than by making my doctrine known amongst guys. You desire," he added, "to know the history of Yüan-shih. I will tell it you. When P'an Ku had finished his work in the primitive Chaos, his spirit left its mortal envelope and found itself tossed about in empty space with no fixed assistance. 'I must,' it said, 'get born-again in noticeable form; till I can go through a brand-new birth I shall remain empty and unclear,' His soul, carried on the wings of the wind, reached Fu-yü T'ai. There it saw a saintly lady named T'ai Yüan, forty years of age, still a virgin, and living alone on Mount Ts' u-o. Air and variegated clouds were the sole nourishment of her vital spirits. A hermaphrodite, at once both the active and the passive principle, she daily scaled the greatest peak of the mountain to collect there the flowery quintessence of the sun and the moon. P'an Ku, mesmerized by her virgin pureness, benefited from a minute when she was breathing to enter her mouth in the form of a ray of light. She was enceinte for 12 years, at the end of which duration the fruit of her womb came out through her spine. From its first moment the kid could walk and speak, and its body was surrounded by a five-coloured cloud. The newly-born took the name of Yüan-shih T'ien- wang, and his mother was generally known as T'ai- yüan Shêng-mu, 'the Holy Mother of the First Cause.'".

Yü Huang.
Yü Huang means 'the Jade Emperor,' or 'the Pure August One,' jade signifying pureness. He is also known by the name Yü-huang Shang-ti, 'the Pure August Emperor on High.'.

The history of this deity, who later received a lot of honorific titles and ended up being the most popular god, a very Chinese Jupiter, appears to be rather as follows: The Emperor Ch' êng Tsung of the Sung dynasty having actually been obliged in A.D. 1005 to sign a disgraceful peace with the Tunguses or Kitans, the dynasty was in danger of losing the support of the nation. In order to hoodwink the people the Emperor constituted himself a seer, and announced with great pomp that he was in direct communication with the gods of Heaven. In doing this he was following the guidance of his crafty and unreliable minister Wang Ch' in-jo, who had often tried to persuade him that the pretended revelations credited to Fu Hsi, Yü Wang, and others were only pure innovations to induce obedience. The Emperor, having studied his part well, assembled his ministers in the tenth moon of the year 1012, and made to them the following statement: "In a dream I had a go to from an Immortal, who brought me a letter from Yü Huang, the profess of which was as follows: 'I have already sent you by your forefather Chao [T'ai Tsu] two celestial missives. Now I am going to send him personally to visit you.'" A bit after his forefather T'ai Tsu, the founder of the dynasty, came according to Yü Huang's guarantee, and Ch' êng Tsung quickened to inform his ministers of it. This is the beginning of Yü Huang. He was born of a scams, and came ready-made from the brain of an emperor.

The Cask of Pearls.
Fearing to be advised for the fraud by another of his ministers, the academic Wang Tan, the Emperor fixed to put a golden gag in his mouth. So one day, having actually welcomed him to a banquet, he overwhelmed him with flattery and made him intoxicated with great white wine. "I

would like the members of your family also to taste this wine," he added, "so I am making you a present of a cask of it." When Wang Tan returned home, he found the cask filled with precious pearls. Out of thankfulness to the Emperor he kept quiet as to the fraud, and made no more opposition to his plans, but when on his death-bed he asked that his head be shaved like a priest's and that he be clothed in priestly robes so that he may expiate his criminal offense of feebleness right before the Emperor.

K'ang Hsi, the great Emperor of the Ch' ing dynasty, who had already declared that if it is really wrong to assign deceit to a man it is still more reprehensible to assign a fraud to Heaven, stigmatized him as follows: "Wang Tan committed two faults: the very first was in demonstrating himself a repellent flatterer of his Prince throughout his life; the second was in ending up being a worshipper of Buddha at his death."

The Legend of Yü Huang

So much for historic record. The legend of Yü Huang relates that in old times there existed a kingdom called Kuang Yen Miao Lo Kuo, whose king was Ching Tê, his queen being called Pao Yüeh. Though getting on in years, the latter had no child. The Taoist priests were summoned by edict to the palace to perform their rites. They recited prayers with the thing of obtaining a successor to the throne. Throughout the occurring night the Queen had a vision. Lao Chün appeared to her, riding a dragon, and carrying a male child in his arms. He drifted down through the air in her direction. The Queen pled him to give her the child as a successor to the throne. "I am rather willing," he said. "Here it is." She fell on her knees and thanked him. On waking she found herself enceinte. At the end of a year the Prince was born. From an early age he revealed to himself thoughtful and generous to the poor. On the death of his father he rose the throne, but after ruling just a couple of days abandoned in favour of his chief minister, and ended up being a hermit at P' u-ming, in Shensi, and also on Mount Hsiu Yen, in Yünnan. Having actually attained to excellence, he passed the rest of his days in curing illness and saving life; and it was in the workout of these charitable deeds that he passed away. The emperors Ch' êng Tsung and Hui Tsung, of the Sung dynasty, loaded him with all the different titles associated with his name at the present day.

Both Buddhists and Taoists claim him as their own, the former determining him with Indra, in which case Yü Huang is a Buddhist deity integrated into the Taoist temple. He has also been required the subject of a 'nature myth.' The Emperor Ching Tê, his father, is the sun, the Queen Pao Yüeh the moon, and the marriage symbolizes the rebirth of the vivifying power which outfits nature with green plants and gorgeous flowers.

T'ung- t' ien Chiao-chu

In modern Taoism T'ung- t' ien Chiao-chu is considered the very first of the Patriarchs and one of the most powerful genii of the sect. His master was Hung-chün Lao-tsu. He wore a red bathrobe embroidered with white cranes, and rode a k' uei niu, a beast resembling a buffalo, with one long horn like a unicorn. His palace, the Pi Yu Kung, was situated on Mount Tzŭ Chih Yai.

This genie took the part of Chou Wang and helped him to resist Wu Wang's armies. First, he sent his disciple To-pao Tao-jên to Chieh-p' ai Kuan. He gave him four valuable swords and the plan of a fort which he was to construct and to call Chu-hsien Chên, 'the Citadel of all the Immortals.'

To-pao Tao-jên performed his orders, but he had to combat a fight with Kuang Ch' êng-tzŭ, and the latter, equipped with a celestial seal, struck his enemy so hard that he fell to the ground and needed to take refuge in flight.

T'ung- t' ien Chiao-chu came to the defence of his disciple and to restore the spirits of his forces. Unfortunately, a posse of gods came to assist Wu Wang's powerful general, Chiang Tzŭ-ya. The very first who attacked T'ung- t' ien Chiao-chu was Lao Tzŭ, who struck him some times with his stick. Then came Chun T' i, armed with his walking stick. The buffalo of T'ung- t' ien Chiao-chu stamped him under foot, and Chun T' i was tossed to the earth, and only just had time to rise up quickly and mount into the air amid a great cloud of dust.

There could be no doubt that the battle was going against T'ung- t' ien Chiao-chu; to finish his discomfiture Jan-têng Tao-jên cleft the air and fell upon him unexpectedly. With a violent blow of his 'Fix-sea' staff he cast him down and obliged him to forfeit the struggle.

T'ung- t' ien Chiao-chu then prepared prepare for a new fortified camp beyond T'ung Kuan, and tried to take the offensive again, but again Lao Tzŭ stopped him with a blow of his stick. Yüan-shih T'ien- tsun wounded his shoulder with his jewel Ju-i, and Chun-t' i Tao-jên waved his 'Branch of the Seven Virtues.' Immediately the magic sword of T'ung- t' ien Chiao-chu was minimized to splinters, and he saved himself only by flight.

Hung-chün Lao-tsu, the master of these 3 genii, seeing his three cherished disciples in the mêlée, fixed to make peace between them. He put together all 3 in a camping tent in Chiang Tzŭ-ya's camp, made them kneel right before him, then reproached T'ung- t' ien Chiao-chu at length for having taken the part of the tyrant Chou, and suggested them in future to reside in consistency. After finishing his speech, he produced three tablets, and ordered each of the genii to swallow one. When they had done so, Hung-chün Lao-tsu said to them: "I have given you these pills to ensure an inviolable truce among you. Know that the very first who captivates an idea of discord in his heart will find that the tablet will explode in his stomach and trigger his immediate death."

Hung-chün Lao-tsu then took T'ung- t' ien Chiao-chu away with him on his cloud to Heaven.

Immortals, Heroes, Saints
A Never-ceasing, according to Taoist tradition, is a solitary man of the mountains. He appears to die, but does not. After 'death' his body keeps all the qualities of the living. The body or dead body is for him only a way of shift, a stage of transformation-- a cocoon or chrysalis, the short-term home of the butterfly.

To reach this state a hygienic regimen both of the body and mind need to be observed. All luxury, greed, and ambition must be avoided. But negation is inadequate. In the system of nutrition all the aspects which enhance the essence of the constituent yin and yang principles need to be found by methods of medicine, chemistry, gymnastic exercises, etc. When the maximum essential force has been gotten the means of maintaining it and keeping it from the attacks of death and disease should be found; in a word, he must spiritualize himself-- render himself totally independent of matter. All the experiments have for their item the saving in the tablets of immortality the aspects essential for the development of the vital force and for the constitution of a new spiritual and super-humanized being. In this rising perfection there are some grades:

(1) The Immortal (Hsien). The very first stage consists in bringing about the birth of the superhuman in the ascetic's person, which reaching excellence leaves the earthly body, like the grasshopper its sheath. This first stage attained, the Never-ceasing journeys at will throughout the universe, enjoys all the advantages of perfect health without fearing disease or death, consumes copiously-- absolutely nothing is wanting to complete his joy.

(2) The Perfect Man, or Hero (Chên-jên). The 2nd stage is a greater one. The entire body is spiritualized. It has ended up being so subtile, so spiritual, that it can fly in the air. Born upon the wings of the wind, seated on the clouds of Paradise, it takes a trip from one world to another and fixes its habitation in the stars. It is freed from all laws of matter, but is, however, not entirely changed into pure spirit.

(3) The Saint (Shêng-jên). The third stage is that of the superhuman entities or saints. They are those who have achieved to amazing intelligence and virtue.

The God of the Immortals
Mu Kung or Tung Wang Kung, the God of the Immortals, was also called I Chün Ming and Yü Huang Chün, the Prince Yü Huang.

The primitive vapour hardened, remained inactive for a time, and after that produced living entities, beginning with the development of Mu Kung, the purest compound of the Eastern Air, and sovereign of the active male principle yang and of all the nations of the East. His palace is in the misty heavens, violet clouds form its dome, blue clouds its walls. Hsien T'ung, 'the Immortal Youth,' and Yü Nü, 'the Jade Maiden,' are his servants. He keeps the register of all the Immortals, male and woman.

Hsi Wang Mu
Hsi Wang Mu was created out of the pure quintessence of the Western Air, in the legendary continent of Shên Chou. She is typically called the Golden Mom of the Tortoise.

Her family name is otherwise given as Hou, Yang, and Ho. Her own name was Hui, and given name Wan-chin. She had 9 sons and twenty-four daughters.

As Mu Kung, formed of the Eastern Air, is the active principle of the male air and sovereign of the Eastern Air, so Hsi Wang Mu, born of the Western Air, is the passive or female principle (yin) and sovereign of the Western Air. These 2 concepts, co-operating, engender Paradise and earth and all the beings of deep space, and hence become the two principles of life and of the subsistence of all that exists. She is the head of the troop of genii house on the K'un- lun Mountains (the Taoist equivalent of the Buddhist Sumêru), and from time to time holds sexual intercourse with favoured royal votaries.

The Banquet of Peaches

Hsi Wang Mu's palace is positioned in the high mountains of the snowy K'un- lun. It is 1000 li (about 333 miles) in circuit; a rampart of massive gold surrounds its battlements of precious stones. Its right wing rises up on the edge of the Kingfishers' River. It is the normal home of the Immortals, who are divided into seven unique categories according to the colour of their garments-- red, blue, black, violet, yellow, green, and 'nature-colour.' There is a marvellous fountain built of jewels, where the periodical banquet of the Immortals is held. This feast is called P'an- t' ao Hui, 'the Banquet of Peaches.' It occurs on the borders of the Yao Ch' ih, Lake of Gems, and is attended by both male and female Immortals. Besides some superfine meats, they are served with bears' paws, monkeys' lips, dragons' liver, phoenix marrow, and peaches gathered in the orchard, endowed with the mystic virtue of conferring longevity on all who have the all the best to taste them. It was by these peaches that the date of the banquet was repaired. The tree put forth leaves once every 3 thousand years, and it needed three 1,000 years after that for the fruit to ripen. These were Hsi Wang Mu's birthdays, when all the Immortals assembled for the great banquet, "the occasion being more joyful than solemn, for there was music on invisible instruments, and songs not from mortal tongues."

Chapter 13: The First Taoist Pope

Chang Tao-ling, the very first Taoist pope, was born in A.D. 35, in the reign of the Emperor Kuang Wu Ti of the Han dynasty. His birth place is variously given as the T'ien- mu Shan, 'Eye of Paradise Mountain,' in Lin-an Hsien, in Chekiang, and Fêng-yang Fu, in Anhui. He committed himself wholly to study and meditation, decreasing all deals to enter the service of the State. He preferred to use up his home in the mountains of Western China, where he persevered in the research study of alchemy and in cultivating the virtues of pureness and mental abstraction. From the hands of Lao Tzŭ he received superly a mystic writing, by following the instructions in which he was successful in his search for the elixir of life.

One day when he was participated in experimenting with the 'Dragon-tiger elixir' a soul appeared to him and said: "On Po-sung Mountain is a stone house in which are hidden the works of the 3 Emperors of antiquity and a canonical work. By getting these you might rise to Heaven, if you go through the course of discipline they prescribe."

Chang Tao-ling found these works, and by methods of them got the power of flying, of hearing far-off noises, and of leaving his body. After going through a 1000 days of discipline, and receiving instruction from a goddess, who taught him to perambulate amongst the stars, he proceeded to eliminate with the king of the devils, to divide mountains and seas, and to command the wind and thunder. All the devils fled right before him. On account of the prodigious massacre of demons by this hero the wind and thunder were decreased to subjection, and different divinities came with eager haste to acknowledge their faults. In nine years he got the power to rise to Heaven.

The Founder of Modern Taoism

Chang Tao-ling might appropriately be thought about as the true founder of contemporary Taoism. The dishes for the tablets of immortality contained in the strange books, and the creation of talismans for the cure of all sorts of maladies, not only exalted him to the high position he has since occupied in the minds of his numerous disciples, but allowed them in turn to exploit effectively this brand-new source of power and wealth. From that time the Taoist sect began to concentrate on the art of healing. Protecting or treating talismans bearing the Master's seal were purchased for huge sums. It is thus seen that he was after all a deceiver of the people, and unbelievers or competing partisans of other sects have called him a 'rice-thief'--which perhaps he was.

He is typically represented as clothed in highly embellished garments, displaying with his right hand his magic sword, keeping in his left a cup including the draught of immortality, and riding a tiger which in one paw understands his magic seal and with the others squashes down the five venomous beings: lizard, snake, spider, toad, and centipede. Pictures of him with these accessories are pasted up in houses on the 5th day of the fifth moon to forfend disaster and sickness.

The Peach-gathering

It is related of him that, not wanting to ascend to Paradise too soon, he took part of only half of the pill of immortality, dividing the other half amongst several of his admirers, and that he had at least two selves or personalities, one of which used to disport itself in a boat on a small lake in front of his home. The other self would receive his visitors, entertaining them with food and drink and instructional discussion. On one occasion this self said to them: "You are unable to quit the world altogether as I can, but by mimicing my example in the matter of family relations you could acquire a medication which would lengthen your lives by some centuries. I have given the crucible in which Huang Ti prepared the draught of immortality to my disciple Wang Ch' ang. Later on, a man will come from the East, who also will use it. He will arrive on the seventh day of the first moon."

Exactly on that day there arrived from the East a man called Chao Shêng, who was the person indicated by Chang Tao-ling. He was acknowledged by a symptom of himself he had caused to appear in advance of his coming. Chang then led all his disciples, to the number of three hundred, to the greatest peak of the Yün-t'ai. Below them they saw a peach-tree growing near a pointed rock, extending its branches like arms above a fathomless abyss. It was a large tree, covered with ripe fruit. Chang said to his disciples: "I will communicate a spiritual formula to the one among you who will dare to collect the fruit of that tree." They all leaned over to look, but each declared the task to be impossible. Chao Shêng alone had the nerve to hurry out to the point of the rock and up the tree stretching out into space. With firm foot he stood and gathered the peaches, putting them in the folds of his cloak, as many as it would hold, but when he wished to climb back up the precipitous slope, his hands slipped on the smooth rock, and all his attempts failed. Appropriately, he threw the peaches, three hundred and 2 in all, one by one up to Chang Tao-ling, who distributed them. Each disciple ate one, as also did Chang, who reserved the remaining one for Chao Shêng, whom he helped to climb again. To do this Chang extended his arm to a length of thirty feet, all present marvelling at the miracle. After Chao had eaten his peach Chang was standing on the edge of the precipice, and said with a laugh: "Chao Shêng was brave enough to climb out to that tree and his foot never tripped. I too will make the effort. If I prosper I will have a big peach as a benefit." Having actually spoken thus, he jumped into space, and alighted in the branches of the peach-tree. Wang Ch'ang and Chao Shêng also jumped into the tree and stood one on each side of him. There Chang communicated to them the strange formula. 3 days later they went back to their homes; then, having made final arrangements, they repaired once again to the mountain peak, whence, in the presence of the other disciples, who followed them with their eyes until they had entirely vanished from view, all three rose to Heaven in the daylight.

Chang Tao-ling's Great Power

The name of Chang Tao-ling, the Heavenly Teacher, is a household word in China. He is on the earth the Vicegerent of the Pearly Emperor in Heaven, and the Commander-in-Chief of the pure hosts of Taoism. He, the leader of the wizards, the 'real [i.e. ideal] man,' as he is called, wields an enormous spiritual power throughout the land. The present pope boasts of an unbroken line for three-score generations. His family obtained possession of the Dragon-tiger Mountain in Kiangsi about A.D. 1000. "This personage," says a pre-Republican writer, "assumes a state which mimics the imperial. He confers buttons like an emperor. Priests pertain to him from numerous cities and temples to get big promotion, whom he invests with titles and presents with seals of office."

Kings of Paradise

The 4 Kings of Heaven, Ssŭ Ta T'ien- wang, reside on Mount Sumêru (Hsü-mi Shan), the centre of deep space. It is 3,360,000 li-- that is, about a million miles-- high.9 Its eastern slope is of gold, its western of silver, its south-eastern of crystal, and its north-eastern of agate. The Four Kings seem the Taoist reflection of the 4 Chin-kang of Buddhism already noticed. Their names are Li, Ma, Chao, and Wên. They are represented as holding a pagoda, sword, 2 swords, and spiked club respectively. Their praise appears to be due to their advantageous appearance and aid on various critical occasions in the dynastic history of the T'ang and Sung Periods.

T'ai I.

Forehead are found in different parts committed to T'ai I, the Great One, or Great Unity. When Emperor Wu Ti (140-- 86 B.C.) of the Han dynasty was in search of the secret of immortality, and various ideas had proved unacceptable, a Taoist priest, Miao Chi, told the Emperor that his really want of success was because of his omission to sacrifice to T'ai I, the first of the celestial spirits, pricing quote the classical precedent of antiquity found in the Book of History. The Emperor, believing his word, ordered the Grand Master of Sacrifices to re-establish this worship at the capital. He followed thoroughly the prescriptions of Miao Chi. This enraged the literati, who fixed to ruin him. One day, when the Emperor was about to drink among his potions, among the chief courtiers seized the cup and drank the contents himself. The Emperor was about to have him killed, when he said: "Your Majesty's order is unnecessary; if the potion gives immortality, I cannot be killed; if, on the other hand, it does not, your Majesty must reimburse me for negating the pretensions of the Taoist priest." The Emperor, however, was not convinced.

One account represents T'ai I as having resided in the time of Shên Nung, the Divine Husbandman, who visited him to speak with him on the subjects of diseases and fortune. He was Hsien Yüan's medical preceptor. His medical knowledge was given to future generations. He was one of those who, with the Immortals, was welcomed to the great Peach Assembly of the Western Royal Mom.

As the spirit of the star T'ai I he resides in the Eastern Palace, listening for the sobs of patients so as to save them. For this purpose he presumes numberless forms in various regions. With a boat of lotus-flowers of nine colours he ferries guys over to the shore of salvation. Keeping in his hand a willow-branch, he scatters from it the dew of the doctrine.

T'ai I is otherwise represented as the Ruler of the Five Celestial Sovereigns, Cosmic Matter before it caked into concrete shapes, the Triune Spirit of Heaven, earth, and T'ai I as 3 different beings, an unknown Spirit, the Spirit of the Pole Star, etc., but virtually the Taoists confine their T'ai I to T'ai- i Chên-jên, in which Perfect Man they personify the abstract philosophical concepts.10.

Goddess of the North Star.
Tou Mu, the Bushel Mother, or Goddess of the North Star, worshipped by both Buddhists and Taoists, is the Indian Maritchi, and was made an excellent divinity by the Taoists. She is said to have been the mother of the nine Jên Huang or Human Sovereigns of wonderful antiquity, who succeeded the lines of Celestial and Terrestrial Sovereigns. She occupies in the Taoist religion the exact same relative position as Kuan Yin, who may be said to be the heart of Buddhism. Having attained to a profound knowledge of celestial mysteries, she shone with divine light, could cross the seas, and pass from the sun to the moon. She also had a kind heart for the sufferings of humanity. The King of Chou Yü, in the north, married her on hearing of her tons of virtues. They had nine sons. Yüan-shih T'ien- tsun came to earth to welcome her, her husband, and 9 sons to enjoy the thrills of Heaven. He placed her in the palace Tou Shu, the Pivot of the Pole, since all the other stars revolve round it, and gave her the title of Queen of the Teaching of Primitive Heaven. Her 9 sons have their palaces in the neighbouring stars.

Tou Mu wears the Buddhist crown, is seated on a lotus throne, has three eyes, eighteen arms, and holds numerous precious things in her many hands, like a bow, spear, sword, flag, dragon's head, pagoda, five chariots, sun's disk, moon's disk, and so on. She has control of the books of life and death, and all who wish to prolong their days praise at her shrine. Her devotees abstain from animal food on the 3rd and twenty-seventh day of every month.

Of her sons, two are the Northern and Southern Bushels; the latter, dressed in red, guidelines birth; the former, in white, guidelines death. "A young Esau once found them on the South Mountain, under a tree, playing chess, and by a deal of venison his lease of life was extended from nineteen to ninety-nine years."

Snorter and Blower
At the time of the defeat of the Shang and facility of the Chou dynasty in 1122 B.C. there lived two marshals, Chêng Lung and Ch' ên Ch' i. These were Hêng and Ha, the Snorter and Blower respectively.

The previous was the primary superintendent of supplies for the armies of the autocrat emperor Chou, the Nero of China. The latter supervised of the victualling department of the exact same army.

From his master, Tu O, the popular Taoist magician of the K'un- lun Mountains, Hêng acquired a wonderful power. When he snorted, his nostrils, with a sound like that of a bell, produced two white columns of light, which damaged his enemies, body and soul. Hence through him the Chou gained many victories. But one day he was caught, bound, and taken to the general of Chou. His life was spared, and he was made general superintendent of army stores as well as generalissimo of 5 army corps. Later he found himself deal with to face with the Blower. The latter had learnt from the magician how to store in his chest a supply of yellow gas which, when he blew it out, annihilated anybody whom it struck. By this means he triggered large spaces to be made in the ranks of the enemy.

Being opposed to one another, the one snorting out great streaks of white light, the other blowing streams of yellow gas, the combat continued till the Blower was injured in the shoulder by No-cha, of the army of Chou, and pierced in the stomach with a spear by Huang Fei-hu, Yellow Flying Tiger

The Snorter in turn was slain in this battle by Marshal Chin Ta-shêng, 'Golden Big Pint,' who was an ox-spirit and endowed with the mystical power of producing in his entrails the renowned niu huang, ox-yellow, or bezoar. Dealing with the Snorter, he spat in his face, with a noise like thunder, a piece of bezoar as large as a rice-bowl. It struck him on the nose and split his nostrils. He fell down to the earth, and was instantly cut in 2 by a blow from his victor's sword.

After the Chou dynasty had been definitely established Chiang Tzŭ-ya canonized the 2 marshals Hêng and Ha, and conferred on them the offices of guardians of the Buddhist temple gates, where their enormous images may be seen.

Blue Dragon and White Tiger.
The functions discharged by Hêng and Ha at the gateways of Buddhist temples are in Taoist temples released by Blue Dragon and White Tiger.

The former, the Spirit of the Blue Dragon Star, was Têng Chiu-kung, one of the chief generals of the last emperor of the Yin dynasty. He had a boy named Têng Hsiu, and a daughter called Ch' an-yü.

The army of Têng Chiu-kung was camped at San-shan Kuan, when he got orders to proceed to the battle then taking place at Hsi Ch'i. There, in withstanding No-cha and Huang Fei-hu, he had his left arm broken by the former's magic bracelet, but, thankfully for him, his subordinate, T'u Hsing-sun, a distinguished magician, gave him a solution which quickly healed the fracture.

His daughter then emerged to avenge her father. She had a magic weapon, the Five-fire Stone, which she tossed full in the face of Yang Chien. But the Immortal was not wounded; on the other hand, his celestial pet dog leapt at Ch'an-yü and bit her neck, so that she was obliged to leave. T'u Hsing-sun, however, recovered the injury.

After a banquet, Têng Chiu-kung promised his daughter in a marriage relationship to T'u Hsing-sun if he would get him the triumph at Hsi Ch'i. Chiang Tzŭ-ya then persuaded T'u's magic master, Chü Liu-sun, to call his disciple over to his camp, where he asked him why he was battling against the brand-new dynasty. "Since," he replied, "Chiu-kung has promised me his daughter in marriage as a benefit of success." Chiang Tzŭ-ya thereupon promised to acquire the bride, and sent a force to take her. As a result of the battling that occurred, Chiu-kung was beaten, and pulled away in confusion, leaving Ch'an-yü in the hands of the victors. Throughout the next couple of days, the marriage was celebrated with great event in the victor's camp. According to custom-made, the bride-to-be returned for some days to her father's home, and while there she earnestly exhorted Chiu-kung to submit. Following her advice, he visited Chiang Tzŭ-ya's party.

In the ensuing battles he combated valiantly on the side of his former enemy, and killed tons of famous warriors, but he was eventually attacked by the Blower, from whose mouth a column of yellow gas struck him, tossing him from his steed. He was made prisoner, and performed by order of General Ch'iu Yin. Chiang Tzŭ-ya provided on him the kingdom of heaven Dragon Star.

The Spirit of the White Tiger Star is Yin Ch'êng-hsiu. His dad, Yin P'o-pai, a high courtier of the tyrant Chou Wang, was sent out to negotiate peace with Chiang Tzŭ-ya but was taken and put to death by Marquis Chiang Wên-huan. His son, attempting to avenge his dad's murder, was pierced by a spear, and his head was cut off and carried in accomplishment to Chiang Tzŭ-ya.

As compensation he was, though rather tardily, canonized as the Spirit of the White Tiger Star.

Chinese Mythology

Mystical Creatures from Oriental Hemispheres

By Sally Stephens

If you like my book, please leave a review. I would appreciate it. Thank you!

Table of Contents

Chapter 1: Apotheosized Theorists *81*
Chapter 2: The 3 Musical Brothers *83*
Chapter 3: Celestial Ministries *90*
Chapter 4: The Many Gods *91*
Chapter 5: Chinese Polytheism *96*
Chapter 6: Star-worship *103*
Chapter 7: Myths of Time *106*
Chapter 8: Understanding the Legend of T'ai Sui *107*
Chapter 9: The Myths of Thunder, Rain, Lightning, and Wind *109*
Chapter 10: The Dragon-kings *115*
Chapter 12: The Great Flood *123*
Chapter 13: The City is Founded *127*
Chapter 14: Fiery Myths *130*
Chapter 15: Myths of Medicine, Epidemics, Exorcism *133*
Chapter 16: The Goddess of Mercy and Grace *139*
Chapter 17: Hell and Paradise *149*

Chapter 1: Apotheosized Theorists

The theorists Lieh Tzŭ, Huai-nan Tzŭ, Chuang Tzŭ, Mo Tzŭ, etc., have also been apotheosized. Nothing really impressive is related of them. The majority of them had several reincarnations and possessed supernatural powers. The second, who was a king, when taken by the 8 Immortals to the genii's Heaven forgot once in a while to resolve them as superiors, and but for their intercession with Yü Ti, the Pearly Emperor, would have been reincarnated. In order to humiliate himself, he afterwards called himself Huai-nan Tzŭ, 'the Sage of the South of the Huai.' The third, Chuang Tzŭ, Chuang Shêng, or Chuang Chou, was a disciple of Lao Tzŭ. Chuang Tzŭ was in the routine of sleeping throughout the day, and in the evening would change himself into a butterfly, which fluttered gaily over the flowers in the garden. On waking, he would still feel the experience of flying in his shoulders. On asking Lao Tzŭ the reason for this, he was told: "Previously you were a white butterfly which, having partaken of the quintessence of flowers and of the yin and the yang, should have been immortalized; but one day you took some peaches and flowers in Wang Mu Niang-niang's garden. The defender of the garden variety you, and that is how you happened reincarnated." At this time he was fifty years of age.

Fanning the Tomb
Among the tales connected with him describes how he saw a young woman in grieving vigorously fanning a recently made grave. On his asking her the reason of the strange conduct, she replied: "I am doing this because my spouse begged me to wait until the earth on his tomb was dry right before I remarried!" Chuang Tzŭ offered to help her, and as soon as he waved the fan once the earth was dry. The young widow thanked him and departed.

On his return home, Chuang Shêng associated this incident to his spouse. She uttered astonishment at such conduct on the part of an other half. "There's absolutely nothing to be shocked at," rejoined the partner; "that's how things enter this world." Seeing that he was poking fun at her, she opposed madly. Some little time after this Chuang Shêng passed away. His wife, much grieved, buried him.

Husband and Wife
Several days later a boy named Ch'u Wang-sun gotten here with the intent, as he said, of positioning himself under the direction of Chuang Shêng. When he heard that he was dead he went and carried out prostrations before his burial place, and afterward used up his residence in an empty room, saying that he wished to study. After half a month had elapsed, the widow asked an old servant who had accompanied Wang-sun if the boy was married. On his responding in the negative, she asked for the old servant to propose a match between them. Wang-sun made some objections, saying that people would criticize their conduct. "Since my husband is dead, what can they say?" responded the widow. She then put off her mourning-garments and gotten ready for the wedding.

Wang-sun took her to the tomb of her partner, and said to her: "The gentleman has returned to life!" She looked at Wang-sun and acknowledged the features of her spouse. She was so overloaded with pity that she hanged herself. Chuang Shêng buried her in an empty burial place, and then began to sing.

He burnt his house, went away to P'u-shui, in Hupei, and occupied himself in fishing. From there he went on to Chung-t'iao Shan, where he met Fêng Hou and her instructor Hsüan Nü, the Mother of Paradise. In their business he checked out the palaces of the stars. One day, when he was going to a banquet at the palace of Wang-mu, Shang Ti gave him as his kingdom the world Jupiter, and assigned to him as his palace the age-old house of Mao Mêng, the stellar god reincarnated throughout the Chou dynasty. He had not yet returned, and had left his palace empty. Shang Ti had cautioned him never ever to missing himself without his consent.

Canonized Generalissimos

A ton of military men also have been canonized as celestial generalissimos. A few will act as examples of the rest.

Chapter 2: The 3 Musical Brothers

There were three brothers: T'ien Yüan-shuai, the oldest; T'ien Hung-i, the 2nd; and T'ien Chih-piao, the youngest. They were all musical artists of unparalleled skill.

In the K'ai- yüa Period (A.D. 713-- 42) the Emperor Hsüan Tsung, of the T'ang dynasty, designated them his music masters. At the noise of their terrific flute the clouds in the sky stopped in their courses; the consistency of their songs caused the odoriferous la mei flower to open in winter. They stood out also in tunes and dances.

The Emperor fell sick. He saw in a dream the three brothers accompanying their singing on a mandolin and violin. The harmony of their songs charmed his ear, and on waking he found himself well again. Out of gratitude for this advantage he provided on each the title of marquis.

The Grand Master of the Taoists was trying to stay the devastations of a plague, but he could not conquer the demons which caused it. Under these situations he attracted the 3 brothers and asked their advice regarding what course to adopt. T'ien Yüan-shuai had a big boat built, called 'Spirit-boat.' He assembled in it a million spirits, and ordered them to beat drums. On hearing this tumult all the satanic forces of the town came out to listen. T'ien Yüan-shuai, seizing the chance, captured them all and, with the assistance of the Grand Master, expelled them from the town.

Besides the canonization of the three T'ien brothers, all the members of their families received posthumous titles.

The Dragon-boat Celebration
This is said to be the origin of the dragon-boats which are to be seen on all the waterways of China on the fifth day of the 5th moon.11 The Celebration of the Dragon-boats, hung on that day, was set up in memory of the statesman-poet Ch' ü Yüan (332-- 296 B.C.), who drowned himself in the Mi-lo River, an affluent of the Tung-t' ing Lake, after having been wrongly implicated by one of the petty princes of the State. The people, out of pity for the unfortunate courtier, sent out these boats looking for his body.

Chiang Tzŭ-ya
In the wars which led to the conquer of the tyrant Chou Wang and his dynasty and the facility of the great Chou dynasty, the most prominent generalissimo was Chiang Tzŭ-ya. His family name was Chiang, and his own name Shang, but owing to his descent from among the ministers of the ancient King Yao, whose beneficiaries owned the fief of Lü, the family came to be called by that name, and he himself was known as Lü Shang. His honorific title was T'ai Kung Wang, 'Hope of T'ai Kung,' given him by Wên Wang, who recognized in the person of Chiang Tzŭ-ya the sensible minister whom his father T'ai Kung had triggered him to expect before his death.

The Battle of Mu Yeh

Chiang Tzŭ-ya was originally in the service of the autocrat Chou Wang, but transferred his services to the Chou cause, and by his terrific ability allowed that house finally to get the success. The decisive fight took place at Mu Yeh, located to the south of Wei-hui Fu, in 1122 B.C. The soldiers of Yin, 700,000 in number, were beat, and Chou, the autocrat, shut himself up in his splendid palace, set it alight, and was burned alive with all his ownerships. For this achievement Chiang Tzŭ-ya was approved by Wu Wang the title of Father and Counsellor, and was appointed Prince of Ch' i, with perpetual succession to his descendants.

A Legend of Chiang Tzŭ-ya

The Feng shên yen i contains a lot of chapters defining in detail the numerous fights which led to the defeat of the last tyrant of the Shang dynasty and the establishment of the remarkable Chou dynasty on the throne of China. This legend and the following one are exemplified from that work.

No-cha beats Chang Kuei-fang

The redoubtable No-cha having, by means of his Heaven-and-earth Bracelet, overcame Fêng Lin, a star-god and secondary officer of Chang Kuei-fang, in spite of the black smoke-clouds which he burnt out of his nostrils, the beat warrior ran away and sought the help of his chief, who combated No-cha in some thirty to forty encounters without being successful in removing him from his Wind-fire Wheel, which enabled him to move about quickly and to perform prodigious feats, such as causing hosts of silver flying dragons like clouds of snow to descend upon his opponent. During one of these battles No-cha heard his name called three times, but paid no hearken. Finally, with his Heaven-and-earth Bracelet he broke Chang Kuei-fang's left arm, following this up by shooting out some stunning rays of light which knocked him off his horse.

When he went back to the city to report his success to Tzŭ-ya, the latter asked him if during the fight Kuei-fang had called his name. "Yes," replied No-cha, "he called, but I took no observe of him." "When Kuei-fang calls," said Tzŭ-ya, "the hun and the p' o [anima and umbra] ended up being separated, and so the body breaks down." "However," responded No-cha, "I had changed myself into a lotus-flower, which has neither hun nor p' o, so he could not succeed in getting me off my magic wheel."

Tzŭ-ya goes to K'un- lun.

Tzŭ-ya, however, still uncertain in mind about the finality of No-cha's victories, went to consult Wu Wang (whose death had not yet happened at this time). After the interview Tzŭ-ya notified Wu Wang of his wish to visit K'un- lun Mountain. Wu Wang warned him of the threat of leaving the kingdom with the opponent so near the capital; but Tzŭ-ya obtained his permission by saying he would be missing only 3 days at most. So he gave directions relating to the defence to No-cha, and went off in his spirit chariot to K'un- lun. On his arrival at the Unicorn Precipice he was much spellbinded with the stunning surroundings, the colours, flowers, trees, bridges, birds, deer, apes, blue lions, white elephants, and so on, all of which appeared to make earth surpass Heaven in loveliness.

He gets the List of Immortals.
From the Unicorn Precipice he went on to the Jade Palace of Abstraction. Here he was presented to Yüan-shih. From him he got the List of Promos to Immortals, which Nan-chi Hsien-wêng, 'Ancient Immortal of the South Pole,' had brought, and was told to go and erect a Fêng Shên T'ai (Spirits' Big promotion Terrace) on which to display it. Yüan-shih also warned him that if anyone called him while he was on the way he was to be most careful not to answer. On reaching the Unicorn Precipice on his way back, he heard some one call: "Chiang Tzŭ-ya!" This occurred 3 times without his paying any heed. Then the voice was heard to say: "Now that you are Prime Minister, how devoid of feeling and forgetful of bygone advantages you must be not to remember one who studied with you in the Jade Palace of Abstraction!" Tzŭ-ya could not but turn his head and look. He then saw that it was Shên Kung-pao. He said: "Sibling, I did not know it was you who were calling me, and I did not observe you as Shih-tsun told me on no account to respond." Shên Kung-pao said: "What is that you hold in your hand?" He told him it was the List of Promotions to Immortals. Shên Kung-pao then tried to lure Tzŭ-ya from his obligation to Chou. Among Shên's techniques was that of persuading Tzŭ-ya of the superiority of the magical arts at the disposal of the advocates of Chou Wang. "You," he said, "can drain the sea, change the hills, and suchlike things, but what are those compared with my powers, who can take off my head, make it mount into space, travel 10,000,000 li, and return to my neck just as complete as before and able to speak? Burn your List of Promotions to Immortals and come with me." Tzŭ-ya, thinking that a head which could travel 10,000,000 li and be the same as before was exceptionally unusual, said: "Bro, you take your head off, and if in reality it can do as you say, rise into space and return and be as before, I shall be willing to burn the List of Promotions to Immortals and return with you to Chao Ko." Shên Kung-pao said: "You will not go back on your word?" Tzŭ-ya said: "When your elder brother has spoken his word is as unchangeable as Mount T'ai, How can there be any going back on my word?"

The Skyrocketing Head.
Shên Kung-pao then doffed his Taoist cap, seized his sword, with his left hand securely comprehended the blue thread binding his hair, and with his right cut off his head. His body did not drop. He then took his head and tossed it up into space. Tzŭ-ya gazed with upturned face as it continued to rise, and was sorely puzzled. But the Ancient Immortal of the South Pole had kept a watch on the procedures. He said: "Tzŭ-ya is a loyal and truthful man; it looks just as if he has been tricked by this charlatan." He ordered White Crane Youth to presume rapidly the form of a crane and fetch Shên Kung-pao's head.

The Ancient Immortal saves the Situation.
Tzŭ-ya was still gazing upward when he felt a slap on his back and, turning round, saw that it was the Ancient Immortalof the South Pole. Tzŭ-ya rapidly asked: "My older brother, why have you returned?" Hsien-wêng said: "You are a fool. Shên Kung-pao is a guy of unholy practices. These couple of small tricks of his you take as realities. But if the head does not go back to the neck within an hour and three-quarters the blood will coagulate, and he will die. Shih-tsun ordered you not to reply to anybody; why did you not hearken to his words? From the Jade Palace of Abstraction, I saw you speaking together, and knew you had promised to burn the List

of Promotions to Immortals. So I ordered White Crane Youth to bring me the head. After an hour and three-quarters Shên Kung-pao will be recompensed."

Tzŭ-ya said: "My elder brother, since you know all you can pardon him. In the Taoist heart there is no place where mercy cannot be worked out. Keep in mind the tons of years during which he has consistently followed the Course."

Eventually the Ancient Immortal was persuaded, but in the meantime Shên Kung-pao, finding that his head did not return, ended up being very much bothered in mind. In an hour and three-quarters the blood would stop flowing and he would die. However, Tzŭ-ya having prospered in his intercession with the Ancient Never-ceasing, the latter signed to White Crane Youth, who was flying in space with the head in his beak, to let it drop. He did so, but when it reached the neck it was facing backwards. Shên Kung-pao quickly installed his hand, took hold of an ear, and turned his head the proper way round. He was then able to open his eyes, when he saw the Ancient Immortal of the South Pole. The latter arraigned him in a loud voice saying: "You as-good-as-dead charlatan, who by methods of corrupt tricks try to trick Tzŭ-ya and make him burn the List of Immortals and help Chou Wang against Chou, what do you mean by all this? You should be taken to the Jade Palace of Abstraction to be punished!"

Shên Kung-pao, ashamed, could not respond; installing his tiger, he made off; but as he left he hurled back a risk that the Chou would yet have their white bones stacked mountains high at Hsi Ch' i. Subsequently Tzŭ-ya, thoroughly preserving the valuable List, after a lot of adventures had a lot of success in building the Fêng Shên T'ai, and posted the List up on it. Having achieved his mission, he returned in time to resist the capture of Hsi Ch' i by Chang Kuei-fang, whose soldiers were beat with great slaughter.

Ch' iung Hsiao's Magic Scissors

In another of the lots of conflicts between the 2 rival states Lao Tzŭ went into the battle, whereupon Ch' iung Hsiao, a goddess who fought for the house of Shang (Chou), tossed into the air her gold scaly-dragon scissors. As these slowly come down, opening and closing in a most threatening manner, Lao Tzŭ waved the sleeve of his jacket and they fell straight into the sea and ended up being definitely still. Many comparable tricks were used by the different contestants. The Gold Bushel of Disorderly Origin succumbed to the Wind-fire Sphere, and so on. Ch' iung Hsiao resumed the attack with some magic two-edged swords, but was killed by a blow from White Crane Youth's Three-precious Jade Sceptre, tossed at her by Lao Tzŭ's orders. Pi Hsiao, her sister, tried to avenge her death, but Yüan-shih, producing from his sleeve a magic box, tossed it into the air and caught Pi Hsiao in it. When it was opened it was found that she had merged blood and water.

Chiang Tzŭ-ya defeats Wên Chung

After this Lao Tzŭ rallied lots of the skilful spirits to help Chiang Tzŭ-ya in his fight with Wên Chung, supplying them with the Ancient Immortalof the South Pole's Sand-blaster and an earth-conquering light which enabled them to travel a thousand li in a day. From the hot sand used the contest ended up being called the Red Sand Battle Jan Têng, on P'êng- lai Mountain, in consultation with Tzŭ-ya, also arranged the plan of fight.

The Red Sand Battle.

The battle started with a challenge from the Ancient Immortalof the South Pole to Chang Shao. The latter, riding his deer, dashed into the fray, and aimed an excellent blow with his sword at Hsien-wêng's head, but White Crane Youth warded it off with his Three-precious Jade Sceptre. Chang then produced a two-edged sword and renewed the attack, but, being deactivated, dismounted from his deer and threw some handfuls of hot sand at Hsien-wêng. The latter, however, easily fanned them away with his Five-fire Seven-feathers Fan, rendering them harmless. Chang then got a whole plantel of the hot sand and spread it over the enemy, but Hsien-wêng counteracted the hazard by simply waving his fan. White Crane Youth struck Chang Shao with his jade sceptre, knocking him off his horse, and then dispatched him with his two-edged sword.

After this battle Wu Wang was found to be already dead. Jan Têng on learning this ordered Lei Chên-tzŭ to take the corpse to Mount P'êng and wash it. He then liquified a tablet in water and poured the solution into Wu Wang's mouth, whereupon he revived and was accompanied back to his palace.

More Fighting

Preparations were then made for resuming the attack on Wên Chung. While the latter was talking to Ts'ai-yün Hsien-tzŭ and Han Chih-hsien, he heard the sound of the Chou weapons and the thunder of their soldiers. Wên Chung, mounting his black unicorn, galloped like a whiff of smoke to meet Tzŭ-ya, but was stopped by blows from two silver hammers wielded by Huang T'ien-hua. Han Chih-hsien came to Wên's aid, but was opposed by Pi Hsiang-yang. Ts'ai-yün Hsien-tzŭ rushed into the fray, but No-cha stepped on to his Wind-fire Wheel and opposed him. From all sides other Immortals participated in the great fight, which was a chaos of longbows and crossbows, iron armour and brass mail, striking whips and falling hammers, weapons cleaving mail and mail resisting weapons. In this fierce contest, while Tzŭ-ya was combating Wên Chung, Han Chih-hsien released a black wind from his magic wind-bag, but he did not know that the Taoist Barge of Mercy (which transports left spirits to the land of happiness), sent out by Kuan Yin, the Goddess of Mercy, had on board the Stop-wind Pearl, by which the black storm was immediately stopped. Thereupon Tzŭ-ya rapidly seized his Vanquish-spirits Whip and struck Han Chih-hsien in the middle of the skull, so that the brain-fluid gushed forth and he died. No-cha then variety Ts'ai-yün Hsien-tzŭ with a spear-thrust.

Thus the stern battle went on, until finally Tzŭ-ya, under cover of night, assaulted Wên Chung's soldiers simultaneously on all 4 sides. The noise of slaughter filled the air. Generals and rank and file, lanterns, torches, swords, spears, guns, and daggers were one baffled mêlée; Heaven could rarely be identified from earth, and dead bodies were stacked mountains high.

Tzŭ-ya, having actually broken through seven lines of the opponent's ranks, forced his way into Wên Chung's camp. The latter mounted his unicorn, and displaying his magic whip rushed to meet him. Tzŭ-ya drew his sword and stopped his onrush, being helped by Lung Hsü-hu, who consistently cast a rain of hot stones on to the troops. In the middle of the fight Tzŭ-ya highlighted his great magic whip, and in spite of Wên Chung's efforts to keep away from it had a lot of success in wounding him in the left arm. The Chou troops were battling like dragons lashing their tails and pythons curling their bodies. To contribute to their disasters, the Chou now saw flames rising behind the camp, and knew that their arrangements were being burned by Yang Chien.

The Chou armies, with gongs beating and drums rolling, advanced for a last effort, the massacre being so great that even the demons wept, and the spirits wailed. Wên Chung was ultimately driven back seventy li to Ch' i Hill. His soldiers could do nothing but sigh and stumble along. He made for Peach-blossom Variety, but as he approached it he saw a yellow banner hoisted, and under it was Kuang Ch' êng-tzŭ. Being stopped from leaving in that direction he signed up with battle, but by use of red-hot sand, his two-edged sword, and his Turn-heaven Seal Kuang Ch' êng-tzŭ put him to flight. He then scampered towards the west, followed by Têng Chung. His design was to produce Swallow Hill, which he reached after several days of tired marching. Here he saw another yellow banner flying, and Ch' ih Ching-tzŭ notified him that Jan Têng had forbidden him to stop at Swallow Hill or to go through the Five Passes. This resulted in another battle royal, Wên Chung using his magic whip and Ch' ih his spiritual two-edged sword. After some bouts Ch' ih highlighted his yin-yang mirror, by use of which irresistible weapon Wên was driven to Yellow Flower Hill and Blue Dragon Pass, and so on from fight to battle, until he was drawn up to Paradise from the top of Dead-dragon Mountain.

Thousand-li Eye and Favourable-wind Ear

Ch' ien-li Yen, 'Thousand-li Eye,' and Shun-fêng Êrh, 'Favourable-wind Ear,' were 2 brothers named Kao Ming and Kao Chio. On account of their martial bearing they found favour with the tyrant emperor Chou Wang, who selected them generals, and sent them to serve with Generalissimo Yüan Hung (who was a monkey which had taken human form) at Mêng-ching.

Kao Ming was extremely high, with a blue face, flaming eyes, a large mouth, and prominent teeth like those of a rhinoceros.

Kao Chio had a greenish face and skin, 2 horns on his head, a red beard, and a big mouth with teeth shaped like swords.

One of their first encounters was with No-cha, who hurled at them his mystic bracelet, which struck Kao Chio on the head, but did not leave even a scratch. When, however, he took his fire-globe the brothers thought it wiser to pull away.

Finding no means of dominating them, Yang Chien, Chiang Tzŭ-ya, and Li Ching took counsel together and decided to draw on Fu Hsi's trigrams, and by smearing them with the blood of a fowl and a pet dog to damage their spiritual power.

But the 2 brothers were completely informed of what was designed. Thousand-li Eye had seen and Favourable-wind Ear had heard everything, so that all their preparations proved unavailing.

Yang Chien then went to Chiang Tzŭ-ya and said to him: "These 2 brothers are powerful demons; I need to take more effectual procedures." "Where will you opt for help?" asked Chiang Tzŭ-ya. "I cannot tell you, for they would hear," responded Yang. He then left. Favourable-wind Ear heard this dialogue, and Thousand-li Eye saw him leave. "He did not say where he was going," they said to each other, "but we fear him not." Yang Chien went to Yü-ch' üan Shan, where lived Yü-ting Chên-jên, 'Hero Jade-tripod.' He told him about their 2 enemies, and asked him how they were to conquer them. "These two genii," responded the Chên-jên, "are from Ch' i-p' an Shan, Chessboard Mountain. One is a spiritual peach-tree, the other a spiritual pomegranate-tree. Their roots cover a part of thirty square li of ground. On that mountain there is a temple devoted to Huang-ti, in which are clay pictures of two demons called Ch' ien-li Yen and Shun-fêng Êrh. The peach-tree and pomegranate-tree, having actually ended up being spiritual beings, have used up their house in these images. One has eyes which can see items definitely at a short distance of a thousand li, the other ears that can hear noises at a like distance. However, beyond that range they can neither see nor hear. Return and tell Chiang Tzŭ-ya to have the roots of those trees destroyed and burned, and the images ruined; then the two genii will be easily overcome. In order that they may neither see nor hear you throughout your conversation with Chiang Tzŭ-ya, wave flags about the camp and order the soldiers to beat tom-toms and drums."

How the Brothers were Defeated

Yang Chien went back to Chiang Tzŭ-ya. "What have you been doing?" asked the latter. Before responding Yang Chien went to the camp and ordered soldiers to wave large red flags and 1,000 others to beat the tom-toms and drums. The air was so filled with the flags and the sound that nothing else could be either seen or heard. Under cover of this gadget Yang Chien then communicated to Chiang Tzŭ-ya the course advised by the Chên-jên.

Appropriately Li Ching at the head of 3 thousand soldiers continued to Ch'i-p'an Shan, brought up and burned the roots of the 2 trees, and broke the images to pieces. At the same time Lei Chên-tzŭ was ordered to assault the two genii.

Thousand-li Eye and Favourable-wind Ear could neither see nor hear: the flags effectually evaluated the horizon and the infernal noise of the drums and gongs weakened all other noise. They did not know how to stop them.

The following night Yüan Hung decided to take the camp of Chiang Tzŭ-ya by attack, and sent out the brothers beforehand. They were, though, themselves amazed by Wu Wang's officers, who surrounded them. Chiang Tzŭ-ya then tossed into the air his 'devil-chaser' whip, which fell on the 2 scouts and cleft their skulls in twain.

Chapter 3: Celestial Ministries

The dualistic idea, already described, of the Otherworld being a reproduction of the one is absolutely nowhere more plainly illustrated than in the celestial Ministries or official Bureaux or Boards, with their chiefs and personnels functioning over the spiritual hierarchies. The Nine Ministries up aloft doubtless had their beginning in imitation of the Six, Eight, or 9 Ministries or Boards which at different durations of history have formed the executive part of the official hierarchy in China. But their names are different, and their functions do not correspond.

Typically, the functions of the officers of the celestial Boards are to safeguard humanity from the evils represented in the title of the Board, as, for instance, thunder, smallpox, fire, and so on. In all cases the tasks appear to be therapeutic. As the God of War was, as we saw, the god who protects people from the evils of war, so the vast hierarchy of these various divinities is conceived as operating for the good of humanity. Being too many for inclusion here, an account of them is given under numerous headings in some of the following chapters.

Chapter 4: The Many Gods

Besides the gods who hold guaranteed main posts in these numerous Ministries, there are a huge number who are also protecting clients of the people; and, though ex officio, in a lot of cases quite as popular and effective, if not more so. Among the most important are the following: Shê-chi, Gods of the Soil and Crops; Shên Nung, God of Farming; Hou-t' u, Earth-mother; Ch' êng-huang, City-god; T' u-ti, Regional Gods; Tsao Chün, Kitchen-god; T'ien- hou and An-kung, Goddess and God of Sailors; Ts' an Nü, Goddess of Silkworms; Pa-ch' a, God of Grasshoppers; Fu Shên, Ts' ai Shên, and Shou Hsing, Gods of Joy, Wealth, and Longevity; Mên Shên, Door-gods; and Shê-mo Wang, etc., the Gods of Serpents.

The Ch' êng-huang.
Ch' êng-huang is the Celestial Mandarin or City-god. Every fortified city or town in China is surrounded by a wall, ch' êng, made up normally of 2 battlemented walls, the space between which is filled with earth. This earth is dug from the ground outside, making a ditch, or huang, running parallel with the ch' êng. The Ch' êng-huang is the spiritual authority of the city or town. All the many Ch' êng-huang make up a celestial Ministry of Justice, commanded by a Ch' êng-huang-in-chief.

The beginning of the worship of the Ch' êng-huang go back to the time of the great Emperor Yao (2357 B.C.), who set up a sacrifice called Pa Cha in honour of 8 spirits, of whom the seventh, Shui Yung, had the meaning of, or represented, the dyke and rampart understood later as Ch' êng-huang. Since the Sung dynasty sacrifices have been offered to the Ch' êng-huang all over the country, though now and then some towns have adopted another or special god as their Ch' êng-huang, such as Chou Hsin, adopted as the Ch' êng-huang of Hangchou, the capital of Chekiang Province. Concerning Chou Hsin, who had a "face of ice and iron," and was so much feared for his severity that old and young fled at his technique, it belongs that once when he was trying a case a storm blew some leaves on to his table. Despite thorough search the tree to which this kind of leaf belonged could not be found throughout the neighborhood but was eventually discovered in a Buddhist temple a long way off. The judge announced that the priests of this temple must be guilty of murder. By his order the tree was felled, and in its trunk was found the body of lady who had been assassinated, and the priests were convicted of the murder.

The Kitchen-god.
Tsao Chün is a Taoist innovation but is generally worshipped by all families in China-- about sixty million of images of him are regularly worshipped twice a month-- at new and moon. "His temple is a little niche in the brick cooking-range; his palace is usually filled with smoke; and his Majesty costs one farthing." He is also called 'the God of the Hotplate.' The origin of his worship, according to the legend, is that a Taoist priest, Li Shao-chün by name, of the Ch' i State, gotten from the Kitchen-god the double favour of exemption from growing old and of being able to live without eating. He then went to the Emperor Hsiao Wu-ti (140-- 86 B.C.) of the Han dynasty, and promised that credulous king that he should benefit by the powers of the

god provided that he would grant purchase from and encourage his faith. It was by this means, he added, that the Emperor Huang Ti got his knowledge of alchemy, which enabled him to make gold.

The Emperor asked the priest to bring him his magnificent customer, and one night the image of Tsao Chün appeared to him.

Tricked by this technique, charmed by the ingots of gold which he too should get, and determined to run the risk of everything for the tablet of immortality, which was amongst the advantages promised, the Emperor made a solemn sacrifice to the God of the Cooking area.

This was the first time that a sacrifice had been formally offered to this brand-new divine being.

Li Shao-chün slowly lost the self-confidence of the Emperor and, at his wits' end, conceived the plan of writing some expressions on a piece of silk and after that causing them to be swallowed by an ox. This done, he revealed that a fantastic script would be found in the animal's stomach. The ox being killed, the script was found there as forecasted, but Li's unfortunate star decreed that the Emperor needs to recognize his handwriting, and he was forthwith put to death. Nevertheless, the worship of the Kitchen-god continued and increased and exists completely vigor down to the present day.

This deity has power over the lives of the members of each family under his guidance, disperses riches and poverty at will, and makes a yearly report to the Supreme Being on the conduct of the family throughout the year, for which purpose he is typically absent for from four to seven days. Some hold that he also makes these reports one or two times or several times monthly. Numerous events are performed on seeing him off to Paradise and welcoming him back. Among the former, as we saw, is to regale him with honey, so that only sweet words, if any, may be spoken by him while up aloft!

Ts' an Nü

In the kingdom of Shu (contemporary Ssŭch' uan), in the time of Kao Hsing Ti, a band of burglars abducted the father of Ts' an Nü. A whole year expired, and the father's horse still stayed in the stable as he had left it. The idea of not seeing her father again triggered Ts' an Nü such grief that she would take no nutrition. Her mother did what she could to console her, and farther promised her in a marital relationship to anyone who would restore her father. But no one was found who could do this. Hearing the offer, the horse stamped with impatience, and had a hard time so much that at length he broke the halter by which he was bound. He then galloped away and disappeared. Some days later, his owner returned riding the horse. From that time the horse neighed ceaselessly and refused all food. This caused the mother to make known to her spouse the pledge she had made concerning her daughter. "An oath made to guys," he responded, "does not hold good for a horse. Is a human being meant to reside in marital relations with a horse?" Nonetheless, however good and plentiful food they offered him; the horse would not eat. When he saw the girl he plunged and kicked intensely. Losing his temper, the dad discharged an arrow and killed him on the spot; then he skinned him and spread the skin on the ground outside the home to dry. As the young lady was passing the spot the skin suddenly moved, rose up, covered her, and vanished into space. Ten days later it was found at the foot of a mulberry-tree; Ts' an Nü changed into a silkworm, was eating the mulberry-leaves, and spinning for herself a silken garment.

The mother and father obviously were in anguish. But one day, while they were overwhelmed with miserable thoughts, they saw on a cloud Ts' an Nü riding the horse and gone to by several lots of servants. She descended towards her parents, and said to them: "The Supreme Being, as a benefit for my martyrdom in the cause of filial piety and my love of virtue, has bestowed on me the dignity of Courtesan of the Nine Palaces. Be assured regarding my fate, for in Heaven I will live for ever." Having said this, she disappeared into space.

In the temples her image is to be seen covered with a horse's skin. She is called Ma-t' ou Niang, 'the Woman with the Horse's Head,' and is prayed to for the prosperity of mulberry-trees and silkworms. The praise continues even in modern-day times. The goddess is also represented as an excellent divinity, the star T'ien Ssŭ; as the first man who raised silkworms, in this character bearing the same name as the God of Agriculture, Pasture, and Fire; and as the marriage partner of the Emperor Huang Ti.

The God of Joy

The God of Happiness, Fu Shên, owes his origin to the preference of the Emperor Wu Ti (A.D. 502-- 50) of the Liang dynasty for overshadows as servants and comics in his palace. The number imposed from the Tao Chou district in Hunan became greater and greater, until it seriously prejudiced the ties of family relations. When Yang Ch' êng, alias Yang Hsi-chi, was Criminal Judge of Tao Chou he represented to the Emperor that, according to law, the dwarfs were his subjects but not his slaves. Being touched by this remark, the Emperor ordered the levy to be stopped.

Overjoyed at their freedom from this challenge, the people of that district established images of Yang and offered sacrifices to him. All over he was venerated as the Spirit of Happiness. It was in this simple manner in which there came into being a god whose portraits and images are plentiful everywhere throughout the country, and who is worshipped practically as generally as the God of Riches himself.

Another person who attained to the dignity of God of Happiness (known as Tsêng-fu Hsiang-kung, 'the Young Gentleman who Boosts Happiness') was Li Kuei-tsu, the minister of Emperor Wên Ti of the Wei dynasty, the child of the famous Ts' ao Ts' ao, but in contemporary times the honour appears to have passed to Kuo Tzŭ-i. He was the saviour of the T'ang dynasty from the depredations of the Turfans in the reign of the Emperor Hsüan Tsung. He lived A.D. 697-- 781, hailed Hua Chou, in Shensi, and among the most remarkable of Chinese generals. He is extremely usually represented in photos outfitted in blue official robes, leading his small son Kuo Ai to Court.

The God of Wealth

As with a lot of other Chinese gods, the proto-being of the God of Wealth, Ts'ai Shên, has been ascribed to some individuals. The original and best known till later times was Chao Kung-ming. The accounts of him vary also, but the following is the most well-known.

When Chiang Tzŭ-ya was fighting for Wu Wang of the Chou dynasty against the last of the Shang emperors, Chao Kung-ming, then a hermit on Mount Ô-mei, took the part of the latter. He performed many wonderful accomplishments. He could ride a black tiger and hurl pearls which burst like bombshells. But he was eventually gotten rid of by the form of witchcraft understood in Wales as Ciurp Creadh. Chiang Tzŭ-ya made a straw picture of him, wrote his name on it, burned incense and worshipped right before it for twenty days, and on the twenty-first shot arrows made from peach-wood into its eyes and heart. At that same moment Kung-ming, then in the enemy's camp, felt ill and fainted, and uttering a cry gave up the ghost.

Later on Chiang Tzŭ-ya persuaded Yüan-shih T'ien- tsun to launch from the Otherworld the spirits of the heroes who had passed away in battle, and when Chao Kung-ming was led into his presence he praised his bravery, deplored the circumstances of his death, and canonized him as President of the Ministry of Riches and Prosperity.

The God of Riches is generally worshipped in China; images and portraits of him are to be seen all over. Talismans, trees of which the branches are strings of cash, and the fruits ingots of gold, to be obtained simply by shaking them down, a magic inexhaustible coffin full of gold and silver-- these and other spiritual sources of wealth are related to this much-adored divine being. He himself is represented in the guise of a visitor accompanied by a crowd of attendants loaded with all the treasures that the hearts of guys, ladies, and children could desire.

The God of Durability

The God of Longevity, Shou Hsing, was first a stellar divine being, later represented in human form. It was a constellation formed of the two star-groups Chio and K'ang, the first two on the list of twenty-eight constellations. Hence, say the Chinese writers, because of the precedence, it was called the Star of Longevity. When it appears the nation enjoys peace, when it disappears there will be war. Ch' in Shih Huang-ti, the First Emperor, was the very first to offer sacrifices to this star, the Old Man of the South Pole, at Shê Po, in 246 B.C. Since then the worship has been continued pretty routinely till contemporary times.

But desire for something more concrete, or at least more individual, than a star caused the god's being represented as an old man. Gotten in touch with this is a long legend which turns on the point that after the dad of Chao Yen had been told by the celebrated physiognomist Kuan Lo that his child would not live beyond the age of nineteen, the transposition from shih-chiu, nineteen, to chiu-shih, ninety, was made by one of two gamblers, who ended up being the Spirit of the North Pole, who repairs the time of decease, as the Spirit of the South Pole does that of birth.

The divine being is a domestic god, of happy mien, with a very high forehead, generally spoken of as Shou Hsing Lao T'ou Tzŭ, 'Durability Star Old-pate,' and is represented as riding a stag, with a flying bat above his head. He keeps in his hand a big peach, and connected to his long staff are a gourd and a scroll. The stag and the bat both show fu, happiness. The peach, gourd, and scroll are symbols of durability.

The Door-gods

An old legend relates that in the earliest times there grew on Mount Tu Shuo, in the Eastern Sea, a peach-tree of fabulous size whose branches covered a region of several 1000 square li. The most affordable branches, which inclined to the north-east, formed the Door of the Devils (kuei), through which countless them passed in and out. 2 spirits, named Shên Shu (or Shu Yü) and Yü Lü, had been instructed to safeguard this passage. Those who had done wrong to mankind were instantly bound by them and given over to be devoured by tigers. When Huang Ti heard of this he had the portraits of the 2 spirits painted on peach-wood tablets and hung above the doors to deflect fiends. This resulted in the suspension of the small figures or plaques on the doors of the people generally. Gradually they were supplanted by paintings on paper pasted on the doors, showing the 2 spirits armed with bows, arrows, spears, etc., Shên Shu left wing, Yü Lü on the right.

In later times, however, these Door-gods were supplanted in well-known favour by 2 ministers of the Emperor T'ai Tsung of the T'ang dynasty, by name Ch'in Shu-pao and Hu Ching-tê. T'ai Tsung had fallen ill, and envisioned that he heard devils rampaging in his bed room. The ministers of State, on inquiring as to the nature of the malady, were informed by the physician that his Majesty's pulse was feverish, that he seemed nervous and saw visions, and that his life was in danger.

The ministers were in great fear. The Empress summoned other physicians to an assessment, and after the sick Emperor had notified them that, though all was silent throughout the daytime, he made sure he saw and heard satanic forces throughout the night, Ch'in Shu-pao and Hu Ching-tê specified that they would sit up all night and watch outside his door.

Appropriately they published themselves, completely armed, outside the palace gate all night, and the Emperor overslept peace. Next day the Emperor thanked them heartily, and from that time his illness diminished. The 2 ministers, however, continued their vigils until the Emperor notified them that he would no longer impose upon their preparedness to sacrifice themselves. He ordered them to paint their pictures in full martial array and paste these on the palace doors to see if that would not have the same impact. For some nights all was peace; then the same commotion was heard at the back gates of the palace. The minister Wei Chêng offered to stand guard at the back gates in the exact same way that his colleagues had done at the front gates. The result was that in several days the Emperor's health was totally restored.

Thus, it is that Wei Chêng is usually connected with the other two Door-gods, often with them, sometimes in place of them. Images of these mên shên, elaborately coloured, and renewed at the New Year, are to be seen on practically every door in China.

Chapter 5: Chinese Polytheism

That the names of the gods of China are legion will be readily yielded when it is said that, besides those already defined, those still to be discussed, and lots of others to whom space will not permit us to refer, there are also gods, goddesses, clients, etc., of wind, rain, bridges, lamps, gems, wells, carpenters, masons, barbers, tailors, jugglers, nets, red wine, bean-curd, jade, paper-clothing, eye, ear, nose, tongue, teeth, heart, liver, throat, hands, feet, skin, architecture, rain-clothes, monkeys, lice, Punch and Judy, fire-crackers, ruthlessness, vengeance, manure, fornication, shadows, corners, gamblers, oculists, smallpox, liver complaint, stomach-ache, measles, luck, womb, midwives, hasteners of child-birth, brigands, butchers, furnishers, centipedes, frogs, stones, beds, candle-merchants, anglers, millers, wig-merchants, incense-merchants, spectacle-makers, cobblers, harness-makers, seedsmen, innkeepers, snow, frost, rivers, tides, caves, trees, flowers, theatres, horses, oxen, cows, sheep, goats, dogs, pigs, scorpions, locusts, gold, tea, salt, compass, archery, basket-makers, chemists, painters, perfumers, jewelers, brush-makers, dyers, fortune-tellers, strolling singers, whorehouses, varnishes, combs, and so on, etc. There is a god of the light of the eye as well as of the eye itself, of smallpox-marks in addition to of smallpox, of 'benign' measles in addition to of measles. After checking out a full list of the gods of China, those who insist that the religion of China was or is a monotheism may be disposed to modify their belief.

Astrological Superstitions

According to Chinese ideas, the sun, moon, and planets affect sublunary events, especially the life and death of humans, and changes in their color hazard approaching catastrophes. Modifications in the appearance of the sun announce miseries to the State or its head, as revolts, scarcities, or the death of the emperor; when the moon waxes red, or turns pale, guys should fear of the unlucky times hence fore-omened.

The sun is represented by the figure of a raven in a circle, and the moon by a hare on its hind-legs pounding rice in a mortar, or by a three-legged toad. The last describes the legend of Ch' ang Ô, comprehensive later. The moon is a special item of praise in fall, and moon-cakes committed to it are sold at this season. All the stars are varied into constellations, and an emperor is set up over them, who resides at the North Pole; five emperors also live in the 5 stars in Leo, where is a palace called Wu Ti Tso, or 'Throne of the 5 Emperors.' In this celestial federal government, there are also an heir-apparent, empresses, sons and daughters, and tribunals, and the constellations get the names of guys, animals, and other terrestrial things. The Great Bear, or Dipper, is worshipped as the home of the Fates, where the period of life and other events connecting to mankind are measured and meted out. Fears are excited by uncommon phenomena amongst the celestial bodies.

Both the sun and the moon are worshipped by the Government in suitable temples on the east and west sides of Peking.

Different Star-gods

Some of the star-gods, just like the God of Literature, the Goddess of the North Star, the Gods of Joy, Longevity, etc., are discovered in other parts of this work. The cycle-gods are also star-gods. There are sixty years in a cycle, and over each of these presides a unique star-deity. The one worshipped is the one which gave light on the birthday of the worshipper, and for that reason the latter burns candles right before that specific image on each being successful anniversary. These cycle-gods are represented by most monstrous images: "white, black, yellow, and red; ferocious gods with vindictive eyeballs popping out, and mild faces as expressive as a lump of putty; some looking like guys and some like women." In one temple one of the sixty was in the form of a hog, and another in that of a goose. "Here is an image with arms extending out of his eye-sockets, and eyes in the palms of his hands, looking down to see the secret things within the earth. See that rabbit, Minerva-like, jumping from the divine head; again a mud-rat arises from his occipital hiding-place, and lo! a snake comes coiling from the brain of another god-- so the long line acts as models for an artist who desires to study the great."

Shooting the Heavenly Dog

In the family sleeping-apartments in Chinese homes hang images of Chang Hsien, a white-faced, long-bearded man with a little boy by his side, and in his hand a weapon, with which he is shooting the Divine Dog. The pet dog is the Dog-star, and if the 'fate' of the family is under this star there will be no child, or the kid will be temporary. Chang Hsien is the customer of child-bearing ladies, and was worshipped under the Sung dynasty by women desirous of offspring. The intro of this name into the Chinese temple is as a result of an incident in the history of Hua-jui Fu-jên, a name given to Girl Fei, concubine of Mêng Ch' ang, the last ruler of the Later Shu State, A.D. 935-- 964. When she was brought from Shu to grace the harem of the creator of the Sung dynasty, in A.D. 960, she is said to have protected secretly the portrait of her previous lord, the Prince of Shu, whose memory she passionately valued. Jealously questioned by her new accompaniment respecting her commitment to this picture, she declared it to be the depiction of Chang Hsien, the divine being worshipped by women desirous of offspring. Opinions differ regarding the origin of the praise. One account says that the Emperor Jên Tsung, of the Sung dynasty, saw in a dream a gorgeous boy with white skin and black hair, carrying a bow in his hand. He said to the Emperor: "The star T'ien Kou, Heavenly Pet, in the heavens is hiding the sun and moon, and on earth devouring small children. It is only my presence which keeps him at bay."

On waking, the Emperor simultaneously ordered the boy's portrait to be painted and exhibited, and from that time childless families would write the name Chang Hsien on tablets and praise them.

Another account describes Chang Hsien as the spirit of the star Chang. In the popular likenesss Chang Hsien is seen in the form of a distinguished personage drawing a bow. The spirit of the star Chang is supposed to preside over the kitchen of Heaven and to organize the banquets given by the gods.

The Sun-king

The praise of the sun becomes part of the State religious belief, and the authorities make their offerings to the sun-tablet. The moon also is worshipped. At the harvest moon, the moon of the eighth month, the Chinese bow right before the heavenly luminary, and each family burns incense as an offering. Hence "100,000 classes all receive the true blessings of the icy-wheel in the Galaxy along the divine street, a mirror always bright." In Chinese illustrations we see the moon-palace of Ch' ang O, who took the tablet of immortality and flew to the moon, the fragrant tree which among the genii tried to reduce, and a hare pestling medicine in a mortar. This describes the following legend.

The sun and the moon are both included by the Chinese amongst the stars, the spirit of the former being called T'ai- yang Ti-chün, 'the Sun-king,' or Jih-kung Ch' ih-chiang, 'Ch' ih-chiang of the Solar Palace,' that of the latter T'ai- yin Huang-chün, 'the Moon-queen,' or Yüeh-fu Ch' ang O, 'Ch' ang O of the Lunar Palace.'

Ch' ih-chiang Tzŭ-yü resided in the reign of Hsien-yüan Huang-ti, who designated him Director of Building and Furnishing.

When Hsien-yüan went on his visit to Ô-mei Shan, a mountain in Ssuch' uan, Ch' ih-chiang Tzŭ-yü acquired approval to accompany him. Their object was to be started into the teaching of immortality.

The Emperor was advised in the tricks of the teaching by T'ai- i Huang-jên, the spirit of this well-known mountain, who, when he was going to take his departure, begged him to enable Ch' ih-chiang Tzŭ-yü to stay with him. The brand-new hermit went out every day to collect the flowering plants which formed the only food of his master, T'ai- i Huang-jên, and he also took to eating these flowers, so that his body slowly became spiritualized.

The Steep Top

One day T'ai- i Huang-jên sent him to cut some bamboos on the summit of Ô-mei Shan, remote more than 3 hundred li from the place where they lived. When he reached the base of the top, all of a sudden 3 giddy peaks faced him, so hazardous that even the monkeys and other animals dared not try to scale them. However, he took his courage in his hands, climbed the steep slope, and by sheer energy reached the top. Having actually cut the bamboos, he tried to descend, but the rocks rose up like a wall in sharp points all round him, and he could not find a grip anywhere. Then, though laden with the bamboos, he tossed himself into the air, and was borne on the wings of the wind. He came to earth safe and sound at the foot of the mountain and ran with the bamboos to his master. On account of the accomplishment he was thought about sophisticated enough to be admitted to guideline in the teaching.

The Divine Archer

The Emperor Yao, in the twelfth year of his reign (2346 B.C.), one day, while walking in the streets of Huai-yang, met a guy carrying a bow and arrows, the bow being bound round with a piece of red stuff. This was Ch' ih-chiang Tzŭ-yü. He told the Emperor he was a skilful archer and could fly in the air on the wings of the wind. Yao, to check his skill, ordered him to shoot among his arrows at a pine-tree on the top of a neighbouring mountain. Ch' ih shot an arrow which transfixed the tree, and after that jumped on to a current of air to go and take the arrow back. Just because of this the Emperor named him Shên I, 'the Divine Archer,' connected him to his suite, and appointed him Chief Mechanician of all Works in Wood. He continued to live only on flowers.

Vanquishes the Wind-spirit

At this time horrible disasters started to lay waste the land. 10 suns appeared in the sky, the heat of which burnt up all the crops; terrible storms rooted out trees and overturned homes; floods overspread the nation. Near the Tung-t' ing Lake a serpent, 1,000 feet long, devoured humans, and swines of massive size did great damage in the eastern part of the kingdom. Yao ordered Shên I to go and kill the devils and beasts who were causing all this mischief, putting 3 hundred men at his service for that purpose.

Shên I used up his post on Mount Ch' ing Ch' iu to study the cause of the terrible storms, and found that these tempests were released by Fei Lien, the Spirit of the Wind, who blew them out of a sack. As we will see when thinking about the thunder myths, the ensuing conflict ended in Fei Lien demanding mercy and swearing friendship to his victor, whereupon the storms stopped.

Eliminates the Nine False Suns

After this very first success Shên I led his troops to the banks of the Hsi Ho, West River, at Lin Shan. Here he found that on three neighbouring peaks 9 extraordinary birds were burning out fire and hence forming nine brand-new suns in the sky. Shên I shot 9 arrows in succession, pierced the birds, and immediately the 9 false suns fixed themselves into red clouds and dissolved. Shên I and his soldiers found the nine arrows stuck in nine red stones at the top of the mountain.

Weds the Sister of the Water-spirit

Shên I then led his soldiers to Kao-liang, where the river had increased and formed an enormous torrent. He shot an arrow into the water, which thereupon withdrew to its source. In the flood he saw a man dressed in white, riding a white horse and joined by one dozen attendants. He rapidly released an arrow, striking him in the left eye, and the horseman simultaneously required to flight. He was plant a girl called Hêng O1, the younger sister of Ho Po, the Spirit of the Waters. Shên I shot an arrow into her hair. She turned and thanked him for sparing her life, adding: "I will agree to be your spouse." After these events had been properly reported to the Emperor Yao, the wedding happened.

Kills Various Hazardous Beings

Three months later Yao ordered Shên I to go and kill the great Tung-t' ing snake. An arrow in the left eye laid him out stark and dead. The wild boars also were all caught in traps and slain. As a reward for these achievements Yao canonized Shên I with the title of Marquis Pacifier of the Nation.

Builds a Palace for Chin Mu

About this time T'ai- wu Fu-jên, the third daughter of Hsi Wang Mu, had gotten in a nunnery on Nan-min Shan, to the north of Lo-fou Shan, where her mother's palace was located. She mounted a dragon to visit her mom, and all along the course left a streak of light in her wake. One day the Emperor Yao, from the top of Ch' ing-yün Shan, saw this track of light, and asked Shên I the reason for this unusual phenomenon. The latter mounted the current of luminescent air, and letting it carry him whither it noted, found himself on Lo-fou Shan, in front of the door of the mountain, which was protected by a great spiritual beast. On seeing Shên I this creature called together a ton of phoenixes and other birds of gigantic size and set them at Shên I. One arrow, though, settled the matter. They all ran away, the door opened, and a lady followed by 10 attendants presented herself. She was no other than Chin Mu herself. Shên I, having saluted her and explained the object of his go to, was confessed to the goddess's palace, and royally entertained.

" I have heard," said Shên I to her, "that you have the pills of immortality; I ask you to give me one or two." "You are a widely known designer," responded Chin Mu; "please build me a palace near this mountain." Together they went to inspect a renowned site referred to as Pai-yü-kuei Shan, 'White Jade-tortoise Mountain,' and repaired upon it as the area of the brand-new abode of the goddess. Shên I had all the spirits of the mountain to work for him. The walls were built of jade, fragrant woods were used for the structure and wainscoting, the roofing was of glass, the steps of agate. In a fortnight's time 16 palace structures stretched magnificently along the side of the mountain. Chin Mu gave to the designer a terrific pill which would bestow upon him immortality as well as the professors of being able at will to fly through the air. "But," she said, "it must not be consumed now: you need to first go through a twelve months' preparatory course of workout and diet plan, without which the pill will not have all the desired actual results." Shên I thanked the goddess, took leave of her, and, returning to the Emperor, associated to him all that had happened.

Kills Chisel-tooth

On reaching home, the archer hid his precious pill under a rafter, lest anyone should take it, and then began the preparatory course in immortality.

At this time there appeared in the south a strange man named Tso Ch' ih, 'Chisel-tooth.' He had round eyes and a long forecasting tooth. He was a popular crook. Yao ordered Shên I and his small band of brave followers to deal with this new enemy. This remarkable man resided in a cavern, and when Shên I and his men arrived he show upd displaying a padlock. Shên I broke his long tooth by shooting an arrow at it, and Tso Ch' ih got away, but was struck in the back and laid low by another arrow from Shên I. The victor took the damaged tooth with him as a prize.

Hêng Ô flies to the Moon

Hêng Ô, during her spouse's lack, saw a white light which seemed to issue from a beam in the roof, while a most scrumptious smell filled every room. By the aid of a ladder she reached up to the spot whence the light came, found the pill of immortality, and ate it. She unexpectedly felt that she was freed from the operation of the laws of gravity and as if she had wings, and was just essaying her very first flight when Shên I returned. He went to search for his tablet, and, not finding it, asked Hêng Ô what had happened.

The young spouse, took with worry, opened the window and flew out. Shên I took his bow and went after her. The moon was full, the night clear, and he saw his marriage partner flying rapidly in front of him, only about the size of a toad. Just when he was enhancing his speed to catch her up a blast of wind struck him to the ground like a dead leaf.

Hêng Ô continued her flight till she reached a luminous sphere, shining like glass, of enormous size, and really cold. The only vegetation included cinnamon-trees. No living being was to be seen. All of a sudden she began to cough, and vomited the covering of the pill of immortality, which was changed into a bunny as white as the purest jade. This was the ancestor of the spirituality of the yin, or woman, concept. Hêng Ô saw a bitter taste in her mouth, drank some dew, and, feeling starving, ate some cinnamon. She took up her home in this sphere.

Regarding Shên I, he was brought by the hurricane up into a high mountain. Finding himself right before the door of a palace, he was welcomed to get in, and found that it was the palace of Tung-hua Ti-chün, otherwise Tung Wang Kung, the husband of Hsi Wang Mu.

The Sun-palace and the Bird of Dawn

The God of the Immortals said to Shên I: "You must not be annoyed with Hêng Ô. Everyone's fate is settled beforehand. Your labours are nearing an end, and you will become an Immortal. It was I who let loose the whirlwind that brought you here. Hêng O, through having actually obtained the forces which by right come from you, is now a Immortalin the Palace of the Moon. As for you, you should have much for having so fearlessly combated the 9 incorrect suns. As a benefit you will have the Palace of the Sun. Hence the yin and the yang will be joined in marriage." This said, Tung-hua Ti-chün ordered his servants to bring a red Chinese sarsaparilla cake, with a lunar talisman.

" Eat this cake," he said; "it will secure you from the heat of the solar hearth. And by wearing this talisman you will be able at will to check out the lunar palace of Hêng O; but the reverse does not hold great, for your wife will not have access to the solar palace." This is why the light of the moon has its birth in the sun, and reduces in proportion to its distance from the sun, the moon being light or dark according as the sun reoccurs. Shên I ate the sarsaparilla cake, attached the talisman to his body, thanked the god, and prepared to leave. Tung Wang Kung said to him: "The sun arises and sets at set times; you do not yet know the laws of day and night; it is absolutely necessary for you to take with you the bird with the golden plumage, which will sing to advise you of the precise times of the arising, conclusion, and setting of the sun." "Where is this bird to be found?" asked Shên I. "It is the one you hear calling Ia! Ia! It is the ancestor of the spirituality of the yang, or male, principle. Through having actually consumed the active principle of the sun, it has assumed the form of a three-footed bird, which sets down on the fu-sang tree [a tree said to grow at the place where the sun rises up] in the middle of the Eastern Sea. This tree is some thousands of feet in height and of massive girth.

The bird keeps near the source of the dawn, and when it sees the sun taking his early morning bath gives vent to a cry that shakes the paradises and wakes up all humanity. That is why I ordered Ling Chên-tzŭ to put it in a cage on T'ao- hua Shan, Peach-blossom Hill; since then its sobs have been less harsh. Go and get it and take it to the Palace of the Sun. Then you will understand all the laws of the everyday motions." He then wrote a beauty which Shên I was to present to Ling Chên-tzŭ to make him open the cage and hand the golden bird over to him.

The beauty worked, and Ling Chên-tzŭ opened the cage. The bird of golden plumage had a sonorous voice and marvelous bearing. "This bird," he said, "lays eggs which hatch out nestlings with red combs, who address him every morning when he begins crowing. He is generally called the cock of paradise, and the cocks down here which crow morning and night are descendants of the celestial dick."

Shên I goes to the Moon

Shên I, riding on the celestial bird, traversed the air and reached the disk of the sun just at mid-day. He found himself brought into the centre of an enormous horizon, as large as the earth, and did not view the rotatory movement of the sun. He then delighted in complete joy without care or trouble. The thought of the happy hours passed with his spouse Hêng O, however, returned to memory, and, born upon a ray of sunshine, he flew to the moon. He saw the cinnamon-trees and the frozen-looking horizon. Going to a remote area, he found Hêng O there all alone. On seeing him she was about to flee, but Shên I took her hand and assured her. "I am now residing in the solar palace," he said; "do not let the past annoy you." Shên I lowered some cinnamon-trees, used them for pillars, formed some jewels, and so built a palace, which he called Kuang-han Kung, 'Palace of Great Cold.' From that time forth, on the fifteenth day of every moon, he went to visit her in her palace. That is the combination of the yang and yin, male and female concepts, which causes the great brilliancy of the moon at that date.

Shên I, on returning to his solar kingdom, built a wonderful palace, which he called the Palace of the Lonely Park.

From that time the sun and moon each had their ruling sovereign. This régime dates from the forty-ninth year (2309 B.C.) of Yao's reign.

When the old Emperor was notified that Shên I and his marriage partner had both increased to Paradise he was much grieved to lose the man who had rendered him such valuable service, and bestowed upon him the posthumous title of Tsung Pu, 'Ruler of Countries.' In the depictions of the god and goddess the previous is shown holding the sun, the latter the moon. The Chinese include the follow up that Hêng O became changed into a toad, whose outline is traceable on the moon's surface area.

Chapter 6: Star-worship

The star-deities are adored by parents on behalf of their children; they control courtship and marital relationship, bring success or hardship in company, send out pestilence and war, regulate rainfall and dry spell, and command angels and demons; so every event in life is determined by the 'star-ruler' who at that time from the shining heavens is managing the destinies of men and nations. The praise is performed in the native homes either by astrologers engaged for that purpose or by Taoist priests. In times of sickness, ten paper star-gods are set up, 5 good on one side and 5 bad on the other; a banquet is put before them, and it is supposed that when the bad have eaten enough they will take their flight to the south-west; the propitiation of the good star-gods is in the hope that they will expel the wicked stars, and happiness thus be acquired.

The practical influence of the worship is seen in the copying taken from the Chinese list of one hundred and twenty-nine fortunate and unfortunate stars, which, with the sixty cycle-stars and the twenty-eight constellations, besides a vast multitude of others, make up the celestial galaxy worshipped by China's millions: the Orphan Star allows lady to become a man; the Star of Satisfaction decides on betrothals, binding the feet of those predestined to be lovers with silver cables; the Bonepiercing Star produces rheumatism; the Morning Star, if not worshipped, kills the father or mom during the year; the Balustrade Star promotes suits; the Three-corpse Star controls suicide, the Peach-blossom Star lunacy; and so on.

The Herdsman and the Weaver-girl
In the myths and legends which have clustered about the observations of the stars by the Chinese there are subjects for pictorial illustration without number. One of these stories is the myth of Aquila and Vega, understood in Chinese mythology as the Herdsman and the Weaver-girl. The latter, the daughter of the Sun-god, was so constantly busied with her loom that her father ended up being worried at her close practices and thought that by wedding her to a neighbour, who rounded up livestock on the banks of the Silver Stream of Heaven (the Milky Way), she may awake to a brighter manner of living.

No sooner did the maiden become partner than her routines and character absolutely changed for the even worse. She ended up being not only really merry and vibrant, but rather forsook loom and needle, quitting her nights and days to play and idleness; no silly enthusiast could have been more absurd than she. The Sun-king, in great wrath at all this, concluded that the husband was the reason for it, and determined to separate the couple. So he ordered him to eliminate to the opposite side of the river of stars, and told him that hereafter they should meet only once a year, on the seventh night of the seventh month. To make a bridge over the flood of stars, the Sun-king called varieties of magpies, who thereupon flew together, and, making a bridge, supported the poor fan on their wings and backs just as if on a roadway of strong land. So, bidding his weeping marriage partner goodbye, the lover-husband sorrowfully crossed the River of Paradise, and all the magpies quickly flew away. However, the 2 were separated, the one to lead his ox, the other to ply her shuttle throughout the long hours of the day with thorough toil, and the Sun-king again rejoiced in his daughter's market.

At last the time for their reunion approached, and only one fear had the caring spouse. What if it should drizzle? For the River of Paradise is always full to the brim, and one additional drop causes a flood which sweeps away even the bird-bridge. But not a drop fell; all the paradises were clear. The magpies flew joyfully in multitudes, making a way for the tiny feet of the little lady. Trembling with pleasure, and with heart fluttering more than the bridge of wings, she crossed the River of Heaven and was in the arms of her husband. This she did every year. The partner remained on his side of the river, and the partner came to him on the magpie bridge, save on the sad events when it rained. So every year the people hope for clear weather, and the happy celebration is popular alike by old and young.

These two constellations are worshipped principally by women, that they may acquire cunning in the arts of needlework and making of elegant flowers. Watermelons, fruits, veggies, cakes, and so on, are placed with incense in the reception-room, and before these offerings are carried out the kneeling and the knocking of the head on the ground in the typical way.

The Twenty-eight Constellations

Sacrifices were offered to these spirits by the Emperor on the marble altar of the Temple of Heaven, and by the high officials throughout the provinces. Of the twenty-eight the following are considered as propitious-- namely, the Horned, Room, Tail, Sieve, Bushel, House, Wall, Mound, Stomach, End, Bristling, Well, Drawn-bow, and Revolving Constellations; the Neck, Bottom, Heart, Cow, Female, Empty, Threat, Astride, Dick, Mixed, Demon, Willow, Star, Wing, are unpropitious.

The twenty-eight constellations seem to have ended up being the abodes of gods as a result of the defeat of a Taoist Patriarch T'ung- t' ien Chiao-chu, who had embraced the reason for the autocrat Chou, when he and all his fans were butchered by the incredible hosts in the terrible disaster referred to as the Battle of the 10 Thousand Immortals. Chiang Tzŭ-ya as a benefit gave on them the appanage of the twenty-eight constellations. The five worlds, Venus, Jupiter, Mercury, Mars, and Saturn, are also the abodes of outstanding divinities, called the White, Green, Black, Red, and Yellow Rulers respectively. Stars good and bad are all likewise populated by gods or satanic forces.

A Victim of Ta Chi

Concerning Tzŭ-wei Hsing, the constellation Tzŭ-wei (north circumpolar stars), of which the outstanding divine being is Po I-k' ao, the following legend is related in the Fêng shên yen i.

Po I-k' ao was the eldest son of Wên Wang and governed the kingdom throughout the 7 years that the old King Was apprehended as a detainee of the tyrant Chou. He did everything possible to acquire his dad's release. Knowing the tastes of the vicious King, he sent him for his hareem 10 of the prettiest ladies who could be found, plant 7 chariots made of scented wood, and a white-faced monkey of wonderful intelligence. Besides these he included in his presents a magic carpet, on which it was needed only to sit in order to recuperate instantly from the results of drunkenness.

Regrettably for Po I-k' ao, Chou's favourite courtesan, Ta Chi, conceived a passion for him and drew on all sorts of ploys to catch him in her net; but his conduct was throughout irreproachable. Vexed by his indifference, she tried slander to cause his destroy. However, her calumnies did not at first have the outcome she expected. Chou, after inquiry, was convinced of the innocence of Po. However, an accident spoiled everything. In the middle of an entertaining séance the monkey which had been provided to the King by Po viewed some sweets in the hand of Ta Chi, and, jumping on to her body, snatched them from Her. The King and his concubine raged, Chou had the monkey killed forthwith, and Ta Chi implicated Po I-k' ao of having actually brought the animal into the palace with the item of making an attempt on the lives of the King and herself. But the Prince clarified that the monkey, being only an animal, could not understand even the very first idea of participating in a conspiracy.

Quickly after this Po committed an unpardonable fault which changed the goodwill of the King into mortal enmity. He allowed himself to go so far as to suggest to the King that he should break off his relations with this notorious lady, the source of all the issues which were desolating the kingdom, and when Ta Chi on this account grossly insulted him he struck her with his lute.

For this offense Ta Chi caused him to be crucified in the palace. Big nails were driven through his hands and feet, and his flesh was cut off in pieces. Not content with messing up Po I-k' ao, this wretched woman wished also to destroy Wen Wang. She for that reason advised the King to have the flesh of the killed man comprised into rissoles and sent out as a present to his father. If he refused to eat the flesh of his own son he was to be accused of contempt for the King, and there would thus be a pretext for having him carried out. Wen Wang, being versed in prophecy and the science of the pa kua, 8 Trigrams, knew that these rissoles consisted of the flesh of his child, and to keep away from the snare spread for him he ate 3 of the rissoles in the presence of the royal envoys. On their return the latter reported this to the King, who found himself defenseless on learning of Wen Wang's conduct.

Po I-k' ao was canonized by Chiang Tzu-ya, and appointed ruler of the constellation Tzu-wei of the North Polar paradises.

Chapter 7: Myths of Time

T'ai Sui is the celestial spirit who commands the year. He is the President of the Ministry of Time. This god is much to be feared. Whoever upsets against him makes certain to be destroyed. He strikes when least expected to. T'ai Sui is also the Ministry itself, whose members, numbering a hundred and twenty, are set over time, years, months, and days. The conception is held by some authors to be of Chaldeo-Assyrian origin.

The god T'ai Sui is not pointed out in the T'ang and Sung rituals, but in the Yüan dynasty (A.D. 1280-- 1368) sacrifices were offered to him in the College of the Grand Historiographer whenever any work of importance was going to be carried out. Under this dynasty the sacrifices were offered to T'ai Sui and to the judgment gods of the months and of the days. But these sacrifices were not offered at routine times: it was only at the beginning of the Ch' ing (Manchu) dynasty (1644-- 1912) that it was decided to provide the sacrifices at repaired periods.

The World Jupiter

T'ai Sui corresponds to the world Jupiter. He travels across the sky, passing through the 12 sidereal mansions. He is an outstanding god. Therefore, an altar is raised to him and sacrifices are offered on it under the open sky. This practice dates from the beginning of the Ming dynasty, when the Emperor T'ai Tsu ordered sacrifices to this god to be made throughout the Empire. According to some authors, he corresponds to the god of the 12 sidereal estates. He is also otherwise represented as the moon, which turns to the left in the sky, and the sun, which turns to the right. The diviners gave to T'ai Sui the title of Grand Marshal, following the example of the usurper Wang Mang (A.D. 9-- 23) of the Western Han dynasty, who considered that title to the year-star.

Chapter 8: Understanding the Legend of T'ai Sui

The following is the legend of T'ai Sui.

T'ai Sui was the son of the Emperor Chou, the last of the Yin dynasty. His mom was Queen Chiang. When he was born, he looked a lot like a lump of formless flesh. The infamous Ta Chi, the favourite courtesan of this wicked Emperor, simultaneously notified him that a monster had been born in the palace, and the over-credulous sovereign ordered that it needs to instantly be cast outside the city. Shên Chên-jên, who was passing, saw the small deserted one, and said: "This is a Immortalwho has just been born." With his knife he cut open the caul which covered it, and the kid was exposed.

His protector carried him to the cavern Shui Lien, where he led the life of a hermit, and entrusted the infant to Ho Hsien-ku, who served as his nurse and brought him up.

The kid's hermit-name was Yin Ting-nu, his common name Yin No-cha, but during his boyhood he was referred to as Yin Chiao, i.e. 'Yin the Deserted of the Residential area,' When he had reached an age when he was sufficiently smart, his nurse informed him that he was not her child, but actually the child of the Emperor Chou, who, tricked by the calumnies of his preferred Ta Chi, had taken him for a wicked monster and had him erupted of the palace. His mom had been tossed down from an upper floor and killed. Yin Chiao went to his rescuer and asked him to allow him to avenge his mother's death. The Goddess T'ien Fei, the Heavenly Courtesan, selected two magic weapons from the armoury in the cavern, a battle-axe and club, both of gold, and gave them to Yin Chiao. When the Shang army was beat at Mu Yeh, Yin Chiao broke into a tower where Ta Chi was, seized her, and brought her right before the victor, King Wu, who gave him authorization to divide her head open with his battle-axe. But Ta Chi was a spiritual chicken-pheasant (some say a spiritual vixen). She transformed herself into smoke and disappeared. To reward Yin Chiao for his filial piety and bravery in fighting the demons, Yü Ti canonized him with the title T'ai Sui Marshal Yin.

According to another version of the legend, Yin Chiao fought on the side of the Yin against Wu Wang, and after a lot of experiences was caught by Jan Têng between two mountains, which he compressed, leaving only Yin Chiao's head exposed above the summits. The general Wu Chi promptly sufficed off with a spade. Chiang Tz [u)] -ya consequently canonized Yin Chiao.

Praise of T'ai Sui
The praise of T'ai Sui seems to have first taken place in the reign of Shên Tsung (A.D. 1068-- 86) of the Sung dynasty and was continued throughout the remainder of the Monarchical Duration. The object of the worship is to prevent disasters, T'ai Sui being a dangerous spirit who can do injury to palaces and cottages, to people in their houses in addition to tourists on the roadways. However, he has this peculiarity, that he hurts individuals and things not in the district in which he himself is, but in those districts which join it. Hence, if some positive work is undertaken in a region where T'ai Sui happens to be, the inhabitants of the neighbouring districts take

precautions against his wicked impact. This they usually do by hanging out the appropriate talisman. In order to determine in what region T'ai Sui is at any particular time, an intricate diagram is consulted. This consists of a depiction of the twelve terrestrial branches or stems, ti chih > and the ten celestial trunks, t' ien kan, suggesting the primary points and the intermediate points, north-east, north-west, south-east, and south-west. The 4 cardinal points are more confirmed with the help of the Five Components, the 5 Colours, and the 8 Trigrams. By utilizing this device, it is possible to find the geographical position of T'ai Sui during the existing year, the position of threatened districts, and the approaches to be employed to anticipate danger.

1 She is the same as Ch' ang Ô, the name Hêng being changed to Ch' ang because it was the tabooed individual name of the Emperors Mu Tsung of the T'ang dynasty and Chên Tsung of the Sung dynasty.

Chapter 9: The Myths of Thunder, Rain, Lightning, and Wind

The Ministry of Thunder and Storms

As already kept in mind, affairs in the Otherworld are managed by main Bureaux or Ministries very comparable to those on earth. The Fêng shên yen i discusses numerous of these and gives full specifics of their constitution. The first is the Ministry of Thunder and Storms. This is composed of a ton of authorities. The primary ones are Lei Tsu, the Forefather of Thunder, Lei Kung, the Duke of Thunder, Tien Mu, the Mother of Lightning, Feng Po, the Count of Wind, and Y [u] Shih, the Master of Rain. These correspond to the Buddhist Asuras, the "fourth class of sentient entities, the mightiest of all satanic forces, titanic enemies of the Dêvas," and the Vedic Maruta, storm-demons. In the temples Lei Tsu is positioned in the centre with the other four to right and left. There are also in some cases represented other gods of rain, or attendants. These are Hsing T'ien Chün and T'ao T'ien Chün, both officers of Wen Chung, or Lei Tsu, Ma Yüan-shuai, Generalissimo Ma, whose exploits are referred to later, and others.

The President of the Ministry of Thunder

This divinity has three eyes, one in the middle of his forehead, from which, when open, a ray of white light profits to a distance of more than 2 feet. Mounted on a black unicorn, he traverses countless miles in the twinkling of an eye.

His origin is ascribed to a guy called Wên Chung, generally known as Wên Chung T'ai- shih, 'the Great Teacher Wên Chung,' He was a minister of the tyrant king Chou (1154-- 1122 B.C.), and battled against the armies of the Chou dynasty. Being beat, he fled to the mountains of Yen, Yen Shan, where he met Ch' ih Ching-tzu, among the alleged originators of fire, and joined fight with him; the latter, though, flashed his yin-yang mirror at the unicorn, and put it out of action. Lei Chên-tzu, one of Wu Wang's marshals, then struck the animal with his personnel, and severed it in twain.

Wên Chung got away in the direction of the mountains of Chüeh-lung Ling, where another marshal, Yün Chung-tzu, disallowed his way. Yün's hands had the power of producing lightning, and eight columns of strange fire all of a sudden came out of the earth, completely enveloping Wên Chung. They were thirty feet high and ten feet in circumference. Ninety fiery dragons came out of each and flew away up into the air. The sky was just like a heating system, and the earth shook with the awful claps of thunder. In this fiery prison Wên Chung died.

When the brand-new dynasty finally showed victorious, Chiang Tzu-ya, by order of Yüan-shih T'ien- tsun, gave on Wên Chung the supreme direction of the Ministry of Thunder, selecting him celestial prince and plenipotentiary protector of the laws governing the distribution of clouds and rain. His full title was Celestial and Highly-honoured Head of the Nine Orbits of the Heavens, Voice of the Thunder, and Regulator of deep space. His birthday is celebrated on the twenty-fourth day of the sixth moon.

The Duke of Thunder

The Spirit of Thunder, for whom Lei Tsu is often mistaken, is represented as an unsightly, black, bat-winged demon, with clawed feet, monkey's head, and eagle's beak, who keeps in one hand a steel chisel, and in the other a spiritual hammer, with which he beats numerous drums strung about him, therefore producing the great sound of thunder. According to Chinese reasoning it is the sound of these drums, and not the lightning, which triggers death.

A. Gruenwedel, in his Guide to the Lamaist Collection of Prince Uchtomsky, p. 161, specifies that the Chino-Japanese God of Thunder, Lei Kung, has the shape of the Indian divine bird Garuda. Are we to expect, then, that the Chinese Lei Kung is of Indian beginning? In modern pictures the God of Thunder is portrayed with a dick's head and claws, carrying in one hand the hammer, in the other the sculpt. We learn, however, from Wang Ch' ung's Lun Hêng that in the very first century B.C., when Buddhism was not yet introduced into China, the 'Thunderer' was represented as a strong man, not as a bird, with one hand dragging a cluster of drums, and with the other displaying a hammer. Thus Lei Kung existed already in China when the latter got her first knowledge of India. Yet his contemporary image might well owe its wings to the Indian rain-god Vajrapani, who in one form appears with Garuda wings.

Lei Kung P' u-sa, the avatar of Lei Kung (whose existence as the Spirit of Thunder is denied by at least one Chinese author), has made various appearances on the earth. One of these is described right below.

Lei Kung in the Tree

A specific Yeh Ch' ien-chao of Hsin Chou, when a youth, used to climb the mountain Chien-ch' ang Shan for the purpose of cutting firewood and collecting medicinal herbs. One day when he had taken haven under a tree throughout a rain-storm there was a loud clap of thunder, and he saw a winged being, with a blue face, big mouth, and bird's claws, caught in a cleft of the tree. This being attended to Yeh, saying: "I am Lei Kung. In splitting this tree I got caught in it; if you will release me I will reward you handsomely." The woodcutter opened the cleft larger by driving in some stones as wedges, and freed the detainee. "Return to this area to-morrow," said the latter, "and I will reward you." The next day the woodcutter kept the appointment, and got from Lei Kung a book. "If you consult this work," he explained, "you will be able at will to bring thunder or rain, cure sickness, or lighten sadness. We are 5 brothers, of whom I am the youngest. When you want to bring rain call one or other of my brothers; but call me only in case of pushing necessity, as I have a bad character; but I will come if it is really essential." Having said these words, he vanished.

Yeh Ch' ien-chao, by methods of the prescriptions contained in the mystical book, could treat health problems as easily as the sun dissipates the early morning mist. One day, when he was intoxicated and had gone to sleep in the temple of Chi-chou Ssŭ, the magistrate wished to apprehend and penalize him. But when he reached the steps of the yamên, Ch' ien-chao called Lei Kung to his help. A dreadful clap of thunder instantly resounded throughout the district. The magistrate, almost dead with fright, simultaneously dismissed the case without punishing the culprit. The four brothers never couldn't come to his aid.

By the usage of his power Ch' ien-chao saved many areas from scarcity by bringing timely rain.

The Mystical Bottle
Another legend relates that an old woman living in Kiangsi had her arm broken through being struck by lightning, when a voice from above was heard saying: "I have made a mistake." A bottle fell out of space, and the voice again said: "Use the contents and you will be recovered simultaneously." This being done, the old lady's arm was immediately healed. The villagers, regarding the contents of the bottle as magnificent medicine, wished to take it away and hide it for future usage, but several of them together could not raise it from the ground. All of a sudden, though, it rose and vanished into space. Other individuals in Kiangsi were also struck, and the exact same voice was heard to say:" Use some grubs to the throat and they will recover." After this had been done the victims returned to consciousness none the worse for their experience.

The worship of Lei Kung seems to have been carried on frequently from about the time of the Christian age.

Lei Chên-tzŭ
Another Son of Thunder is Lei Chên-tzŭ, mentioned above, whose name when a child was Wên Yü, who was hatched from an egg after a clap of thunder and found by the soldiers of Wên Wang in some brushwood near an old tomb. The infant's chief quality was its dazzling eyes. Wên Wang, who already had ninety-nine children, adopted it as his hundredth, but gave it to a hermit named Yün Chung-tzŭ to rear as his disciple. The hermit revealed to him the way to rescue his adopted dad from the tyrant who held him prisoner. In seeking for some effective weapon the child found on the hillside two apricots, and ate them both. He then saw that wings had grown on his shoulders, and was way too much embarrassed to return home.

However the hermit, who knew intuitively what had occurred, sent out a servant to seek him. When they met the servant said: "Do you know that your face is totally altered?" The mysterious fruit had not only triggered Lei Chên-tzŭ to grow wings, known as Wings of the Wind and Thunder, but his face had ended up being green, his nose long and pointed, and 2 tusks extended horizontally from each side of his mouth, while his eyes shone like mirrors.

Lei Chên-tzŭ now went and rescued Wên Wang, dispersing his enemies by ways of his mystical power and bringing the old man back on his shoulders. Having positioned him in security he returned to the hermit.

The Mother of Lightning
This divinity is represented as a female figure, beautifully apparelled in blue, green, red, and white, keeping in either hand a mirror from which proceed two broad streams or flashes of light. Lightning, say the Chinese, is triggered by the rubbing together of the yin and the yang, just as triggers of fire may be produced by the tension of 2 compounds.

The Origin of the Spirit of Lightning

Tung Wang Kung, the King of the Immortals, was playing at pitch-pot1 with Yü Nü. He lost; whereupon Paradise smiled, and from its half-open mouth a ray of light came out. This was lightning; it is considered feminine as it is supposed to come from the earth, which is of the yin, or woman, principle.

The God of the Wind

Fêng Po, the God of the Wind, is represented as an old man with a white beard, yellow cloak, and blue and red cap. He holds a large sack, and directs the wind which originates from its mouth in any direction he pleases.

There are different ideas regarding the nature of this deity. He is considered as an outstanding divinity under the control of the star Ch' i,2 because the wind blows at the time when the moon leaves that celestial estate. He is also said to be a dragon called Fei Lien, initially among the fans of the rebel Ch' ih Yu, who was defeated by Huang Ti. Having actually been transformed into a spiritual monster, he stirred up remarkable winds in the southern regions. The Emperor Yao sent Shên I with three hundred soldiers to silent the storms and appease Ch' ih Yu's relatives, who were wreaking their vengeance on the people. Shên I ordered the people to spread out a long fabric in front of their homes, fixing it with stones. The wind, blowing against this, had to change its direction. Shên I then flew on the wind to the top of a high mountain, whence he saw a beast at the base. It had the shape of a huge yellow and white sack, and kept breathing in and breathing out in great gusts. Shên I, concluding that this was the cause of all these storms, shot an arrow and hit the monster, whereupon it took sanctuary in a deep cavern. Here it turned on Shên I and, drawing a sword, dared him to assault the Mother of the Winds. Shên I, however, fearlessly dealt with the monster and released another arrow, this time hitting it in the knee. The monster instantly threw down its sword and begged that its life may be spared.

Fei Lien is somewhere else referred to as a dragon who was originally among the wicked ministers of the autocrat Chou and could walk with unheard-of speed. Both he and his child Ô Lai, who was so strong that he could tear a tiger or rhinoceros to pieces with his hands, were killed when in the service of Chou Wang. Fei Lien is also said to have the body of a stag, about the size of a leopard, with a bird's head, horns, and a serpent's tail, and to be able to make the wind blow whenever he wishes.

The Master of Rain

Yü Shih, the Master of Rain, dressed in yellow scale-armour, with a blue hat and yellow busby, stands on a cloud and from a watering-can pours rain upon the earth. Like lots of other gods, however, he is represented in different types. Sometimes he holds a plate, on which is a small dragon, in his left hand, while with his right he pours down the rain. He is undoubtedly the Parjanya of Vedism.

According to a native account, the God of Rain is one Ch' ih Sung-tzŭ, who appeared during a terrible dry spell in the reign of Shên Nung (2838-- 2698 B.C.), and owing to his reputed magical power was requested by the latter to bring rain from the sky. "Absolutely nothing is much easier," he replied; "put a bottleful of water into an earthen bowl and give it to me." This being done, he plucked from a neighbouring mountain a branch of a tree, soaked it in the water, and with it sprayed the earth. Instantly clouds gathered and rain fell in gushes, filling the rivers to overruning. Ch' ih Sung-tzŭ was then honoured as the God of Rain, and his images show him holding the mystic bowl. He lives in the K'un- lun Mountains, and has many remarkable peculiarities, like the power to go through water without getting wet, to travel through fire without being burned, and to float in space.

This Rain-god also assumes the form of a silkworm chrysalis in another account. He is there believed to possess a concubine who has a black face, holds a serpent in each hand, and has other serpents, red and green, reposing on her right and left ears respectively; also a mystical bird, with only one leg, the shang yang, which can change its height at will and drink the seas dry. The following legend belongs of the bird.

The One-legged Bird

At the time when Hsüan-ming Ta-jên instructed Fei Lien in the tricks of magic, the latter saw a wonderful bird which drew in water with its beak and blew it out again in the shape of rain. Fei lien tamed it, and would take it about in his sleeve.

Later a one-legged bird was seen in the palace of the Prince of Ch' i walking up and down and hopping in front of the throne. Being much puzzled, the Prince sent a messenger to Lu to inquire of Confucius concerning this odd behaviour. "This bird is a shang yang" said Confucius; "its appearance signifies rain. In previous times the children used to entertain themselves by hopping on one foot, knitting their eyebrows, and saying: 'It will rain, as the shang yang is disporting himself.' Since this bird has gone to Ch' i, heavy rain will fall, and the people should be told to dig channels and fix the dykes, for the entire country will be inundated." Not only Ch' i, but all the adjacent kingdoms were flooded; all continual severe damage other than Ch' i, where the necessary precautions had been taken. This caused Duke Ching to exclaim: "Sadly! how few listen to the words of the sages!"

Ma Yüan-shuai

Ma Yüan-shuai is a three-eyed beast condemned by Ju Lai to reincarnation for extreme ruthlessness in the extermination of fiends. In order to follow this command he got in the womb of Ma Chin-mu in the form of 5 worlds of fire. Being a precocious youth, he could fight when only three days old, and killed the Dragon-king of the Eastern Sea. From his instructor he received a spiritual work dealing with wind, thunder, snakes, and so on, and a triangular piece of stone which he could at will become anything he liked. By order of Yü Ti he controlled the Spirits of the Wind and Fire, heaven Dragon, the King of the Five Dragons, and the Spirit of the 5 Hundred Fire Ducks, all without injury to himself. For these and tons of other business he was rewarded by Yü Ti with different magic articles and with the title of Generalissimo of the West, and is considered so effective an interceder with Yü Ti that he is hoped to for all sorts of benefits.

Myths of the Waters

The Dragons
The dragons are spirits of the waters. "The dragon is a sort of being whose miraculous changes are inscrutable." In a sense the dragon is the type of a man, self-controlled, and with powers that verge upon the super. In China the dragon, except as kept in mind below, is not a power for evil, but a beneficent being producing rain and representing the fecundating concept in nature. He is the essence of the yang, or male, principle. "He controls the rain, and so holds in his power success and peace." The evil dragons are those introduced by the Buddhists, who used the existing dragon legends to the nagas living in the mountains. These mountain nagas, or dragons (perhaps initially dreadful mountain people), are hazardous, those populating lakes and rivers friendly and valuable. The dragon, the "chief of the 3 hundred and sixty scaly reptiles," is most normally represented as having the head of a horse and the tail of a serpent, with wings on its sides. It has four legs. The imperial dragon has 5 claws on each foot, other dragons only four. The dragon is also said to have nine 'resemblances': "its horns resemble those of a deer, its head that of a camel, its eyes those of a devil, its neck that of a serpent, its abdominal areas that of a large cockle, its scales those of a carp, its claws those of an eagle, the soles of its feet those of a tiger, its ears those of an ox;" but some have no ears, the organ of hearing being said to be in the horns, or the being "hears through its horns." These numerous properties are supposed to suggest the "fossil remnants of primitive worship of tons of animals." The small dragon is a lot like the silk caterpillar. The large dragon fills the Heaven and the earth. Before the dragon, often suspended from his neck, is a pearl. This represents the sun. There are azure, scaly, horned, hornless, winged, and so on, dragons, which apparently evolve one out of the other: "a horned dragon," for example, "in a 1,000 years changes to a flying dragon."

The dragon is also represented as the father of the great emperors of ancient times. His bones, teeth, and saliva are employed as a medicine. He has the power of change and of rendering himself noticeable or unnoticeable at pleasure. In the spring he ascends to the skies, and in the fall buries himself in the watery depths. Some are wingless, and arise into the air by their own intrinsic power. There is the celestial dragon, who secures the estates of the gods and supports them so that they do not fall; the divine dragon, who causes the winds to blow and produces rain for the advantage of humanity; the earth-dragon, who defines the courses of rivers and streams; and the dragon of the concealed treasures, who watches over the wealth hidden from mortals.

The Buddhists count their dragons in number equivalent to the fish of the great deep, which defies arithmetical computation, and can be uttered only by their holy numerals. The people have a more certain faith in them than in most of their divinities, because they see them so typically; every cloud with a curious setup or serpentine tail is a dragon. "We see him," they say. The scattering of the cloud is his disappearance. He rules the hills, is gotten in touch with fêng-shui (geomancy), dwells round the tombs, is related to the Confucian worship, is the Neptune of the sea, and appears on dry land.

Chapter 10: The Dragon-kings

The Sea-dragon Kings live in gorgeous palaces in the depths of the sea, where they feed on pearls and opals. There are 5 of these divinities, the chief being in the center, and the other four occupying the north, the west, the south, and the east. Each is a league in length, and so bulky that in shifting its posture it tosses one mountain against another. It has 5 feet, one of them remaining in the middle of its stomach, and each foot is armed with five sharp claws. It can reach into the paradises, and stretch itself into all quarters of the sea. It has a glowing armour of yellow scales, a beard under its long snout, a hairy tail, and shaggy legs. Its forehead projects over its blazing eyes, its ears are little and thick, its mouth gaping, its tongue long, and its teeth sharp. Fish are boiled by the blast of its breath, and roasted by the intense exhalations of its body. When it rises up to the surface the whole ocean rises, waterspouts foam, and tropical cyclones rage. When it flies, wingless, through the air, the winds howl, torrents of rain descend, houses are unroofed, the firmament is filled with a din, and whatever lies along its route is swept away with a roar in the typhoon created by the speed of its passage.

The 5 Sea-dragon Kings are all never-ceasing. They know each other's thoughts, plans, and wishes without intercommunication. Like all the other gods they go once a year to the superior Heavens, to make a yearly report to the Supreme Ruler; but they go in the 3rd month, at which time none of the other gods dare appear, and their stay above is but brief. They generally remain in the depths of the ocean, where their courts are filled with their kids, their dependents, and their attendants, and where the gods and genii sometimes visit them. Their palaces, of divers coloured transparent stones, with crystal doors, are said to have been seen in the morning by persons gazing into the deep waters.

The Silly Dragon
The part of the great Buddha legend describing the dragon is as follows:

In years past, a dragon living in the great sea saw that his wife's health was not that good. He, seeing her color vanish, said: "My dear, what shall I get you to eat?" Mrs Dragon was quiet. Just tell me and I will get it," pleaded the caring spouse. "You can't do it; why trouble?" asked she. "Believe me, and you shall have your heart's desire," said the dragon. "Well, I really want a monkey's heart to eat." "Why, Mrs. Dragon, the monkeys live in the mountain forests! How can I get one of their hearts?" "Well, I am going to die; I know I am."

Forthwith the dragon went on coast, and, spying a monkey on the top of a tree, said: "Hail, shining one, are you not afraid you will fall?" "No, I have no such worry." "Why eat of one tree? Cross the sea, and you will find forests of fruit and flowers." "How can I cross?" "Get on my back." The dragon with his tiny load went seaward, and after that suddenly dived down. "Where are you going?" said the monkey, with the seawater in his eyes and mouth. "Oh! my dear sir! my partner is very miserable and ill, and has taken an elegant to your heart." "What shall I do?" thought the monkey. He then spoke, "Remarkable good friend, why did not you tell me? I left my heart on the top of the tree; take me back, and I will get it for Mrs. Dragon." The dragon returned to the coast. As the monkey was tardy in coming down from the tree, the dragon said: "Rush, little friend, I am waiting." Then the monkey thought within himself, "What a fool this dragon is!"

Then Buddha said to his followers: "At this time I was the monkey."

The Ministry of Waters

In the spirit-world there is a Ministry which controls all things connected with the waters on earth, salt or fresh. Its primary departments are the Department of Salt Waters, presided over by 4 Dragon-kings-- those of the East, South, West, and North-- and the Department of Sweet Waters, commanded by the 4 Kings (Ssŭ Tu) of the 4 great rivers-- the Blue (Chiang), Yellow (Ho), Huai, and Ch' i-- and the Dragon-spirits who control the Secondary Waters, the rivers, springs, lakes, pools, rapids. Into the names and functions of the very large number of authorities gotten in touch with these departments it is unneeded to get in. It will be sufficient here to refer only to those whose names are gotten in touch with myth or legend.

An Unapproved Portrait

One of these legends associates with the go to of Ch'in Shih Huang-ti, the First Emperor, to the Spirit of the Sea, Yang Hou, initially a marquis (bou) of the State Yang, who ended up being a god through being drowned in the sea.

Po Shih, a Taoist priest, told the Emperor that a huge oyster threw up from the sea a mystical substance which built up in the form of a tower, and was referred to as 'the market of the sea' (Chinese for 'mirage'). Every year, at a certain duration, the breath from his mouth was like the rays of the sun. The Emperor expressed a dream to see it, and Po Shih said he would write a letter to the God of the Sea, and the next day the Emperor could witness the fantastic sight.

The Emperor then remembered a dream he had had the year right before in which he saw 2 guys defending the sun. The one killed the other, and brought it off. He for that reason wished to check out the nation where the sun rose up. Po Shih said that all that was needed was to throw rocks into the sea and build a bridge right across them. Thereupon he rang his magic bell, the earth shook, and rocks began to rise; but as they moved too slowly he struck them with his whip, and blood originated from them which left red marks in lots of spots. The row of rocks extended as far as the shore of the sun-country, but to build the bridge right across them was found to be beyond the reach of human skill.

So Po Shih sent another messenger to the God of the Sea, requesting him to raise a pillar and place a beam across it which could be used as a bridge. The submarine spirits came and placed themselves at the service of the Emperor, who requested for an interview with the god. To this the latter agreed on condition that nobody should make an example of him, he being extremely ugly. Immediately a stone gangway 100,000 feet long arose out of the sea, and the Emperor, installing his horse, chose his courtiers to the palace of the god. Amongst his followers was one Lu Tung-shih, who tried to draw a portrait of the god by using his foot under the surface of the water. Finding this maneuver, the god was incensed, and said to the Emperor: "You have broken your word; did you bring Lu here to insult me? Retire simultaneously, or evil will befall you." The Emperor, seeing that the situation was precarious, mounted his horse and galloped off. As quickly as he reached the beach, the stone cause-way sank, and all his suite died in the waves. One of the Court magicians said to the Emperor: "This god ought to be feared as much as the God of Thunder; then he could be made to help us. To-day a grave error has been made." For several days after this occurrence the waves beat upon the beach with increasing anger. The Emperor then built a temple and a pagoda to the god on Chih-fu Shan and Wên-têng Shan respectively; by which act of propitiation he was apparently calmed.

The Shipwrecked Servant

As Soon As the 8 Immortals were on their way to Ch' ang-li Shan to celebrate the birthday anniversary of Hsien Wêng, the God of Longevity. They had with them a servant who bore the presents they meant to provide to the god. When they reached the seashore, the Immortals walked on the waves without any difficulty, but Lan Ts' ai-ho said that the servant was unable to follow them and said that a means of transportation should be found for him. So Ts' ao Kuo-chiu took a slab of cypress-wood and made a raft. But when they were in mid-ocean a tropical cyclone arose and upset the raft, and servant and presents sank to the bottom of the sea.

Regarding this as the hostile act of a water-devil, the Immortals said they need to need an explanation from the Dragon-king, Ao Ch' in. Li T'ieh- kuai took his gourd, and, directing the mouth towards the bottom of the sea, created so fantastic a light that it lit up the entire palace of the Sea-king. Ao Ch' in, surprised, asked where this powerful light stemmed, and deputed a courier to determine its cause.

To this messenger the Immortals made their problem. "All we want," they added, "is that the Dragon-king shall restore to us our servant and the presents." On this being reported to Ao Ch' in he presumed his child of being the cause, and, having developed his regret, significantly reprimanded him. The young Prince took his sword, and, followed by an escort, went to find those who had made the grievance to his dad. As soon as he caught sight of the Immortals he started to inveigh against them.

A Fight and its Actual results

Han Hsiang Tzŭ, not liking this unjust abuse, changed his flute into a fishing-line, and as quickly as the Dragon-prince was within reach caught him on the hook, with intent to retain him as a captive. The Prince's escort returned in great haste and notified Ao Ch' in of what had occurred. The latter declared that his son was in the wrong, and proposed to restore the shipwrecked servant and the presents. The Court officers, though, held a different opinion. "These Immortals," they said, "dare to hold captive your Majesty's child merely on account of a few lost presents and a shipwrecked servant. This is a great insult, which we ask authorization to avenge." Eventually they won over Ao Ch' in, and the armies of the deep gathered for the fray. The Immortals called to their help the other Taoist Immortals and Heroes, and therefore two powerful armies found themselves face to deal with.

Some efforts were made by other divinities to avert the dispute, but without success. The fight was a difficult one. Ao Ch' in gotten a ball of fire full on his head, and his army was threatened with catastrophe when Tz' ŭ-hang Ta-shih appeared with his bottle of lustral water. He sprayed the contenders with this magic fluid, using a willow-branch for the purpose, thus triggering all their magic powers to vanish.

Shui Kuan, the Ruler of the Watery Components, then arrived, and reproached Ao Ch' in; he guaranteed him that if the matter were to come to the knowledge of Shang Ti, the Supreme Ruler, he would not only be severely penalized, but would run the risk of losing his post. Ao Ch' in uttered repentance, brought back the servant and the presents, and made full apology to the 8 Immortals.

The Dragon in the Pond

One day Chang Tao-ling, the 'father of modern-day Taoism,' was on Ho-ming Shan with his disciple Wang Ch'ang. "See," he said, "that shaft of white light on Yang Shan yonder! There are unquestionably some bad spirits there. Let us go and bring them to reason." When they reached the foot of the mountain they met twelve women who had the appearance of fiends. Chang Tao-ling asked whence came the shaft of white light. They answered that it was the yin, or woman, concept of the earth. "Where is the source of the salt water?" he asked again. "That pond in front of you," they replied, "in which lives a very wicked dragon." Chang Tao-ling tried to require the dragon to come out, but without success. Then he drew a phœnix with golden wings on a beauty and hurled it into the air over the pond. Thereupon the dragon took scare and left, the pond instantly drying up. After that Chang Tao-ling took his sword and stuck it in the ground, whereupon a well full of salt water appeared on the area.

The Spirits of the Well

The twelve ladies each offered Chang Tao-ling a jade ring, and asked that they may become his spouses. He took the rings, and pushing them together in his hands made from them one big single ring. "I will toss this ring into the well," he said, "and the among you who recuperates it shall be my spouse." All the twelve ladies delved into the well to get the ring; whereupon Chang Tao-ling put a cover over it and attached it down, telling them that henceforth they should be the spirits of the well and would never be enabled to come out.

Shortly after this Chang Tao-ling met a hunter. He exhorted him not to kill living entities, but to change his profession to that of a salt-burner, advising him how to extract the salt from salt-water wells. Therefore the people of that district were advantaged both by being able to get the salt and by being no longer molested by the 12 female spirits. A temple, called Temple of the Prince of Ch' ing Ho, was built by them, and the area of Ling Chou was offered to Chang Tao-ling in acknowledgment of the benefits he had conferred upon the people.

The Dragon-king's Daughter

A graduate called Liu I, in the reign-period I Fêng (A.D. 676-- 679) of the Emperor Kao Tsung of the T'ang dynasty, having failed in his assessment for his licentiate's degree, when travelling through Ching-yang Hsien, in Ch' ang-an, Shensi, on his way home, saw a young woman tending goats by the roadside. She said to him: "I am the youngest daughter of the Dragonking of the Tung-t' ing Lake. My mom and dad married me to the son of the God of the River Ching, but my partner, misinformed by the slanders of the servants, repudiated me. I have heard that you are returning to the Kingdom of Wu, which is quite near to my native district, so I want to ask you to take this letter to my father. To the north of the Tung-t' ing Lake you will find a big orange-tree, called by the locals Protector of the Soil. Strike it 3 times with your girdle and some one will appear."

Some months later the graduate went to the spot, found the orange-tree, and struck it three times, whereupon a warrior occurred from the lake and, saluting him, asked what he wanted. "I wish to see your great King," the graduate responded. The warrior struck the waters, opening a passage for Liu I, and led him to a palace. "This," he said, "is the palace of Ling Hsü." In a few minutes there appeared an individual dressed in violet-coloured outfits and holding in his hand a piece of jade. "This is our King," said the warrior. "I am your Majesty's neighbour," responded Liu I. "I spent my youth in Ch' u and studied in Ch' in. I have just stopped working in my licentiate evaluation. On my way home I saw your daughter tending some goats; she was all dishevelled, and in so pitiable a condition that it hurt me to see her, She has sent you this letter."

Golden Dragon Great Prince
On checking out the letter the King wept, and all the courtiers followed his example. "Stop wailing," said the King, "lest Ch' ien-t' ang hear." "Who is Ch' ien-t' ang?" asked Liu I. "He is my dear brother," replied the King; "formerly he was just one of the chief administrators of the Ch' ien-t' ang River; now he is the chief God of Rivers." "Why are you so afraid that he might hear what I have just told you?" "Since he has a terrible mood. It was he who, in the reign of Yao, triggered a nine-years flood."

Right before he had completed speaking, a red dragon, a 1000 feet long, with red scales, mane of fire, bloody tongue, and eyes blazing like lightning, gone through the air with fast flight and vanished. Barely several moment had elapsed when it returned with a girl whom Liu I acknowledged as the one who had entrusted him with the letter. The Dragon-king, overjoyed, said to him: "This is my daughter; her spouse is no more, and she offers you her hand." Liu did not dare to accept, since it appeared that they had just killed her husband. He took his departure, and wed woman named Chang, who soon passed away. He then wed another named Han, who also passed away. He then went to live at Nanking, and, his solitude preying upon his spirits, he chose to marry yet again. A middleman talked to him of a lady of Fang Yang, in Chihli, whose dad, Hao, had been Magistrate of Ch' ing Liu, in Anhui. This man was always absent on his travels, no one knew whither. The girl's mom, Cheng, had married her two years before to a guy named Chang of Ch' ing Ho, in Chihli, who had just passed away. Distressed at her daughter being left a widow so young, the mother wished to find another partner for her.

Liu I agreed to wed this young woman, and at the end of a year they had a boy. She then said to her partner: "I am the daughter of the King of the Tung-t' ing Lake. It was you who saved me from my miserable plight on the bank of the Ching, and I swore I would reward you. Formerly you refused to accept my hand, and my mother and father decided to marry me to the child of a silk-merchant. I cut my hair, and never ceased to hope that I might some time or other be joined to you in order that I might show you my gratitude."

In A.D. 712, in the reign-period K'ai- yüan of the Emperor Hsüan Tsung of the T'ang dynasty, they both went back to the Tung-t' ing Lake; but the legend says absolutely nothing further with regard to them.

Shang Ti, the Supreme Ruler, conferred on Liu I the title of Chin Lung Ta Wang, 'Golden Dragon Great Prince.'

The Old Mom of the Waters

The Old Mom of the Waters, Shul-mu Niang-niang, is the legendary spirit of Ssŭ-chou, in Anhui. To her is commonly ascribed the damage of the ancient city of Ssŭ-chou, which was entirely immersed by the waters of the Hung-tsê Lake in A.D. 1574.

One author states that this Goddess of the Waters is the more youthful sister of the White Spiritual Elephant, a defender of the Door of Buddha. This elephant is the "subtle principle of metamorphosed water."

In his Recherches sur Us Superstitions en Chine, Père Henri Doré, S.J., relates the legends he had heard with regard to this deity. One of these is as follows:

Shui-mu Niang-niang flooded the town of Ssŭ-chou nearly every year. A report was shown to Yu Huang, Lord of the Skies, begging him to put an end to the scourge which devastated the country and cost so many lives. The Lord of the Skies commanded the Great Kings of the Skies and their generals to raise soldiers and take the field so as to catch this goddess and deprive her of the power of doing more mischief. But her tricks triumphed over force, and the city continued to be regularly devastated by inundations.

One day Shui-mu Niang-niang was seen near the city gate carrying two pails of water. Li Lao-chün suspected some plot, but, an open attack being too risky, he preferred to adopt a ruse. He went and purchased a donkey, led it to the buckets of water, and let it drink their contents. Regrettably the animal could not drink all the water, so that a little remained at the bottom of the buckets. Now these magical containers included the sources of the 5 great lakes, which held enough water to swamp the entire of China. Shui-mu Niang-niang with her foot overturned one of the containers, and the water that had stayed in it was enough to cause a powerful flood, which immersed the unfortunate town, and buried it for ever under the tremendous sheet of water called the Lake of Hung-tsê.

So great a criminal offense really deserved an excellent penalty, and appropriately Yü Huang sent reinforcements to his armies, and a pursuit of the goddess was methodically organized.

The Magic Vermicelli

Sun Hou-tzŭ, the Monkey Sun,1 the rapid courier, who in a single skip could pass through 108,000 li (36,000 miles), started in pursuit and caught her up, but the astute goddess was clever sufficient to slip through his fingers. Sun Hou-tzŭ, furious at this problem, went to ask Kuan-yin P' u-sa to come to his aid. She promised to do so. As one may imagine, the furious race she had had to escape from her opponent had given Shui-mu Niang-niang a really good hunger. Exhausted with tiredness, and with an empty stomach, she saw lady selling vermicelli, who had just prepared two bowls of it and was waiting for consumers. Shui-mu Niang-niang went up to her and started to eat the strength-giving food with avidity. No faster had she consumed half of the vermicelli than it changed in her stomach into iron chains, which wound round her intestinal tracts. The end of the chain protruded from her mouth, and the contents of the bowl ended up being another long chain which welded itself to the end which stood out beyond her lips. The vermicelli-seller was no other than Kuan-yin P' u-sa herself, who had conceived this stratagem as a means of ridding herself of this evil-working goddess. She ordered Sun Hou-tzŭ to take her down a deep well at the foot of a mountain in Hsü-i Hsien and to attach her securely there. It is there that Shui-mu Niang-niang remains in her liquid prison. The end of the chain is to be seen when the water is low.

Hsü, the Dragon-slayer

Hsü Chên-chün was a native either of Ju-ning Fu in Honan, or of Nan-ch'ang Fu in Kiangsi. His dad was Hsü Su. His personal name was Ching-chih, and his ordinary name Sun.

At forty-one years of age, when he was Magistrate of Ching-yang, near the modern-day Chih-chiang Hsien, in Hupei, throughout times of dry spell he had only to touch a piece of tile to turn it into gold, and hence eliminate the people of their distress. He also saved lots of lives by curing sickness through the use of talismans and magic formulæ.

During the duration of the dynastic troubles he resigned and joined the well-known magician Kuo P'o. Together they continued to the minister Wang Tun, who had increased against the Eastern Chin dynasty. Kuo P'o's remonstrances only irritated the minister, who cut off his head.

Hsü Sun then threw his chalice on the ridgepole of the room, causing it to be whirled into the air. As Wang Tun was watching the career of the chalice, Hsü vanished and escaped. When he reached Lu-chiang K'ou, in Anhui, he boarded a boat, which two dragons towed into the offing and after that raised into the air. In an immediate they had borne it to the Lü Shan Mountains, to the south of Kiukiang, in Kiangsi. The perplexed boatman opened the window of his boat and took a furtive keep an eye out. Thereupon the dragons, finding themselves discovered by an infidel, set the boat down on the top of the mountain and fled.

The Spiritual Alligator

In this nation was a dragon, or spiritual alligator, which changed itself into a boy called Shên Lang, and married Chia Yü, daughter of the Chief Judge of T'an Chou (Ch' ang-sha Fu, capital of Hunan). The youths lived in rooms right below the main apartment or condos. Throughout spring and summer season Shên Lang, as dragons are wont to do, wandered in the rivers and lakes. One day Hsü Chên-chün met him, recognized him as a dragon, and knew that he was the reason for the numerous floods which were ravaging Kiangsi Province. He determined to find a way of getting rid of him.

Shên Lang, familiar with the steps being taken against him, changed himself into a yellow ox and left. Hsü Chên-chün simultaneously changed himself into a black ox and started in pursuit. The yellow ox leapt down a well to hide, but the black ox did the same. The yellow ox then leapt out again, and escaped to Ch' ang-sha, where he reassumed a human form and lived with Ms wife in the home of his father-in-law, Hsü Sun, returning to the town, hastened to the yamên, and called to Shên Lang to come out and show himself, addressing him in a serious intonation as follows: "Dragon, how dare you hide yourself there under a borrowed form?" Shên Lang then reassumed the form of a spiritual alligator, and Hsü Sun ordered the spiritual soldiers to kill him. He then commanded his two sons to come out of their abode. By merely spurting a mouthful of water on them he transformed them into young dragons. Chia Yü was told to leave the spaces with all speed, and in the twinkling of an eye the entire yamên sank underneath the earth, and there stayed absolutely nothing but a lake where it had been.

Hsü Chên-chün, after his success over the dragon, assembled the members of his family, to the number of forty-two, on Hsi Shan, outside the city of Nan-ch' ang Fu, and all rose to Paradise in full daylight, taking with them even the dogs and chickens. He was then 133 years of age. This occurred on the first day of the 8th moon of the 2nd year (A.D. 374) of the reign-period Ning-K' ang of the reign of the Emperor Hsiao Wu Ti of the Eastern Chin dynasty.

Subsequently a temple was put up to him, and in A.D. 1111 he was canonized as Just Prince, Admirable and Beneficent.

Chapter 12: The Great Flood

The fixing of the paradises by Nü Kua, in other places alluded to, is also attributed to the following incident.

Prior To the Chinese Empire was founded a noble and fantastic queen combated with the chief of the tribes who populated the nation round about Ô-mei Shan. In a strong battle the chief and his followers met defeat; raging with anger at being beaten by woman, he rushed up the mountain-side; the Queen chased after him with her army, and overtook him at the top; finding no place to hide himself, he tried in desperation both to wreak vengeance upon his enemies and to end his own life by beating his head strongly against the walking stick of the Heavenly Bamboo which grew there. By his mad damaging he at last succeeded in tearing down the towering trunk of the tree, and as he did so its top tore great leas in the canopy of the sky, through which poured great floods of water, swamping the whole earth and drowning all the inhabitants other than the triumphant Queen and her soldiers. The floods had no power to damage her or her followers, as she herself was an all-powerful divinity and was known as the 'Mom of the Gods,' and the 'Defender of the Gods.' From the mountainside she gathered together stones of a kind having five colors, and ground them into powder; of this she made a plaster or mortar, with which she fixed the tears in the heavens, and the floods instantly ceased.

The Marriage of the River-god
In Yeh Hsien there was a witch and some main attendants who gathered cash from the people annual for the marital relationship of the River-god.

The witch would select a pretty girl of low birth and say that she must be the Queen of the River-god. The girl was bathed and clothed in a gorgeous gown of gay and costly silk. She was then brought to the bank of the river, to a monastery which was magnificently embellished with scrolls and banners. A feast was held, and the girl was put on a bed which was drifted out upon the tide till it vanished under the waters.

Tons of families having lovely daughters transferred to remote spots, and gradually the city became deserted. The typical belief in Yeh was that if no queen was offered to the River-god a flood would come and drown the people.

One day Hsi-mên Pao, Magistrate of Yeh Hsien, said to his attendants: "When the marriage of the River-god occurs I wish to say farewell to the chosen girl."

Accordingly, Hsi-mên Pao existed to witness the event. About three thousand people had come together. Standing next to the old witch were ten of her female disciples, "Call the girl out," said Hsi-mên Pao. After seeing her, Hsi-mên Pao said to the witch: "She is unfair. Go you to the River-god and tell him that we will find a fairer house maid and present her to him later on." His attendants then took the witch and tossed her into the river.

After a little while Hsi-mên Pao said: "Why does she stay so long? Send out a disciple to call her back." One of the disciples was tossed into the river. Another and yet another followed. The magistrate then said:" The witches are females and therefore cannot bring me a reply." So one of the main attendants of the witch was thrown into the river.

Hsi-mên Pao was standing on the bank for a long time, apparently awaiting a reply. The spectators were alarmed. Hsi-mên Pao then bade his attendants send out the remaining disciples of the witch and the other official attendants to recall their mistress. The scoundrels threw themselves on their knees and knocked their heads on the ground, which was stained with the blood from their foreheads, and with tears confessed their sin.

" The River-god apprehends his visitor too long," said Hsi-mên Pao at length. "Let us adjourn."

Afterwards none attempted to celebrate the marriage of the River-god.

Legend of the Structure of Peking

When the Mongol Yüan dynasty had been damaged, and the Emperor Hung Wu had prospered in securely developing that of the Great Ming, Ta Ming, he made Chin-ling, the present Nanking, his capital, and held his Court there with great splendor, envoys from every province within the '4 Seas' (the Chinese Empire) putting together there to witness his greatness and to prostrate themselves before the Dragon Throne.

The Emperor had tons of sons and daughters by his different accompaniments and concubines, each mother, in her inmost heart, fondly hoping that her own son would be chosen by his dad to prosper him.

Although the Empress had a child, who was the heir-apparent, yet she felt jealous of those girls who had likewise been blessed with kids, for fear one of the princes should supplant her child in the affection of the Emperor and in the succession. This envy displayed itself on every occasion; she was considerably beloved by the Emperor, and exerted all her influence with him, as the other young princes grew up, to get them eliminated from Court. Through her ways the majority of them were sent to the different provinces as rulers; those provinces under their federal government being so many principalities or kingdoms.

Chu-ti

Among the consorts of Hung Wu, the Woman Wêng, had a son called Chu-ti. This young prince was extremely handsome and graceful in his deportment; he was, moreover, of a pleasant disposition. He was the 4th child of the Emperor, and his pleasing manner and address had made him a great favorite, not only with his father, but with each about the Court. The Empress discovered the evident affection the Emperor evinced for this prince and determined to get him eliminated from the Court as soon as possible. By a judicious usage of flattery and cajolery, she eventually persuaded the Emperor to appoint the prince governor of the Yen country, and thenceforth he was styled Yen Wang, Prince of Yen.

The Sealed Packet

The young Prince, quickly after, taking a caring leave of the Emperor, left Chin-ling to proceed to his post. Ere he departed, though, a Taoist priest, called Liu Po-wên, who had a great affection for the Prince, put a sealed package into his hand, and told him to open it when he found himself in difficulty, distress, or threat; the perusal of the very first part that came to his hand would inevitably suggest some solution for the evil, whatever it was. After doing so, he was again to seal the packet, without further looking into its contents, till some other emergency situation occurred necessitating guidance or support, when he would again find it. The Prince departed on his journey, and in the course of time, without conference with any experiences worth tape-recording, showed up securely at his destination.

A Desolate Region

The place where Peking now stands was originally called Yu Chou; in the T'ang dynasty it was called Pei-p' ing Fu; and afterward became known as Shun-t' ien Fu-- but that was after the city now called Peking was built. The name of the nation in which this place was located was Yen. It was a mere barren wilderness, with extremely couple of inhabitants; these lived in huts and scattered hamlets, and there was no city to afford security to the people and to check the depredations of robbers.

When the Prince saw what a desolate-looking spot he had been appointed to, and idea of the long years he was most likely predestined to spend there, he grew extremely melancholy, and nothing his attendants essayed to do in hope of minimizing his sorrow had success.

The Prince opens the Sealed Packet

At one time the Prince bethought himself of the packet which the old Taoist priest had given him; he forthwith continued to make search for it-- for in the bustle and excitement of travelling he had forgotten really all about it-- in hope that it may suggest something to better the potential customers right before him. Having actually found the package, he quickly broke it available to see what directions it contained; taking out the very first paper which came to hand, he read the following:

" When you reach Pei-p' ing Fu you should build a city there and name it No-cha Ch' êng, the City of No-cha.2 But, as the work will be expensive, you need to issue a proclamation welcoming the rich to subscribe the required funds for building it. At the back of this paper is a plan of the city; you should be careful to act according to the instructions accompanying it."

The Prince examined the strategy, thoroughly read the guidelines, and found even the smallest specifics completely explained. He was struck with the splendor of the design of the proposed city, and simultaneously acted on the guidelines contained in the package; proclamations were posted up, and large amounts were speedily subscribed, 10 of the wealthiest families who had accompanied him from Chin-ling being the largest contributors, supporting the strategy not only with their purses, by giving immense amounts, but by their influence among their less wealthy neighbors.

Chapter 13: The City is Founded

When adequate cash had been subscribed, a propitious day was chosen on which to begin the undertaking. Trenches where the foundations of the walls were to be were first removed, according to the strategy found in the packet. The structures themselves included layers of stone quarried from the western hills; bricks of an immense size were made and burnt in the neighborhood; the moat was dug out, and the earth from it used to fill in the center of the walls, which, when complete, were forty-eight li in area, fifty cubits in height, and fifty in breadth; the entire circuit of the walls having battlements and embrasures. Above each of the nine gates of the city immense three-storied towers were built, each tower being ninety-nine cubits in height.

Near the front entrance of the city, facing one another, were built the Foreheads of Heaven and of Earth. In rear of it the stunning 'Coal Hill' (better known as 'Prospect Hill') was raised; while in the square in front of the Great Gate of the palace was buried an enormous quantity of charcoal (that and the coal being kept as a preventative measure in case of siege).

The palace, consisting of lots of exceptional structures, was constructed in a style of exceeding splendor; in the different enclosures were stunning gardens and lakes; in the different yards, too, seventy-two wells were dug, and thirty-six golden tanks positioned. The entire of the buildings and premises was surrounded by a lofty wall and a stone-paved moat, in which the lotus and other flowers flowered in great charm and abundance, and in the clear waters of which myriads of gold and silver fish disported themselves.

The geomancy of the city resembled that of Chin-ling, when everything was completed the Prince compared it with the strategy and found that the city tallied with it in every respect. He was much delighted and required the ten rich persons who had been the chief contributors, and gave each of them a pair of 'couchant dragon' silk- or satin-embroidered cuffs, and permitted them great benefits. As much as the present time there is the common phrase: "Ever since the 'dragon-cuffed' gentlefolks have flourished."

General Success
All the people were loud in praise of the charm and strength of the recently built city. Merchants from every province accelerated to Peking, attracted by the news they heard of its majesty and the prospect there was of profitably dealing with their items. Simply put, the people were prosperous and happy, food was plentiful, the soldiers brave, the king just, his ministers virtuous, and all took pleasure in the blessings of peace.

A Dry spell and its Cause
While every little thing was hence relaxing, an unexpected and unfortunate event happened which spread out discouragement and consternation on all sides. One day when the Prince entered into the hall of audience among his ministers reported that "the wells are thirsty and the rivers dried up"-- there was no water, and the people were all in the best alarm. The Prince

at the same time called his counsellors together to create some means of correcting this disaster and triggering the water to go back to the wells and springs, but no one could suggest a suitable strategy.

It is necessary to explain the reason for this deficiency of water. There was a dragon's cave outside the east gate of the city at a place called Lei-chên K'ou, 'Thunder-clap Mouth' or 'Pass' (the name of a village). The dragon had not been seen for varieties of years, yet it was well known that he lived there.

In digging out the earth to build the wall the workers had broken into this dragon's cavern, little thinking about the repercussions which would result. The dragon was exceptionally wroth and determined to shift his residence, but the female dragon said: "We have lived here countless years, and shall we suffer the Prince of Yen to drive us forth therefore? If we do go we will collect all the water, place it in our yin-yang baskets [used for drawing water], and at midnight we will appear in a dream to the Prince, asking for permission to retire. If he gives us approval to do so, and allows us also to take our baskets of water with us, he will fall into our trap, for we will take the water with his own authorization,"

The Prince's Dream

The two dragons then changed themselves into an old man and an old female, went to the chamber of the Prince, who was asleep, and appeared to him in a dream. Kneeling right before him, they cried: "O Lord of a Thousand Years, we have come before you to beg leave to retire from this spot, and to beseech you out of your great bounty to give us authorization to take these two baskets of water with us."

The Prince readily assented, little imagining the risk he was sustaining. The dragons were highly pleased and hastened out of his presence; they filled the baskets with all the water there was in Peking, and brought them off with them.

When the Prince awoke he ignored his dream till he heard the report of the shortage of water, when, reflecting on the singularity of his dream, he thought there may be some covert meaning in it. He therefore drew on the package again, and found that his dream-visitors had been dragons, who had taken the waters of Peking away with them in their magic baskets; the packet, though, included directions for the recovery of the water, and he at once prepared to follow them.

The Pursuit of the Dragons

In haste the Prince wore his armour, installed his black horse, and, spear in hand, rushed out of the west gate of the city. He pressed on his horse, which went swift as the wind, nor did he subside speed till he thought of the water-stealing dragons, who still maintained the forms in which they had appeared to him in his dream. On a cart were the 2 similar baskets he had seen; in front of the cart, dragging it, was the old lady, while behind, pushing it, was the old man.

An Unanticipated Flood

When the Prince saw them he galloped up to the cart, and, without stopping briefly, thrust his spear into one of the baskets, making a great hole, out of which the water rushed so quickly that the Prince was much scared. He rushed off at full speed to save himself from being swallowed up by the waters, which in a very brief time had risen more than thirty feet and had flooded the surrounding nation. On galloped the Prince, followed by the roaring water, till he reached a hill, up which he advised his startled horse. When he got the top he found that it stood out of the water like an island, totally surrounded; the water was seething and swirling round the hill in a shocking manner, but no vestige could he see of either of the dragons.

The Waters Subside

The Prince was very much alarmed at his perilous position, when suddenly a Buddhist priest appeared before him, with clasped hands and bent head, who bade him not be alarmed, just like Paradise's support he would soon distribute the water. Hereupon the priest recited a short prayer or spell, and the waters declined as rapidly as they had risen, and finally returned to their appropriate channels.

The Origin of Chên-shui T' a.

The damaged basket ended up being a big deep hole, some three mu (about half an English acre) in extent, in the centre of which was a water fountain which tossed up a vast body of clear water. From the midst of this there emerged a pagoda, which rose and fell with the water, floating on the top like a vessel; the spire thrusting itself far up into the sky, and swaying about like the mast of a ship in a storm.

The Prince returned to the city filled with wonder at what he had seen, and with happiness at having so effectively carried out the directions consisted of in the packet. On all sides he was welcomed by the acclamations of the people, who hailed him as the saviour of Peking. Since that time Peking has never ever had the bad luck to be without water.

The pagoda is called the Pagoda on the Hill of the Imperial Spring (Yü Ch' üan Shan T' a; more typically Chên-shui T' a, 'Water-repressing Pagoda').3 The spring is still there, and day and night, unceasingly, its clear waters bubble up and flow eastward to Peking, which would now be a barren wilderness but for Yen Wang's pursuit of the water.

Chapter 14: Fiery Myths

The Ministry of Fire

The celestial organization of Fire is the 5th Ministry, and is presided over by a President, Lo Hsüan, whose titular classification is Huo-tê Hsing-chün, 'Excellent Sovereign of the Fire-virtue,' with five subordinate ministers, four of whom are star-gods, and the fifth a "celestial prince who gets fire": Chieh-huo T'ien- chün. Like so tons of other Chinese deities, the 5 were all ministers of the autocrat emperor Chou.

It belongs that Lo Hsüan was originally a Taoist priest known as Yen-chung Hsien, of the isle Huo-lung, 'Fire-dragon.' His face was the colour of ripe fruit of the jujube-tree, his hair and beard red, the previous done up in the shape of a fish-tail, and he had 3 eyes. He wore a red cloak ornamented with the pa kua; his horse snorted flames from its nostrils and fire darted from its hoofs.

While fighting in the service of the son of the autocrat emperor, Lo Hsüa suddenly changed himself into a giant with 3 heads and 6 arms. In each of his hands he held a magic weapon. These were a seal which reflected the heavens and the earth, a wheel of the five fire-dragons, a gourd including ten 1000 fire-crows, and, in the other hands, two swords which drifted like smoke, and a column of smoke some countless li long enclosing swords of fire.

A Blaze

Having actually gotten to the city of Hsi Ch' i, Lo Hsüa sent forth his smoke-column, the air was filled with swords of fire, the ten thousand fire-crows, emerging from the gourd, spread themselves over the town, and an awful blaze broke out, the whole spot being ablaze in a few minutes.

At this juncture there appeared in the sky the Princess Lung Chi, daughter of Wang-mu Niang-niang; forthwith she topped the city her shroud of mist and dew, and the fire was snuffed out by a heavy downpour of rain. All the strange systems of Lo Hsüan lost their effectiveness, and the magician required to his heels down the side of the mountain. There he was met by Li, the Pagoda-bearer,1 who tossed his golden pagoda into the air. The pagoda fell on Lo Hsüan's head and broke his skull.

C'ih Ching-tzŭ

Of the various fire-gods, Ch' ih Ching-tzŭ, the concept of spiritual fire, is one of the five spirits representing the 5 Aspects. He is Fire personified, which has its birth in the south, on Mount Shih-t' ang. He himself and every little thing connected with him-- his skin, hair, beard, pants, cape of leaves, etc.-- are all of the colour of fire, though he is sometimes represented with a blue cap resembling the blue suggestion of a flame. He appeared in the presence of Huang Lao in a fire-cloud. He it was who obtained fire from the wood of the mulberry-tree, and the heat of the fire, joined with the wetness of water, developed the bacteria of terrestrial entities.

The Red Emperor

Chu Jung, though also otherwise personified, is usually considered as having been a legendary emperor who made his first appearance in the time of Hsien Yuan (2698-- 2598 B.C.). In his youth he asked Kuang-shou Lao-jên, 'Old Durability,' to grant him immortality. "The time has not yet come," responded Old Longevity; "right before it does you need to become an emperor. I will give you the means of reaching the end you prefer. Offer orders that after you are dead you are to be buried on the southern slope of the sacred mountain Hêng Shan; there you will discover the teaching of Ch' ih Ching-tzŭ and will become immortal."

The Emperor Hsien Yüan, having actually relinquished the throne, sent out for Chu Jung, and bestowed upon him the crown. Chu Jung, having actually become emperor, taught the people making use of fire and the advantages to be derived therefrom. In those early times the forests were filled with poisonous reptiles and savage animals; he ordered the peasants to set fire to the brushwood to drive away these unsafe neighbours and keep them at a short distance. He also taught his subjects the art of purifying, creating, and welding metals by the action of fire. He was nicknamed Ch' ih Ti, 'the Red Emperor.' He ruled for more than 2 hundred years, and ended up being an Immortal, His capital was the ancient city of Kuei, thirty li north-east of Hsin-chêng Hsien, in the Prefecture of K'ai- fêng Fu, Honan. His burial place is on the southern slope of Heng Shan. The peak is called Chu Jung Peak. His descendants, who went to reside in the south, were the forefathers of the Directors of Fire.

Hui Lu

The most popular God of Fire, though, is Hui Lu, a renowned magician who, according to the Shên hsien t' ung chien, lived a long time right before the reign of Ti K' u (2436-- 2366 B.C.), the father of Yao the Great, and had a mysterious bird called Pi Fang and a hundred other fire-birds shut up in a gourd. He had only to let them out to set up a blaze which would extend over the entire nation.

Huang Ti ordered Chu Jung to eliminate Hui Lu and also to suppress the rebel Chih Yu. Chu Jung had a big bracelet of pure gold-- a most wonderful and efficient weapon. He tossed it into the air, and it fell on Hui Lu's neck, throwing him to the ground and rendering him incapable of moving. Finding resistance impossible, he asked mercy from his victor and promised to be his follower in the spiritual contests. Consequently he always called himself Huo-shih Chih T' u, 'the Disciple of the Master of Fire.'

The Fire-emperor

Shen Nung, the God of Agriculture, also contributes to his other functions those appertaining to the God of Fire, the reason being that when he succeeded the Emperor Fu Hsi on the throne he adopted fire as the symbol of his federal government, just as Huang Ti adopted the symbol of Earth. Thus he happened called Huo Ti, the 'Fire-emperor.' He taught his subjects making use of fire for heating metals and making carries out and weapons, and the use of oil in lights, etc. All the divisions of his main hierarchy were linked in some way with this element; hence, there were the Ministers of Fire usually, the officers of Fire of the North, South, and so on. Ending up being hence two times as the patron of fire, a 2nd fire symbol (huo) was added to his name, changing it from Huo Ti, 'Fire-emperor,' to Yen Ti, 'Blazing Emperor.'

Chapter 15: Myths of Medicine, Epidemics, Exorcism

The Ministry of Epidemics

The gods of upsurges, etc., come from the sixth, ninth, second, and 3rd celestial Ministries. The composition of the Ministry of Epidemics is set up in a different way in different works as Upsurges (regarded as epidemics in the world, but as satanic forces in Heaven) of the Centre, Spring, Summer Season, Fall, and Winter season, or as the marshals outfitted in yellow, green, red, white, and blue respectively, or as the Officers of the East, West, South, and North, with 2 additional members: a Taoist who stops the plague epidemic, and the Grand Master who exhorts people to do right.

With regard to the Ministry of Seasonal Upsurges, it belongs that in the sixth moon of the eleventh year (A.D. 599) of the reign of Kao Tsu, creator of the Sui dynasty, 5 stalwart persons appeared in the air, outfitted in robes of 5 colors, each carrying different things in his hands: the first a spoon and earthenware vase, the second a leather bag and sword, the 3rd a fan, the fourth a club, the fifth a container of fire. The Emperor asked Chang Chü-jên, his Grand Historiographer, who these were and if they were humane or fiends. The official replied: "These are the five powers of the 5 directions. Their appearance suggests the imminence of upsurges, which will last throughout the 4 times of the year of the year." "What solution is there, and how am I to safeguard the people?" asked the Emperor. "There is no remedy," replied the authority, "for epidemics are sent by Heaven." During that year the death was extremely great. The Emperor built a temple to the five individuals and bestowed upon them the title of Marshals to the Five Spirits of the Plague. During that and the following dynasty sacrifices were offered to them on the fifth day of the 5th moon.

The President of the Ministry

The following details are given concerning the President of the Ministry, whose name was Lü Yüeh. He was an old Taoist hermit, living at Chiu-lung Tao, 'Nine-dragon Island,' who ended up being an Immortal. The 4 members of the Ministry were his disciples. He wore a red garment, had a blue face, red hair, long teeth, and 3 eyes. His war-horse was called the Myopic Camel. He carried a magic sword, and was in the service of Chou Wang, whose armies were concentrated at Hsi Ch' i. In a battle with Mu-cha, brother of No-cha, he had his arm severed by a sword-cut. In another battle with Huang T'ien- hua, child of Huang Fei-hu, he appeared with 3 heads and six arms. In a lot of hands, he held the celestial seal, pester microorganisms, the flag of afflict, the plague sword, and two strange swords. His faces were green, and big teeth extended from his mouths. Huang T'ien- hua threw his magic weapon, Huo-lung Piao, and hit him on the leg. Just at that moment Chiang Tzŭ-ya came with his goblin-dispelling whip and dropped him with a blow. He was able, however, to rise again, and required to flight.

The Plague-disseminating Umbrellas

Fixed to avenge his defeat, he signed up with General Hsü Fang, who was commanding an army corps at Ch' uan-yün Kuan. Round the mountain he organized a system of entrenchments and of infection against their opponents. Yang Chien released his celestial hound, which bit Lü Yüeh on the crown of his head. Then Yang Jên, equipped with his magic fan, chased after Lü Yüeh and compelled him to retreat to his fortress. Lü Yüeh installed the main raised part of the embattled wall and opened all his plague-disseminating umbrellas, with the object of contaminating Yang Jên, but the latter, just by waving his fan, reduced all the umbrellas to dust, and also burned the fort, and with it Lü Yüeh.

Similar terrific accomplishments are related in other words notices in the Fêng shên yen i of the 4 other officers of the Ministry.

Li P'ing, the sixth officer of the Ministry, met a like fate to that of Lü Yüeh after having failed to cause the latter to abandon the reason for the Shang dynasty for that of Chou.

The 5 Graduates

In Père Henri Doré's Recherches sur les Superstitions en Chine is given an interesting legend concerning five other gods of epidemics. These gods are called the Wu Yüeh, '5 Mountains,' and are worshipped in the temple San-i Ko at Ju-kao, particularly in break outs of infectious illnesses and fevers. A patient goes to the temple and guarantees offerings to the gods in the event of recovery. The traditional offering is five little wheaten loaves, called shao ping, and a pound of meat.

The Wu Yüeh are stellar demons whom Yü Huang sent out to be reincarnated in the world. Their names were T'ien Po-hsüeh, Tung Hung-wên, Ts' ai Wên-chü, Chao Wu-chên, and Huang Ying-tu, and they were reincarnated at Nan-ch' ang Fu, Chien-ch' ang Fu, Yen-mên Kuan, Yang Chou, and Nanking respectively. They were all noted for their brilliant intellects, and were creative academics who passed their graduate's evaluation with success.

When Li Shih-min rose the throne, in A.D. 627, he called together all the literati of the Empire to take the Doctor's Evaluation in the capital. Our five graduates began for the metropolis, but, losing their way, were robbed by brigands, and had to plead aid so as to reach the end of their journey. By good luck they all met in the temple San-i Ko, and related to each other the numerous challenges they had undergone. But when they eventually reached the capital the evaluation was over, and they were out in the streets without resources. So they took an oath of brotherhood for life and death. They pawned some of the few clothes they possessed, and buying some musical instruments formed themselves into a band of strolling musical artists.

The first purchased a drum, the 2nd a seven-stringed guitar, the third a mandolin, the fourth a clarinet, and the fifth and youngest made up songs.

Therefore, they went through the streets of the capital giving their shows, and Fate decreed that Li Shih-min should hear their tunes. Charmed with the sweet sounds, he asked Hsü Mao-kung whence came this band of musical artists, whose ability was certainly remarkable. Having made inquiries, the minister related their experiences to the Emperor. Li Shih-min ordered them to be brought into his presence, and after hearing them play and sing selected them to his personal suite, and from that time on, they accompanied him wherever he went.

The Emperor’s Strategy

The Emperor bore malice towards Chang T'ien- shih, the Master of the Taoists, as he refused to pay the taxes on his property, and conceived a strategy to produce his destruction. He caused a spacious subterranean chamber to be dug under the reception-hall of his palace. A wire gone through the ceiling to where the Emperor sat. He could hence at will give the signal for the music to begin or stop. Having actually stationed the 5 musical artists in this subterranean chamber, he summoned the Master of the Taoists to his presence and welcomed him to a banquet. During the course of this he pulled the wire, and a subterranean babel began.

The Emperor pretended to be terrified and enabled himself to be up to the ground. Then, resolving himself to the T'ien- shih, he said: "I know that you can at will catch the diabolical hobgoblins which molest human beings. You can hear for yourself the infernal row they make in my palace. I order you under penalty of death to put a stop to their pranks and to annihilate them."

The Musicians are Slain

Having actually spoken thus, the Emperor arose and left. The Master of the Taoists brought his forecasting mirror and began to seek for the evil spirits. In vain he examined the palace and its precincts; he could find nothing. Fearing that he was lost, he in anguish tossed his mirror on the floor of the reception-hall.

A minute later, sad and pensive, he stooped to pick it up; what was his happy surprise when he saw shown in it the subterranean room and the musical artists! Simultaneously he drew 5 talismans on yellow paper, burned them, and ordered his celestial general, Chao Kung-ming, to take his sword and kill the 5 musical artists. The order was immediately carried out, and the T'ien- shih notified the Emperor, who received the news with ridicule, not believing it to be real. He went to his seat and pulled the wire, but all remained silent. A second and third time he gave the signal, but without reaction. He then ordered his Grand Officer to ascertain what had happened. The officer found the five graduates bathed in their blood, and lifeless.

The Emperor, furious, reproached the Master of the Taoists. "But," replied the T'ien- shih, "was it not your Majesty who ordered me under real pain of death to exterminate the authors of this pandemonium?" Li Shih-min could not respond. He dismissed the Master of the Taoists and ordered the five victims to be buried.

The Emperor Tormented

After the funeral ceremonies, apparitions appeared in the evening in the place where they had been killed, and the palace became a babel. The spirits threw bricks and broke the tiles on the roofing systems.

The Emperor ordered his awkward visitors to go to the T'ien- shih who had murdered them. They obeyed, and, seizing the garments of the Master of the Taoists, swore not to enable him any rest if he would not restore them to life.

To appease them the Taoist said: "I am going to give each of you a terrific object. You are then to return and spread out upsurges amongst wicked people, beginning in the imperial palace and with the Emperor himself, with the object of forcing him to canonize you."

One received a fan, another a gourd filled with fire, the 3rd a metal ring to surround people's heads, the fourth a stick made from wolves' teeth, and the 5th a cup of lustral water.

The spirit-graduates left full of delight, and made their first experiment on Li Shih-min. The very first gave him feverish chills by waving his fan, the 2nd burned him with the fire from his gourd, the 3rd surrounded his head with the ring, causing him violent headache, the 4th struck him with his stick, and the 5th put out his cup of lustral water on his head.

The exact same night a similar catastrophe took place in the palace of the Empress and the 2 chief royal courtesans.

T'ai- po Chin-hsing, though, informed Yü Huang what had happened, and, touched with compassion, he sent three Immortals with tablets and talismans which cured the Empress and the women of the palace.

The Graduates Canonized

Li Shih-min, having also recuperated his health, summoned the five deceased graduates and expressed his remorse for the unfortunate issue of his design against the T'ien- shih. He proceeded: "To the south of the capital is the temple San-i Ko. I will change its name to Hsiang Shan Wu Yüeh Shên, 'Fragrant Hill of the Five Mountain Spirits.' On the twenty-eighth day of the ninth moon betake yourselves to that temple to get the seals of your canonization." He conferred upon them the title of Ti, 'Em peror.'.

The Ministry of Medication.

The celestial Ministry of Medication is made up of three primary divisions consisting of: (1) the Ancestral Gods of the Chinese race; (2) the King of Remedies, Yao Wang; and (3) the Specialists. There is a different Ministry of Smallpox. This latter controls and remedies smallpox, and the facility of a different celestial Ministry is significant of the frequency and significance of the condition. The devastations of smallpox in China, undoubtedly, have been terrific: so much so, that, till recent years, it was considered as natural and unavoidable for a child to have smallpox when it comes to it to cut its teeth. One of the ceremonial questions addressed by a visitor to the parent of a child was always Ch' u la hua' rh mei yu? "Has he had the smallpox?" and a kid who got away the scourge was typically, if not as a guideline, related to with disfavour and, curiously enough, as a weakling. Most likely the train of thought in the Chinese mind was that, as it is the fittest who endure, those who have successfully travelled through the process of "putting out the flowers" have shown their fitness in the battle for presence. Nowadays vaccination is general, and the number of pockmarked faces seen is much tinier than it used to be-- in simple fact, the pockmarked are now the exception. But, as far as I have had the ability to ascertain, the Ministry of Smallpox has not been abolished, and potentially its members, like those of some more mundane ministries, continue to draw big salaries for doing little or no work.

The Medicine-gods.

The primary gods of medicine are the legendary kings P'an Ku, Fu Hsi, Shên Nung, and Huang Ti. The very first 2, being by different authors considered as the very first progenitor or creator of the Chinese people, are alternatives, so that Fu Hsi, Shên Nung, and Huang Ti might be said to be a sort of ancestral triad of medicine-gods, superior to the actual God or King of Medicine, Yao Wang. Of P'an Ku we have spoken sufficiently at some earlier point, and with regard to Fu Hsi, also called T'ien Huang Shih, 'the Celestial Emperor,' the legendary sovereign and supposed creator of cooking, musical instruments, the calendar, hunting, fishing, etc., the chief interest for our present purpose centres in his discovery of the pa kua, or Eight Trigrams. It is on the strength of these trigrams that Fu Hsi is considered as the chief god of medication, since it is by their mystical power that the Chinese doctors influence the minds and ailments of their clients. He is represented as holding in front of him a disk on which the signs are painted.

The Ministry of Exorcism.

The Ministry of Exorcism is a Taoist development and is composed of 7 chief ministers, whose duty is to expel fiends from residences and usually to counteract the inconveniences of infernal demons. The 2 gods normally described in the well-known legends are P'an Kuan and Chung K'uei. The first is actually the Guardian of the Living and the Dead in the Otherworld, Fêng-tu P'an Kuan (Fêng-tu or Fêng-tu Ch' êng being the area beyond the tomb). He was initially a expert named Ts' ui Chio, who became Magistrate of Tz' ŭ Chou, and later Minister of Ceremonies. After his death he was selected to the spiritual post above discussed. His best-known achievement is his prolongation of the life of the Emperor T'ai Tsung of the T'ang dynasty by twenty years by changing i, 'one,' into san, 'three,' in the life-register kept by the gods. The term P'an Kuan is, however, more usually used as the classification of an officer or civil or military attendant upon a god than of any unique individual, and the initial P'an Kuan, 'the Decider of Life in Hades,' has been gradually supplanted in popular favour by Chung K'uei, 'the Protector against Evil Spirits.'.

The Exorcism of 'Em ptiness and Destruction'

The Emperor Ming Huang of the T'ang dynasty, also known as T'ang Hsüan Tsung, in the reign-period K'ai Yüan (A.D. 712-- 742), after an expedition to Mount Li in Shensi, was attacked by fever. During a bad nightmare he saw a little devil remarkably dressed in red trousers, with a shoe on one foot but none on the other, and a shoe hanging from his girdle. Having broken through a bamboo gate, he seized an embroidered box and a jade flute, and after that started to make a tour of the palace, sporting and gambolling. The Emperor grew mad and questioned him. "Your simple servant," responded the little satanic force, "is named Hsü Hao, 'Em ptiness and Destruction,'" "I have never ever heard of such a person," said the Emperor. The satanic force rejoined, "Hsü means to prefer Emptiness, as in Emptiness one can fly just as one desires; Hao, 'Devastation,' changes people's happiness to sadness. "The Emperor, irritated by this flippancy, was about to call his guard, when unexpectedly a great devil appeared, wearing a scruffy head-covering and a blue bathrobe, a horn clasp on his belt, and official boots on his feet. He went up to the sprite, tore out one of his eyes, crushed it up, and ate it. The Emperor asked the beginner who he was. "Your modest servant," he responded, "is Chung K'uei, Doctor of Tung-nan Shan in Shensi. In the reign-period Wu Tê (A.D. 618-- 627) of the Emperor Kao Tsu of the T'ang dynasty I was ignominiously turned down and unjustly defrauded of a first class in the general public evaluations. Overwhelmed with pity, I committed suicide on the steps of the royal palace. The Emperor ordered me to be buried in a green robe [reserved for members of the royal clan], and out of gratitude for that favor I testified safeguard the sovereign in any part of the Empire against the evil machinations of the demon Hsü Hao." At these words the Emperor awoke and found that the fever had left him. His Majesty required Wu Tao-tzŭ (among the most celebrated Chinese artists) to paint the picture of the person he had seen in his dream. The work was so well done that the Emperor recognized it as the real satanic force he had seen in his sleep and rewarded the artist with a hundred teals of gold. The picture is said to have been still in the royal palace throughout the Sung dynasty.

Another variation of the legend says that Chung K'uefs essay was recognized by the examiners as equal to the work of the best authors of antiquity, but that the Emperor declined him on account of his extremely ugly features, whereupon he committed suicide in his presence, was honoured by the Emperor and accorded a funeral service as if he had been the successful first candidate, and canonized with the title of Great Spiritual Chaser of Demons for the Whole Empire.

Chapter 16: The Goddess of Mercy and Grace

The Guardian Angel of Buddhism

As Mary is the assisting spirit of Roman Catholicism, so is Kuan Yin of the Buddhist faith.

According to a gorgeous Chinese legend, Kuan Yin. when ready to enter Paradise, heard a cry of anguish rising from the earth beneath her, and, moved by pity, paused as her feet touched the wonderful limit. For this reason, her name 'Kuan (Shih) Yin' (one who notices or hears the cry, or prayer, of the world).

Kuan Yin was at one time always represented as a guy; but in the T'ang dynasty and Five Dynasties we find him represented as lady, and he has been usually, though not inevitably, so represented since that time.

In old Buddhism Shâkyamuni was the primary god, and in a lot of temples he still nominally inhabits the seat of honour, but he is entirely eclipsed by the God or Goddess of Mercy.

" The guys really love her, the children adore her, and the women chant her prayers. Whatever the temple may be, there is almost always a chapel for Kuan Yin within its precincts; she lives in lots of homes, and in a lot of, a lot of hearts she sits enshrined. She is the patron goddess of mothers, and when we keep in mind the relative value of a child in Chinese estimation, we can appreciate the heartiness of the praise. She secures in sadness, and so countless times the prayer is offered, 'Fantastic mercy, great pity, save from sadness, save from suffering,' or, as it is in the books, 'Excellent mercy, great pity, save from misery, save from evil, broad, great, effective, responsive Kuan Yin Buddha,' She saves the tempest-tossed sailor, and so has eclipsed the Empress of Heaven, who, as the female Neptune, is the patroness of seamen; in drought the mandarins praise the Dragon and the Pearly Emperor, but if they fail the bronze Goddess of Grace from the hills brings rain. Other gods are feared, she is loved; other ones have black, scornful faces, her countenance is radiant as gold, and mild as the moon-beam; she draws near to the people and the people approach to her. Her throne is upon the Isle of Pootoo [P' u T' o], to which she came drifting upon a water-lily. She is the model of Chinese beauty, and to say a girl or a little girl is a 'Kuan Yin' is the highest compliment that can be paid to grace and loveliness. She is lucky in having 3 birthdays, the nineteenth of the second, sixth, and ninth moons." There are lots of transformations of the goddess.

The Buddhist Savior

" She is called Kuan Yin as at any cry of suffering she 'hears the voice and eliminates the grief.' Her appellation is 'Taking-away-fear Buddha,' If in the midst of the fire the name of Kuan Yin is called, the fire cannot burn; if tossed by mountain billows, call her name, and shallow waters will be reached. If merchants go across the sea looking for gold, silver, pearls, and precious stones, and a storm shows up and threatens to carry the crew to the evil devil's kingdom, if one on board contacts the name of Kuan Yin, the ship will be conserved. If one goes into a conflict and calls on the name of Kuan Yin, the sword and spear of the opponent fall harmless. If the 3 thousand great kingdoms are gone to by demons, get in touch with her name, and these devils cannot with an evil eye look on a guy. If, within, you have evil ideas, only contact Kuan Yin, and your heart will be purified, Anger and wrath might be dispelled by contacting the name of Kuan Yin. A lunatic who hopes to Kuan Yin will become sane. Kuan Yin gives sons to mothers, and if the mother asks for a child, she will be lovely. Two guys-- one chanting the names of the 6,200,000 Buddhas, in number like the sands of the Ganges, and the other simply calling on Kuan Yin-- have equivalent benefit. Kuan Yin might take the form of a Buddha, a prince, a priest, a nun, a scholar, any form or shape, go to any kingdom, and preach the law throughout the earth."

Miao Chuang desires a Beneficiary

In the twenty-first year of the reign of Ta Hao, the Great One, of the Golden Heavenly Dynasty, a guy called P' o Chia, whose given name was Lo Yü, an enterprising kinglet of Hsi Yii, took the throne for twenty years, after continuing a war for a space of three years. His kingdom was known as Hsing Lin, and the title of his reign as Miao Chuang.

The kingdom of Hsing Lin was, so says the Chinese writer, positioned between India on the west, the kingdom of T'ien Cheng on the south, and the kingdom of Siam on the north, and was 3000 li in length. The limits vary according to different authors. Of this kingdom the 2 pillars of State were the Grand Minister Chao Chen and the General Ch' u Chieh. The Queen Pao Tê, whose first name was Po Ya, and the King Miao Chuang had lived nearly half a century without having any male issue to succeed to the throne. This was a source of great grief to them. Po Ya suggested to the King that the God of Hua Shan, the sacred mountain in the west, had the track record of being always prepared to help; and that if he hoped to him and asked his pardon for having shed so much blood during the wars which preceded his accession to the throne he might acquire an heir.

Inviting this idea, the King sent for Chao Chên and ordered him to dispatch to the temple of Hua Shan the 2 Chief Ministers of Ceremonies, Hsi Hêng-nan and Chih Tu, with guidelines to demand fifty Buddhist and Taoist priests to wish seven days and 7 nights in order that the King may acquire a boy. When that period was over, the King and Queen would go in person to provide sacrifices in the temple.

Prayers to the Gods

The envoys took with them lots of uncommon and valuable presents, and for 7 days and 7 nights the temple resounded with the sound of drums, bells, and all kinds of instruments, intermingled with the voices of the praying priests. On their arrival the King and Queen offered sacrifices to the god of the spiritual mountain.

But the God of Hua Shan knew that the King had been denied of a male heir as a penalty for the bloody hecatombs during his three years' war. The priests, though, interceded for him, advising that the King had can be found in person to offer the sacrifices, wherefore the God could not completely reject his prayer. So he ordered Ch' ien-li Yen, 'Thousand-li Eye,' and Shun-fêng Erh,

'Favourable-wind Ear,' 1 to go rapidly and determine if there were not some worthy person who was on the point of being reincarnated into this world.

The two messengers quickly returned, and mentioned that in India, in the Chiu Ling Mountains, in the town of Chih-shu Yüan, there lived a pretty good man named Shih Ch' in-ch' ang, whose ancestors for 3 generations had observed all the ascetic guidelines of the Buddhists. This man was the father of three children, the eldest Shih Wên, the 2nd Shih Chin, and the 3rd Shih Shan, all worthy fans of the great Buddha.

The Murder of the Tais

Wang Chê, a brigand chief, and thirty of his fans, finding themselves chased after and pestered by the Indian soldiers, without arrangements or shelter, passing away of hunger, went to Shih Wên and begged for something to eat. Understanding that they were lawbreakers, Shih Wên and his 2 brothers refused to provide anything; if they starved, they said, the peasants would no longer struggle with their depredations. Thereupon the brigands chose that it was a case of life for life, and burglarized the house of a wealthy family of the name of Tai, burning their home, eliminating a hundred men, women, and children, and carrying off every little thing they possessed.

The regional t' u-ti at the same time made a report to Yü Huang.

" This Shih family," replied the god, "for 3 generations has given itself up to good works, and certainly the brigands were not deserving of any pity. However, it is unrealistic to deny that the 3 brothers Shih, in declining them food, ethically forced them to loot the Tai family's house, putting all to the sword or flames. Is not this the same as if they had committed the crime themselves? Let them be arrested and put in chains in the celestial jail and let them never ever see the light of the sun again."

" Since," said the messenger to the God of Hua Shan," your appreciation towards Miao Chuang forces you to grant him an heir, why not ask Yü Huang to pardon their criminal offense and reincarnate them in the womb of the Queen Po Ya, so that they may start a new terrestrial presence and give themselves as much as good works?" As a result, the God of Hua Shan called the Spirit of the Wind and gave him a message for Yü Huang

A Message for Yü Huang.

The message was as follows: "King Miao Chuang has offered sacrifice to me and pled me to grant him a beneficiary. However, since by his wars he has triggered the deaths of a great deal of people, he does not deserve to have his demand granted. Now these 3 brothers Shih have offended your Majesty by constraining the brigand Wang Che to be guilty of murder and break-in. I hope you to consider their past good works and pardon their criminal activity, providing a chance of expiating it by triggering them all 3 to be born-again, but of the female sex, in the womb of Po Ya the Queen.2 In this way they will have the ability to atone for their criminal activity and save tons of souls." Yü Huang was pleased to comply, and he ordered the Spirit of the North Pole to launch the three slaves and take their spirits to the palace of King Miao

Chuang, where in three years' time they would be changed into women in the womb of Queen Po Ya.

Birth of the Three Daughters

The King, who was anxiously expecting day by day the birth of a successor, was informed one morning that a daughter had been born to him. She was called Miao Ch' ing. A year went by, and another daughter was born. This one was called Miao Yin. When, at the end of the third year, another daughter was born, the King, next to himself with rage, called his Grand Minister Chao Chên and, all disconsolate, said to him, "I am past fifty, and have no male child to succeed me on the throne. My dynasty will therefore become extinct. Of what use have been all my labours and all my triumphes?" Chao Chen tried to console him, saying, "Heaven has granted you 3 daughters: no human power can change this divine decree. When these princesses have grown up, we will choose 3 sons-in-law for your Majesty, and you can elect your inheritor from amongst them. Who will dare to contest his right to the throne?"

The King named the 3rd daughter Miao Shan. She ended up being kept in mind for her modesty and tons of other good qualities, and scrupulously observed all the tenets of the Buddhist doctrines. Virtuous living seemed, certainly, to be to her a second nature.

Miao Shan's Ambition

One day, when the three sisters were playing in the palace garden of Perpetual Spring, Miao Shan, with a pretty serious mien, said to her sisters, "Riches and splendor are a lot like the rain in spring or the early morning dew; a little while, and all is gone. Kings and emperors believe to take pleasure in to the end the good luck which puts them in a rank apart from other humans; but sickness lays them low in their coffins, and all is over. Where are now all those powerful dynasties which have laid down the law to the world? As for me, I want nothing more than a peaceful retreat on a lone mountain, there to try the attainment of excellence. If someday I can reach a high degree of goodness, then, borne on the clouds of Heaven, I will travel throughout deep space, passing in the twinkling of an eye from east to west. I will rescue my father and mother, and bring them to Paradise; I will save the unhappy and afflicted in the world; I will transform the spirits which do evil, and trigger them to do good. That is my only ambition."

Her Sisters Marry

No quicker had she completed speaking than a girl of the Court came to reveal that the King had found sons-in-law to his preference for his two elder daughters. The wedding-feast was to be the very next day. "Be quick," she added, "and prepare your presents, your dresses, etc, for the King's order is essential." The partner chosen for Miao Ch' ing was a First Academician named Chao K'uei. His individual name was Tê Ta, and he was the child of a well-known minister of the ruling dynasty. Miao Yin's husband-elect was a military officer named Ho Fêng, whose individual name was Ch' ao Yang. He had passed initially in the assessment for the Military Doctorate. The marriage ceremonies were of a splendid character. Festivity followed festivity; the newly-wed were appropriately set up in their palaces, and general happiness dominated.

Miao Shan's Renunciation

There now remained only Miao Shan. The King and Queen wished to find for her a man popular for knowledge and virtue, capable of ruling the kingdom, and worthy of being the inheritor to the throne. So the King called her and explained to her all his strategies concerning her, and how all his hopes rested on her.

" It is a criminal offense," she responded, "for me not to comply with my dad's desires; but you must pardon me if my ideas vary from yours."

" Tell me what your ideas are," said the King.

" I do not wish to marry," she rejoined. "I wish to get to perfection and to Buddhahood. Then I promise that I will not be unthankful to you."

" Scoundrel of a daughter," wept the King in anger, "you believe you can teach me, the head of the State and ruler of so great a people! Has anybody ever known a child of a king become a nun? Can a good lady be found in that class? Put aside all these mad ideas of a nunnery and tell me at the same time if you will wed a Very first Academician or an Armed Force First Graduate."

" Who is there," replied the girl, "who does not really love the royal self-respect? -- what person who does not aspire to the joy of marriage? Nevertheless, I wish to become a nun. With respect to the riches and glory of the world, my heart is as cold as a dead cinder, and I feel an eager desire to make it ever purer and purer."

The King rose in rage and wished to cast her out from his presence. Miao Shan, understanding she could not honestly disobey his orders, took another course. "If you absolutely insist upon my marrying," she said, "I will consent; only I should wed a doctor."

" A physician!" grumbled the King. "Are men of great family and talents desiring in my kingdom? What an unreasonable idea, to want to wed a physician!"

" My wish is," said Miao Shan, "to recover humanity of all its ills; of cold, heat, lust, old age, and all imperfections. I wish to equalize all classes, putting wealthy and poor on the same footing, to have community of items, without difference of persons. If you will grant me my desire, I can still in this way become a Buddha, a Savior of Humanity. There is no necessity to hire the diviners to choose an auspicious day. I am all set to be married now."

She is Banished to the Garden

At these words the King seethed with rage. "Wicked imbecile!" he wept, "what diabolical tips are these that you dare to make in my presence?"

Without more ado he called Ho T'ao, who on that day was officer of the palace guard. When he had arrived and kneeled to get the King's commands, the latter said: "This wicked nun dishonors me. Take from her Court robes and drive her from my presence. Take her to the Queen's garden and let her perish there of cold: that will be one care less for my distressed heart."

Miao Shan fell on her face and thanked the King, and then chose the officer to the Queen's garden, where she started to lead her retired hermit life, with the moon for companion and the wind for friend, content to see all obstacles overthrown on her way to Nirvāna, the greatest state of spiritual bliss, and happy to exchange the satisfaction of the palace for the sweetness of privacy.

The Nunnery of the White Bird

After futile efforts to dissuade her from her purpose by the Court ladies, her mother and father, and sisters, the King and Queen next deputed Miao Hung and Ts' ui Hung to make a last effort to bring their misguided daughter to her senses. Miao Shan, annoyed at this restored solicitation, in a hoity-toity manner ordered them never ever again to come and torture her with their ridiculous prattle. "I have discovered," she added, "that there is a well-known temple at Ju Chou in Lung-shu Hsien. This Buddhist temple is known as the Nunnery of the White Bird, Po-ch' iao Ch' an-ssŭ. In it 5 hundred nuns give themselves up to the research study of the real doctrine and the way of excellence. Go then and ask the Queen on my behalf to obtain the King's permission for me to retire thither. If you can procure me this favour, I will not fail to reward you later."

Miao Chuang summoned the messengers and asked the result of their efforts. "She is more unapproachable than ever," they replied; "she has even ordered us to ask the Queen to obtain your Majesty's authorization to retire to the Nunnery of the White Bird in Lung-shu Hsien."

The King gave his consent, but sent rigorous orders to the nunnery, instructing the nuns to do all in their power to discourage the Princess when she arrived from carrying out her objective to stay.

Her Reception at the Nunnery

This Nunnery of the White Bird had been built by Huang Ti, and the five hundred nuns who lived in it had as Superior a lady called I Yu, who was amazing for her virtue. On receipt of the royal mandate, she had summoned Chêng Chêng-ch' ang, the choir-mistress, and informed her that Princess Miao Shan, owing to a disagreement with her dad, would quickly arrive at the temple. She requested her to receive the visitor courteously, but at the exact same time to do all she could to deter her from adopting the life of a nun. Having given these guidelines, the Superior, plant two novices, went to meet Miao Shan at the gate of the temple. On her arrival they saluted her. The Princess returned the salute, but said: "I have just left the world so as to put myself under your orders: why do you come and salute me on my arrival? I ask you to be so good as to take me into the temple, in order that I may pay my aspects to the Buddha" I Yu led her into the principal hall, and advised the nuns to light incense-sticks, ring the bells, and beat the drums. The check out to the temple completed, she went into the preaching-hall, where she greeted her instructresses. The latter obeyed the King's command and endeavoured to persuade the Princess to return to her home, but, as none of their arguments had any impact, it was at length chose to give her a trial, and to put her in charge of the kitchen area, where she could prepare the food for the nunnery, and generally be at the service of all. If she did not give satisfaction they could dismiss her.

She makes Offering to the Buddha.
Miao Shan joyfully concurred, and continued to make her humble submission to the Buddha. She knelt right before Ju Lai, and made offering to him, praying as follows: "Great Buddha, filled with goodness and mercy, your simple servant desires to leave the world. Grant that I might never ever accept the temptations which will be sent out to try my faith." Miao Shan further promised to observe all the regulations of the nunnery and to obey the superiors.

Spiritual Help
This generous self-sacrifice touched the heart of Yü Huang, the Master of Heaven, who summoned the Spirit of the North Star and advised him as follows: " Miao Shan, the third daughter of King Miao Chuang, has renounced the world in order to devote herself to the achievement of perfection. Her father has consigned her to the Nunnery of the White Bird. She has undertaken without grumbling the problem of all the work in the nunnery. If she is left without aid, who is there who will be willing to adopt the virtuous life? Do you go rapidly and order the Three Agents, the Gods of the Five Spiritual Peaks, the 8 Ministers of the Heavenly Dragon, Ch' ieh Lan, and the t' u-ti to send her aid at once. Tell the Sea-dragon to dig her a well near the kitchen, a tiger to bring her firewood, birds to collect vegetables for the prisoners of the nunnery, and all the spirits of Paradise to help her in her responsibilities, that she may give herself up without disturbance to the pursuit of perfection. See that my commands are without delay obeyed." The Spirit of the North Star complied without hold-up.

The Nunnery on Fire
Seeing all these gods arrive to help the novice, the Superior, I Yu, held assessment with the choir-mistress, saying: "We designated to the Princess the burdensome work of the cooking area as she refused to return to the world; but since she has entered upon her tasks the gods of the 8 caverns of Paradise have concerned offer her fruit, Ch' ieh Lan sweeps the cooking area, the dragon has dug a well, the God of the Hearth and the tiger bring her fuel, birds gather veggies for her, the nunnery bell every night at dusk booms of itself, just as if struck by some mystical hand. Undoubtedly miracles are being performed. Speed up and take the King, and beg his Majesty to recall his daughter."

Chêng Chêng-ch' ang started on her way, and, on arrival, notified the King of all that had happened. The King called Hu Pi-li, the chief of the guard, and ordered him to go to the sub-prefecture of Lung-shu Hsien at the head of an army corps of 5000 infantry and cavalry. He was to surround the Nunnery of the White Bird and burn it to the ground, together with the nuns. When he reached the spot the leader surrounded the nunnery with his soldiers and set fire to it. The five hundred doomed nuns conjured up the help of Paradise and earth, and after that, attending to Miao Shan, said: "It is you who have brought upon us this dreadful disaster."

" It is actually true," said Miao Shan. "I alone am the cause of your damage." She then knelt down and prayed to Heaven: "Great Sovereign of deep space, your servant is the daughter of King Miao Chuang; you are the grandson of King Lun. Will you not save your more youthful sister? You have left your palace; I also have left mine. You in previous times betook yourself to the snowy mountains to get perfection; I came here with the same item. Will you not save us from this intense damage?"

Her prayer ended, Miao Shan took a bamboo barrette from her hair, punctured the roof of her mouth with it, and spat the flowing blood toward Paradise. Instantly great clouds gathered in all parts of the sky and sent down swamping showers, which put out the fire that threatened the nunnery. The nuns tossed themselves on their knees and thanked her effusively for having saved their lives.

Hu Pi-li retired, and went in rush to notify the King of this remarkable incident. The King, enraged, ordered him to return at once, bring his daughter in chains, and behead her on the area.

The Execution of Miao Shan

But the Queen, who had heard about this brand-new plot, pled the King to grant her daughter a last chance. "If you will permit," she said, "I will have a magnificent structure built at the side of the road where Miao Shan will pass in chains en route to her execution and will go there with our 2 other daughters and our sons-in-law. As she passes, we will have music, tunes, feasting, everything very likely to impress her and make her contrast our glamorous life with her unhappy predicament. This will surely bring her to repentance."

" I concur," said the King, "to counter-order her execution until your preparations are complete." Nonetheless, when the time came, Miao Shan showed absolutely nothing but contempt for all this worldly program, and to all advances responded only: "I love not these pompous vanities; I swear that I choose death to the so-called joys of this world." She was then resulted in the place of execution. All the Court existed. Sacrifices were made to her as to one already dead. A Grand Minister pronounced the sacrificial oration.

In the middle of all this the Queen appeared, and ordered the authorities to return to their posts, that she might once again exhort her daughter to repent. But Miao Shan only listened in silence with downcast eyes.

The King felt great repugnance to shedding his daughter's blood, and ordered her to be imprisoned in the palace, in order that he might make a last effort to save her. "I am the King," he said; "my orders cannot be gently reserved. Disobedience to them involves penalty, and in spite of my paternal love for you, if you persist in your present attitude, you will be performed to-morrow in front of the palace gate."

The t' u-ti, hearing the King's decision, opted for all speed to Yü Huang, and reported to him the sentence which had been pronounced against Miao Shan. Yü Huang exclaimed: "Save Buddha, there is none in the west so honorable as this Princess. To-morrow, at the designated hour, go to the scene of execution, break the swords, and splinter the lances they will use to kill her. See that she suffers no pain. At the moment of her death transform yourself into a tiger and bring her body to the pinewood. Having actually deposited it in a safe spot, put a magic pill in her mouth to detain decay. Her triumphant soul on its return from the lower areas should find it in an ideal state of conservation to have the ability to re-enter it and animate it afresh. After that, she must betake herself to Hsiang Shan on P' u T' o Island, where she will reach the greatest state of excellence."

On the day appointed, Leader Hu Pi-li led the condemned Princess to the place of execution. A body of troops had been stationed there to keep order. The t' u-ti was in attendance at the palace gates. Miao Shan was glowing with joy. "To-day," she said, "I leave the world for a better life. Quicken to take my life, but beware of damaging my body."

The King's warrant showed up, and suddenly the sky ended up being overcast and darkness fell upon the earth. An intense light surrounded Miao Shan, and when the sword of the executioner fell upon the neck of the victim it was broken in two. Then they thrust at her with a spear, but the weapon fell down to pieces. After that the King ordered that she be strangled with a silken cable. A few moment later a tiger leapt into the execution ground, dispersed the executioners, put the inanimate body of Miao Shan on his back, and disappeared into the pine-forest. Hu Pi-li hurried to the palace, recounted to the King full specifics of all that had taken place, and received a reward of two ingots of gold.

Miao Shan goes to the Infernal Areas

Meantime, Miao Shan's soul, which remained safe, was born upon a cloud; when, waking as from a dream, she raised her head and looked round, she could not see her body. "My dad has just had me strangled," she sighed. "How is it that I find myself in this spot? Here are neither mountains, nor trees, nor plants; no sun, moon, nor stars; no habitation, no noise, no cackling of a fowl nor barking of a dog. How can I live in this desolate area?"

Suddenly a boy dressed in blue, shining with a dazzling light, and carrying a big banner, appeared and said to her: "By order of Yen Wang, the King of the Hells, I concern take you to the eighteen infernal areas."

" What is this cursed place where I am now?" asked Miao Shan.

" This is the lower world, Hell," he responded. "Your refusal to wed, and the magnanimity with which you chose an ignominious death rather than break your resolutions, are worthy of the acknowledgment of Yü Huang, and the ten gods of the lower areas, amazed and delighted at your distinguished virtue, have sent me to you. Worry absolutely nothing and follow me."

Therefore, Miao Shan began her see to all the infernal areas. The Gods of the Ten Hells came to congratulate her.

" Who am I," asked Miao Shan, "that you should deign to take the trouble to show me such respect?"

" We have heard," they replied, "that when you recite your prayers all wicked disappears just as if by magic. We should like to hear you pray."

" I consent," responded Miao Shan, "on condition that all the condemned ones in the ten infernal regions be released from their chains so as to listen to me."

At the designated time the condemned were led in by Niu T'ou (' Ox-head') and Ma Mien (' Horse-face'), the two chief constables of Hell, and Miao Shan began her prayers. No quicker had she completed than Hell was suddenly transformed into a paradise of pleasure, and the instruments of abuse into lotus-flowers.

Chapter 17: Hell and Paradise

P'an Kuan, the keeper of the Register of the Living and the Dead, presented a memorial to Yen Wang stating that since Miao Shan's arrival there was no more strong pain in Hell; and all the condemned were beside themselves with happiness. "Given that it has always been decreed," he added, "that, in justice, there should be both a Paradise and a Hell, if you do not send this saint back to earth, there will no longer be any Hell, but only a Paradise."

" Since that is so," said Yen Wang, "let forty-eight flag-bearers escort her across the Styx Bridge [Nai-ho Ch' iao], that she might be brought to the pine-forest to reenter her body and resume her life in the upper world."

The King of the Hells having paid his aspects to her, the youth in blue conducted her soul back to her body, which she found lying under a pine-tree. Having reentered it, Miao Shan found herself alive again. A bitter sigh got away from her lips. "I keep in mind," she said, "all that I saw and heard in Hell. I sigh for the moment which will find me devoid of all obstacles, and yet my soul has re-entered my body. Here, without any lonesome mountain on which to give myself up to the pursuit of excellence, what will become of me?" Great tears welled from her eyes.

A Test of Virtue
Just then Ju Lai Buddha appeared. "Why have you come to this spot?" he asked. Miao Shan clarified why the King had put her to death, and how after her descent into Hell her soul had re-entered her body. "I considerably pity your misfortune," Ju Lai said, "but there is nobody to help you. I also am alone. Why should we not wed? We could build ourselves a hut and pass our days in peace. What say you?" "Sir," she responded, "you need to not make impossible tips. I died and came to life again. How can you speak so lightly? Do me the enjoyment of withdrawing from my presence."

" Well," said the visitor, "he to whom you are speaking is no other than the Buddha of the West. I came to check your virtue. This spot is not ideal for your devotional exercises; I invite you to come to Hsiang Shan."

Miao Shan tossed herself on her knees and said: "My physical eyes tricked me. I never ever thought that your Majesty would pertain to a place like this. Pardon my seeming want of respect. Where is this Hsiang Shan?"

" Hsiang Shan is an older abbey," Ju Lai replied, "constructed in the earliest historical times. It is lived in by Immortals. It is positioned in the sea, on P' u T' o Island, a reliance of the kingdom of Annam. There you will have the ability to reach the highest excellence."

" How far off is this island?" Miao Shan asked. "More than three thousand li," Ju Lai replied. "I fear," she said, "I could not bear the tiredness of so long a journey." "Calm yourself," he rejoined. "I have brought with me a magic peach, of a kind not to be found in any earthly orchard. Once you have eaten it, you will experience neither hunger nor thirst; old age and death will have no power over you: you will live for ever."

Miao Shan ate the magic peach, departed of Ju Lai, and started on the way to Hsiang Shan. From the clouds the Spirit of the North Star saw her wending her way painfully towards P' u T' o. He called the Guardian of the Soil of Hsiang Shan and said to him: "Miao Shan is on her way to your country; the way is long and hard. Do you take the form of a tiger, and carry her to her journey's end."

The t' u-ti transformed himself into a tiger and stationed himself in the middle of the roadway along which Miao Shan should pass, giving vent to relentless roars.

" I am a bad girl lacking filial piety," said Miao Shan when she turned up. "I have disobeyed my father's commands; devour me, and make an end of me."

The tiger then spoke, saying: "I am not a real tiger, but the Guardian of the Soil of Hsiang Shan. I have received instructions to carry you there. Get on my back."

" Since you have received these instructions," said the girl, "I will obey, and when I have achieved to excellence I will not forget your compassion."

The tiger went off like a flash of lightning, and in the twinkling of an eye Miao Shan found herself at the foot of the rocky slopes of P' u T' o Island.

Miao Shan obtains to Excellence

After 9 years in this retreat Miao Shan had reached the acme of excellence. Ti-tsang Wang then came to Hsiang Shan, and was so astonished at her virtue that he inquired of the regional t' u-ti regarding what had produced this terrific outcome. "With the exception of Ju Lai, in all the west no one equals her in self-respect and perfection. She is the Queen of the three thousand P' u-sa's and of all the entities on earth who have skin and blood. We regard her as our sovereign in all things. Therefore, on the 19th day of the l lth moon we will enthrone her, that the whole world might profit by her beneficence."

The t' u-ti sent his invites for the ceremony. The Dragon-king of the Western Sea, the Gods of the Five Sacred Mountains, the Emperor-saints to the number of one hundred and twenty, the thirty-six officials of the Ministry of Time, the celestial functionaries in charge of wind, rain, thunder, and lightning, the 3 Causes, the Five Saints, the Eight Immortals, the Ten Kings of the Hells-- all were present on the designated day. Miao Shan took her seat on the lotus-throne, and the assembled gods proclaimed her sovereign of Heaven and earth, and a Buddha. Furthermore, they decided that it was not meet that she needs to stay alone at Hsiang Shan; so they pled her to choose a worthwhile boy and a virtuous damsel to serve her in the temple.

The t' u-ti was turned over with the job of finding them. While making search, he met a young priest named Shan Ts' ai. After the death of his mother and father he had ended up being a hermit on Ta-hua Shan, and was still a beginner in the science of perfection.

Miao Shan ordered him to be given her. "Who are you?" she asked.

" I am a bad orphan priest of no benefit," he replied. "From my earliest youth I have led the life of a hermit. I have been told that your power is equalled only by your goodness, so I have ventured to come to pray you to show me how to get to excellence."

" My only worry," replied Miao Shan, "is that your desire for excellence may not be genuine."

" I have now no mom and dad," the priest continued, "and I have come more than a thousand li to find you. How can I be desiring in sincerity?"

" What unique degree of ability have you attained during your course of excellence?" asked Miao Shan.

" I have no skill," responded Shan Ts' ai, "but I rely for every little thing on your great pity, and under your guidance I hope to reach the required ability."

" Well," said Miao Shan, "use up your station on the top of yonder peak and wait till I find a method of transferring you."

A Ruse

Miao Shan called the t' u-ti and bade him go and plead all the Immortals to camouflage themselves as pirates and to besiege the mountain, waving torches, and threatening with swords and spears to kill her. "Then I will look for sanctuary on the summit, and thence leap over the precipice to prove Shan Ts' ai's fidelity and affection."

A minute later a horde of brigands of ferocious aspect rushed up to the temple of Hsiang Shan. Miao Shan wept for assistance, rushed up the high incline, missed her footing, and rolled down into the ravine. Shan Ts' ai, seeing her fall into the void, without doubt flung himself after her so as to rescue her. When he reached her, he asked: "What have you to fear from the burglars? You have absolutely nothing for them to take; why toss yourself over the precipice, exposing yourself to certain death?"

Miao Shan saw that he was weeping and wept too. "I need to abide by the dream of Heaven," she said.

The Transformation of Shan Ts' ai.

Shan Ts' ai, heartbroken, hoped Paradise and earth to save his protectress. Miao Shan said to him: "You should not have risked your life by throwing yourself over the precipice, I have not yet changed you. But you did a brave thing, and I know that you have a good heart. Now, look down there." "Oh," said he, "if I mistake not, that is a lifeless body." "Yes," she responded, "that is your former body. Now you are transformed you can rise up at will and fly in the air." Shan Ts' ai bowed low to thank his benefactress, who said to him: "Henceforth you should say your prayers by my side, and not leave me for a single day."

' Brother and Sister'.
With her spiritual sight Miao Shan viewed at the bottom of the Southern Sea the third child of Lung Wang, who, in performing his father's orders, was cleaving the waves in the form of a carp. While doing so, he was caught in a fisherman's net, brought to the marketplace at Yüeh Chou, and marketed. Miao Shan at the same time sent her faithful Shan Ts' ai, in the guise of a servant, to buy him, giving him a 1000 money to acquire the fish, which he was to require to the foot of the rocks at P' u T' o and release in the sea. The son of Lung Wang heartily thanked his deliverer, and on his return to the palace associated to his dad what had happened. The King said: "As a benefit, make her a present of a luminescent pearl, so that she may recite her prayers by its light at night-time."

Lung Nü, the daughter of Lung Wang's third child, acquired her grandfather's permission to take the gift to Miao Shan and ask that she might be enabled to study the teaching of the sages under her guidance. After having proved her sincerity, she was accepted as a pupil. Shan Ts' ai called her his sister, and Lung Nü reciprocated by calling him her dear brother. Both lived as brother and sister by Miao Shan's side.

The King's Punishment.
After King Miao Chuang had burned the Nunnery of the White Bird and killed his daughter, Ch' ieh Lan Buddha presented a petition to Yü Huang hoping that the criminal offense be not enabled to go unpunished. Yü Huang, justly inflamed, ordered P'an Kuan to speak with the Register of the Living and the Dead to see how long this homicidal King had yet to live. P'an Kuan turned over the pages of his register, and saw that according to the divine regulations the King's reign on the throne of Hsing Lin should last for twenty years, but that this duration had not yet ended.3 "That which has been decreed is immutable," said Yü Huang, "but I will penalize him by sending him health problem." He called the God of Epidemics, and ordered him to afflict the King's body with ulcers, of a kind which could not be recovered other than by remedies to be given him by his daughter Miao Shan.

The order was promptly executed, and the King could get no rest by day or by night. His 2 daughters and their spouses spent their time in feasting while he tossed about in agony on his sick bed. Fruitless the most popular physicians were hired; the condition only grew worse, and misery grabbed the patient. He then caused a proclamation to be made that he would grant the succession to the throne to anybody who would supply him with an effectual treatment to restore him to health.

The Disguised Priest-doctor.
Miao Shan had discovered by discovery at Hsiang Shan all that was occurring at the palace. She presumed the form of a priest-doctor, outfitted herself in a priest's gown, with the regulation

headdress and straw shoes, and connected to her girdle a gourd consisting of pills and other medications. In this clothing she went straight to the palace gate, read the royal edict posted there, and tore it down. Some members of the palace guard seized her, and inquired madly: "Who are you that you should dare to take down the royal proclamation?"

" I, a poor priest, am also a physician," she replied. "I check out the edict published on the palace gates. The King is asking for a physician who can recover him. I am a doctor of an old cultured family, and propose to restore him to health."

" If you are of a cultured family, why did you become a priest?" they asked. "Would it not have been better to gain your living honestly in practicing your art than to shave your head and go loafing about the world? Besides, all the greatest doctors have tried in vain to treat the King; do you imagine that you will be more skilful than all the aged professionals?"

" Set your minds at ease," she replied. "I have received from my ancestors the most efficacious solutions, and I guarantee that I shall restore the King to health," The palace guard then granted send her petition to the Queen, who notified the King, and in the end the pretended priest was admitted. Having reached the royal bed-chamber, he sat still some time so as to calm himself before feeling the pulse, and to have complete control of all his faculties while examining the King. When he felt rather sure of himself, he approached the King's bed, took the King's hand, felt his pulse, thoroughly identified the nature of the disease, and assured himself that it was quickly treatable.

Odd Medicine.

One serious trouble, though, presented itself, and that was that the right medication was practically impossible to acquire. The King showed his annoyance by saying: "For every disease there is a medical prescription, and for every single prescription a particular medicine; how can you say that the diagnosis is simple, but that there is no remedy?"

" Your Majesty," replied the priest, "the treatment for your disease is not to be found in any drug store, and no one would consent to sell it."

The King blew up, really believed that he was being enforced upon, and ordered those about him to repel the priest, who left smiling.

The following night the King saw in a dream an old man who said to him: "This priest alone can treat your disease, and if you ask him he himself will give you the right solution."

The King awoke as soon as these words had been uttered, and pled the Queen to remember the priest. When the latter had returned, the King associated his dream, and asked the priest to obtain for him the solution required." What, after all, is this solution that I must have so as to be treated?" he asked.

" There should be the hand and eye of a living person, from which to intensify the lotion which alone can save you," replied the priest.

The King called out in indignation: "This priest is tricking me! Who would ever give his hand or his eye? Even if anybody would, I could never have the heart to utilize them."

" Nonetheless," said the priest, "there is no other efficient remedy."

" Then where can I acquire this remedy?" asked the King.

" Your Majesty must send your ministers, who must observe the Buddhist guidelines of abstaining, to Hsiang Shan, where they will be given what is needed."

" Where is Hsiang Shan, and how far from here?"

" About 3 1000 or more li, but I myself will suggest the route to be followed; in a really brief time they will return."

The King, who was suffering terribly, was more pleased when he heard that the journey could be rapidly accomplished. He called his two ministers, Chao Chên and Liu Ch' in, and advised them to lose no time in starting for Hsiang Shan and to observe scrupulously the Buddhist rules of abstinence. He ordered the Minister of Ceremonies to apprehend the priest in the palace until their return.

A Conspiracy that Stopped working

The two sons-in-law of the King, Ho Fêng and Chao K'uei, who had already made secret preparations to be successful to the throne as quickly as the King should breathe his last, learned without any little surprise that the priest had hopes of curing the King's illness, and that he was waiting in the palace until the saving solution was brought to him. Fearing that they might be dissatisfied in their ambition, and that after his healing the King, faithful to his guarantee, would give the crown to the priest, they participated in a conspiracy with a dishonest courtier called Ho Li. They were obliged to act quickly, since the ministers were travelling by pushed marches, and would quickly be back. That exact same night Ho Li was to offer to the King a poisoned drink, composed, he would say, by the priest with the item of assuaging the King's strong pain until the return of his two ministers. Quickly after, an assassin, Su Ta, was to murder the priest. Therefore, at one stroke both the King and the priest would meet their death, and the kingdom would pass to the King's 2 sons-in-law.

Miao Shan had gone back to Hsiang Shan, leaving in the palace the physical form of the priest. She saw the 2 traitors Ho Fêng and Chao K'uei preparing the toxin and knew their wicked objectives. Calling the spirit Yu I, who was on duty that day, she told him to fly to the palace and change into a harmless soup the toxin about to be administered to the King and to bind the assassin hand and foot.

At midnight Ho Li, carrying in his hand the poisoned beverage, knocked at the door of the royal apartment, and said to the Queen that the priest had prepared a calming potion while awaiting the return of the ministers. "I come," he said, "to provide it to his Majesty." The Queen took the bowl in her hands and was going to give it to the King, when Yu I showed up unannounced. Het thought quickly and he took the bowl from the Queen and poured the contents on the ground; at the same moment he knocked over those present in the room, so that they all rolled on the floor.

At the time this was going on the assassin Su Ta got in the priest's room, and struck him with his sword. Immediately the assassin, without knowing how, found himself enwrapped in the priest's robe and tossed to the ground. He struggled and tried to totally free himself but found that his hands had been rendered useless by some strange power, and that flight was impossible. The spirit Yu I, having actually satisfied the mission turned over to him, now returned to Hsiang Shan and reported to Miao Shan.

A Confession and its Actual results

Next morning, the two sons-in-law of the King heard about the turn things had taken during the night. The whole palace was in a state of the best confusion.

When he was notified that the priest had been killed, the King called Ch' u Ting-lieh and ordered him to have the killer jailed. Su Ta was put to the abuse and confessed all that he knew. Together with Ho Li he was condemned to be cut into a thousand pieces.

The 2 sons-in-law were seized and ordered to instantaneous execution, and it was only on the Queen's intercession that their wives were spared. The irritated King, however, ordered that his two daughters should be locked up in the palace.

The Gruesome Solution

Meantime Chao Chên and Liu Ch' in had reached Hsiang Shan. When they were given Miao Shan the ministers took the King's letter and read it to her." I, Miao Chuang, King of Hsing Lin, have learned that there stays at Hsiang Shan a Immortalwhose power and empathy have no equal in the whole world. I have passed my fiftieth year, and am afflicted with ulcers that all remedies have could not cure. To-day a priest has ensured me that at Hsiang Shan I can obtain the hand and eye of a living person, with which he will prepare a lotion able to restore me to my usual state of health. Relying upon his word and upon the goodness of the Immortal to whom he has directed me, I venture to beg that those two parts of a living body essential to heal my ulcers be sent out to me. I guarantee you of my everlasting gratitude, fully positive that my request will not be refused."

The next early morning Miao Shan bade the ministers take a knife and cut off her left hand and gouge out her left eye. Liu Ch' in took the knife offered him, but did not dare to obey the order. "Fast," prompted the Immortal; "you have been commanded to return as quickly as possible; why do you wait as though you were a young girl?" Liu Ch' in was pushed to continue. He plunged in the knife, and the red blood flooded the ground, spreading out a smell like sweet incense. The hand and eye were put on a golden plate, and, having actually paid their grateful aspects to the Never-ceasing, the envoys sped up to return.

When they had left, Miao Shan, who had changed herself in order to enable the envoys to eliminate her hand and eye, told Shan Ts' ai that she was now going to prepare the ointment required for the treatment of the King. "Must the Queen," she added, "send for another eye and hand, I will transform myself again, and you can provide to her." No faster had she completed speaking than she installed a cloud and disappeared in space. The two ministers reached the palace and presented to the Queen the gruesome treatment which they had brought from the temple. She, conquered with appreciation and emotion, wept copiously. "What Immortal," she asked, "can have been so charitable as to sacrifice a hand and eye for the King's benefit?" Then all of a sudden her tears gushed forth with redoubled vigour, and she uttered a great cry, for she acknowledged the hand of her daughter by a black scar which was on it.

Half-measures

" Who else, in fact, but his kid," she continued in the middle of her sobs, "could have had the guts to give her hand to save her father's life?" "What are you saying?" said the King. "On the planet there are lots of hands like this." While they thus reasoned, the priest got in the King's apartment or condo. "This great Immortal has long devoted herself to the attainment of perfection," he said. "Those she has recovered are many. Provide me the hand and eye." He took them and quickly produced a lotion which, he told the King, was to be applied to his left side. No sooner had it touched his skin than the real pain on his left side disappeared just as if by magic; no indication of ulcers was to be seen on that side, but his right side remained swollen and painful as previously.

" Why is it," asked the King, "that this solution, which is so effective for the left side, should not be applied to the right?" "Since," replied the priest, "the left hand and eye of the saint treatments only the left side. If you wish to be entirely treated, you must send your officers to acquire the right eye and right hand also." The King appropriately dispatched his envoys anew with a letter of thanks, and asking as an additional favour that the treatment should be completed by the healing also of his right side.

The King Cured

On the arrival of the envoys Shan Ts' ai met them in the mutilated form of Miao Shan, and he bade them cut off his right-hand man, pluck out his right eye, and put them on a plate. At the sight of the four bleeding wounds Liu Ch' in could not avoid calling out indignantly: "This priest is a wicked man, therefore to make a martyr of lady so as to obtain the succession!"

Having hence spoken, he left with his companion for the kingdom of Hsing Lin. On their return the King was overwhelmed with delight. The priest rapidly prepared the ointment, and the King, without hold-up, applied it to his right side. At once the ulcers disappeared like the darkness of night right before the rising sun. The whole Court praised the King and eulogized the priest. The King gave upon the latter the title Priest of the Brilliant Eye. He fell on his face to return thanks, and added: "I, a bad priest, have left the world, and have only one desire, particularly, that your Majesty ought to govern your subjects with justice and sympathy and that all the officials of the world should prove themselves men of integrity. As for me, I am used to wandering about. I have no desire for any royal estate. My joy surpasses all earthly joys."

Having actually therefore spoken, the priest waved the sleeve of his cloak, a cloud came down from Heaven, and seating himself upon it he disappeared in the sky. From the cloud a note containing the following words was seen to fall: "I are among the Teachers of the West. I came to treat the King's disease, and so to glorify the True Doctrine."

The King's Daughter
All who experienced this wonder exclaimed with one voice: "This priest is the Living Buddha, who is returning to Heaven!" The note was taken to King Miao Chuang, who exclaimed: "Who am I that I should be worthy of that one of the rulers of Heaven should deign to descend and cure me by the sacrifice of hands and eyes?"

" What was the face of the saintly person like who gave you the remedy?" he then asked Chao Chên.

" It was like unto that of your deceased daughter, Miao Shan," he responded.

" When you eliminated her hands and eyes did she appear to suffer?"

" I saw a great flow of blood, and my heart stopped working, but the face of the victim appeared glowing with joy."

" This definitely need to be my daughter Miao Shan, who has obtained to excellence," said the King. "Who but she would have given hands and eyes? Cleanse yourselves and observe the guidelines of abstinence, and go rapidly to Hsiang Shan to return thanks to the saint for this inestimable favour. I myself will ere long make a trip thither to return thanks face to face."

The King and Queen taken Prisoners
3 years later the King and Queen, with the grandees of their Court, set out to go to Hsiang Shan, but on the way the emperors were caught by the Green Lion, or God of Fire, and the White Elephant, or Spirit of the Water, the two guardians of the Temple of Buddha, who transported them to a dark cavern in the mountains. A terrific fight then happened between the evil spirits on the one side and some hosts of divine genii, who had been summoned to the rescue, on the other. While its problem was still unpredictable, reinforcements under the Red Kid Devil, who could resist fire, and the Dragon-king of the Eastern Sea, who could control water, finally routed the enemy, and the detainees were released.

The King's Repentance
The King and Queen now resumed their pilgrimage, and Miao Shan advised Shan Ts' ai to get the kings when they arrived to offer incense. She herself used up her put on the altar, her eyes

torn out, her hands cut off, and her wrists all leaking with blood. The King acknowledged his daughter, and bitterly reproached himself; the Queen fell swooning at her feet. Miao Shan then spoke and tried to comfort them. She told them of all that she had experienced since the day when she had been executed, and how she had obtained to never-ceasing perfection. She then went on: "In order to penalize you for having caused the deaths of all those who perished in the wars preceding your accession to the throne, and also to avenge the burning of the Nunnery of the White Bird, Yü Huang afflicted you with those severe ulcers. It was then that I changed myself into a priest to recover you, and gave my eyes and hands, with which I prepared the ointment that treated you. It was I, furthermore, who procured your liberty from Buddha when you were sent to prison in the cave by the Green Lion and the White Elephant."

Sackcloth and Ashes

At these words the King threw himself with his face on the ground, offered incense, worshipped Heaven, earth, the sun, and the moon, saying with a voice broken by sobs: "I committed a great crime in killing my daughter, who has sacrificed her eyes and hands so as to cure my sickness."

No earlier were these words said than Miao Shan reassumed her normal form, and, coming down from the altar, approached her mother and father and sisters. Her body had again its initial completeness; and in the presence of its flawless appeal, and at finding themselves reunited as one family, all wept for joy.

" Well," said Miao Shan to her dad, "will you now force me to marry and prevent my dedicating myself to the attainment of excellence?"

" Speak no more of that," replied the King. "I was in the wrong. If you had not reached excellence, I should not now live. I have made up my mind to exchange my sceptre for the pursuit of the best life, which I wish to lead henceforth together with you."

The King renounces the Throne

Then, in the presence of all, he resolved his Grand Minister Chao Chên, saying: "Your dedication to the service of the State has rendered you deserving to wear the crown: I surrender it to you." The Court announced Chao Chên King of Hsing Lin, bade farewell to Miao Chuang, and set out for their kingdom accompanied by their new sovereign.

Pardon of the Green Lion and the White Elephant

Buddha had summoned the White Elephant and the Green Lion, and was on the point of sentencing them to everlasting damnation when the compassionate Miao Shan interceded for them. "Definitely you should have no forgiveness," he said, "but I cannot refuse a request made by Miao Shan, whose clemency was actually without limitation. I give you over to her, to serve and follow her in everything. Follow her."

Miao Shan becomes a Buddha

The defender spirit on duty that day then announced the arrival of a messenger from Yü Huang. It was T'ai- po Chin-hsing, who was the bearer of a divine decree, which he handed to Miao

Shan. It read as follows: "I, the august Emperor, make known to you this decree: Miao Chuang, King of Hsing Lin, forgetful alike of Paradise and Hell, the six virtues, and metempsychosis, has led a blameworthy life; but your 9 years of penitence, the filial piety which triggered you to sacrifice your own body to effect his treatment, in other words, all your virtues, have redeemed his faults. Your eyes can see and your ears can hear all the great and bad deeds and words of guys. You are the thing of my especial regard. For that reason I make proclamation of the decree of canonization.

" Miao Shan will have the title of Extremely Merciful and Extremely Caring P' u-sa, Saviour of the Afflicted, Miraculous and Always Helpful Protectress of Mortals. On your lofty valuable lotus-flower throne, you will be the Sovereign of the Southern Seas and of P' u T' o Isle.

" Your 2 sisters, hitherto polluted with earthly enjoyments, will gradually progress till they reach real excellence.

" Miao Ch' ing will have the title of Very Virtuous P' u-sa, the Completely Beautiful, Rider of the Green Lion.

" Miao Yin will be honoured with the title of Extremely Virtuous and Entirely Resplendent P' u-sa, Rider of the White Elephant.

" King Miao Chuang is raised to the self-respect of Virtuous Dominating P' u-sa, Property surveyor of Mortals.

" Queen Po Ya gets the title of P' u-sa of Ten Thousand Virtues, Property Surveyor of Famous Women.

" Shan Ts' ai has bestowed upon him the title of Golden Youth.

" Lung Nü has the title of Jade Maiden.

" Throughout perpetuity incense is to be burned right before all the members of the canonized group."

Chinese Mythology

Myths, Goddesses, and Gods from China

By Sally Stephens

If you like my book, please leave a review. I would appreciate it. Thank you!

Table of Contents

Chapter 1: The 8 Immortals 163

Chapter 2: The Guardian of the Eviction of Heaven 172

Chapter 3: Fighting amongst Themselves 181

Chapter 4: From Monkey to God 184

Chapter 5: Legendary Foxes 207

Chapter 6: The Alchemist 213

Chapter 7: The City-god of Yen Ch' êng 223

Chapter 1: The 8 Immortals

Pa Hsien

Either singly or in groups the 8 Immortals, Pa Hsien, of the Taoist religious belief are one of the most popular subjects of representation in China; their pictures are to be seen everywhere-- on porcelain vases, teapots, teacups, fans, scrolls, embroidery, and so on. Images of them are made in porcelain, earthenware, roots, wood, metals. The term 'Eight Immortals' is figuratively used for joy. The number eight has ended up being fortunate in association with this custom, and individuals or things eight in number are graced appropriately. Therefore we check out of respect shown to the '8 Genii Table' (Pa Hsien Cho), the '8 Genii Bridge' (Pa Hsien Ch' iao), '8 Genii Vermicelli' (Pa Hsien Mien), the '8 Genii of the Wine-cup' (Tin Chung Pa Hsien)-- wine-bibbers of the T'ang dynasty celebrated by Tu Fu, the poet. They are favorite subjects of love, and special things of love. In them we see "the personification of the ideas of flawless but imaginary joy which have the minds of the Chinese people." 3 of them (Chung-li Ch' üan, Chang Kuo, and Lü Yen) were historical personages; the other ones are discussed only in fables or romances. They represent all kinds of people-- old, young, male, female, civil, military, rich, poor, afflicted, cultured, noble. They are also representative of early, middle, and later historic durations.

The legend of the 8 Immortals is definitely not older than the time of the Sung dynasty (A.D. 960-- 1280) and is most likely to be appointed to that of the Yüan dynasty (1280-- 1368). But some, if not all, of the group seem to have been formerly celebrated as Immortals in the Taoist legends. Their bios are generally arranged in the order of their main eminence or seniority in age. Here I follow that adopted in Hsiu hsiang Pa Hsien tung yu chi1 in which they are defined in the order in which they ended up being Immortals.

Li T'ieh- kuai.

Li T'ieh- kuai, illustrated always with his crutch and gourd loaded with magic medicines, was of the family name of Li, his own name being Li Yüan (Hs' üan, now check out Yüan). He is also referred to as K'ung- mu. Hsi Wang Mu cured him of an ulcer on the leg and taught him the art of becoming immortal. He was canonized as Rector of the East. He is said to have been of commanding stature and dignified mien, committing himself entirely to the research study of Taoist tradition. Hsi Wang Mu made him a present of an iron crutch, and sent him to the capital to teach the teaching of immortality to Han Chung-li.

He is also identified with Li Ning-yang, to whom Lao Tzŭ descended from Paradise to instruct him in the wisdom of the gods. Right after he had finished his course of guideline his soul left his body to go on a see to Hua Shan. Some say he was summoned by Lao Tzŭ, other ones that Lao Tzŭ engaged him as escort to the nations of Hsi Yü. He left his disciple Lang Ling in charge of his body, saying that if he did not return within seven days he was to have the body cremated. Regrettably, when only 6 days had elapsed the disciple was called away to the death-bed of his mom. In order to be able to leave at the same time he cremated the body forthwith, and when the soul returned it found only a stack of ashes. Some say the body was not cremated, but only ended up being devitalized through overlook or through being unoccupied for so long a time. The thing of the setting of the watch was not only to prevent injury to or theft of the body, but also to stop any other soul from taking up its home in it.

In a forest near by a beggar had just passed away of appetite. Finding this dead body untenanted, the wandering spirit entered it through the temples, and made off. When he found that his head was long and pointed, his face black, his beard and hair woolly and dishevelled, his eyes of gigantic size, and among his legs lame, he wished to get out of this repellent body; but Lao Tzŭ advised him not to make the attempt and gave him a gold band to keep his hair in order, and an iron crutch to help his lame leg. On lifting his hand to his eyes, he found they were as large as buckles. That is why he was called Li K'ung- mu, 'Li Hollow Eyes.' Widely he is referred to as Li T'ieh- kuai, 'Li with the Iron Crutch.' No accurate period appears to be assigned to his profession on earth, though one tradition spots him in the Yüan dynasty. Another account says that he was changed into a dragon, and in that form rose to Heaven.

In other places it belongs that T'ieh- kuai, after going into the body of the lame beggar, benevolently continued to revive the mother of Yang, his negligent disciple. Leaning on his iron personnel and carrying a gourd of medications on his back he went to Yang's house, where preparations were being made for the funeral service. The contents of the gourd, put into the mouth, restored the dead lady. He then made himself known, and, giving Yang another tablet, vanished in a gust of wind. 2 a century later he effected the immortalization of his disciple.

Throughout his peregrinations on earth he would hang a bottle on the wall during the night and delve into it, emerging on the following early morning. He often went back to earth, and sometimes tried to bring about the transmigration of others.

An example is the case of Ch' ao Tu, the watchman. T'ieh- kuai walked into an intense heater and bade Ch' ao follow. The latter, being afraid of mimicing an act evidently associated with the transcendent world of evil spirits, refused to do so. T'ieh- kuai then told Ch' ao to step on to a leaf drifting on the surface of the river, saying that it was a boat that would bear him across securely. Again the watchman refused, whereupon T'ieh- kuai, remarking that the cares of this world were seemingly too weighty for him to be able to rise to immortality, stepped on to the leaf himself and vanished.

Chung-li Ch' üan.

Relating to the beginning and life of the Immortal some different accounts are given. One states that his family name was Chung-li, and that he resided in the Han dynasty, being therefore called Han Chung-li. His cognomen was Ch' üan, his literary appellation Chi Tao, and his pseudonyms Ho-ho Tzŭ and Wang-yang Tzŭ; his style Yün-fang.

He was born in the district of Hsien-yang Hsien (a sub-prefecture of the old capital Hsi-an Fu) in Shensi. He became Marshal of the Empire in the cyclic year 2496. In his old age he ended up being a hermit on Yang-chio Shan, thirty li north-east of I-ch' êng Hsien in the prefecture of

P'ing- yang Fu in Shansi. He is referred to by the title of King-emperor of the True Active Principle.

Another account defines Chung-li Ch' üan as simply a vice-marshal in the service of Duke Chou Hsiao. He was defeated in battle, and escaped to Chung-nan Shan, where he met the 5 Heroes, the Flowers of the East, who advised him in the doctrine of immortality. At the end of the T'ang dynasty Han Chung-li taught this same science of immortality to Lü Tung-pin (see p. 297), and took the pompous title of the Only Independent One Under Heaven.

Other versions specify that Han Chung-li is not the name of a person, but of a country; that he was a Taoist priest Chung Li-tzŭ; and that he was a beggar, Chung-li by name, who gave to one Lao Chih a pill of immortality. No earlier had the latter swallowed it than he went mad, left his wife, and ascended to Paradise.

During a great scarcity he transmuted copper and pewter into silver by amalgamating them with some mystical drug. This treasure he distributed among the poor, and countless lives were thus saved.

One day, while he was practicing meditation, the stone wall of his house in the mountains was lease asunder, and a jade casket exposed to view. This was found to consist of secret information regarding how to become an Immortal.

When he had followed these guidelines for some time, his room was filled with many-coloured clouds, music was heard, and a celestial stork came and bore him away on its back to the areas of immortality.

He is sometimes represented holding his feather-fan, Yü-mao Shan; at other times the peach of immortality. Since his admission to the ranks of the gods, he has appeared in the world at different times as the messenger of Heaven.

Lan Ts' ai-ho.

Lan Ts' ai-ho is otherwise specified to have been woman and an hermaphrodite. She is the strolling vocalist or mountebank of the Immortals. Generally, she plays a flute or a set of cymbals. Her origin is unidentified, but her personal name is said to have been Yang Su, and her career is appointed to the period of the T'ang dynasty. She roamed abroad outfitted in a tattered blue gown held by a black wood belt 3 inches wide, with one foot shoeless and the other shod, wearing in summer season an undergarment of wadded product, and in winter sleeping on the snow, her breath rising in a dazzling cloud like the steam from a boiling cauldron. In this guise she made her income by singing in the streets, keeping time with a wand three feet long. Though considered a lunatic, the doggerel verse she sang negated the well-known slanders. It knocked this fleeting life and its delusive satisfaction. When given cash, she either strung it on a cable and waved it to the time of her song or spread it on the ground for the poor to pick up.

One day she was found to have become intoxicated in an inn at Fêng-yang Fu in Anhui, and while in that state vanished on a cloud, having actually tossed down to earth her shoe, bathrobe, belt, and castanets.

According to common belief, however, only one of the Eight Immortals, namely, Ho Hsien-ku, was woman, Lan Ts' ai-ho being represented as a young adult of about sixteen, bearing a basket of fruit. According to the Hsiu hsiang Pa Hsien tung yu chi, he was 'the Red-footed Great Genius,' Ch' ih-chiao Ta-hsien incarnate. Though he was a man, adds the writer, he could not understand how to be a guy (which is perhaps the reason that he has been supposed to be lady).

Chang Kuo.

The duration appointed to Chang Kuo is the middle or close of the seventh to the middle of the 8th century A.D. He lived as a hermit on Chung-t' iao Shan, in the prefecture of P'ing- yang Fu in Shansi. The Emperors T'ai Tsung and Kao Tsung of the T'ang dynasty frequently welcomed him to Court, but he constantly refused to go. At last, pressed once more by the Empress Wu (A.D. 684-- 705), he consented to leave his retreat, but was struck down by death at the big gate of the Temple of the Envious Woman. His body began to decay and to be eaten by worms, when lo! he was seen again, alive and well, on the mountains of Hêng Chou in P'ing- yang Fu. He rode on a white mule, which carried him thousands of miles in a day, and which, when the journey was finished, he folded like a sheet of paper and put away in his wallet. When he again required its services, he had only to spurt water upon the packet from his mouth and the animal at once assumed its appropriate shape. At all times he carried out wonderful tasks of necromancy and announced that he had been Grand Minister to the Emperor Yao (2357-- 2255 B.C.) during a previous presence.

In the twenty-third year (A.D. 735) of the reign-period K'ai Yüan of the Emperor Hsüan Tsung of the T'ang dynasty, he was contacted us to Lo-yang in Honan, and elected Chief of the Imperial Academy, with the honourable title of Really Perspicacious Teacher.

It was just at this time that the well-known Taoist Yeh Fa-shan, thanks to his skill in necromancy, was in great favour at Court. The Emperor asked him who this Chang Kuo Lao (he normally has the epithet Lao, 'old,' contributed to his name) was. "I know," replied the magician; "but if I were to tell your Majesty I should fall dead at your feet, so I dare not speak unless your Majesty will guarantee that you will choose bare feet and bare head to ask Chang Kuo to forgive you, in which case I should instantly revive." Hsüan Tsung having actually promised, Fa-shan then said: "Chang Kuo is a white spiritual bat which came out of primeval turmoil." No faster had he spoken than he dropped dead at the Emperor's feet.

Hsüan Tsung, with bare head and feet, went to Chang Kuo as he had promised, and begged forgiveness for his indiscretion. The latter then sprayed water on Fa-shan's face and he revived. Not long after Chang fell sick and returned to die in the Hêng Chou Mountains during the period A.D. 742-- 746. When his disciples opened his burial place, they found it empty.

He is typically seen installed on his white mule, in some cases facing its head, in some cases its tail. He carries a phœnix-feather or a peach of immortality.

At his interviews with the Emperor Ming Huang in A.D. 723 (when he lived still) Chang Kuo "entertained the Emperor with a variety of magical tricks, such as rendering himself invisible, drinking off a cup of aconite, and felling birds or flowers by pointing at them. He refused the hand of a royal princess, and also decreased to have his portrait positioned in the Hall of Worthies."

An image of Chang Kuo sitting on a donkey and offering a descendant to the newlywed couple is typically found in the nuptial chamber. It seems rather incongruous that an old ascetic should be associated with matrimonial joy and the giving of offspring, but the clarification may potentially be gotten in touch with his efficiency of wonderful accomplishments of mysticism, though he is said not to have given motivation to others in these things during his lifetime.

Ho Hsien Ku
A first holding in her hand a magic lotus-blossom, the flower of open-heartedness, or the peach of immortality given her by Lü Tung-pin in the mountain-gorge as a sign of identity, playing at times the shêng or reed-organ, or drinking white wine-- this is the image the Chinese paint of the Never-ceasing Ho Hsien Ku.

She was the daughter of Ho T'ai, a native of Tsêng-ch' êng Hsien in Kuangtung. Others say her father was a storekeeper at Ling-ling in Hunan. She resided in the time of the usurping empress Wu (A.D. 684-- 705) of the T'ang dynasty. At her birth six hairs were found growing on the crown of her head, and the account says she never had any more, though the photos represent her with a full head of hair. She elected to are on Yün-mu Ling, twenty li west of Tsêng-ch' êng Hsien. On that mountain was found a stone called yün-mu shih, 'mother-of-pearl.' In a dream she saw a spirit who ordered her to powder and eat one of these stones, by doing which she could obtain both dexterity and immortality. She complied with this injunction, and also vowed herself to a life of virginity. Her days were thenceforth passed in drifting from one peak to another, bringing home in the evening to her mother the fruits she collected on the mountain. She slowly found that she had no need to eat so as to live. Her fame having reached the ears of the Empress, she was welcomed to Court, but while travelling thither unexpectedly vanished from mortal view and ended up being an Immortal. She is said to have been seen again in A.D. 750 drifting upon a cloud of a lot of colours at the temple of Ma Ku, the well-known female Taoist magician, and again, some years later, in the city of Canton.

She is represented as a very stunning maiden, and is amazing as inhabiting so popular a position in a cult in which no system of female asceticism is developed.

Lü Tung-pin
Lü Tung-pin's family name was Lü; his personal name Tung-pin; also Yen; and his pseudonym Avoid Yang Tzŭ. He was born in A.D. 798 at Yung-lo Hsien, in the prefecture of Ho-chung Fu in Shansi, a hundred and twenty li south-east of the present sub-prefecture of Yung-chi Hsien (P' u

Chou). He came of a main family, his grandfather having been President of the Ministry of Ceremonies, and his father Prefect of Hai Chou. He was 5 feet 2 inches in height, and at twenty was still not married. At this time he made a journey to Lu Shan in Kiangsi, where he met the Fire-dragon, who presented him with a magic sword, which allowed him at will to hide himself in the heavens.

During his see to the capital, Ch' ang-an in Shensi, he met the Immortal Han Chung-li, who advised him in the mysteries of alchemy and the elixir of life. When he revealed himself as Yün-fang Hsien-shêng, Lü Yen uttered an ardent desire to assist in converting mankind to the real teaching but was very first exposed to a series of ten temptations. These being successfully overcome, he was invested with superpower and magic weapons, with which he passed through the Empire, slaying dragons and ridding the earth of divers kinds of evils, throughout a period of upward of four hundred years. Another variation says that Han Chung-li was in an inn, warming a jug of rice-wine. Here Lü met him and going to sleep dreamed that he was promoted to a really high office and was incredibly favoured by fortune in every way. This had gone on for fifty years when all of a sudden, a very serious fault caused him to be condemned to exile, and his family was annihilated. Alone in the world, he was sighing bitterly, when he awoke with a start. All had occurred in so brief a space of time that Han Chung-li's red wine was not yet hot. This is the event described in Chinese literature in the expression 'rice-wine dream.' Persuaded of the hollowness of worldly self-respects, he followed Han Chung-li to the Ho Ling Mountains at Chung-nan in Shensi, where he was initiated into the magnificent secrets, and ended up being a Never-ceasing.

In A.D. 1115 the Emperor Hui Tsung gave on him the title of Hero of Marvelous Knowledge; and later he was proclaimed King-emperor and Strong Protector.

There are various versions of the legend of Lü Tung-pin. One of these adds that so as to fulfil his guarantee made to Chung-li to do what he could to help in the work of converting his fellow-creatures to the true doctrine, he went to Yüch Yang in the guise of an oil-seller, planning to celebrate all those who did not request additional weight to the amount of oil acquired. During a whole year he met only self-centered and extortionate clients, with the exception of one old woman who alone did not ask for more than was her due. So he went to her home, and seeing a well in the courtyard threw several grains of rice into it. The water amazingly turned into wine, from the sale of which the dame accumulated great wealth.

He was extremely expert in fencing, and is always represented with his magic Excalibur called Chan-yao Kuai, 'Devil-slaying Sabre,' and in one hand holds a fly-whisk, Yün-chou, or 'Cloud-sweeper,' a symbol common in Taoism of being able to fly at will through the air and to walk on the clouds of Heaven.

Like Kuan Kung, he is revealed bearing in his arms a male child-- suggesting a pledge of many children, consisting of literati and popular authorities. Consequently, he is one of the spiritual entities honoured by the literati.

Han Hsiang Tzŭ

Han Hsiang Tzŭ, who is illustrated with a bouquet of flowers or a basket of peaches of immortality, is stated to have been a grand-nephew of Han Yü (A.D. 768-- 824), the great statesman, theorist, and poet of the T'ang dynasty, and an ardent votary of transcendental study. His own name was Ch' ing Fu. The kid was delegated to his uncle to be informed and prepared for the public assessments. He excelled his instructor in intelligence and the performance of terrific feats, just like the production from a little earth in a flower-pot of some marvellous blooming plants, on the leaves of which were written in letters of gold some verses to this impact:

The clouds hide Mount Ch' in Ling.
Where is your home?
The snow is deep on Lan Kuan;
Your horse refuses to advance.

" What is the meaning of these verses?" asked Han Yü. "You will see," responded Han Hsiang Tzŭ.

Some time afterward Han Yü was sent out in disgrace to the prefecture of Ch' ao-chou Fu in Kuangtung. When he reached the foot of Lan Kuan the snow was so deep that he could not go on. Han Hsiang Tzŭ appeared, and, sweeping away the snow, made a path for him. Han Yü then understood the prediction in his pupil's verses.

When Han Hsiang Tzŭ was leaving his uncle, he gave him the following in verse:

A lot of certainly are the noteworthy men who have served their nation, but which of them surpasses you in his knowledge of literature? When you have reached a high position, you will be buried in a damp and foggy land.

Han Yü also gave his pupil a farewell verse:

How many here right below allow themselves to be inebriated by the love of honours and pelf! Alone and careful you persevere in the right course. But a time will come when, taking your flight to the sky, you will open in the heavenly blue a luminescent highway.

Han Yü was depressed at the idea of the wet climate of his place of exile. "I fear there is no doubt," he said, "that I shall die without seeing my family again."

Han Hsiang Tzŭ consoled him, gave him a prescription, and said: "Not only will you return in flawless health to the bosom of your family, but you will be reinstated in your previous offices." All this happened exactly as he had predicted.

Another account specifies that he ended up being the disciple of Lü Tung-pin, and, having actually been brought approximately the super peach-tree of the genii, fell from its branches, but during his descent obtained to the state of immortality. Still another variation says that he was killed by the fall, was transformed, and then went through the different experiences with Han Yü already associated.

Ts' ao Kuo-chiu

Ts'ao Kuo-chiu was gotten in touch with the royal family of the Sungs and is shown with the tablet of admission to Court in his hand. He became one of the Eight Immortals since the other seven, who occupied seven of the eight grottos of the Upper Spheres, wished to see the eighth occupied, and nominated him since "his disposition looked like that of a genie." The legend relates that the Empress Ts'ao, wife of the Emperor Jên Tsung (A.D. 1023-- 64), had 2 more youthful brothers. The elder of the two, Ching-hsiu, did not issue himself with the affairs of State; the younger, Ching-chih, was notorious for his misbehaviour. Despite all cautions he refused to reform and being at last guilty of murder was condemned to death. His brother, ashamed at what had taken place, went and hid in the mountains, where he clothed his head and body with wild plants, dealt with to lead the life of a hermit. One day Han Chung-li and Lü Tung-pin found him in his retreat and asked him what he was doing. "I am engaged in studying the Way," he responded. "What way, and where is it?" they asked. He pointed to the sky. "Where is the sky?" they went on. He pointed to his heart. The two visitors smiled and said: "The heart is the sky, and the sky is the Way; you understand the origin of things." They then gave him a recipe for excellence, to allow him to take his spot amongst the Perfect Ones. In several days only he had reached this much-sought-after condition.

In another version we find fuller specifics concerning this Never-ceasing. A graduate called Yüan Wên-chêng of Ch'ao-yang Hsien, in the sub-prefecture of Ch'ao-chou Fu in Kuangtung, was taking a trip with his wife to take his assessments at the capital. Ts'ao Ching-chih, the younger brother of the Empress, saw the girl, and was struck with her appeal. In order to gratify his enthusiasm he invited the graduate and his young spouse to the palace, where he strangled the spouse and tried to force the partner to cohabit with him. She refused obstinately, and as a last resort he had her put behind bars in a noisome dungeon. The soul of the graduate appeared to the imperial Censor Pao Lao-yeh, and asked him to specific vengeance for the execrable crime. The senior brother, Ching-hsiu, seeing the case put in the hands of the upright Pao Lao-yeh, and knowing his brother to be guilty of murder, advised him to put the female to death, so as to cut off all sources of information and so to prevent more proceedings. The young voluptuary thereupon caused the lady to be thrown down a deep well, but the star T'ai-po Chin-hsing, in the form of an old man, drew her out again. While making her escape, she met on the road a main procession which she mistook for that of Pao Lao-yeh, and, going up to the sedan chair, made her accusation. This authority was no other than the older brother of the killer. Ching-hsiu, terrified, attempted not contradict the charge, but on the pretext that the lady had not placed herself respectfully by the side of the official chair, and hence had not left a way clear for the passage of his retinue, he had her beaten with iron-spiked whips, and she was cast away for dead in a neighboring lane. This time also she revived and went to inform Pao Lao-yeh. The latter immediately had Ts'ao Ching-hsiu apprehended, cangued, and fettered. Without loss of time he wrote an invitation to the 2nd brother, Ts'ao Ching-chih, and on his arrival faced him with the graduate's partner, who implicated him to his face. Pao Lao-yeh had him put in a pit, and remained deaf to all entreaties of the Emperor and Empress on his behalf. A few days later the killer was taken to the place of execution, and his head rolled in the dust. The problem now was how to get Ts'ao Ching-hsiu out of the hands of the horrible Censor. The Emperor Jên Tsung, to please the Empress, had a universal amnesty proclaimed throughout the Empire, under which all prisoners were set free. On invoice of the edict, Pao Lao-yeh freed Ts'ao Ching-hsiu from the cangue and enabled him to go free. As one increased from the dead, he gave himself approximately the practice of excellence, ended up being a hermit, and, through the guideline of the Perfect Ones, turned into one of the 8 Immortals.

Pa Hsien Kuo Hai

The phrase Pa Hsien kuo hai, 'the Eight Immortals crossing the sea,' describes the legend of an exploration made by these deities. Their thing was to witness the fascinating things of the sea not to be found in the celestial sphere.

The typical mode of celestial mobility-- by taking a seat on a cloud-- was discarded at the suggestion of Lü Yen who suggested that they should show the limitless range of their skills by putting things on the surface of the sea and stepping on them.

Li T'ieh- kuai threw down his crutch, and scudded rapidly over the waves. Chung-li Ch' üa used his feather-fan, Chang Kuo his paper mule, Lü Tung-pin his sword, Han Hsiang Tzŭ his flower-basket, Ho Hsien Ku her lotus-flower, Lan Ts' ai-ho his musical instrument, and Ts' ao Kuo-chiu his tablet of admission to Court. The well-known pictures usually represent the majority of these short articles turned into numerous kinds of sea-monsters. The musical instrument was discovered by the child of the Dragon-king of the Eastern Sea. This avaricious prince conceived the idea of taking the instrument and imprisoning its owner. The Immortals thereupon announced war, the details of which are described at length by the Chinese writers, the result being that the Dragon-king was absolutely defeated. After this the Eight Immortals continued their submarine exploits for an indefinite time, experiencing numberless adventures; but here the author takes a trip far into the fertile region of romance, beyond the frontiers of our present province.

Chapter 2: The Guardian of the Eviction of Heaven

Li, the Pagoda-bearer
In Buddhist temples there is to be seen a highly attired figure of a man holding in his hand a model of a pagoda. He is Li, the Prime Minister of Heaven and dad of No-cha.

He was a general under the autocrat Chou and leader of Ch' ên-t' ang Kuan at the time when the bloody war was being waged which resulted in the extinction of the Yin dynasty.

No-cha is just one of the most frequently pointed out heroes in Chinese romance; he is represented in one account as being Yü Huang's shield-bearer, sixty feet in height, his three heads with nine eyes crowned by a golden wheel, his 8 hands each holding a magic weapon, and his mouth throwing up blue clouds. At the sound of his Voice, we are told, the heavens shook, and the foundations of the earth shivered. His duty was to bring into submission all the satanic forces which desolated the world.

His birth was in this smart. Li Ching's wife, Yin Shih, bore him 3 sons, the oldest Chin-cha, the 2nd Mu-cha, and the 3rd No-cha, typically referred to as 'the Third Prince.'

Yin Shih dreamed one night that a Taoist priest entered her room. She indignantly exclaimed: "How dare you enter my room in this hasty manner?" The priest responded: "Female, get the kid of the unicorn!" Before she could respond the Taoist pushed a challenge her bosom.

Yin Shih awoke in a shock, a cold sweat all over her body. Having awakened her partner, she told him what she had dreamed. At that moment she was taken with the discomforts of childbirth. Li Ching withdrew to an adjacent room, anxious at what appeared to be inauspicious omens. A little later two servants ran to him, crying out: "Your wife has given birth to a monstrous freak!"

An Avatar of the Intelligent Pearl
Li Ching took his sword and entered into his wife's room, which he found filled with a traffic signal breathing out a most amazing smell. A ball of flesh was rolling on the floor like a wheel; with a blow of his sword he cut it open, and a babe appeard, surrounded by a halo of red light. Its face was very white, a gold bracelet was on its right wrist, and it wore a set of red silk trousers, from which continued rays of spectacular golden light. The bracelet was 'the horizon of Heaven and earth,' and the two precious items belonged to the cavern Chin-kuang Tung of T'ai- i Chên-jên, the priest who had bestowed them upon him when he appeared to his mother throughout her sleep. The kid itself was an avatar of Ling Chu-tzŭ, 'the Intelligent Pearl.'

On the morrow T'ai- i Chên-jên returned and asked Li Ching's consent to see the new-born babe. "He shall be called No-cha," he said, "and will become my disciple."

A Precocious Youth

At seven years of age No-cha was already six feet in height. One day he asked his mom if he might choose a walk outside the town. His mother granted him authorization on condition that he was joined by a servant. She also counselled him not to stay too long outside the wall, lest his dad must become anxious.

It was in the fifth moon: the heat was excessive. No-cha had not gone a li right before he was in a profuse sweating. Some way ahead he saw a clump of trees, to which he sped up, and, settling himself in the shade, opened his coat, and breathed with relief the fresher air. In front of him he saw a stream of limpid green water running between two rows of willows, carefully upset by the movement of the wind, and streaming round a rock. The child went to the banks of the stream, and said to his defender: "I am covered with perspiration, and will bathe from the rock." "Be quick," said the servant; "if your father returns home right before you he will be anxious." No-cha stripped himself, took his red silk trousers, several feet long, and dipped them in the water, meaning to use them as a towel. No sooner were the magic pants immersed in the stream than the water began to boil, and Heaven and earth trembled. The water of the river, the Chiu-wan Ho, 'Nine-bends River,' which communicated with the Eastern Sea, turned completely red, and Lung Wang's palace shook to its structures. The Dragon-king, surprised at seeing the walls of his crystal palace shaking, called his officers and inquired: "How is it that the palace threatens to collapse? There should not be an earthquake at this time." He ordered among his attendants to address once and discover what evil was triggering the turmoil. When the officer reached the river he saw that the water was red, but discovered nothing else except a boy dipping a band of silk in the stream. He cleft the water and called out angrily: "That kid ought to be tossed into the water for making the river red and causing Lung Wang's palace to shake."

" Who is that who speaks so brutally?" said No-cha. Then, seeing that the man meant to take him, he leapt aside, took his gold bracelet, and tossed it in the air. It fell on the head of the officer, and No-cha left him dead on the rock. Then he picked up his bracelet and said smiling: "His blood has stained my precious horizon of Paradise and earth." He then cleaned it in the water.

The Slaying of the Dragon-king's Child

" How is it that the officer does not return?" asked Lung Wang. At that moment attendants came to notify him that his retainer had been murdered by a kid.

Thereupon Ao Ping, the third child of Lung Wang, putting himself at the head of a troop of marines, his spear in his hand, left the palace precincts. The warriors dashed into the river, raising on every side waves mountains high. Seeing the water rising up, No-cha stood on the rock and was confronted by Ao Ping installed on a sea-monster.

" Who slew my messenger?" wept the warrior.

" I did," answered No-cha.

" Who are you?" demanded Ao Ping.

" I am No-cha, the third son of Li Ching of Ch' ên-t' ang Kuan. I came here to shower and revitalize myself; your messenger cursed me, and I killed him. Then--".

" Rascal! do you not know that your victim was a deputy of the King of Paradise? How dare you kill him, and after that boast of your criminal activity?"

So saying, Ao Ping thrust at the boy with his trident. No-cha, by a brisk relocation, averted the thrust.

" Who are you?" he asked in turn.

" I am Ao Ping, the third son of Lung Wang."

" Ah, you are a blusterer," mocked the boy; "if you dare to touch me I will skin you alive, you and your mud-eels!"

" You make me choke with rage," rejoined Ao Ping, at the exact same time thrusting again with his spear.

Furious at this renewed attack, No-cha spread his silk trousers in the air, and countless balls of fire flew out of them, felling Lung Wang's son. No-cha put his foot on Ao Ping's head and struck it with his magic bracelet, whereupon he appeared in his real form of a dragon.

" I am now going to pull out your sinews," he said, "in order to make a belt for my dad to use to bind on his cuirass."

No-cha was as good as his word, and Ao Ping's escort ran and informed Lung Wang of the fate of his child. The Dragon-king went to Li Ching and demanded a description.

Being totally oblivious of what had happened, Li Ching sought No-cha to question him.

A Rowdy Son

No-cha was in the garden, occupied in weaving the belt of dragon-sinew. The stupefaction of Li Ching might be imagined. "You have brought most dreadful miseries upon us," he exclaimed. "Come and give an account of your conduct." "Have no fear," replied No-cha superciliously; "his son's sinews are still undamaged; I will provide back to him if he wants."

When they went into the house, he saluted the Dragon-king, made a curt apology, and offered to return his son's sinews. The dad, moved with grief at the sight of the proofs of the tragedy, said bitterly to Li Ching: " You have such a child and yet dare to deny his guilt, though you heard him haughtily confessing! To-morrow I shall report the matter to Yü Huang." Having actually spoken hence, he left.

Li Ching was overwhelmed at the enormity of his child's criminal offense. His spouse, in an adjoining room, hearing his lamentations, went to her husband. "What obnoxious being is this that you have brought into the world?" he said to her madly. "He has killed two spirits, the son of Lung Wang and a steward sent out by the King of Paradise. To-morrow the Dragon-king is to lodge a problem with Yü Huang, and 2 or 3 days for this reason will see the end of our presence."

The poor mother began to weep copiously. "What!" she sobbed, "you whom I suffered so much for, you are to be the reason for our destroy and death!"

No-cha, seeing his mom and dad so sidetracked, fell on his knees. "Let me tell you once for all," he said, "that I am no common mortal. I am the disciple of T'ai- i Chên-jên; my magic weapons I received from him; it is they which brought upon me the undying hatred of Lung Wang. But he cannot dominate. To-day I will go and ask my master's guidance. The guilty alone should suffer the charge; it is unjustified that his parents should suffer in his stead."

Drastic Procedures

He then left for Ch' ien-yüan Shan and got in the cave of his master T'ai- i Chên-jên, to whom he related his experiences. The master dwelt upon the grave effects of the murders, and then ordered No-cha to bare his breast. With his finger he drew on the skin a magic formula, after which he gave him some secret instructions. "Now," he said, "go to the big gate of Heaven and wait for the arrival of Lung Wang, who functions to implicate you right before Yü Huang. Then you need to return to consult me, that your father and mother may not be molested just because of your misdeeds."

When No-cha reached the gate of Paradise it was closed. Fruitless he sought for Lung Wang, but after a while he saw him approaching. Lung Wang did not see No-cha, for the formula written by T'ai- i Chên-jên rendered him invisible. As Lung Wang approached the large gate No-cha ran up to him and struck him so hard a blow with his golden bracelet that he fell down to the ground. Then No-cha marked on him, cursing him vehemently.

The Dragon-king now acknowledged his assailant and dramatically reproached him with his crimes, but the only reparation he got was a renewal of kicks and blows. Then, partially raising Lung Wang's cape and raising his shield, No-cha detached from his body about forty scales. Blood flowed copiously, and the Dragon-king, under tension of the pain, asked his enemy to spare his life. To this No-cha consented on condition that he relinquished his purpose of implicating him right before Yü Huang.

" Now," went on No-cha, "change yourself into a little serpent that I might take you back without fear of your leaving."

Lung Wang took the form of a little blue dragon, and followed No-cha to his dad's house, upon getting in which Lung Wang resumed his normal form, and accused No-cha of having belaboured him. "I will choose all the Dragon-kings and lay an accusation right before Yü Huang," he said. Thereupon he changed himself into a gust of wind, and disappeared.

No-cha draws a Bow at an Endeavor

" Things are going from bad to even worse," sighed Li Ching, His son, though, consoled him: "I beg you, my dad, not to let the future trouble you. I am the chosen one of the gods. My master is T'ai- i Chên-jên, and he has guaranteed me that he can easily protect us."

No-cha now went out and ascended a tower which commanded a view of the entrance of the fort. There he found a wonderful bow and three magic arrows. No-cha did not know that this was the spiritual weapon belonging to the fort. "My master notified me that I am predestined to combat to establish the coming Chou dynasty; I ought therefore to flawless myself in using weapons. This is a great chance." He accordingly seized the bow and shot an arrow towards the south-west. A red path showed the course of the arrow, which hissed as it flew. At that moment Pi Yün, a servant of Shih-chi Niang-niang, happened to be at the foot of K' u-lou Shan (Skeleton Hill), in front of the cave of his mistress. The arrow pierced his throat, and he fell dead, bathed in his blood. Shih-chi Niang-niang came out of her cavern, and analyzing the arrow found that it bore the engraving: "Arrow which shakes the paradises." She thus knew that it must have originated from Ch' ên-t' ang Kuan, where the magic bow was kept.

Another Encounter

The goddess mounted her blue phœnix, flew over the fort, seized Li Ching, and brought him to her cavern. There she made him kneel before her, and reminded him how she had safeguarded him that he might gain honour and glory in the world right before he obtained to immortality." It is therefore that you show your gratitude-- by killing my servant!"

Li Ching swore that he was innocent; but the tell-tale arrow was there, and it could not but have come from the fortress. Li Ching pled the goddess to set him at liberty, in order that he might find the offender and bring him to her. "If I cannot find him," he added, "you might take my life."

Once again No-cha honestly admitted his deed to his dad, and followed him to the cave of Shih-chi Niang-niang. When he reached the entrance the second servant reproached him with the criminal offense, whereupon No-cha struck him a heavy blow. Shih-chi Niang-niang, exasperated, tossed herself at No-cha, sword in hand; one after the other she wrenched from him his bracelet and magic pants.

Deprived of his magic weapons, No-cha fled to his master, T'ai- i Chên-jên. The goddess followed and required that he be put to death. A terrible dispute occurred between the two champs, until T'ai- i Chên-jên tossed into the air his world of nine fire-dragons, which, falling on Shih-chi Niang-niang, covered her in a whirlwind of flame. When this had passed it was seen that she was changed into stone.

" Now you are safe," said T'ai- i Chên-jên to No-cha, "but return rapidly, for the 4 Dragon-kings have laid their allegation before Yü Huang, and they are going to carry off your mom and dad. Follow my guidance, and you will save your parents from their misfortune."

No-cha commits Hara-Kiri

On his return No-cha found the 4 Dragon-kings on the point of carrying off his mother and father. "It is I," he said, "who killed Ao Ping, and I who should pay the charge. Why are you molesting my father and mother? I will return to them what I received from them. Will it please you?"

Lung Wang agreed, whereupon No-cha took a sword, and right before their eyes cut off an arm, sliced open his stomach, and fell unconscious. His soul, borne on the wind, went straight to the cavern of T'ai- i Chên-jên, while his mom busied herself with burying his body.

" Your home is not here," said his master to him; "go back to Ch' ên-t' ang Kuan, and ask your mom to build a temple on Ts' ui-p' ing Shan, forty li farther on. Incense will be burned to you for three years; at the end of which time you will be reincarnated."

A Habitation for the Soul

Throughout the night, towards the 3rd watch, while his mom was in a deep sleep, No-cha appeared to her in a dream and said: "My mom, pity me; since my death, my soul, separated from my body, wanders about without a house. Build me, I pray you, a temple on Ts' ui-p' ing Shan, that I may be reincarnated." His mom awoke in tears, and associated her vision to Li Ching, who reproached her for her blind attachment to her abnormal son, the cause of so much disaster.

For five or 6 nights the child appeared to his mom, each time repeating his demand. The last time he added: "Do not forget that by nature I am ferocious; if you refuse my request evil will befall you."

His mother then sent out contractors to the mountain to construct a temple to No-cha, and his image was established in it. Miracles were not wanting, and the number of pilgrims who went to the shrine increased daily.

Li Ching ruins his Child's Statue

One day Li Ching, with a troop of his soldiers, was passing this mountain, and saw the roadways crowded with pilgrims of both sexes. "Where are these people going?" he asked. "For 6 months past," he was told, "the spirit of the temple on this mountain has went on to perform miracles. Individuals originate from far and near to worship and supplicate him."

" What is the name of this spirit?" asked Li Ching.

" No-cha," they responded.

" No-cha!" exclaimed the father. "I will go and see him myself."

In a rage Li Ching went into the temple and examined the statue, which was a speaking image of his child. By its side were images of 2 of his servants. He took his whip and began to beat the statue, cursing everything the while. "It is not enough, apparently, for you to have been a source of catastrophe to us," he said; "but even after your death you must trick the wide variety." He whipped the statue until it fell to pieces; he then kicked over the images of the servants, and went back, advising the people not to worship so wicked a man, the pity and destroy of his family. By his orders the temple was scorched to the ground.

When he reached Ch' ên-t' ang Kuan his spouse came to him, but he received her coldly. "You brought to life that cursed child," he said, "who has been the plague disease of our lives, and after his death you build him a temple in which he tricks the people. Do you wish to have me disgraced? If I were to be accused at Court of having set up the worship of false gods, would not my damage be certain? I have burned the temple, and mean that shall settle the matter once for all; if ever you think of restoring it I will break off all relations with you."

No-cha consults his Master

At the time of his father's check out No-cha was absent from the temple. On his return he found only its smoking residues. The spirits of his two servants ran up regretting. "Who has destroyed my temple?" he asked. "Li Ching," they responded. "In doing this he has exceeded his powers," said No-cha. "I gave him back the substance I got from him; why did he come with violence to break up my image? I will have absolutely nothing more to do with him."

No-cha's soul had already started to be spiritualised. So he determined to go to T'ai- i Chên-jên and ask for his assistance. "The worship rendered to you there," responded the Taoist, "had absolutely nothing in it which should have offended your dad; it did not concern him. He was in the wrong. Before long Chiang Tzŭ-ya will descend to inaugurate the new dynasty, and since you must throw in your lot with him I will find a way to help you."

A New No-cha

T'ai- i Chên-jên had two water-lily stalks and three lotus-leaves gave him. He spread these on the ground in the form of a human and put the soul of No-cha in this lotus skeleton, uttering magic necromancies the while. There arised a new No-cha full of life, with a fresh skin tone, purple lips, keen glance, and sixteen feet of height. "Follow me to my peach-garden," said T'ai- i Chên-jên, "and I will give you your weapons." He handed him an intense spear, extremely sharp, and 2 wind-and-fire wheels which, placed under his feet, acted as a Car. A brick of gold in a panther-skin bag completed his magic armament. The new warrior, after thanking his master, mounted his wind-and-fire wheels and went back to Ch' ên-t' ang Kuan.

A Fight between Father and Child

Li Ching was informed that his child No-cha had returned and was threatening revenge. So he took his weapons, mounted his horse, and went forth to meet him. Having actually cursed each other profusely, they joined battle, but Li Ching was worsted and forced to get away. No-cha chased after his dad, but as he was on the point of overtaking him Li Ching's 2nd son, Mu-cha, emerged, and acutely reproached his brother for his unfilial conduct.

" Li Ching is no longer my dad," responded No-cha. "I gave him back my compound; why did he burn my temple and smash up my image?"

Mu-cha thereupon prepared to defend his dad, but got on his back a blow from the golden brick, and fell unconscious. No-cha then resumed his pursuit of Li Ching.

His strength exhausted, and in danger of falling into the hands of his opponent, Li Ching drew his sword and was going to kill himself. "Stop!" cried a Taoist priest. "Come into my cavern, and I will secure you."

When No-cha showed up he could not see Li Ching and required his surrender from the Taoist. But he had to do with one stronger than himself, no less a being than Wên-chu T'ien- tsun, whom T'ai- i Chên-jên had sent out in order that No-cha might receive a lesson. The Taoist, with the help of his magic weapon, seized No-cha, and in a minute, he found a gold ring secured round his neck, two chains on his feet, and he was bound to a pillar of gold.

Peace at the Last

At this moment, just as if by mishap, T'ai-i Chên-jên appeared upon the scene. His master had No-cha brought before Wên-chu T'ien-tsun and Li Ching and advised him to live at peace with his dad, but he also rebuked the dad for having burned the temple on Ts'ui-p'ing Shan. This done, he ordered Li Ching to go home, and No-cha to go back to his cavern. The latter, overflowing with anger, his heart full of revenge, started again in pursuit of Li Ching, swearing that he would penalize him. However, the Taoist came back and prepared to safeguard Li Ching.

No-cha, bristling like a savage cat, tossed himself at his opponent and tried to pierce him with his spear, but a white lotus-flower arose from the Taoist's mouth and jailed the course of the weapon. As No-cha went on to threaten him, the Taoist drew from his sleeve a mystical thing which rose in the air, and, falling at the feet of No-cha, covered him in flames. Then No-cha wished mercy. The Taoist exacted from him three different promises: to live in consistency with his father, to acknowledge and address him as his dad, and to toss himself at his, the Taoist's, feet, to suggest his reconciliation with himself.

After this act of reconciliation had been carried out, Wên-chu T'ien-tsun promised Li Ching that he should leave his main post to become an Immortal able to place his services at the disposal of the brand-new Chou dynasty, shortly to come into power. In order to guarantee that their reconciliation should last for ever, and to position it beyond No-cha's power to seek vengeance, he gave Li Ching the fantastic object by whose firm No-cha's feet had been burned, and which had been the means of bringing him into subjection. It was a golden pagoda, which became the particular weapon of Li Ching, and gave rise to his label, Li the Pagoda-bearer. Finally, Yü Huang appointed him Generalissimo of the Twenty-six Celestial Officers, Grand Marshal of the Skies, and Guardian of the Gate of Paradise.

Chapter 3: Fighting amongst Themselves

Multifarious Versatile Divinities

The Fêng shên yen i defines at length how, during the wars which preceded the accession of the Chou dynasty in 1122 B.C., a multitude of demigods, Buddhas, Immortals, and so on, took part on one side or the other, some defending the old, some for the new dynasty. They were wonderful creatures, talented with wonderful powers. They could at will change their form, multiply their heads and limbs, become undetectable, and produce, by merely uttering a word, awful beasts who bit and ruined, or sent out forth toxin gases, or given off flames from their nostrils. In these battles there is much lightning, thunder, flight of fire-dragons, dark clouds which throw up burning hails of murderous weapons; swords, spears, and arrows fall from the sky on to the heads of the combatants; the earth shivers, the pillars of Heaven shake.

Chun T' i.

One of these gifted warriors was Chun T' i, a Taoist of the Western Paradise, who appeared on the scene when the armies of the competing dynasties were facing each other. K'ung Hsüan was gallantly holding the pass of the Chin-chi Ling; Chiang Tzŭ-ya was attempting to take it by attack-- up until now without success.

Chun T' i's mission was to take K'ung Hsüan to the home of the blest, his knowledge and general development having now reached the required degree of excellence. This was a means of breaking down the invincible resistance of this powerful opponent and at the same time of rewarding his dazzling talents.

However, K'ung Hsüan did not authorize of this strategy, and a fight happened between the two champions. At one moment Chun T' i was seized by a luminous bow and carried into the air, but while covered in a cloud of fire he appeared with eighteen arms and twenty-four heads, holding in each hand a powerful talisman.

The One-eyed Peacock.

He put a silk cord round K'ung Hsüan's neck, touched him with his wand, and pushed him to reassume his initial form of a red one-eyed peacock. Chun T' i seated himself on the peacock's back, and it flew across the sky, bearing its saviour and master to the Western Paradise. Brilliantly variegated clouds marked its track through space.

Arrangements for the Siege.

On the disappearance of its protector the defile of Chin-chi Ling was captured, and the town of Chieh-p' ai Kuan, the bulwark of the opponent's forces, reached. This spot was safeguarded by a host of genii and Immortals, the most prominent among them being the Taoist T'ung- t' ien Chiao-chu, whose specifically efficient appeals had so far kept the fort protect against every attempt upon it.

Lao Tzŭ himself had deigned to come down from dwelling in happiness, together with Yüan-shih T'ien- tsun and Chieh-yin Tao-jên, to take part in the siege. But the town had four gates, and these incredible rulers were only 3 in number. So Chun T' i was recalled, and each member of the quartette was entrusted with the job of recording one of the gates.

Impediments.
Chun T' i's duty was to take the Chüeh-hsien Mên, safeguarded by T'ung- t' ien Chiao-chu. The warriors who had tried to enter the town by this gate had one and all paid for their temerity with their lives. The moment each had crossed the limit a clap of thunder had resounded, and a mysterious sword, moving with lightning rapidity, had slain him.

Offence and Defence.
As Chun T' i advanced at the head of his warriors terrible lightning rent the air and the mysterious sword came down like a thunderbolt upon his head. But Chun T' i held on high his Seven-precious Branch, whereupon there appeard from it countless lotus-flowers, which formed an impenetrable covering and stopped the sword in its fall. This and the other gates were then pushed, and a grand assault was now directed against the chief protector of the town.

T'ung- t' ien Chiao-chu, riding his ox and surrounded by his warriors, for the last time risked the chance of war and bravely faced his four horrible adversaries. With his sword held aloft, he tossed himself on Chieh-yin Tao-jên, whose only weapon was his fly-whisk. But there show upd from this a five-coloured lotus-flower, which stopped the sword-thrust. While Lao Tzŭ struck the hero with his personnel, Yüan-shih T'ien- tsun warded off the dreadful sword with his jade ju-i.

Chun T' i now called to his help the spiritual peacock and took the form of a warrior with twenty-four heads and eighteen arms. His mystical weapons surrounded T'ung- t' ien Chiao-chu, and Lao Tzŭ struck the hero so hard that fire came out from his eyes, nose, and mouth. Unable to parry the assaults of his foes, he next received a blow from Chun T' i's magic wand, which felled him, and he took flight in a whirlwind of dust.

The defenders now offered no further resistance, and Yüan-shih T'ien- tsun thanked Chun T' i for the valuable assistance he had rendered in the capture of the village, after which the gods went back to their palace in the Western Heaven.

Attempts at Revenge.
T'ung- t' ien Chiao-chu, overcome and routed, testified have his revenge. He called to his aid the spirits of the twenty-eight constellations and marched to assault Wu Wang's army. The honour of the success that ensued come from Chun T' i, who disarmed both the Immortal Wu Yün and T'ung- t' ien Chiao-chu.

Wu Yün, armed with his magic sword, entered the lists against Chun T' i; but the latter opened his mouth and a blue lotus-flower came out and stopped the blows targeted at him. Other thrusts were met by similar miracles.

" Why continue so useless a fight?" said Chun T' i at last. "Desert the reason for the Shang, and come with me to the Western Paradise. I came to save you, and you should not oblige me to make you resume your initial form."

An insulting flow of words was the reply; again the magic sword came down like lightning, and again the stroke was avoided by a timely lotus-flower. Chun T' i now waved his wand, and the magic sword was broken to bits, the deal with only staying in Wu Yün's hand.

The Golden-bearded Turtle.
Mad with rage, Wu Yün took his club and tried to fell his enemy. But Chun T' i summoned a disciple, who appeared with a bamboo pole. This he thrust out like a fishing-rod, and on a hook at the end of the line connected to the pole dangled a big golden-bearded turtle. This was the Immortal Wu Yün, now in his original form of a spiritual turtle. The disciple seated himself on its back, and both, disappearing into space, went back to the Western Heavens.

The Fight Won.
To dominate T'ung- t' ien Chiao-chu was harder, but after a long fight Chun T' i waved his Wand of the 7 Treasures and broke his adversary's sword. The latter, disarmed and beat, disappeared in a cloud of dust. Chun T' i did not trouble to go after him. The battle was won.

Buddhahood.
A disciple of T'ung- t' ien Chiao-chu, P' i-lu Hsien, 'the Immortal P' i-lu,' seeing his master beaten in 2 succeeding engagements, left the battlefield and followed Chun T' i to the Western Paradise, to become a Buddha. He is referred to as P' i-lu Fo, one of the primary gods of Buddhism.

Chun T' i's celebration is celebrated on the sixth day of the 3rd moon. He is usually revealed with 8 hands and three faces, one of the latter being that of a pig.

Chapter 4: From Monkey to God

The Hsi Yu Chi

In handling the gods of China, we discovered the monkey among them. Why and in what way he obtained to that exalted rank is stated in detail in the Hsi yu chi1-- a work the contents of which have ended up being woven into the fabric of Chinese legendary lore and are known and really loved by every intelligent native. Its pages are filled with ghosts, devils, and fairies, great and bad, but "it contains no greater than the average Chinese really believes to exist, and his belief in such manifestations is so firm that from the cradle to the grave he lives and moves and has his being in with reference to them." Its characters are said to be allegorical, though it may be questioned whether these implications might appropriately read into the Chinese text. Therefore:

Hsüan (or Yüan) Chuang, or T'ang Sêng, is the pilgrim of the Hsi yu chi, who symbolizes conscience, to which all actions are brought for trial. The priestly garment of Hsüan Chuang symbolizes the good work of the corrected human nature. It is held to be a great protection to the new heart from the multitudes of wicked beings which surround it, seeking its damage.

Sun Hou-tzŭ, the Monkey Fairy, represents humanity, which is vulnerable to all evil. His unreasonable vagaries moved Hsüan Chuang to compel him to wear a Head-splitting Helmet which would contract upon his head in moment of waywardness. The painful pressure thus triggered would bring him to his senses, irrespective of his distance from his master.

The iron wand of Sun Hou-tzŭ is said to represent the use that can be made of doctrine. It was useful for all functions, great or small. By a word it could be made undetectable, and by a word it could become long enough to cover the distance between Paradise and earth.

Chu Pa-chieh, the Pig Fairy, with his muck-rake, stands for the coarser enthusiasms, which are continuously at war with the conscience in their endeavours to cast off all restraint.

Sha Ho-shang, Priest Sha, is a very good likeness of Mr Faithful in The Pilgrim's Progress. In the Hsi yu chi he means the human character, which is naturally weak, and which needs continuous motivation.

Legend of Sun Hou-tzŭ

The deeds of this wonderful being, the hero of the Hsi yu chi, are to be met with constantly in Chinese popular literature, and they are very much alive in the well-known mind. In certain parts a routine praise is offered to him, and in lots of temples likenesss of or legends concerning him are to be seen or heard.

Other names by which Sun Hou-tzŭ is described are: Sun Hsing-chê, Sun Wu-k' ung, Mei Hou-wang, Ch' i-t' ien Ta Shêng, and Pi-ma Wên, the last-mentioned being a title which triggered him annoyance by recalling the derisive self-respect conferred upon him by Yü Huang.2 Throughout the rest of this chapter Sun Hou-tzŭ will be shortly referred to as 'Sun.'.

Beyond the seas, in the Eastern continent, in the kingdom of Ao-lai, is the mountain Hua-kuo Shan. On the high sides of this mountain there is a rocky point 36 feet 5 inches high and 24 feet in area. At the extremely top an egg formed, and, fructified by the breath of the wind, gave birth to a stone monkey. The newly born saluted the four points of the horizon; from his eyes shone golden streaks of lightning, which filled the palace of the North Pole Star with light. This light diminished as soon as he was able to take nourishment.

" To-day," said Yü Huang to himself, "I am going to complete the wonderful variety of the beings engendered by Paradise and earth. This monkey will skip and gambol to the greatest peaks of mountains, leap about in the waters, and, eating the fruit of the trees, will be the companion of the gibbon and the crane. Like the deer he will pass his nights on the mountain slopes, and throughout the day will be seen leaping on their summits or in their caverns. That will be the finest accessory of all for the mountains!"

The creature's exploits quickly triggered him to be proclaimed king of the monkeys. He then began to try to find some methods of ending up being immortal. After taking a trip for eighteen years by land and sea he met the Immortal P' u-t' i Tsu-shih on the mountain Ling-t' ai-fang-ts' un. Throughout his travels the monkey had slowly obtained human characteristics; his face stayed always as it had been originally but dressed in human apparel he began to be civilized. His brand-new master gave him the family name of Sun, and personal name of Wu-k' ung, 'Originator of Tricks.' He taught him how to fly through the air, and to change into seventy-two different forms. With one leap he could cover 108,000 li (about 36,000 miles).

A Rod of Iron

Sun, after his return to Hua-kuo Shan, multitude the satanic force Hun-shih Mo-wang, who had been molesting the monkeys during his long lack. Then he organized his subjects into a regular army, 47,000 all told. Hence the peace of the simian kingdom was assured. When it comes to himself, he could not find a weapon to suit him, and went to speak with Ao Kuang, the Lung Wang, or Dragon-king of the Eastern Sea, about it. It was from him that he obtained the formidable rod of iron, previously planted in the ocean-bed by the Great Yü (Yü Wang) to regulate the level of the waters. He pulled it out, and customized it to suit his tastes. The two extremities he bound round with gold bands, and on it engraved the words: 'Gold-bound Wand of my Desires.' This magic weapon could accommodate itself to all his desires; being able to assume the most extraordinary proportions or to decrease itself to the form of the finest of needles, which he kept hidden in his ear. He terrified the Four Kings of the sea, and dressed himself at their cost. The neighbouring kings allied themselves with him. A splendid banquet with copious libations of red wine sealed the alliance of friendship with the seven kings; but alas! Sun had taken part so freely that when he was seeing his visitors off, no faster had he taken several steps than he fell straight into an inebriated sleep. The undertakers of Yen Wang, the King of the Hells, to whom Lung Wang had accused him as the disturber of his watery kingdom, seized his soul, put chains round its neck, and led it down to the infernal areas. Sun woke up in front of the large gate of the kingdom of the dead, broke his fetters, killed his two custodians, and, equipped with his magic personnel, permeated into the realm of Yen Wang, where he threatened to carry out general damage. He contacted us to the 10 infernal gods to bring him the Register of the Living and the Dead, removed with his own hand the page on which were written his name and those of his monkey subjects, and then told the King of the Hells that he was no longer subject to the laws of death. Yen Wang yielded, though with bad grace, and Sun returned victorious from his expedition beyond the burial place.

Eventually Sun's adventures came to the knowledge of Yü Huang. Ao Kuang and Yen Wang each sent deputies to the Master of Paradise, who bore in mind of the double accusation, and sent out T'ai- po Chin-hsing to summon before him this disturber of the incredible peace.

Grand Master of the Heavenly Stables
In order to keep him occupied, Sun was selected Grand Master of the Heavenly Stables, and was entrusted with the feeding of Yü Huang's horses; his official celestial title being Pi-ma Wên. In the future, learning the item of the creation of this derisory appointment, he reversed the Master's throne, took his personnel, broke down the South Gate of Paradise, and descended on a cloud to Hua-kuo Shan.

Grand Superintendent of the Heavenly Peach-garden
Yü Huang in great indignation organized a siege of Hua-kuo Shan, but the Kings of Paradise and the generals with their celestial armies were repulsed some times. Sun now arrogated to himself the pompous title of Grand Saint, Governor of Paradise. He had this emblazoned on his banners, and threatened Yü Huang that he would carry destruction into his kingdom if he refused to recognize his brand-new dignity. Yü Huang, alarmed at the result of the military operations, consented to the condition put down by Sun. The latter was then designated Grand Superintendent of the Incredible Peach-garden, the fruit of which provided immortality, and a new palace was built for him.

Double Immortality
Having actually made minute observations on the secret properties of the peaches, Sun ate of them and was therefore assured against death. The time was ripe for him to delight in his tricks without restraint, and an opportunity quickly presented itself. Deeply hurt at not having actually been invited to the feast of the Peach Festival, P'an- t' ao Hui, given occasionally to the Immortals by Wang-mu Niang-niang, the Goddess of the Immortals, he dealt with upon revenge. When the preparations for the feast were complete, he cast a spell over the servants, causing them to fall into a deep sleep, and after that ate up all the most juicy meats and drank the great wines provided for the heavenly guests. Sun had, though, indulged himself too liberally; with heavy head and bleary eye he missed the road back to his incredible home, and came unaware to the large gate of Lao Chün, who was, however, missing from his palace. It was only a matter of a few minutes for Sun to enter and swallow the pills of immortality which Lao Chün kept in 5 gourds. Thus Sun, twice as immortal, riding on the mist, again descended to Hua-kuo Shan.

Sun Hou-tzŭ Captured

These numerous misbehaviours excited the indignation of all the gods and goddesses. Allegations poured in upon Yü Huang, and he ordered the Four Gods of the Heavens and their chief generals to bring Sun to him. The armies laid siege to Hua-kuo Shan, an internet was spread in the heavens, great fights happened, but the resistance of the enemy was as difficult and obstinate as previously.

Lao Chün and Êrh-lang, nephew of Yü Huang, then appeared on the scene. Sun's warriors resisted gallantly, but the forces of Paradise were way too much for them, and at length they were overcome. At this point Sun changed his form, and in spite of the net in the sky managed to find an escape. Fruitless search was made everywhere, till Li T'ien-wang, by the help of his devil-finding mirror, found the quarry and notified Êrh-lang, who rushed off in pursuit. Lao Chün tossed his magic ring on to the head of the fugitive, who stumbled and fell. Quick as lightning, the celestial dog, T'ien Kou, who was in Êrh-lang's service, threw himself on him, bit him in the calf, and caused him to stumble afresh. This was the end of the fight. Sun, surrounded on all sides, was seized and chained. The battle was won.

Sun leaves from Lao Chün's Furnace

The celestial armies now raised the siege, and went back to their quarters. However, a brand-new and unexpected trouble occurred. Yü Huang condemned the criminal to death, but when they went to carry out the sentence the executioners learned that he was invulnerable; swords, iron, fire, even lightning, could make no impression on his skin. Yü Huang, alarmed, asked Lao Chün the reason of this. The latter replied that there was nothing unexpected about it, seeing that the knave had eaten the peaches of life in the garden of Paradise and the tablets of immortality which he had composed. "Hand him over to me," he added. "I will distil him in my furnace of the 8 Trigrams, and extract from his structure the components which render him immortal."

Yü Huang ordered that the detainee be handed over, and in the sight of all he was stopped talking in Lao Chün's alchemical heater, which for forty-nine days was heated white-hot. But at an unguarded moment Sun raised the cover, arised in a rage, seized his magic staff, and threatened to destroy Heaven and eradicate its inhabitants. Yü Huang, at the end of his resources, summoned Buddha, who came and addressed Sun as follows: "Why do you wish to possess yourself of the Kingdom of the Heavens?"

" Have I not power enough to be the God of Paradise?" was the big-headed reply.

" What qualifications have you?" asked Buddha. "Enumerate them."

" My certifications are numerous," replied Sun. "I am invulnerable, I am immortal, I can change myself into seventy-two different forms, I can ride on the clouds of Paradise and pass through the air at will, with one leap I can traverse a hundred and 8 thousand li."

" Well," replied Buddha, "have a match with me; I bet that in one leap you cannot even jump out of the palm of my hand. If you succeed, I will bestow upon you the sovereignty of Paradise."

Broad-jump Competitors

Sun arose into space, flew like lightning in the great vastness, and reached the confines of Paradise, opposite the 5 great red pillars which are the limits of the created universe. On among them he wrote his name, as irrefutable proof that he could reach this severe limitation; this done, he returned triumphant to demand of Buddha the desirable inheritance.

" But, miscreant," said Buddha, "you never ever went out of my hand!"

" How is that?" rejoined Sun. "I reached the pillars of Paradise, and even took the preventative measure of writing my name on one of them as proof in case of need."

" Look then at the words you have written," said Buddha, raising a finger on which Sun read with stupefaction his name as he had engraved it.

Buddha then took Sun, transferred him out of Paradise, and changed his five fingers into the five elements, metal, wood, water, fire, and earth, which instantly formed five high mountains contiguous to each other. The mountains were called Wu Hsing Shan, and Buddha shut Sun up in them.

Conditions of Release

Thus controlled, Sun would not have had the ability to get out of his stone prison but for the intercession of Kuan Yin P' u-sa, who obtained his release on his solemn guarantee that he would serve as guide, philosopher, and good friend to Hsüan Chuang, the priest who was to undertake the challenging journey of 108,000 li to the Western Heaven. This promise, on the whole, he satisfied in the service of Hsüan Chuang throughout the fourteen years of the long journey. Now faithful, now restive and unrestrained, he was always the one to triumph in the end over the eighty-one fantastical adversities which beset them as they journeyed.

Sha Ho-shang

Among the principal of Sun's fellow-servants of the Master was Sha Ho-shang.

He is illustrated wearing a necklace of skulls, the heads of the 9 Chinese deputies sent in previous centuries to find the Buddhist canon, but whom Sha Ho-shang had devoured on the banks of Liu-sha River when they had tried to cross it.

He is also known by the name of Sha Wu-ching, and was originally Grand Superintendent of the Manufactory of Stores for Yü Huang's palace. During a great banquet given on the Peach Festival to all the gods and Immortals of the Chinese Olympus he let fall a crystal bowl, which was smashed to atoms. Yü Huang triggered him to be beaten with 8 hundred blows, drove him out of Paradise, and banished him to earth. He lived on the banks of the Liu-sha Ho, where every seventh day a mystical sword appeared and wounded him in the neck. Having no other means of subsistence, he used to devour the passers-by.

Sha Ho-shang becomes Baggage-coolie

When Kuan Yin travelled through that region on her way to China to find the priest who was predestined to devote himself to the tiresome undertaking of the mission of the spiritual Buddhist books, Sha Ho-shang threw himself on his knees before her and pled her to put an end to all his woes.

The goddess promised that he ought to be delivered by the priest, her envoy, supplied he would engage himself in the service of the pilgrim. On his guaranteeing to do this, and to lead a much better life, she herself ordained him priest. In the end it came about that Hsüan Chuang, when passing the Sha Ho, took him into his suite as coolie to carry his baggage. Yü Huang pardoned him in consideration of the service he was rendering to the Buddhist cause.

Chu Pa-chieh

Chu Pa-chieh is a grotesque, even gross, personage, with all the instincts of animalism. One day, while he was inhabiting the high office of Overseer-general of the Navigation of the Galaxy, he, during a fit of drunkenness, vilely attacked the daughter of Yü Huang. The latter had him beaten with 2 thousand blows from an iron hammer, and exiled to earth to be reincarnated.

Throughout his transition an error was made, and going into the womb of a plant he was born half-man, half-pig, with the head and ears of a pig and a body. He began by killing and eating his mom, and then devoured his little porcine brothers. Then he went to live on the wild mountain Fu-ling Shan, where, equipped with an iron rake, he first robbed and after that ate the travellers who travelled through that area.

Mao Êrh-chieh, who resided in the cavern Yün-chan Tung, engaged him as provider of her individual effects, which she later bequeathed to him.

Accepting the exhortations of the Goddess Kuan Yin, who, at the time of her journey to China, convinced him to lead a less dissolute life, he was ordained a priest by the goddess herself, who gave him the name of Chu (Pig), and the spiritual name of Wu-nêng, 'Hunter after Strength.' This monster was torn down by Sun when the latter was passing over the mountain plant Hsüan Chuang, and he announced himself a disciple of the pilgrim priest. He accompanied him throughout the journey, and was also gotten in the Western Paradise as a benefit for his aid to the Buddhist propaganda.

Hsüan Chuang, the Master

The beginning of this priest was as follows: In the reign of the Emperor T'ai Tsung of the T'ang dynasty, Ch' ên Kuang-jui, a graduate of Hai Chou, in his examination for the doctor's degree came out as chuang yüan, first on the list. Wên Chiao (also named Man-t' ang Chiao), the daughter of the minister Yin K'ai- shan, meeting the young academician, fell for him, and wed him. Several days after the wedding event the Emperor designated Ch' ên Kuang-jui Governor of Chiang Chou (modern Chên-chiang Fu), in Kiangsu. After a short visit to his native town he began to take up his post. His old mom and his wife accompanied him. When they reached Hung Chou his mother fell sick and they were pushed to stay for a time at the Inn of Ten Thousand Flowers, kept by one Liu Hsiao-êrh. Days passed; the sickness did not leave her, and as the time for her son to take control of the seals of office was approaching, he needed to proceed without her.

The Released Carp

Before his departure he saw an angler holding in his hand a fine carp; this he bought for a little amount to provide to his mom. All of a sudden, he noticed that the fish had a very amazing look, and, changing his mind, he let it go in the waters of the Hung Chiang, later telling his mother what he had done. She praised him on his action and guaranteed him that the kind deed would not go unrewarded.

The Chuang Yüan Murdered

Ch' ên Kuang-jui re-entered his boat with his wife and a servant. They were stopped by the chief waterman, Liu Hung, and his assistant. Struck with the great beauty of Ch' ên Kuang-jui's partner, the previous planned a criminal activity which he carried out with the assistance of his assistant. At the dead of night he took the boat to a retired spot, killed Ch' ên and his servant, threw their bodies into the river, seized his main documents of title and the lady he wished for, passed himself off as the real chuang yüan, and acquired the magistracy of Chiang Chou. The widow, who was with child, had two options-- silence or death. Meantime she chose the former. Before she gave birth to her kid, T'ai- po Chin-hsing, the Spirit of the South Pole Star, appeared to her, and said he had been sent by Kuan Yin, the Goddess of Grace, to present her with a son whose popularity would fill the Empire. "Above all," he added, "take every safety measure lest Liu Hung kill the child, for he will definitely do so if he can." When the kid was born the mom, throughout the absence of Liu Hung, determined to expose it instead of see it slain. Accordingly, she wrapped it up carefully in a shirt, and carried it to the bank of heaven River. She then bit her finger, and with the blood wrote a short note mentioning the child's beginning and hid it in its breast. Additionally, she bit off the baby's left little toe, as an enduring mark of identity. No faster had this been done than a gust of wind blew a big plank to the river's edge. The poor mom tied her baby securely to this plank and abandoned it to the mercy of the waves. The waif was brought to the shore of the isle of Chin Shan, on which stands the well-known monastery of Chin-shan Ssŭ, near Chinkiang. The sobs of the baby drew in the attention of an old monk called Chang Lao, who saved it and gave it the name of Chiang Liu, 'Waif of the River.' He reared it with much care, and cherished the note its mom had written with her blood. The child grew up, and Chang Lao made him a priest, naming him Hsüan Chuang on the day of his taking the vows. When he was eighteen years of age, having one day quarrelled with another priest, who had cursed him and reproached him with having neither father nor mother, he, much hurt, went to his protector Chang Lao. The latter said to him: "The time has concerned expose to you your origin." He then told him all, showed him the note, and made him assure to avenge his assassinated father. To this end he was made a roving priest, went to the main Court, and eventually got into touch with his mother, who was still dealing with the prefect Liu Hung. The letter placed in his bosom, and the t-shirt in which he had been covered, easily proved the truth of his declarations. The mother, happy at having found her son, promised to drop in him at Chin Shan. In order to do this, she pretended to be ill, and told Liu Hung that formerly, when still young, she had taken a vow which she had not yet had the ability to satisfy. Liu Hung himself helped her to do so by sending a large gift of cash to the priests, and permitted her to opt for her servants to perform her devotions at Chin-shan Ssŭ. On this second check out, during which she could speak more easily with her child, she wished to see for herself the injury she had made on his foot. This eliminated the last shadow of doubt.

Hsüan Chuang finds his Grandma

She told Hsüan Chuang that he should to start with go to Hung Chou and find his grandmother, previously left at the Inn of 10 Thousand Flowers, and after that on to Ch' ang-an to take to her dad Yin K'ai- shan a letter, putting him in ownership of the chief truths concerning Liu Hung, and praying him to avenge her.

She gave him a stick of incense to take to her mother-in-law. The old woman lived the life of a beggar in a wretched hovel near the city gate, and had ended up being blind from weeping. The priest told her of the terrible death of her son, then touched her eyes with the stick of incense, and her sight was brought back. "And I," she exclaimed, "have so often implicated my son of ingratitude, thinking him to be still alive!" He took her back to the Inn of 10 Thousand Flowers and settled the account, then sped up to the palace of Yin K'ai- shan. Having actually gotten an audience, he showed the minister the letter, and notified him of all that had occurred.

The Killer Performed

The following day a report was revealed to the Emperor, who gave orders for the immediate arrest and execution of the murderer of Ch' ên Kuang-jui.

Yin K'ai- shan went with all rush to Chên-chiang, where he came during the night, surrounded the main home, and took the perpetrator, whom he sent to the spot where he had committed the murder. His heart and liver were torn out and sacrificed to the victim.

The Carp's Thankfulness

Now it occurred that Ch' ên Kuang-jui was not dead after all. The carp released by him was in simple fact no other than Lung Wang, the God of the River, who had been going through his kingdom in that guise and had been caught in the angler's net. On learning that his rescuer had been cast into the river, Lung Wang had saved him, and designated him an officer of his Court. On that day, when his child, marriage partner, and father-in-law were sacrificing the heart of his assassin to his hairs on the river-bank, Lung Wang ordered that he return to earth. His body all of a sudden appeared on the surface of the water, floated to the bank, revived, and came out full of life and health. The joy of the family reunited under such unforeseen circumstances might well be thought of. Ch' ên Kuang-jui returned with his father-in-law to Chên-chiang, where he used up his official post, eighteen years after his nomination to it.

Hsüan Chuang became the Emperor's favourite priest. He was kept in great respect at the capital, and had many honours bestowed upon him, and in the end was chosen for the journey to the Western Paradise, where Buddha face to face gave him the sacred books of Buddhism.

Pai Ma, the White Horse

When he left the capital, Hsüan Chuang had been presented by the Emperor with a white horse to carry him on his long pilgrimage. One day, when he reached Shê-p' an Shan, near a gush, a dragon show upd from the deep river-bed and feasted on both the horse and its saddle. Sun tried fruitless to find the dragon, and at last had to look for the aid of Kuan Yin.

Now Yü Lung San T'ai- tzǔ, child of Ao Jun, Dragonking of the Western Sea, having actually burnt a precious pearl on the roofing of his father's palace, was knocked to Yü Huang, who had him beaten with 3 hundred blows and suspended in the air. He was awaiting death when Kuan Yin handed down her way to China. The regrettable dragon asked for the goddess to have pity on him, whereupon she prevailed upon Yü Huang to spare his life on condition that he worked as steed for her pilgrim on the exploration to the Western Paradise. The dragon was turned over to Kuan Yin, who revealed to him the deep pool in which he was to dwell while waiting for the arrival of the priest. It was this dragon who had feasted on Hsüan Chuang's horse, and Kuan Yin now bade him change himself into a horse of the same colour to carry the priest to his destination. He had the honor of bearing on his back the spiritual books that Buddha gave to T'ai Tsung's deputy, and the very first Buddhist temple built at the capital bore the name of Pai-ma Miao, 'Temple of the White Horse.'

Hazards by the Way

It is natural to expect that numberless interesting experiences should befall such a fascinating quartette, and certainly the Hsi yu chi, which contains a hundred chapters, is full of them. The pilgrims encountered eighty difficulties on the journey out and one on the journey home. The copying are characteristic of the rest.

The Grove of Cypress-trees

The travelers were making their way westward through shining waters and over green hills, where they found limitless luxuriance of greenery and flowers of all colors in profusion. However, the way was long and lonely, and as darkness began with no sign of habitation the Priest said: "Where shall we find a resting-place for the night?" The Monkey responded: "My Master, he who has left home and become a priest must dine on the wind and lodge on the water, lie down under the moon and sleep in the forest; all over is his home; why then ask where shall we rest?" But Pa-chieh, who was the bearer of the pilgrim's baggage, was not pleased with this reply, and tried to get his load transferred to the horse but was silenced when told that the latter's sole duty was to carry the Master.

Nevertheless, the Monkey gave Pai Ma a blow with his rod, triggering him to start forward at a great rate, and in a few minutes from the eyebrow of a hill Hsüan Chuang espied in the distance a grove of cypress-trees, beneath the shade of which was a big enclosure. This appeared a suitable spot to pass the night, so they made towards it, and as they approached observed in the enclosure a spacious and glamorous facility. There being no signs that the spot was then inhabited, the Monkey made his way inside.

A Proposition of Marital relationship

He was met by a girl of charming appearance, who came out of an inner room, and said: "Who is this that endeavors to intrude upon a widow's household?" The situation was humiliating, but the girl showed to be most affable, welcomed them all very heartily, told them how she became a widow and had been left in belongings of riches in abundance, and that she had three daughters, Truth, Love, and Pity by name. She then proceeded to make a proposal of marital relationship, not only on behalf of herself, but of her 3 daughters too. They were 4 guys, and here were 4 ladies; she had mountain lands for fruit-trees, dry lands for grain, flooded fields for rice-- more than five thousand acres of each; horses, oxen, sheep, pigs countless; sixty or seventy plantations; granaries choked with grain; storehouses full of silks and satins; gold and silver enough to last some lifetimes however extravagantly they lived. Why should the four visitors not finish their journey there, and enjoy ever later? The temptation was great, especially as the 3 daughters were girls of exceeding appeal along with adepts at needlework and embroidery, well read, and able to sing sweetly.

But Hsüan Chuang sat just as if listening to frogs after rain, unmoved except by anger that she should attempt to divert him from his incredible purpose, and in the end the lady retired in a rage, slamming the door behind her.

The covetous Pa-chieh, though, uttered himself in favour of accepting the widow's terms. Finding it unrealistic to do so openly, he stole round to the back and protected a personal interview. His individual appearance was against him, but the widow was not entirely uncompliant. She not only amused the visitors but consented to Pa-chieh retiring within the home in the character of a son-in-law, the other three remaining as guests in the guestrooms.

Blind Man's Enthusiast

But a new problem now occurred. If Pa-chieh were wedded to one of the three daughters, the others would feel aggrieved. So the widow proposed to blindfold him with a scarf, and marry him to whichever he had success in catching. But, with the plaster connected over his eyes, Pa-chieh only found himself groping in darkness. "The tinkling noise of female ornaments was all around him, the odour of musk was in his nostrils; like fairy kinds they fluttered about him, but he could no more grasp one than he could a shadow. One way and another he ran till he was too giddy to stand and could only stumble helplessly about."

The prospective mother-in-law then unloosed the bandage, and informed Pa-chieh that it was not her daughters' 'slipperiness,' as he had called it, which prevented their capture, but the severe modesty of each in being generous enough to forgo her claims in favour of among her sisters. Pa-chieh thereupon ended up being really importunate, advising his suit for any among the daughters or for the mom herself or for all three or all four. This was beyond all conscience, but the widow amounted to the emergency, and suggested another solution. Each of her daughters wore a waistlinecoat embroidered in gems and gold. Pa-chieh was to try these on in turn, and to marry the owner of the one which fitted him. Pa-chieh put one on, but as he was connecting the cable round his waist it transformed itself into strong coils of rope which bound him tightly in every limb. He rolled about in agonizing misery, and as he did so the drape of enchantment fell and the beauties and the palace vanished.

Next morning the rest of the party on awakening also found that all had changed and saw that they had been sleeping on the ground in the cypress-grove. On making search they found Pa-chieh bound fast to a tree. They cut him down, to chase after the journey a sadder and smarter Pig, and the butt of many a quip from his fellow-travelers.

The Lotus Cave

When the party left the Elephant Country, seeing a mountain ahead, the Master alerted his disciples to be cautious. Sun said: "Master, say not so; keep in mind the text of the Sacred Book, 'So long as the heart is right there is absolutely nothing to fear.'" After this Sun kept a close watch on Pa-chieh, who, while professing to be on guard, slept most of the time. When they came to Ping-ting Shan they were approached by a woodcutter, who alerted them that in the mountain, which extended for 600 li (200 miles), there was a Lotus Cavern, inhabited by a band of devils under two chiefs, who were lying in wait to feast on the travellers. The woodcutter then vanished. Accordingly, Pa-chieh was ordered to keep watch. But, seeing some hay, he set and went to sleep, and the mountain demons carried him away to the Lotus Cave.

On seeing Pa-chieh, the 2nd chief said: "He is no good; you should enter search of the Master and the Monkey." All this time the Monkey, to safeguard his Master, was walking ahead of the horse, swinging his club up and down and to right and left. The Demon-king saw him from the top of the mountain and said to himself: "This Monkey is well-known for his magic, but I will prove that he is no match for me; I will yet feast on his Master." So, coming down the mountain, he transformed himself into a lame beggar and waited by the roadside. The Master, out of pity, convinced the Monkey to carry him. While on the Monkey's back the Devil, by magic skill, threw Mount Mêru on to Sun's head, but the Monkey warded it off with his left shoulder, and walked on. Then the Devil threw Mount Ô-mei on to Sun's head, and this he warded off with his right shoulder, and walked on, much to the Satanic force's surprise. Finally the Devil triggered T'ai Shan to fall on to his head. This at last stunned the Monkey. Sha Ho-shang now defended the Master with his personnel, which was, though, no match for the Satanic force's stellar sword. The Satanic Force seized the Master and carried him under one arm and Sha Ho-shang under the other to the Lotus Cavern.

The two Demons then planned to take their two most valuable things, a yellow gourd and a jade vase, and try to bottle the Monkey. They arranged to carry them upside down and call out the Monkey's name. If he replied, then he would be inside, and they could seal him up, using the seal of the great Ancient of Days, the resident in the mansion of T'ai Sui.3.

The Monkey under the Mountain.

When the Monkey found that he was being squashed under the mountain he was greatly distressed about his Master, and wept out: "Oh, Master, you provided me from under the mountain before, and trained me in religious belief; how is it that you have brought me to this pass? If you must die, why should Sha Ho-shang and Pa-chieh and the Dragon-horse also suffer?" Then his tears put down like rain.

The spirits of the mountain were amazed at hearing these words. The protector angels of the Five Religions asked: "Whose is this mountain, and who is crushed beneath it?" The local gods replied: "The mountain is ours, but who is under it we do not know." "If you do not know," the angels replied, "we will tell you. It is the Great Holy One, the Equal of Paradise, who rebelled there 5 hundred years ago. He is now transformed, and is the disciple of the Chinese ambassador. How dare you provide your mountain to the Satanic force for such a function?" The defender angels and regional gods then recited some prayers, and the mountain was removed. The Monkey emerged, displaying his spear, and the spirits at once said sorry, saying that they were under enforced service to the Demons.

While they were speaking Sun saw a light approaching and asked what it was. The spirits responded: "This light originates from the Satanic forces' magic treasures. We fear they are bringing them to catch you." Sun then said: "Now we shall have some sport. Who is the Demon-chief's associate?" "He is a Taoist," they responded, "who is always occupied in preparing chemicals." The Monkey said: "Leave me, and I will catch them myself." He then changed himself into a duplicate of the Taoist.

The Magic Gourd.

Sun went to meet the Satanic forces, and in conversation gained from them that they were on their way to catch the famous Monkey, and that the magic gourd and vase were for that purpose. They showed these treasures to him, and explained that the gourd, though little, could hold a 1000 people. "That is absolutely nothing," responded Sun. "I have a gourd which can consist of all the heavens." At this they marvelled greatly, and made a bargain with him, according to which he was to provide his gourd, after it had been tested regarding its capability to contain the heavens, in exchange for their precious gourd and vase. Going up to Paradise, the Monkey obtained authorization to extinguish the light of the sun, moon, and stars for one hour. At midday the next day there was complete darkness, and the Demons actually believed Sun when he mentioned that he had put the whole paradises into his gourd so that there could be no light. They then handed over to the Monkey their magic gourd and vase, and in exchange he gave them his incorrect gourd.

The Magic Rope.

On discovering that they had been tricked, the Demons made complaint to their chiefs, who informed them that Sun, by pretending to be among the Immortals, had outsmarted them. They had now lost 2 out of their 5 magic treasures. There remained three, the magic sword, the magic palm fan, and the magic rope. "Go," said they, "and welcome our dear grandma to come and dine on human flesh." Personating one of the Demons, Sun himself went on this errand. He told the old lady that he wanted her to bring with her the magic rope, with which to catch Sun. She was thrilled, and set out in her chair carried by two fairies.

When they had gone some few li, Sun killed the women, and after that saw that they were foxes. He took the magic rope, and hence had three of the magic treasures. Having actually changed the dead so that they looked like living creatures, he returned to the Lotus Cavern. Lots of little demons came adding, saying that the old woman had been slain. The Demon-king, alarmed, proposed to release the whole party. But his younger brother said: "No, let me fight Sun. If I win, we can eat them; if I struggle, we can let them go."

After thirty bouts Sun lost the magic rope, and the Satanic force lassoed him with it and carried him to the cavern, and took back the magic gourd and vase. Sun now transformed himself into 2 false demons. One he positioned instead of himself in the lasso bound to a pillar, and then went and reported to the 2nd Demon-chief that Sun was struggling hard, and that he needs to be bound with a more powerful rope lest he make his escape. Hence, by this method, Sun acquired possession of the magic rope again. By a similar technique he also returned the magic gourd and vase.

The Master Rescued.
Sun and the Devils now started to wrangle about the respective merits of their gourds, which, each ensured the other, could lock up men and make them follow their desires. Finally, Sun had success in putting one of the Satanic forces into his gourd.

There took place another battle concerning the magic sword and palm fan, during which the fan was scorched to ashes. After more encounters Sun had success in bottling the second Devil in the magic vase, and sealed him up with the seal of the Ancient of Days. Then the magic sword was delivered, and the Demons submitted. Sun returned to the cave, took his Master out, swept the cave tidy of all fiends, and they then started again on their westward journey. On the roadway they met a blind man, who resolved them saying: "Whither away, Buddhist Priest? I am the Ancient of Days. Give me back my magic treasures. In the gourd I keep the pills of immortality. In the vase I keep the water of life. The sword I use to suppress devils. With the fan I stir up interest. With the cable I bind packages. One of these two Devils had charge of the gold crucible. They stole my magic treasures and got away to the ordinary sphere of mortals. You, having actually caught them, are deserving of great benefit." But Sun responded: "You should be seriously punished for allowing your servants to do this evil on the planet." The Ancient of Days responded: "No, without these trials your Master and his disciples could never attain to perfection."

Sun understood and said: "Since you have been available in person for the magic treasures, I return them to you." After receiving them, the Ancient of Days returned to his T'ai Sui mansion in the skies.

The Red Child Satanic Force.
By the autumn the travellers arrived at a great mountain. They saw on the roadway a red cloud which the Monkey thought should be a satanic force. It was in fact a satanic force child who, so as to allure the Master, had had himself bound and connected to the branch of a tree. The kid consistently sobbed out to the passers-by to deliver him. Sun believed that it was a trick; but

the Master could no longer endure the pitiful wails; he ordered his disciples to loose the kid, and the Monkey to carry him.

As they continued on their way the Satanic force triggered a strong whirlwind to emerge, and throughout this he brought off the Master. Sun discovered that the Demon was an old friend of his, who, centuries previously, had vowed himself to eternal friendship. So he consoled his comrades by saying that he felt sure no harm would concern the Master.

A Potential Feast.

Quickly Sun and his companions reached a mountain covered with pine-forests. Here they found the Demon in his cave, intent upon delighting in the Priest. The Satanic force refused to recognize his ancient friendship with Sun, so the 2 came to blows. The Satanic force set fire to every little thing, so that the Monkey might be blinded by the smoke. Therefore he was unable to find his Master. In despair he said: "I should get the aid of some another expert than myself." Pa-chieh was sent to get Kuan Yin. The Satanic force then seized a magic bag, transformed himself into the shape of Kuan Yin, and welcomed Pa-chieh to get in the cave. The simpleton fell straight into the trap and was seized and positioned in the bag. Then the Satanic force appeared in his real form, and said: "I am the beggar kid, and mean to cook you for my dinner. A great man to protect his Master you are!" The Satanic force then summoned 6 of his most doughty generals and ordered them to accompany him to take his father, King Ox-head, to dine off the pilgrim. When they had gone Sun opened the bag, released Pa-chieh, and both followed the six generals.

The Generals Tricked

Sun thought that as the Demon had fooled Pa-chieh, he would play one on his generals. So he rushed on in front of them, and changed himself into the form of King Ox-head. The Satanic force and his generals were invited into his presence, and Red Child said: "If anyone eats of the pilgrim's flesh, his life will be prolonged indefinitely. Now he is caught and I invite you to feast on him." Sun, personifying the dad, said: "No, I cannot come. I am fasting to-day. Furthermore, Sun has charge of the pilgrim, and if any damage befall him it will be the even worse for you, for he has seventy-two magic arts. He can make himself so big that your cavern cannot include him, and he can make himself as little as a fly, a mosquito, a bee, or a butterfly."

Sun then went to Kuan Yin and appealed for assistance. She gave him a bottle, but he found he could not move it. "No," said Kuan Yin, "for all the forces of the ocean are kept in it."

Kuan Yin lifted it with ease, and said: "This dew water is different from dragon water, and can extinguish the fire of enthusiasm. I will send out a fairy with you on your boat. You need no sails. The fairy needs only to blow a little, and the boat moves along with no effort." Finally, the Red Child, having been overcome, repented and begged to be received as a disciple. Kuan Yin got him and blessed him, giving him the name of Steward.

The Demons of Blackwater River

One day the Master all of a sudden exclaimed: "What is that noise?" Sun replied: "You are afraid; you have forgotten the Heart Prayer, according to which we are to be indifferent to all the calls of the 6 senses-- the eye, ear, nose, tongue, body, mind. These are the 6 Burglars. If you cannot reduce them, how do you expect to see the Great Lord?" The Master thought a while and then said: "O disciple, when shall we see the Incarnate Model (Ju Lai) face to face?"

Pa-chieh said: "If we are to meet such demons as these, it will take us a thousand years to get to the West." But Sha Ho-shang rejoined: "Both you and I are silly; if we stand firm and travel on, shoulder to shoulder, we will reach there at last." While therefore talking, they saw right before them a dark river in flood, which the horse could not cross. Seeing a little boat, the Master said: "Let us engage that boat to take us right across." While crossing the river in it, they found that it was a boat sent out by the Satanic force of Blackwater River to allure them in midstream, and the Master would have been killed had not Sun and the Western Dragon pertain to the rescue.

The Slow-carts Country

Having actually crossed the Blackwater River, they travelled westward, facing wind and snow. Unexpectedly they heard a great shout as of ten 1,000 voices. The Master was alarmed, but Sun laughingly went to investigate. Resting on a cloud, he rose up in the air, and saw a city, outside of which there were countless priests and carts loaded with bricks and all types of structure materials. This was the city where Taoists were appreciated, and Buddhists were not wanted. The Monkey, who appeared amongst the people as a Taoist, was informed that the nation was called the Ch' ê Ch' ih, 'Slow-carts Nation,' and for twenty years had been ruled by 3 Taoists who could acquire rain throughout times of dry spell. Their names were Tiger, Deer, and Sheep. They could also command the wind, and change stones into gold. The Monkey said to the two leading Taoists: "I really wonder if I shall be so lucky regarding see your Emperor?" They responded: "We will see to that when we have attended to our company." The Monkey inquired what service the priests could have. "In previous times," they said, "when our King ordered the Buddhists to wish rain, their prayers were not answered. Then the Taoists prayed, and generous showers fell. Ever since all the Buddhist priests have been our servants, and need to carry the structure products, as you see. We must designate them their work, and then will pertain to you." Sun responded: "Never ever mind; I remain in search of an uncle of mine, from whom I have not heard for many years. Perhaps he is here amongst your slaves." They said: "You may see if you can find him."

Restraints on Liberty

Sun went to try to find his uncle. Hearing this, tons of Buddhist priests surrounded him, wanting to be acknowledged as his lost relative. After a while he smiled. They asked him the reason. He said: "Why do you make no progress? Life is not meant for idleness." They said: "We cannot really do anything. We are awfully oppressed." " What power have your masters?" "By using their magic they can call up wind or rain." "That is a little matter," said Sun. "What else can they do?" "They can make the tablets of immortality, and change stone into gold."

Sun said: "These are also small matters; many can do the same. How did these Taoists deceive your King?" "The King attends their prayers night and day, expecting thereby to attain to immortality." "Why do you not leave the place?" "It is impossible, for the King has ordered pictures of us to be hung up everywhere. In all the many prefectures, magistracies, and market-places in Slow-carts Nation are images of the Buddhist priests, and any official who captures a runaway priest is promoted 3 degrees, while every non-official receives fifty taels. The pronouncement is signed by the King. So you see we are helpless." Sun then said: "You might as well die and end all of it."

Immortal for Suffering

They responded: "A great number have died. At one time we numbered more than two 1000. But through deaths and suicides there now stay only about five hundred. And we who remain cannot die. Ropes cannot strangle us; swords cannot cut us; if we plunge into the river we cannot sink; poison does not kill us." Sun said: "Then you are fortunate, for you are all Immortals." "Sadly!" said they, "we are immortal only for suffering. We get poor food. We have only sand to sleep on. But in the night hours spirits appear to us and tell us not to kill ourselves, for an Arhat will come from the East to deliver us. With him, there is a disciple, the Great Holy One, the Equal of Heaven, most effective and tender-hearted. He will put an end to these Taoists and have pity on us Buddhists."

The Saviour of the Buddhists

Inwardly Sun was happy that his popularity had gone abroad. Going back to the city, he met the 2 chief Taoists. They asked him if he had found his relative. "Yes," he replied, "they are all my family members!" They smiled and said: "How is it that you have so many family members?" Sun said: "One hundred are my father's loved ones, one hundred my mother's family members, and the rest my adopted loved ones. If you will let all these priests depart with me, then I will go into the city with you; otherwise I will not enter." "You should be mad to talk to us in this way. The priests were given us by the King. If you had asked for several only, we may have consented, but your demand is completely unreasonable." Sun then asked three times if they would liberate the priests. When they finally refused, he grew extremely upset, took his magic spear from his ear and displayed it in the air, when all their heads fell off and rolled on the ground.

Anger of the Buddhist Priests

The Buddhist priests saw from a distance what had occurred, and screamed: "Murder, murder! The Taoist superintendents are being killed." They surrounded Sun, saying: "These priests are our masters; they go to the temple without visiting the King, and return home without departing of the King. The King is the high priest. Why have you killed his disciples? The Taoist chief priest will certainly accuse us Buddhist priests of the murders. What are we to do? If we go into the city with you, they will make you pay for this with your life."

Sun laughed. "My good friends," he said, "do not trouble yourselves over this matter. I am not the Master of the Clouds, but the Great Holy One, a disciple of the Holy Master from China, going to the Western Paradise to take the sacred books, and have pertained to save you."

" No, no," said they, "this cannot be, for we know him." Sun responded: "Having never ever met him, how can you know him?" They responded: "We have seen him in our dreams. The spirit of the planet Venus has defined him to us and warned us not to slip up." "What description did he give?" asked Sun. They replied: "He has a very hard head, bright eyes, a round, hairy face without cheeks, sharp teeth, popular mouth, a hot temper, and is uglier than the Thunder-god. He has a rod of iron, caused a disruption in Paradise itself, but later repented, and is featuring the Buddhist pilgrim in order to save mankind from catastrophes and suffering." With mixed emotions Sun replied: "My good friends, no doubt you are right in saying I am not Sun. I am only his disciple, who has pertained to discover how to perform his plans. But," he added, pointing with his hand, "is not that Sun coming yonder?" They all looked in the direction in which he had pointed.

Sun bestows Talismans

Sun rapidly changed himself from a Taoist priest and appeared in his natural form. At this they all fell down and worshipped him, asking his forgiveness because their mortal eyes could not acknowledge him. They then asked him to go into the city and force the demons to repent. Sun told them to follow him. He then went with them to a sandy place, cleared two carts and smashed them into splinters, and threw all the bricks, tiles, and wood into a heap, calling upon all the priests to disperse. "Tomorrow," he said, "I am visiting the King and will ruin the Taoists!" Then they said: "Sir, we dare not go any farther, lest they try to take you and trigger trouble." "Have no worry," he responded; "but if you believe so I will give you a charm to safeguard you." He took out some hairs, and gave one to each to hold firmly on the ring finger. "If anyone tries to seize you," he said, "keep tight hold of it, call out 'Great Holy One, the Equal of Heaven,' and I will at once concerned your rescue, even though I be ten 1000 miles away." Some of them tried the beauty, and, sure enough, there he was before them like the God of Thunder. In his hand he held a rod of iron, and he could keep ten 1,000 guys and horses at bay.

The Magic Circle

It was now winter season. The pilgrims were crossing a high mountain by a narrow pass, and the Master was scared of wild monsters. The three disciples bade him fear not, as they were joined, and were all great guys seeking truth. Being cold and hungry they rejoiced to see a great building ahead of them, but Sun said: "It is another devil's trap. I will make a ring round you. Inside that you will be safe. Do not roam outside it. I will go and search for food." Sun returned with his bowl filled with rice, but found that his buddies had got tired of waiting, and had vanished. They had gone forward to the fine structure, which Pa-chieh gotten in. Not a soul was to be seen, but on going upstairs he was terrified to see a human skeleton of tremendous size lying on the floor. At this moment the Satanic force of the house came down on them, bound the Master, and said: "We have been told that if we eat of your flesh our white hair will become black again, and our lost teeth grow anew." So he ordered the little fiends who accompanied him to bind the other ones. This they did, and thrust the pilgrims into a cavern, and after that lay in wait for Sun. It was not long right before the Monkey turned up, when a great battle ensued. In the end, having stopped working, regardless of the exercise of many magic arts, to launch his companions, Sun betook himself to the Spiritual Mountain and besought Ju Lai's help. Eighteen lohan were sent to help him against the Satanic force. When Sun restored the attack, the lohan tossed diamond dust into the air, which blinded the Devil and also half buried him. But, by expert use of his magic coil, he gathered all the diamond dust and brought it back to his cave.

The lohan then advised Sun to seek the help of the Ancient of Days. Accordingly, Sun ascended to the thirty-third Heaven, where was the palace of the god. He there discovered that the Devil was none other than among the god's ox-spirits who had taken the magic coil. It was, in simple fact, the same coil with which Sun himself had at last been subdued when he had rebelled against Heaven.

Help from Ju Lai

The Ancient of Days mounted a cloud and chose Sun to the cavern. When the Devil saw who had come he was horrified. The Ancient of Days then recited an incantation, and the Satanic force surrendered the magic coil to him. On the recitation of a 2nd incantation all his strength left him, and he looked like a bull and was led away by a ring in his nose. The Master and his disciples were then set at liberty, and proceeded on their journey.

The Fire-quenching Fan

In the autumn the pilgrims found themselves in the Ssŭ Ha Li Nation, where everything was red-- red walls, red tiles, red varnish on doors and furniture. Sixty li from this spot was the Flaming Mountain, which lay on their road westward.

An old man they met told them that it was possible to cross the Flaming Mountain only if they had the Magic Iron Fan, which, waved once, quenched fire, waved a second time produced strong wind, and waved a third time produced rain. This magic fan was kept by the Iron-fan Princess in a cave on Ts' ui-yün Shan, 1500 li far-off. On hearing this, Sun mounted a cloud, and in an instant was transferred to the cave. The Iron-fan Princess was one of the lochas (wives and daughters of devils), and the mother of the Red Child Satanic Force, who had ended up being a disciple of Kuan Yin. On seeing Sun she was very mad, and determined to be revenged for the outwitting of her husband, King Ox-head, and for the carrying away of her child. The Monkey said: "If you provide me the Iron Fan I will bring your child to see you." For answer she struck him with a sword. They then fell to battling, the contest lasting a long while, till at length, feeling her strength failing, the Princess took out the Iron Fan and waved it. The wind it raised blew Sun to a distance of 84,000 li and whirled him about like a leaf in a whirlwind. But he quickly returned, reinforced by more magic power lent him by the Buddhist saints. The Princess, though, deceived him by giving him a fan which increased the flames of the mountain instead of satiating them. Sun and his friends needed to pull back more than 20 li, or they would have been burned.

The regional mountain-gods now appeared, bringing beverages, and advising the pilgrims to get the Fan so as to enable them to proceed on their journey. Sun pointed to his fan and said: "Is not this the Fan?" They smiled and said: "No, this is a false one which the Princess has given you." They added: "Originally there was no Flaming Mountain, but when you distress the furnace in Paradise five hundred years ago the fire fell here, and has been burning ever since. For not having actually taken more care in Paradise, we have been set to secure it. The Demon-king Ox-head, though he married the Iocha Princess, deserted her some 2 years ago for the only daughter of a fox-king. They live at Chi-lei Shan, some three 1000 li from here. If you can get the real Iron Fan through his assistance you will have the ability to snuff out the flames, take your Master to the West, save the lives of lots of people round here, and enable us to go back to Paradise once more."

Sun simultaneously installed a cloud and was quickly at Chi-lei Shan. There he met the Fox-princess, whom he upbraided and went after back to her cavern. The Ox-demon came out and became extremely upset with Sun for having terrified her. Sun asked him to return with him to the Iocha Princess and persuade her to give him the Magic Fan, This he refused to do. They then combated three fights, in all of which Sun succeeded. He changed into the Ox-demon's shape and visited the Iocha Princess. She, thinking he was the Ox-demon, gladly received him, and finally gave him the Magic Fan; he then set out to go back to his Master.

The Power of the Magic Fan

The Ox-demon, following after Sun, saw him walking along, joyfully carrying the Magic Fan on his shoulder. Now Sun had forgotten to ask how to make it small, like an apricot leaf, as it was at first. The Ox-demon changed himself into the form of Pa-chieh, and going up to Sun he said: "Brother Sun, I am glad to see you back; I hope you have prospered." "Yes," replied Sun, and described his fights, and how he had fooled the Ox-demon's marriage partner into giving him the Fan. The seeming Pa-chieh said: "You must be extremely exhausted after all your efforts; let me carry the Magic Fan for you." As soon as he had got ownership of it he appeared in his true form, and tried to use it to blow Sun away 84,000 li, for he did not know that the Great Holy One had swallowed a wind-resisting tablet, and was for that reason unmovable. He then put the Magic Fan in his mouth and fought with his 2 swords. He was a match for Sun in all the magic arts, but through the aid of Pa-chieh and the help of the local gods sent by the Master the Monkey had the ability to dominate against him. The Ox-demon changed himself lots of times into a number of birds, but for each of these Sun changed himself into a swifter and more powerful one. The Ox-demon then changed himself into a lot of monsters, like tigers, leopards, bears, elephants, and an ox 10,000 feet long. He then said to Sun, with a laugh: "What can you do to me now?" Sun seized his rod of iron, and cried: "Grow!" He immediately became 100,000 feet high, with eyes like the sun and moon. They fought till the heavens and the earth shook with their onslaughts.

Defeat of the Ox-demon

The Ox-demon being of so strong and dreadful a nature, both Buddha in Heaven and the Taoist Celestial Ruler sent down entire legions of celebrated warriors to help the Master's servant. The Ox-demon tried to escape in every direction, one after the other, but his efforts failed. Finally beat, he was made to assure for himself and his spouse to forfeit their wicked methods and to follow the holy precepts of the Buddhist teaching.

The Magic Fan was provided to Sun, who at the same time proceeded to test its powers. When he waved it once the fires on Flaming Mountain passed away out. When he waved it a second time a gentle breeze emerged. When he waved it a third time refreshing rain fell everywhere, and the pilgrims continued on their method comfort.

The Lovely Ladies

Having actually taken a trip over many mountains, the visitors came to a town. The Master said: "You, my disciples, are always extremely kind, taking round the begging-bowl and getting food for me. To-day I will take the begging-bowl myself." But Sun said: "That is not right; you should let us, your disciples, do this for you." But the Master firmly insisted.

When he reached the village, there was not a man to be seen, but only some lovely ladies. He did not believe that it was right for him to speak with women. On the other hand, if he did not obtain anything for their meal, his disciples would tease him. So, after long hesitation, he moved forward and asked food of them. They invited him to their cavern home, and, having discovered who he was, ordered food for him, but it was all human flesh. The Master informed them that he was a vegetarian, and rose to take his departure, but instead of letting him go they surrounded and bound him, thinking that he would be a fine meal for them next day.

An Awkward Circumstance

Then seven of the ladies went out to bathe in a swimming pool. There Sun, searching for his Master, found them and would have killed them, only he thought it was wrong to kill ladies. So he changed himself into an eagle and brought away their outfits to his nest. This so scared the women that they bent in the pool and did not dare to come out.

But Pa-chieh, also looking for his Master, found the ladies bathing. He changed himself into a fish, which the ladies tried to catch, chasing him hither and thither round the pool. After a while Pa-chieh jumped out of the pool and, appearing in his real form, threatened the ladies for having actually bound his Master. In their scare the ladies left to a structure, round which they spun spiders' threads so heavily that Pa-chieh became entangled and fell. They then escaped to their cave and put on some outfits.

How the Master was Saved

When Pa-chieh at length had disentangled himself from the webs, he saw Sun and Sha Ho-shang approaching. Having discovered what had happened, they feared the women may do some injury to the Master, so they ran to the cave to rescue him. En route they were besieged by the seven dwarf sons of the 7 ladies, who transformed themselves into a swarm of dragon-flies, bees, and other bugs. But Sun took out some hairs and, changing them into seven different swarms of flying insects, destroyed the hostile swarm, and the ground was covered a foot deep with the dead bodies. On reaching the cave, the pilgrims found it had been deserted by the women. They released the Master and made him promise never to beg for food again. Having actually given the guarantee, he installed his horse, and they proceeded on their journey.

The Spiders and the Extinguisher

When they had gone a brief distance they perceived a great building of great architecture ahead of them. It proved to be a Taoist temple. Sha Ho-shang said: "Let us get in, for Buddhism and Taoism teach the exact same things. They differ only in their vestments." The Taoist abbot got them with civility and ordered five cups of tea. Now he was in league with the 7 women, and when the servant had made the tea they put poison in each cup. Sun, though, believed a conspiracy and did not drink his tea. Seeing that the rest had been poisoned, he went and assaulted the sisters, who changed themselves into substantial spiders. They had the ability to spin ropes rather than webs with which to bind their opponents. But Sun assaulted and killed them all.

The Taoist abbot then showed himself in his real form, a satanic force with a 1000 eyes. He joined fight with Sun, and a horrible contest ensued, the outcome being that the Satanic force had a lot of success in putting an extinguisher on his enemy. This was a brand-new technique which Sun did not comprehend. Nevertheless, after attempting fruitless to break out through the top and sides, he started to bore downward, and, finding that the extinguisher was not deep in the ground, he had success in effecting his escape from right below. But he feared that his Master and the others would die of the poison. At this juncture, while he was suffering psychological tortures on their behalf, a Bodhisattva, Girl Pi Lan, came to his rescue. By the help of her magic he broke the extinguisher, gave his Master and fellow-disciples pills to neutralize the toxin, and so rescued them.

Shaving a Whole City

The summer had now gotten here. On the road the pilgrims met an old lady and a little boy. The old lady said: "You are priests; do not go forward, for you are about to pass into the country known as the Country that eradicates Religious belief. The residents have vowed to kill 10 thousand priests. They have already slain that number all but 4 noted ones whose arrival they expect; then their number will be complete."

This old woman was Kuan Yin, with Shên Tsai (Steward), who had concerned provide alerting. Sun thereupon changed himself into a candle-moth and flew into the city to take a look at for himself. He got in an inn, and heard the innkeeper cautioning his visitors to take care of their own clothes and personal belongings when they went to sleep. In order to travel securely through the city, Sun chose that they should all put on turbans and clothes looking like that of the residents. Viewing from the innkeeper's warning that thieving prevailed, Sun stole some clothing and turbans for his Master and pals. Then they all came to the inn at sunset, Sun representing himself as a horse-dealer.

Fearing that in their sleep their turbans would fall off, and their shaven heads be exposed, Sun set up that they should sleep in a cupboard, which he asked the landlady to lock.

During the night burglars came and brought the cabinet away, thinking to find in it silver to buy horses. A watchman saw a lot of guys carrying this cabinet, and became suspicious, and called out the soldiers. The robbers fled, leaving the cabinet in the open. The Master was extremely angry with Sun for getting him into this threat. He feared that at daylight they would be discovered and all be carried out. But Sun said: "Do not be alarmed; I will save you yet!" He changed himself into an ant, and got away from the cabinet. Then he plucked out some hairs and changed them into a 1,000 monkeys like himself. To each he gave a razor and a charm for inducing sleep. When the King and all the officials and their spouses had succumbed to this appeal, the monkeys were to shave their heads.

On the morrow there was a terrible commotion throughout the city, as all the leaders and their families found themselves shaved like Buddhists.

Thus the Master was saved again.

The Return to China

The pilgrims having actually overcome the anticipated eighty problems of their outside journey, there remained only one to be gotten rid of on the homeward way.

They were now returning upon a cloud which had been positioned at their disposal, and which had been credited bear them securely home. But alas! the cloud broke and precipitated them to the earth by the side of a broad river which they should cross. There were no ferry-boats or rafts to be seen, so they were happy to get themselves of the kind offices of a turtle, who offered to take them right across on his back. But in midstream the turtle reminded Hsüan Chuang of a guarantee he had made him when on his outside journey, particularly, that he would intercede for him before the Ruler of the West, and ask his Majesty to forgive all past offences and enable him to resume his mankind again. The turtle asked him if he had remembered to keep his word. Hsüan Chuang responded: "I remember our conversation, but I am sorry to say that under great pressure I rather forgot to keep my promise." "Then," said the turtle, "you are at liberty to ignore my services." He then vanished below the water, leaving the pilgrims floundering in the stream with their precious books. They swam the river, and with great problem managed to save some volumes, which they dried in the sun.

The Travellers Honoured

The pilgrims reached the capital of their nation without more trouble. As soon as they appeared in sight the whole population ended up being greatly excited, and reducing branches of willow-trees went out to meet them. As a mark of unique distinction the Emperor sent his own horse for Hsüan Chuang to ride on, and the pilgrims were escorted with royal honours into the city, where the Emperor and his grateful Court were waiting to get them. Hsüan Chuang's queer trio of converts at first triggered great amusement among the crowds who thronged to see them, but when they learned of Sun's superhuman achievements, and his brave defence of the Master, their amusement was become wondering affection.

But the greatest honours were conferred upon the visitors at a conference of the Immortals presided over by Mi-lo Fo, the Coming Buddha. Dealing With Hsüan Chuang, the Buddha said, "In a previous existence you was among my chief disciples. But for disobedience and for gently esteeming the great teaching your soul was locked up in the Eastern Land. Now a memorial has been presented to me mentioning that you have acquired the True Classics of Redemption, therefore, by your faithfulness, finishing your meritorious labours. You are designated to the high office of Controller of Sacrifices to his Supreme Majesty the Pearly Emperor."

Turning to Sun, the Buddha said, "You, Sun, for creating a disruption in the palace of Paradise, were put behind bars beneath the Mountain of the 5 Aspects, till the fullness of Paradise's disasters had come down upon you, and you had repented and had signed up with the holy faith of Buddha. From that time you have endeavoured to suppress evil and cherish virtue. And on your journey to the West you have ruled over fiends, ghosts, and satanic forces. For your services you are designated God of Victorious Strife."

For his repentance, and for his support to his Master, Chu Pa-chieh, the Pig Fairy, was selected Head Altar-washer to the Gods. This was the highest office for which he was qualified, on account of his inherent greed.

Sha Ho-shang was elevated to the rank of Golden Body Perpetual Saint.

Pai Ma, the white horse who had patiently carried Hsüan Chuang and his problem of books, was led by a god down the Spirit Mountain to the banks of the Pool of Dragon-transformation. Pai Ma plunged in, when he changed at the same time into a four-footed dragon, with horns, scales, claws, and wings complete. From this time he ended up being the chief of the celestial dragon tribe.

Sun's first idea upon receiving his promotion was to get rid of the Head-splitting Helmet. Appropriately he said to his Master, "Now that I am, like yourself, a Buddha, I really want you to ease my head of the helmet you imposed upon me throughout the years of my waywardness." Hsüan Chuang responded, "If you have really become a Buddha, your helmet should have vanished of itself. Are you sure it is still upon your head?" Sun raised his hand, and lo! the helmet was gone.

After this the great assembly separated, and each of the Immortals returned in peace to his own celestial residence.

Chapter 5: Legendary Foxes

The Fox

Amongst the many animals worshipped by the Chinese, those at times seen emerging from caskets or graves naturally hold a prominent place. They are supposed to be the transmigrated souls of deceased people. We should for that reason expect such animals as the fox, stoat, weasel, etc., to be carefully related to the worship of ghosts, spirits, and suchlike creatures, and that they should be the subjects of, or included in, a great deal of Chinese legends. This we find. Of these animals the fox is pointed out in Chinese legendary tradition perhaps more often than any other.

The topic of fox-lore has been handled extensively by my respected coworker, the late Mr Thomas Watters (previously H.B.M. Consul-General at Canton, a man of vast knowing and extreme modesty, insufficiently appreciated in his generation), in the Journal of the North China Branch of the Royal Asiatic Society, viii, 45-- 65, to which the reader is referred for specifics. Usually, the fox is an animal of ill omen, long-lived (living to eight hundred or perhaps a thousand years), with a peculiar virtue in every part of his body, able to produce fire by striking the ground with his tail, cunning, cautious, skeptical, able to see into the future, to transform himself (usually into old guys, or academics, or pretty young maidens), and fond of playing tricks and tormenting humanity.

Fox Legends

Lots of fascinating fox legends are to be found in a collection of stories entitled Liao chai chih i, by P' u Sung-ling (seventeenth century A.D.), part of which was translated into English many years ago by Professor H.A. Giles and appeared in 2 interesting volumes called Strange Stories from a Chinese Studio. These legends were connected to the Chinese author by different people as their own experiences.

Friendship with Foxes

A specific man had a massive stack of straw, as big as a hill, in which his servants, taking what was everyday required for usage, had made quite a large hole. In this hole a fox fixed his home, and would usually show himself to the master of the house under the form of an old man. One day the latter welcomed the master to walk into his abode; he at first decreased but accepted on being pressed; and when he got inside, lo! he saw a long suite of handsome apartments. They then sat down, and exquisitely perfumed tea and wine were brought; but the spot was so bleak that there was no distinction between night and day. By and by, the home entertainment being over, the guest took his leave; and on looking back the lovely rooms and their contents had all disappeared. The old man himself was in the routine of going away in the evening and returning with the very first streaks of morning; and as no one was able to follow him, the master of the home asked him one day whither he went. To this he replied that a good friend invited him to take wine; and then the master asked to be enabled to accompany him, a proposition to which the old man very reluctantly consented. However, he seized the master by the arm, and away they went as though riding on the wings of the wind; and in about the time it requires to prepare a pot of millet they reached a city and walked into a restaurant, where there were certain people drinking together and making a great noise. The old man led his companion to a gallery above, from which they could look down on the feasters below; and he himself decreased and brought away from the tables all kinds of good food and white wine, without seeming seen or observed by any of the business. After a while a man dressed in red garments came forward and laid upon the table some meals of cumquats; 1 the master at once requested the old man to go down and get him some of these. "Ah," replied the latter, "that is an upright man: I cannot approach him." Thereupon the master said to himself, "By therefore seeking the companionship of a fox, I then am deflected from the real course. Henceforth I too will be an upright man." No faster had he formed this resolution than he unexpectedly lost all control over his body and fell from the gallery down amongst the revelers below. These gentlemen were much astonished by his unexpected descent; and he himself, searching for, saw there was no gallery to the house, but only a big beam upon which he had been sitting. He now detailed the entire of the situations, and those present comprised a handbag for him to pay his taking a trip costs; for he was at Yü-t' ai-- a 1000 li from home.

The Marriage Lottery game
A specific laborer, called Ma T'ien- jung, lost his spouse when he was only about twenty years of age, and was too poor to take another. One day, when out hoeing in the fields, he witnessed a nice-looking girl leave the path and come tripping across the furrows towards him. Her face was well painted,2 and she had entirely such a refined appearance that Ma concluded she must have lost her way and started to make some lively remarks in effect. "You go along home," wept the girl, "and I'll be with you by and by." Ma questioned this rather remarkable promise, but she swore and announced she would not break her word; and then Ma went off, telling her that his front door faced the north, and so on. At midnight the girl arrived, and then Ma saw that her hands and face were covered with great hair, that made him presume at once that she was a fox. She did not deny the accusation; and accordingly Ma said to her, "If you really are among those terrific beings you will have the ability to get me anything I really want; and I should be much obliged if you would begin by giving me some cash to relieve my hardship." The girl said she would; and next night, when she came again, Ma asked her where the cash was. "Dear me!" replied she, "I rather forgot it." When she was going away Ma reminded her of what he wanted, but on the following evening she made precisely the same excuse, promising to bring it another day. A few nights later Ma asked her again for the cash, and after that she drew from her sleeve two pieces of silver, each weighing about 5 or 6 ounces. They were both of great quality, with turned-up edges,3 and Ma was really pleased, and stored them away in a cabinet. Some months after this he happened to need some money for use and took out these pieces; but the person to whom he revealed them said they were only pewter, and quickly bit off a portion of among them with his teeth. Ma was much alarmed and put the pieces away straight, seizing the day when night came of abusing the young lady roundly. "It's all your bad luck," retorted she." Real gold would be too much for your inferior destiny." There was an end of that; but Ma went on to say, "I always heard that fox-girls were of exceeding appeal; how is it you are not?" "Oh," responded the girl, "we always adapt ourselves to our business. Now you haven't the luck of an ounce of silver to call your own; and what would you do, for example,

with a lovely princess? My beauty might not be good enough for the upper class; but among your big-footed, bent-backed rustics,4 why, it may safely be called 'exceeding'!"

A few months passed away, and then one day the girl came and gave Ma 3 ounces of silver, saying, "You have typically asked me for cash, but in effect of your misfortune I have always abstained from giving you any. Now, however, your marriage is at hand, and I here give you the expense of a partner, which you may also consider as a parting gift from me." Ma responded that he was not engaged, to which the girl answered that in a few days a go-between would visit him to organize the affair. "And what will she be a lot like?" asked Ma. "Why, as your goals are for 'exceeding' beauty," responded the girl, "naturally she will be possessed of exceeding appeal." "I barely expect that," said Ma; "at any rate, three ounces of silver will not be enough to get a spouse." "Marital relationships," clarified the young lady, "are made in the moon; 5 mortals have absolutely nothing to do with them." "And why must you be going away like this?" asked Ma. "Because," addressed she, "for us to meet only by night is not the proper thing. I had better get you another wife and have done with you." Then when morning came she left, giving Ma a pinch of yellow powder, saying, "In case you are ill after we are separated, this will cure you." Next day, sure enough, a go-between did come, and Ma at once asked what the proposed bride was like; to which the previous responded that she was extremely passable-looking. Four or five ounces of silver was repaired as the marriage present, Ma making no trouble on that score, but declaring he must have a peep at the young lady.6 The go-between said she was a respectable girl, and would never ever enable herself to be seen; nevertheless, it was set up that they should go to the home together, and await a very good chance. So off they went, Ma staying outside while the go-between went in, returning in a little while to tell him it was all right. "A relative of mine lives in the exact same court, and recently I saw the girl sitting in the hall. We have only got to pretend we are visiting my relative, and you will be able to get a look of her." Ma consented, and they accordingly passed through the hall, where he saw the girl sitting down with her head bent forward while some one was scratching her back. She appeared to be all that the go-between had said; but when they came to discuss the cash it appeared that the young lady wanted only one or two ounces of silver, just to purchase herself several outfits, and so on, which Ma thought was a very percentage; so he gave the go-between a present for her trouble, which just finished up the 3 ounces his fox-friend had provided. An advantageous day was chosen, and the young lady came by to his house; when lo! she was humpbacked and pigeon-breasted, with a brief neck like a tortoise, and feet which were totally 10 inches long. The meaning of his fox-friend's remarks then flashed upon him.

The Magnanimous Girl.

At Chin-ling there lived a boy named Ku, who had substantial ability, but was really poor; and having an old mom, he was extremely loth to leave home. So he employed himself in writing or painting7 for people, and gave his mom the profits, going on thus till he was twenty-five years of age without taking a wife. Reverse to their home was another structure, which had long been untenanted; and one day an old lady and a young girl came to inhabit it, but there being no gentleman with them young Ku did not make any inquiries regarding who they were or whence they hailed. Soon later it chanced that just as Ku was getting in the home he observed a girl come out of his mother's door. She was all about eighteen or nineteen, extremely creative and refined-looking, and completely such a girl as one seldom sets eyes on; and when she noticed Mr Ku she did not flee, but appeared rather self-possessed. "It was the girl over the way; she came to obtain my scissors and step," said his mother, "and she told me that there is only her mom and herself. They do not seem to belong to the lower classes. I asked her why she didn't get wed, to which she replied that her mother was old. I should go and call on her to-morrow, and discover how the land lies. If she does not expect way too much, you could take care of her mother for her." So next day Ku's mother went, and found that the girl's mom was deaf, and that they were evidently poor, obviously not having a day's food in the house. Ku's mother asked what their employment was, and the old woman said they relied on for food to her daughter's ten fingers. She then threw out some tips about joining the 2 families, to which the old woman appeared to agree; but, on assessment with her daughter, the latter would not consent. Mrs Ku returned home and told her child, saying, "Perhaps she thinks we are too poor. She does not speak or laugh, is really nice-looking, and as pure as snow; truly no common girl." There ended that; till one day, as Ku was sitting in his research study, up came a really acceptable young fellow, who said he was from a neighbouring town, and engaged Ku to illustrate for him. The two youths soon struck up a firm friendship and met constantly, and later it happened that the complete stranger chanced to see the young lady of over the way. "Who is that?" said he, following her with his eyes. Ku told him, and after that he said, "She is certainly pretty, but rather stern in her appearance." By and by Ku went in, and his mom told him the girl had concerned plead a little rice, as they had had absolutely nothing to eat throughout the day. "She's a great daughter," said his mom, "and I'm really sorry for her. We should try and help them a little." Ku thereupon shouldered a peck of rice, and, knocking at their door, presented it with his mother's compliments. The young lady got the rice, but said absolutely nothing; and then she got into the routine of coming over and assisting Ku's mom with her work and household affairs, nearly just as if she had been her daughter-in-law, for which Ku was extremely grateful to her, and whenever he had anything good he always sent out some of it in to her mom, though the young lady herself never ever once took the trouble to thank him. So things went on until Ku's mom got an abscess on her leg, and lay wincing in misery day and night. Then the girl dedicated herself to the void, waiting on her and giving her medication with such care and attention that at last the sick woman wept out, "O that I could protect such a daughter-in-law as you to see this old body into its grave!" The girl relieved her, and replied, "Your child is a hundred times more filial than I, a poor widow's only daughter." "However even a filial son makes a bad nurse," replied the patient; "besides, I am now drawing towards the night of my life, when my body will be exposed to the mists and the dews, and I am vexed in spirit about our ancestral praise and the continuation of our line." As she was speaking Ku walked in; and his mom, weeping, said, "I am deeply indebted to this young lady; do not forget to repay her goodness." Ku made a low bow, but the young lady said, "Sir, when you were kind to my mother, I did not thank you; why then thank me?" Ku thereupon became more than ever connected to her; but could never ever get her to leave in the tiniest degree from her cold demeanor toward himself. One day, though, he managed to squeeze her hand, upon which she told him never to do so again; and after that for some time he neither saw nor heard anything of her. She had conceived a violent dislike to the young stranger above mentioned; and one evening, when he was sitting talking with Ku, the girl appeared. After a while she snapped at something he said and drew from her robe a flashing knife about a foot long. The young man, seeing her do this, went out in a fright and she after him, only to find that he had disappeared. She then tossed her dagger up into the air, and whish! a streak of light like a rainbow, and something came toppling down with a flop. Ku got a light, and ran to see what it was; and lo! there lay a white fox, head in one place and body in another. "There is your good friend," wept the girl; "I knew he would trigger me to ruin him eventually." Ku dragged it into the house, and said, "Let us wait till to-morrow to talk it over; we will then be calmer." Next day the girl arrived, and Ku asked about her knowledge of the black art; but she told Ku not to trouble himself about such affairs, and to keep it secret or it might be prejudicial to his happiness. Ku then entreated her to consent to their union, to which she replied that she had already been as it were a daughter-in-law to his mother, and there was no requirement to push the thing farther. "Is it since I am poor?" asked Ku. "Well, I am not rich," addressed she, "but the simple fact is I had rather not." She then took her leave, and the next night when Ku went across to their house to try again to persuade her the young lady had disappeared and was never ever seen again.

The Boon-companion

Once upon a time there was a young man called Ch'ê, who was not especially well off, but at the same time extremely fond of his white wine; so much so that without his three stoups of alcohol every night he was quite not able to sleep, and bottles were seldom absent from the head of his bed. One night he had awakened and was turning over and over, when he fancied someone was in the bed with him; but then, thinking it was only the outfits which had slipped off, he put out his hand to feel, and in doing so touched something smooth like a pet cat. Striking a light, he found it was a fox, lying in an inebriated sleep like a dog; and then taking a look at his bottle he saw that it had been cleared. "A boon-companion," said he, laughing, as he avoided stunning the animal, and, covering it up, lay down to sleep with his arm right across it, and the candle light alight so as to see what transformation it might go through. About midnight the fox stretched itself, and Ch'ê wept, "Well, to be sure, you've had a great sleep!" He then drained the clothes and saw a sophisticated young man in a scholar's gown; but the boy jumped up, and, making a low obeisance, returned his host many thanks for not cutting off his head. "Oh," replied Ch'ê, "I am not averse to liquor myself; in simple fact they say I'm way too much provided to it. If you have no objection, we'll be a set of bottle-and-glass buddies." So they put down and went to sleep again, Ch'ê prompting the boy to visit him usually, and saying that they need to have faith in one another. The fox agreed to this, but when Ch'ê woke up in the morning his bedfellow had already vanished. So he prepared a goblet of premium red wine in expectation of his friend's arrival, and at nightfall sure enough he came. They then sat together drinking, and the fox split so many jokes that Ch'ê said he regretted he had not understood him before. "And truly I do not know how to repay your generosity," responded the previous, "in preparing all this good white wine for me." "Oh," said Ch'ê, "what's a pint or so of white wine?-- nothing worth speaking of." "Well," rejoined the fox, "you are only a bad scholar, and money isn't so quickly to be got. I need to see if I can't secure a little wine capital for you." Next night, when he arrived, he said to Ch'ê, "2 miles down towards the south-east you will find some silver lying by the wayside. Go early in the morning and get it." So on the morrow Ch'ê triggered, and actually obtained 2 swellings of silver, with which he bought some choice morsels to help them out with their red wine that evening. The fox now told him that there was a vault in his yard which he ought to open; and when he did so he found therein more than a hundred strings of money.8 "Now then," cried Ch'ê, pleased, "I will have no more stress and anxiety about funds for buying wine with all this in my bag!" "Ah," replied the fox, "the water in a puddle is not endless. I must do something further for you." Some days afterward the fox said to Ch'ê, "Buckwheat is very cheap in the market just now. Something is to be done in that line." Accordingly, Ch'ê bought over forty tons, and thus incurred general ridicule; but by and by there was a bad drought, and all types of grain and beans were ruined. Just buckwheat would grow, and Ch'ê sold his stock at a profit of 1000 percent. His wealth hence began to increase; he bought 2 hundred acres of wealthy land, and always planted his crops, corn, millet, or what not, upon the guidance of the fox secretly given him ahead of time. The fox looked on Ch'ê's wife as a sister, and on Ch'ê's kids as his own; but when subsequently Ch'ê died it never ever came to the home again.

Chapter 6: The Alchemist

At Ch'ang-an there lived a expert named Chia Tzŭ-lung, who one day saw a very refined-looking stranger; and, on investigating about him, learned that he was a Mr Chên who had taken accommodations hard by. Accordingly, Chia called next day and sent out in his card, but did not see Chên, who happened to be out at the time. The same thing happened thrice; and at length Chia engaged someone to watch and let him know when Mr Chên was at home. However, even then the latter would not come forth to receive his visitor, and Chia had to go in and rout him out. The 2 now participated in discussion, and quickly became mutually charmed with one another; and by and by Chia sent off a servant to bring wine from a neighbouring wine-shop. Mr Chên proved himself an enjoyable boon-companion, and when the white wine was almost finished he went to a box and drew from it some wine-cups and a large and lovely jade tankard; into the latter he poured a single cup of white wine, and instantly it was stuffed. They then continued to help themselves from the tankard; but nevertheless, much they took, the contents never ever seemed to lessen. Chia was amazed at this, and asked Mr Chên to tell him how it was done. "Ah," responded Mr Chên, "I tried to avoid making your acquaintance entirely because of your one bad quality-- avarice. The art I practise is a secret understood to the Immortals only: how can I reveal it to you?" "You do me really wrong," rejoined Chia, "in therefore attributing avarice to me. The avaricious, indeed, are always poor." Mr Chên chuckled, and they separated for that day; but from that time they were constantly together, and all event was laid aside between them. Whenever Chia wanted money Mr Chên would draw out a black stone, and, whispering a charm, would rub it on a tile or a brick, which was forthwith changed into a swelling of silver. This silver he would offer to Chia, and it was always just as much as he actually required, neither more nor less; and if ever the latter requested more Mr Chên would rally him on the topic of avarice. Finally, Chia determined to try to get belongings of the stone; and one day, when Mr Chên was sleeping off the fumes of a drinking-bout, he tried to extract it from his outfits. Nevertheless, Chên discovered him at the same time, and announced that they could be friends no more, and next day he left the place entirely. About a year afterward Chia was one day wandering by the riverbank, when he saw a handsome-looking stone, marvellously like that in the ownership of Mr Chên; and he took it at once and brought it home with him. A few days passed away, and suddenly Mr Chên presented himself at Chia's home, and clarified that the stone in question had the property of changing anything into gold, and had been bestowed upon him long in the past by a certain Taoist priest whom he had followed as a disciple. "Sadly!" added he, "I got tipsy and lost it; but prophecy told me where it was, and if you will now restore it to me, I will take care to repay your compassion." "You have divined appropriately," responded Chia; "the stone is with me; but recollect, if you please, that the indigent Kuan Chung10 shared the wealth of his good friend Pao Shu." At this tip Mr Chên said he would give Chia one hundred ounces of silver; to which the latter replied that one hundred ounces was a fair offer, but that he would far earlier have Mr Chên teach him the formula to utter when rubbing the stone on anything, so that he might try the thing once himself. Mr Chên was scared to do this; whereupon Chia cried out, "You are an Immortal yourself; you must know well enough that I would never trick a friend." So Mr Chên was prevailed upon to teach him the formula, and then Chia would have tried the art upon the tremendous stone washing-block11 which was lying near at hand had not Mr Chên took his arm and pled him not to do anything so outrageous. Chia then picked up half a brick and laid it on the washing-block, saying to Mr Chên, "This little piece is not too much, certainly?" Appropriately Mr Chên relaxed his hold and let Chia proceed; which he did by promptly ignoring the half-brick and rapidly rubbing the stone on the washing-block. Mr Chên turned pale when he saw him do this, and made a dash forward to acquire the stone, but it was too late; the washing-block was already a strong mass of silver, and Chia quietly handed him back the stone. "Unfortunately! alas!" cried Mr Chên in anguish, "what is to be done now? For, having hence irregularly conferred wealth upon a mortal, Paradise will definitely penalize me. Oh, if you would save me, give away one hundred coffins12 and one hundred suits of wadded clothes." "My good friend," responded Chia, "my thing in getting money was not to hoard it up like a miser." Mr Chên was thrilled at this; and during the next three years Chia engaged in trade, making sure to satisfy always his promise to Mr Chên. At the expiration of that time Mr Chên himself came back, and, comprehending Chia's hand, said to him, "Trustworthy and noble good friend, when we last parted the Spirit of Happiness impeached me before God,13 and my name was erased from the list of angels. Yet now that you have performed my request that sentence has been rescinded. Go on as you have started, without ceasing." Chia asked Mr Chên what office he filled out Paradise; to which the latter replied that he was only a fox who, by a sinless life, had finally obtained to that clear understanding of the truth which results in immortality. Wine was then brought, and the two good friends enjoyed themselves together since old; and even when Chia had passed the age of ninety years the fox still used to visit him from time to time.

Miscellaneous Legends

The Unnatural People

The Shan hai ching, or Hill and River Classic, includes descriptions of some curious people supposed to populate the areas on the maps represented on the nine tripod vases of the Great Yü, first emperor of the Hsia dynasty.

The Pygmies

The pygmies occupy lots of mountainous regions of the Empire, but are few in number. They are less than nine inches high, but are well formed. They live in thatched homes that look like ants' nests. When they walk out they go in companies of from 6 to 10, joining hands in a line for mutual protection against birds that might carry them away, or other beings that may attack them. Their tone of voice is too low to be differentiated by a normal human ear. They inhabit themselves in working in wood, gold, silver, and gemstones, but a little percentage are tillers of the dirt. They wear clothes of a red colour. The sexes are distinguishable by a slight beard on the men, and long tresses on the ladies, the latter in many cases reaching 4 to five inches in length. Their heads are unduly big, being quite out of proportion to their little bodies. A husband and wife generally tackle hand in hand. A Hakka charcoal-burner once found 3 of the kids playing in his tobacco-box. He kept them there, and later, when he was demonstrating them to a good friend, he laughed so that drops of saliva flew from his mouth and shot 2 of them dead. He then pled his friend to take the 3rd and put it in a place of safety before he should laugh again. His good friend attempted to lift it from the box, but it passed away on being touched.

The Giants

In the Country of the Giants the people are fifty feet in height. Their footprints are 6 feet in length. Their teeth are a lot like those of a saw. Their finger-nails present the appearance of connected claws, while their diet consists completely of raw animal food. Their eyebrows are of such length regarding protrude from the front of the carts in which they ride, big though it is essential for these cars to be. Their bodies are covered with long black hair resembling that of the bear. They live to the sophisticated age of eighteen thousand years. Though cannibals, they never eat members of their own people, confining their extravagance in human flesh chiefly to enemies taken in fight. Their country extends some thousands of miles along certain mountain ranges in North-eastern Asia, in the passes of which they have strong iron gates, simple to close, but tough to open; thus, though their neighbours keep large standing armies, they have thus far never ever been conquered.

The Headless People

The Headless People populate the Long Sheep variety, to which their ancestors were banished in the remote past for an offense against the gods. One of the said forefathers had entered into a debate with the rulers of the heavens, and they in their anger had changed his 2 breasts into eyes and his navel into a mouth, eliminated his head, leaving him without nose and ears, thus cutting him off from smell and sound, and banished him to the Long Sheep Mountains, where with a shield and axe, the only weapons vouchsafed to the people of the Headless Country, he and his posterity were obliged to protect themselves from their enemies and provide their subsistence. This, however, does not in the least appear to have affected their tempers, as their bodies are wreathed in continuous smiles, other than when they thrive their warlike weapons on the method of an enemy. They are not without understanding, because, according to Chinese concepts of physiology, "their bellies have lots of knowledge."

The Armless People

In the Mountains of the Sun and Moon, which are in the Centre of the Great Waste, are the people who have no arms, but whose legs instead outgrow their shoulders. They choose flowers with their toes. They bow by raising the body horizontal with the shoulders, thus turning the face to the ground.

The Long-armed and Long-legged People

The Long-armed People are about thirty feet high, their arms reaching from the shoulders to the ground. Once when a company of explorers was passing through the country which verges on the Eastern Sea they inquired of an old man if he knew whether there were people home beyond the waters. He replied that a fabric garment, in fashion and texture not unlike that of a Chinese coat, with sleeves thirty feet in length, had been found in the sea. The explorers fitted out an exploration, and the discovery of the Long-armed Nation was the outcome.

The natives survive typically on fish, which they obtain by pitching in the water, and taking the fish with their hands instead of with hooks or nets.

The arms of the Long-legged People are of a regular length, the legs are developed to a length representing that of the arms of the Long-armed People.

The country of the latter verge on that of the Long-legs. The practices and food of the 2 are comparable. The difference in their physical structure makes them of shared assistance, those with the long arms being able to take the shellfish of the shallow waters, while those with the long legs take the surface fish from the much deeper regions; thus the 2 gather a harvest otherwise unobtainable.

The One-eyed People and Others

A little to the east of the Country of the Long-legs are to be found the One-eyed People. They have but one eye, rather larger than the regular human eye, put in the centre of the forehead, directly above the nose. Other clans or families have but one arm and one leg, some having a best arm and left leg, others a left arm and right leg, while still other ones have both on the same side, and go in pairs, like shoes. Another species not only has but one arm and one leg, but is of such fashion regarding have but one eye, one nostril, and beard on but one side of the face, there being as it were rights and lefts, the 2 in reality being one, for it is in this way that they pair. The Long-eared Individuals look like Chinese in all except their ears. They live in the far West among mountains and in caves. Their pendant, loose and flabby ears encompass the ground and would hamper their feet in walking if they did not support them on their hands. They are sensitive to the faintest sound. Still another people in this area are identified by having six toes on each foot.

The Feathered People, and so on. The Feathered People are extremely high and are covered with fluffy down. They have wings in place of arms and can fly short distances. On the points of the wings are claws, which work as hands. Their noses are a lot like beaks. Gentle and timid, they do not leave their own country. They have good voices and like to sing ballads. If one dreams to visit this people, he should go far to the south-east and after that inquire. There is also the Land of individuals with Three Faces, who live in the centre of the Great Waste and never die; the Land of the Three-heads, east of the K'un- lun Mountains; the Three-body Country, the inhabitants of which have one head with three bodies, 3 arms and but 2 legs; and yet another where the people have square heads, broad shoulders, and 3 legs, and the stones on the land are all gold and jade.

Individuals of the Punctured Bodies

Another community is said to be composed of people who have holes through their chests. They can be brought about on a pole put through the orifice, or might be conveniently hung upon a peg. They sometimes string themselves on a rope, and hence leave in file. They are harmless people, and eat snakes that they kill with weapons, and they are very long-lived.

The Women's Kingdom

The Women's Kingdom, the nation occupied exclusively by ladies, is said to be surrounded by a sea of less thickness than regular water, so that ships sink on approaching the coasts. It has been reached only by boats brought thither in whirlwinds, and but few of those damaged on its rocks have made it through and gone back to tell of its marvels. The ladies have homes, gardens, and stores. Instead of money they use gems, perforated and strung like beads. They reproduce their kind by sleeping where the south wind blows upon them.

The Land of the Flying Cart

Positioned to the north of the Plain of Great Delight, the Land of the Flying Cart joins the Country of the One-armed People on the south-west and that of the Three-bodied People on the south-east. The inhabitants have but one arm, and an extra eye of large size in the centre of the forehead, making three eyes in all. Their carts, though wheeled, do not run along the ground, but go after each other in mid-air as gracefully as a flock of swallows. The automobiles have a type of winged structure at each end, and the one-armed occupants, each understanding a flag, talk and laugh one to another in great glee during what might be called their aerial entertainment were it not for the fact that it seems to be their sole occupation.

The Expectant Spouse

A curious legend is told concerning a solitary, weird figure which sticks out, rudely weatherworn, from a hill-top in the pass called Shao-hsing Canyon, Canton Province. This point of the pass is called Lung-mên, or Dragon's Mouth, and the hill the Husband-expecting Hill. The figure itself, which is called the Expectant Marriage partner, resembles that of lady. Her bent head and figure down to the waistline are really natural.

The story, commonly understood in this and the neighboring province, runs as follows. Centuries ago a certain poor woman was left by her spouse, who went on a journey into Kwangsi, close by, but in those days considered a wild and distant area, filled with dangers. He promised to return in three years. The time went slowly and sadly past, for she a lot loved her lord, but no spouse appeared. He, ungrateful and unfaithful partner, had fallen for a reasonable one in Kwangsi, a sorceress or witch, who tossed a spell over him and charmed him to his destruction, turning him at length into stone. To this day his figure might be seen standing near a cave nearby the river which is understood by the name of the Apprehended Man Cavern.

The marriage partner, broken by grief at her husband's failure to return, was also turned into a stone, and it is said that a transcendent power will one day bring the couple to life again and reward the ever-faithful wife. The legend gets entire credence from the easy boatmen miserable country people.

The Wild Guys

The wild beasts of the mountain have a king. He is a wild man, with long, thick locks, fiery red in colour, and his body is covered with hair. He is really strong: with a single blow of his substantial fist, he can break large rocks to pieces; he also can bring up the trees of the forest by the root. His flesh is as hard as iron and is invulnerable to the thrusts of knife, spear, or sword. He rides upon a tiger when he leaves his home; he rules over the wolves, leopards, and tigers, and governs all their affairs. Many other wild men, like him in appearance, live in these mountains, but on account of his great strength he alone is king. These wild men kill and eat all human entities they meet, and other hill tribes reside in horror of conference them. Certainly, who of all these mountain people would have been left alive had not some guys, craftier than their fellows, developed a way of overpowering these fierce savages?

This is the technique referred to: On leaving his home the herb-gatherer of the mountains arms himself with two big hollow bamboo tubes which he slips over his wrists and arms; he also brings a jar of very strong white wine. When he meets one of the wild guys he stalls and enables the giant to comprehend him by the arm. As the giant holds him fast, as he supposes, in his firm grasp, he quietly and gradually withdraws one arm from the bamboo cuff, and, taking the pot of white wine from the other hand, rapidly puts it down the throat of the stooping giant, whose mouth is broad open with immoderate laughter at the thought of having caught a victim so easily. The powerful draught of white wine acts simultaneously, triggering the victim to drop to the ground in a dead sleep, whereupon the herb-gatherer either dispatches him summarily with a thrust through the heart, or leaves the intoxicated tyrant to sleep off the influence of his draught, while he returns again to his work of gathering the health-restoring herbs. In this way have the numbers of these wild guys become less and less, until at the present time but few remain.

The Jointed Snake

The people on Ô-mei Shan tell of a fantastic type of serpent that is said to live there. Part of its life is spent among the branches of the trees; if by chance it drops to the ground it separates into 2 or more pieces. These separate sections later on come together again and unify.

A lot of other marvelous and interesting tales relate of this mountain and its inhabitants.

The Casting of the Great Bell

In every province of China there is a legend relating to the casting of the great bell swung in the bell tower of the primary city. These legends are curiously identical in almost every detail. The following is the one current in Peking.

It was in the reign of Yung Lo, the third emperor of the Ming dynasty, that Peking first ended up being the capital of China. Till that duration the 'Child of Paradise' had held his Court at Nanking, and Peking had been of relatively little note. Now, however, on being honored by the 'Spiritual Presence,' stately buildings emerged in all directions for the lodging of the Emperor and his courtiers. Clever guys from all parts of the Empire were drawn in to the capital, and like possessed talent were sure of rewarding employment. About this time the Drum Tower and the Bell Tower were built; both of them as 'look-out' and 'alarm' towers. The Drum Tower was provided with a monster drum, which it still has, of such a size that the thunder of its tones may be heard all over the city, the noise being practically enough to waken the dead.

The Belfry had been completed some time before attempts were made to cast a bell proportionate to the size of the building. At length Yung Lo ordered Kuan Yu, a mandarin of the

2nd grade, who was experienced in casting guns, to cast a bell the sound of which should be heard, on the least alarm, in every part of the city. Kuan Yu at once began the endeavor. He protected the services of a great number of skilled workmen, and gathered immense amounts of material. Months passed, and at length it was announced to the Emperor that everything was all set for the casting. A day was appointed; the Emperor, surrounded by a crowd of courtiers, and preceded by the Court musicians, went to witness the event. At an offered signal, and to the crash of music, the melted metal hurried into the mould prepared for it. The Emperor and his Court then retired, leaving Kuan Yu and his subordinates to wait for the cooling of the metal, which would tell of failure or success. At length the metal was adequately cool to separate the mold from it. Kuan Yu, in breathless uneasiness, quickened to inspect it, but to his mortification and grief discovered it to be honeycombed in a lot of spots. The circumstance was reported to the Emperor, who was naturally vexed at the expenditure of so much time, labor, and money with so unacceptable a result. However, he ordered Kuan Yu to try again.

The mandarin accelerated to obey, and, thinking the failure of the very first attempt should have resulted from some oversight or omission on his part, he watched every detail with redoubled care and attention, completely determined that no overlook or remissness should mar the success of this 2nd casting.

After months of labour the mold was again prepared, and the metal put into it, but again with the exact same result. Kuan Yu was sidetracked, not only at the loss of his track record, but at the certain loss of the Emperor's favour. Yung Lo, when he heard of this 2nd failure, was really wroth, and at once ordered Kuan Yu into his presence, and told him he would give him a 3rd and last trial, and if he did not succeed this time, he would behead him. Kuan Yu went home in a despairing state of mind, asking himself what criminal activity he or any of his forefathers could have committed to have validated this calamity.

Now Kuan Yu had an only daughter, about sixteen years of age, and, having no sons, the whole of his love was centered in this girl, for he had hopes of perpetuating his name and fame through her marital relationship with some deserving young nobleman. Truly she deserved being loved. She had "almond-shaped eyes, like the fall waves, which, gleaming and dancing in the sun, appear to leap up in really happiness and wantonness to kiss the aromatic reeds that grow upon the rivers' banks, yet of such limpid openness that one's form could be seen in their liquid depths just as if reflected in a mirror. These were surrounded by long silken lashes-- now drooping in coy modesty, anon rising up in youthful gaiety and revealing the chuckling eyes but just before hidden below them. Eyebrows like the willow leaf; cheeks of snowy whiteness, yet tinged with the gentlest coloring of the rose; teeth like pearls of the finest water were seen peeping from between half-open lips, so luscious and juicy that they resembled 2 cherries; hair of the jettiest blackness and of the silkiest texture. Her form was such as poets really love to define and painters limn; there was grace and ease in every movement; she appeared to glide instead of walk, so light was she of foot. Add to her other charms that she was skillful in verse-making, exceptional in embroidery, and unequalled in the execution of her household duties, and we have but a faint description of Ko-ai, the stunning daughter of Kuan Yu."

Well might the dad be proud of and love his stunning kid, and she returned his love with all the ardour of her affectionate nature; usually cheering him with her innocent gaiety when he returned from his day-to-day occupations wearied or vexed. Seeing him now return with misery depicted in his countenance, she tenderly asked the cause, not without hope of being the methods of relieving it. When her father told her of his failures, and of the Emperor's risk, she exclaimed: "Oh, my father, be comforted! Heaven will not always be hence unrelenting. Are we not told that 'out of evil cometh great'? These 2 failures will but enhance the splendor of your ultimate success, for success this time need to crown your efforts. I am only a girl, and cannot assist you but with my prayers; these I will daily and per hour offer up for your success; and the prayers of a daughter for a liked moms and dad must be heard." Rather soothed by the endearments of Ko-ai, Kuan Yu again devoted himself to his task with redoubled energy, Ko-ai meanwhile constantly wishing him in his lack, and ministering to his wants when he returned home. One day it struck the maiden to go to a well-known astrologist to establish the reason for these failures, and to ask what means could be taken to prevent a recurrence of them. She thus learned that the next casting would also be a frustration if the blood of a maiden were not mixed with the components. She returned home full of horror at this information, yet inwardly resolving to immolate herself instead of enable her dad to flop. The day for the casting at length came, and Ko-ai requested her father to allow her to witness the event and "to exult in his success," as she laughingly said. Kuan Yu gave his consent, and accompanied by several servants she went, taking up a position near the mould.

Everything was prepared as before. A tremendous concourse put together to witness the third and final casting, which was to result either in honour or degradation and death for Kuan Yu. A dead silence dominated through the large assemblage as the melted metal once again hurried to its location; this was broken by a scream, and a cry, "For my father!" and Ko-ai was seen to throw herself headlong into the seething, hissing metal. Among her servants attempted to take her while in the act of plunging into the boiling fluid, but succeeded only in grasping one of her shoes, which came off in his hand. The father was frenzied, and needed to be kept by force from following her example; he was taken home a raving maniac. The prediction of the astrologist was fulfilled, for, on uncovering the bell after it had cooled, it was found to be perfect, but not a vestige of Ko-ai was to be seen; the blood of a maiden had indeed been instilled with the ingredients.

After a time the bell was suspended by order of the Emperor, and expectation was at its height to hear it called for the first time. The Emperor himself existed. The bell was struck, and far and near was heard the deep tone of its sonorous boom. This indeed was a triumph! Here was a bell surpassing in size and sound any other that had ever been cast! But-- and the surrounding multitudes were horror-struck as they listened-- the heavy boom of the bell was followed by a low wailing seem like the agonized cry of woman, and the word hsieh (shoe) was definitely heard. To this day the bell, each time it is rung, after every boom appears to utter the word 'hsieh,' and people when they hear it shudder and say, "There's poor Ko-ai's voice requiring her shoe."

The Cursed Temple

The reign of Ch' ung Chêng, the last queen of the Ming dynasty, was much struggling both by internal broils and by wars. He was constantly threatened by Tartar hordes from without, though these were usually repelled by the well known general Wu San-kuei, and the nation was perpetually in a state of anarchy and confusion, being overrun by bands of marauding rebels; indeed, so vibrant did these ended up being under a chief called Li Tzŭ-ch' êng that they actually marched on the capital with the avowed objective of positioning their leader on the Dragon Throne. Ch' ung Chêng, on the reception of this shocking news, with no one that he could rely on such an arisency (for Wu San-kuei was absent on an expedition against the Tartars), was at his wits' end. The insurgents were nearly in sight of Peking, and at any moment may show up. Rebellion threatened in the city itself. If he went out boldly to attack the oncoming rebels his own troops might go over to the opponent, or provide him into their hands; if he remained in the city the people would naturally associate it to pusillanimity, and probably open the gates to the rebels.

In this strait he solved to go to the San Kuan Miao, a royal temple located near the Ch' ao-yang Mên, and inquire of the gods as to what he should do, and choose his fate by 'drawing the slip.' If he drew a long slip, this would be a promise, and he would boldly march out to meet the rebels, positive of success; if a middle length one, he would stay silently in the palace and passively await whatever might happen; but if he ought to regrettably draw a short one he would take his own life instead of suffer death at the hands of the rebels.

Upon arrival at the temple, in the presence of the high officers of his Court, the sacrifices were offered up, and the incense scorched, previous to drawing the slip on which hung the fate of an empire, while Ch' ung Chêng himself remained on his knees in prayer. At the conclusion of the sacrificial ceremony the tube containing the bamboo fortune-telling sticks was placed in the Emperor's hand by one of the priests. His courtiers and the attendant priests stood round in breathless thriller, watching him as he swayed television to and fro; at length one fell down to the ground; there was dead silence as it was raised by a priest and handed to the Emperor. It was a brief one! Dismay fell on every one present, nobody daring to break the uncomfortable, terrible silence. After a long pause the Emperor, with a cry of mingled rage and misery, rushed the slip to the ground, exclaiming: "Might this temple built by my forefathers evermore be accursed! Henceforward may every suppliant be denied what he entreats, as I have been! Those who come in sadness, may that sorrow be doubled; in happiness, may that joy be changed to suffering; in hope, may they meet despair; in health, illness; in the pride of life and strength, death! I, Ch' ung Chêng, the last of the Mings, curse it!"

Without another word he retired, followed by his courtiers, proceeded at the same time to the palace, and went straight to the homes of the Empress. The next early morning he and his Empress were found suspended from a tree on Prospect Hill. "In their death they were not divided." The scenes that followed; how the rebels seized the city and were driven out again by the Chinese general, helped by the Tartars; how the Tartars finally succeeded in establishing the Manchu dynasty, are all matters of history. The words used by the Emperor at the temple were prophetic; he was the last of the Mings. The tree on which the monarch of a magnificent

Empire closed his profession and brought the Ming dynasty to an end was ordered to be surrounded with chains; it still exists, and is still in chains. Upward of two hundred and seventy years have passed because that time, yet the temple is standing since old; but the halls that at one time were crowded with worshippers are now silent, no one ever venturing to praise there; it is the resort of the fox and the bat, and people in the evening pass it shudderingly--" It is the cursed temple!"

The Maniac's Mite

An intriguing story is told of a woman called Ch'ên, who was a Buddhist nun celebrated for her virtue and austerity. Between the years 1628 and 1643 she left her nunnery near Wei-hai city and set out on a long journey for the purpose of gathering memberships for casting a brand-new image of the Buddha. She roamed through Shantung and Chihli and finally reached Peking, and there-- subscription-book in hand-- she stationed herself at the great south gate in order to take toll from those who wished to lay up for themselves treasures in the Western Paradise. The first passer-by who took any notice of her was a pleasant maniac. His dress was made of coloured shreds and patches, and his general appearance was wild and tacky. "Wither away, nun?" he asked. She clarified that she was gathering subscriptions for the casting of a great picture of Buddha, and had come all the way from Shantung. "Throughout my life," said the madman, "I was ever a generous provider." So, taking the nun's subscription-book, he headed a page with his own name (in very large characters) and the amount subscribed. The amount in question was two money, equivalent to a small portion of a farthing. He then turned over the two little coins and went on his way.

In course of time the nun returned to Wei-hai-wei with her subscriptions, and the work of casting the image was properly begun. When the time had come for the procedure of smelting, it was observed that the copper stayed hard and intractable. Once again and again the furnace was fed with fuel, but the shapeless mass of metal remained firm as a rock. The head workman, who was a guy of large experience, offered an explanation of the secret. "An offering of great value must be missing," he said. "Let the collection-book be examined so that it might be seen whose membership has been kept." The nun, who was standing by, immediately produced the madman's money, which on account of its minute value she had not taken the trouble to hand over. "There is one cash," she said, "and there is another. Certainly, the offering of these must have been an act of the greatest benefit, and the provider must be a holy man who will some day attain Buddhahood." As she said this she tossed the two cash into the middle of the cauldron. Great bubbles arose and burst, the metal melted and ran like the sap from a tree, limpid as streaming water, and in several moment the work was accomplished and the new Buddha successfully cast.

Chapter 7: The City-god of Yen Ch' êng

The following story of the Ch' êng-huang P' u-sa of Yen Ch' êng (Salt City) is told by Helena von Poseck in the East of Asia Publication, vol. iii (1904), pp. 169-- 171. This legend is also related of some other cities in China.

The Ch' êng-huang P' u-sa is, as already noted, the tutelary god of a city, his position in the unseen world responsing to that of a chih hsien, or district magistrate, among men, if the city under his care be a hsien; but if the city hold the rank of a fu, it has (or used to have until just recently) two Ch' êng-huang P' u-sas, one a prefect, and the other a district magistrate. One part of his duty consists of sending out little satanic forces to carry off the spirits of the passing away, of which spirits he afterward serves as ruler and judge. He is supposed to exercise unique care over the k' u kuei, or spirits which have no descendants to praise and offer sacrifices to them, and on the celebration of the Seventh Month Celebration he is brought round the city in his chair to maintain order amongst them, while the people provide food to them, and burn paper currency for their benefit. He is also brought in procession at the Ch' ing Ming Festival, and on the first day of the tenth month.

The Ch' êng-huang P' u-sa of the city of Yen Ch' êng is in the exceptionally regrettable dilemma of having no skin to his face, which fact is therefore represented:

Once upon a time there lived at Yen Ch' êng an orphan boy who was raised by his uncle and aunt. He was just going into upon his teens when his aunt lost a gold hairpin, and implicated him of having stolen it. The boy, whose conscience was clear in the matter, idea of a plan by which his innocence might be proved.

" Let us go to-morrow to Ch' êng-huang P' u-sa's temple," he said, "and I will there swear an oath before the god, so that he may manifest my innocence."

They appropriately fixed to the temple, and the boy, solemnly addressing the idol, said:

" If I have taken my aunt's gold pin, may my foot twist, and may I fall as I go out of your temple door!"

Unfortunately for the poor suppliant! As he stepped over the threshold his foot twisted, and he fell down to the ground. Naturally, everybody was securely convinced of his guilt, and what could the poor boy say when his own attract the god therefore turned against him?

After such a proof of his depravity his auntie had no room in her house for her orphan nephew, neither did he himself wish to stick with people who thought him of theft. So he left the home which had protected him for years, and roamed out alone into the cold tough world. Lots of a hardship did he experience, but with rare pluck he persevered in his studies, and at the age of twenty odd years ended up being a mandarin.

In course of time our hero went back to Yen Ch' êng to visit his uncle and auntie. While there he betook himself to the temple of the divine being who had dealt so barely with him, and prayed for a revelation as to the location of the lost hairpin. He slept that night in the temple, and was rewarded by a vision in which the Ch' êng-huang P' u-sa told him that the pin would be found under the floor of his auntie's house.

He quickened back, and informed his family members, who took up the boards in the spot indicated, and lo! there lay the long-lost pin! The women of the house then bore in mind that the pin had been used in pasting together the various layers of the soles of shoes, and, when night came, had been carelessly left on the table. No doubt rats, drawn in by the odor of the paste which clung to it, had carried it off to their domains under the floor.

The young mandarin joyfully returned to the temple, and offered sacrifices by way of thanksgiving to the Ch' êng-huang P' u-sa for bringing his innocence to light, but he could not refrain from addressing to him what one is gotten rid of to consider a well-merited reproach.

" You made me fall down," he said, "and so led people to believe I was guilty, and now you accept my presents. Aren't you embarrassed to do such a thing? You have no face!"

As he uttered the words all the plaster fell from the face of the idol, and was smashed into pieces.

From that day forward the Ch' êng-huang P' u-sa of Yen Ch' êng has had no skin on his face. People have tried to repair the disfigured countenance, but in vain: the plaster always falls off, and the face remains skinless.

Some try to defend the Ch' êng-huang P' u-sa by saying that he was not in the house on the day when his temple was gone to by the accused boy and his relatives, and that among the little devils employed by him in carrying off dead individuals' spirits out of sheer mischief committed a prank on the poor boy.

In that case it is certainly hard that his skin should so persistently affirm against him by declining to remain on his face!

The Origin of a Lake.
In the city of Ta-yeh Hsien, Hupei, there is a large sheet of water called the Liang-ti Lake. The people of the district give the following account of its beginning:

About five hundred years ago, during the Ming dynasty, there was no lake where the broad waters now spread out. A prospering hsien city stood in the center of a populous country. The city was noted for its wickedness, but amidst the wicked population stayed one exemplary woman, a rigorous vegetarian and a follower of all greats. In a vision of the night it was exposed to her that the city and area would be damaged by water, and the sign promised was that when the stone lions in front of the yamên wept tears of blood, then destruction was near at hand. Like Jonah at Nineveh, the female, known to-day simply as Niang-tzŭ, paced the streets of the city, warning all of the coming catastrophe. She was laughed at and looked upon as mad by the negligent people. A pork-butcher in the town, a noted wag, took some pig's blood and sprinkled it round the eyes of the stone lions. This had the preferred impact, for when Niang-tzŭ saw the blood she fled from the city amid the jeers and laughter of the inhabitants. Right before tons of hours had passed, though, the face of the sky darkened, a magnificent earthquake shook the country-side, there was a great subsidence of the earth's surface area, and the waters of the Yangtzŭ River flowed into the hollow, burying the city and towns out of sight. But a spot of ground on which the good female stood, after getting away from the doomed city, stayed at its regular level, and it stands to-day in the middle of the lake, an isle called Niang-tzŭ, a place at which boats anchor in the evening, or to which they fly for shelter from the storms that sweep the lake. They are saved to-day because of one good woman helped by the gods so long ago.

As a proof of the truth of the above story, it is asserted that on clear days traces of the buried city may be seen, while sometimes a fisherman casting his net hauls up some home utensil or antique of bygone days.

Miao Creation Legends.

If the Miao have no written records, they have lots of legends in verse, which they learn to repeat and sing. The Hei Miao (or Black Miao, so called from their dark chocolate-coloured clothes) treasure poetical legends of the Creation and of a deluge. These are made up in lines of 5 syllables, in stanzas of unequal length, one interrogative and one responsive. They are sung or recited by two persons or 2 groups at feasts and festivals, usually by a group of youths and a group of maidens. The legend of the Creation starts:

Who made Heaven and earth?
Who made pests?
Who made guys?
Made male and made woman?
I who speak don't know.

Heavenly King made Paradise and earth,
Ziene made bugs,
Ziene made guys and devils,
Made male and made woman.
How is it you do not know?

How made Paradise and earth?
How made bugs?
How made men and devils?
Made male and made female?
I who speak don't know.

Heavenly King was smart,
Spat a ton of spittle into his hand,
Clapped his hands with a sound,
Produced Heaven and earth,
High grass made bugs,
Stories made men and devils,
Made male and made woman.
How is it you do not know?

The legend proceeds to mention how and by whom the heavens were propped up and how the sun was made and repaired in its spot, but the continuation is exceedingly ridiculous.

The legend of the Flood is another very ridiculous composition, but it is fascinating to keep in mind that it tells of a great deluge. It begins:

Who came to the bad disposition,
To send fire and burn the hill?
Who came to the bad disposition,
To send out water and destroy the earth?
I who sing don't know.

Zie did. Zie was of bad personality,
Zie sent fire and burned the hill;
Thunder did. Thunder was of bad personality,
Thunder sent out water and damaged the earth.
Why don't you know?

In this story of the flood only two persons were saved in a large bottle gourd used as a boat, and these were A Zie and his sister. After the flood the brother wished his sister to become his partner, but she objected to this as not appertaining. At length she proposed that one should take the upper and one the nether millstone and going to opposite hills should set the stones rolling to the valley between. If these should be found in the valley effectively adjusted one above the other she would be his wife, but not if they came to rest apart. The boy, considering it unlikely that two stones hence rolled down from opposite hills would be found in the valley one upon another, while pretending to accept the test suggested, secretly positioned two other stones in the valley one upon the other. The stones rolled from the hills were lost in the high wild grass, and on coming down into the valley A Zie called his sister to come and see the stones he had put. She, though, was not satisfied, and suggested as another test that each needs to take a knife from a double sheath and, going again to the opposite hill-tops, hurl them into the valley below. If both these knives were found in the sheath in the valley she would marry him, but if the knives were found apart they would live apart. Once again the brother surreptitiously positioned 2 knives in the sheath, and, the experiment ending as A Zie wished, his sister became his spouse. They had one child, a misshapen thing without arms or legs, which A Zie in great anger killed and cut to pieces. He threw the pieces all over the hill, and next morning, on waking up, he found these pieces transformed into women and men; hence the earth was populated again.

The Imagine the South Branch

The dawn of Chinese romantic literature must be credited the period between the 8th and tenth centuries of our era, when the cultivation of the liberal arts got encouragement at the hands of sovereigns who had reunited the Empire under the sway of a single ruler, and whose conquests and far-off embassies attracted representatives from every Asiatic country to their superb Court. It was during this duration that the large bulk of Indian literature was effectively attacked by a host of Buddhist translators, and that the alchemists and mechanicals of Central Asia, Persia, and the Byzantine Empire introduced their varied acquirements to the knowledge of the Chinese. With the flow of new learning which hence gained admittance to certify the freezing and monotonous growing of the old classics and their analysts, there came also a motivation to indulgence in the license of creativity in which it is unrealistic to error the impact of Western minds. While the Sanskrit fables, on the one hand, passed into a Chinese gown, and added to the coloring of the popular mythology, the legends which distributed from mouth to mouth in the dynamic Arabian exchanges found, in like way, an echo in the heart of China. Side by side with the mechanical efforts of rhythmical composition which constitute the national ideal of poetry there started, throughout the middle period of the T'ang dynasty (A.D. 618--907), to grow up a class of romantic tales in which the kinship of ideas with those that distinguish the products of Arabian genius is too significant to be overlooked. The unnoticeable world appears suddenly to open right before the Chinese eye; the relations of the sexes overstep for a moment the chilling limitation enforced by the traditions of Confucian etiquette; a certain degree of liberty and geniality is, in a word, for the first time and only for a quick period infused into the intellectual expression of a nation hitherto closely constrained in the bonds of a narrow pedantry. It was at this period that the drama started to flourish, and the bacteria of the modern author's art made their very first appearance. Amongst the works of imagination dating from the period in question which have boiled down to the present day there is maybe none which better shows the impact of an exotic fancy upon the sober and methodical authorship of the Chinese, or which has left a more enduring mark upon the language, than the little tale which is given in translation in the following pages.

The Nan k' o mêng, or Imagine the South Branch (as the title, actually translated, should read), is the work of an author named Li Kung-tso, who, from an incidental mention of his own experiences in Kiangsi which appears in another of his tales, is ascertained to have lived at the beginning of the ninth century of our age. The nan k' o, or South Branch, is the portion of a huai tree (Sophora Japdonica, a tree popular in China, and rather looking like the American locust-tree) in which the adventures told in the story are supposed to have taken place; and from this narrative of a dream, remembering more than among the incidents stated in the Arabian Nights, the Chinese have obtained a metaphor to enhance the vocabulary of their literature. The equivalent of our own expression "the baseless material of a vision" is in Chinese nan k' o chih mêng-- a dream of the south branch.

Ch' un-yü Fên gets in the Locust-tree

Ch' un-yü Fên, a native of Tung-p' ing, was by nature a gallant who had little regard for the proprieties of life, and whose primary pleasure was found in extravagance in wine-bibbing in the society of boon-companions. At one time he held a commission in the army, but this he lost through his dissipated conduct, and from that time he more than ever gave himself approximately the enjoyments of the wine-cup.

One day-- it was in the ninth moon of the seventh year of Chêng Yüan (A.D. 791)-- after drinking greatly with a celebration of good friends under a wide-spreading old locust-tree near his home, he had to be carried to bed and there left to recuperate, his friends saying that they would leave him while they went to bathe their feet. The moment he put down his head he fell straight into a deep sleep. In his dream appeared to him two men dressed in purple, who kneeling down informed him that they had been sent out by their master the King of Huai-an (' Locust-tree Peace') to request his presence. Unconsciously he rose, and, arranging his gown, followed his visitors to the door, where he saw a varnished chariot drawn by a white horse. On each side were varied seven attendants, by whom he was assisted to mount, whereupon the carriage drove away, and, going out of the garden gate, gone through a hole in the trunk of the locust-tree already mentioned. Filled with awe, but too much scared to speak, Ch' un-yü saw that he was going by hills and rivers, trees and roads, but of quite a different kind from those he was accustomed to. A few miles brought them to the walls of a city, the method to which was lined with men and vehicles, who fell back at once the moment the order was given. Over the large gate of the city was a pavilion on which was written in gold letters "The Capital of Huai-an." As he went through, the guard turned out, and a mounted officer, shouting that the spouse of the King's daughter had gotten here, revealed to him the way into a hall where he was to rest some time. The room contained fruits and flowers of every description, and on the tables was laid out an excessive display of refreshments.

While Ch' un-yü still remained lost in awe, a cry was raised that the Prime Minister was coming. Ch' un-yü got up to meet him, and the two got one another with every demonstration of politeness.

He marries the King's Daughter

The minister, looking at Ch' un-yü, said: "The King, my master, has brought you to this remote region so as to give his daughter in a marriage to you." "How could I, a poor worthless lowlife," replied Ch' un-yü, "have ever desired such honour?" With these words both proceeded towards the audience-chamber, passing through a hall lined with soldiers, among whom, to his great joy and surprise, Ch' un-yü recognized an old good friend of his former drinking days, to whom he did not, though, then venture to speak; and, following the Prime Minister, he was ushered into the King's presence. The King, a man of worthy bearing and enforcing stature, was dressed in plain silk, a jewelled crown reposing on his head. Ch' un-yü was so awe-stricken that he was powerless even to look up, and the attendants on either side were required to remind him to make his prostrations. The King, addressing him, said: "Your father, little as my kingdom is, did not disdain to promise that you should wed my daughter." Ch' un-yü could not utter a word; he merely lay prostrate on the ground. After several moment he was reclaimed to his apartments, and he busied his thoughts in trying to discover what all this meant. "My dad," he said to himself, "battled on the northern frontier, and was taken prisoner; but whether his life was saved or not I do not know. It might be that this affair was settled while he was in those distant areas."

That exact same night preparations were made for the marriage; and the spaces and passages were filled with damsels who passed and repassed, filling the air with the sound of their dancing and music. They surrounded Ch' un-yü and kept up a continuous fire of witty remarks, while he sat there gotten rid of by their grace and appeal, not able to say a word. "Do you keep in mind," said among them, coming near Ch' un-yü, "the other day when with the Lady Ling-chi I was listening to the service in the yard of a temple, and while I, with all the other girls, was resting on the window step, you came near us, talking rubbish, and trying to get up a flirtation? Don't you remember how we connected a handkerchief on the stem of a bamboo?" Then she continued: "Another time at a temple, when I tossed down 2 gold hairpins and an ivory box as an offering, you asked the priest to let you take a look at the important things, and after admiring them for a very long time you turned towards me, and said that neither the presents nor the donor were of this world; and you would like to know my name, and where I lived, but I would not tell you; and then you looked on me so tenderly, and could not take your eyes off me. You remember this, without doubt?" "I have ever valued the recollection in my heart; how could I possibly forget it?" was Ch' un-yü's reply, whereat all the maidens exclaimed that they had never expected to see him in their midst on this happy celebration.

At this moment 3 guys came near Ch' un-yü and mentioned that they had been selected his ministers. He stepped up to one of them and asked him if his name was not Tzŭ-hua. "It is," was the reply; whereupon Ch' un-yü, taking him by the hands, recalled to him their old friendship, and questioned him as to how he had found his way to this area. He then proceeded to ask him if Chou-pien was also here. "He is," responded the other, " and holding extremely high office; he has often used his influence on my behalf."

As they were talking, Ch' un-yü was summoned to the palace, and as he passed within, a curtain in front of him was drawn aside, divulging a girl of about fourteen years of age. She was called the Princess of the Golden Stem, and her dazzling beauty was well in keeping with her incomparable grace.

He writes to his Dad

The marital relationship was celebrated with all majesty, and the young couple grew fonder from day to day. Their facility was maintained in baronial style, their primary amusement being the chase, the King himself regularly inviting Ch' un-yü to join him in searching explorations to the Tortoise-back Hill. As they were returning one day from among these excursions, Ch' un-yü said to the King: "On my marriage day your Majesty told me that it was my father's desire that I should embrace your daughter. My father was worsted in fight on the frontier, and for seventeen years we have had no news of him. If your Majesty understands his location, I would beg consent to go and see him."

" Your dad," replied the King, "is regularly heard about; you may send him a letter; it is not required to go to him." Accordingly a letter and some presents were got ready and sent, and in due time a reply was gotten, in which Ch' un-yü's dad asked a lot of questions about his relations, his child's profession, but manifested no desire that the latter should pertain to him.

He takes Office

One day Ch' un-yü's wife asked him if he would not like to hold office. His answer was to the influence that he had always been a wanderer, and had no experience of main affairs, but the Princess promised to give him her assistance, and found celebration to speak on the based on her dad. In consequence the King one day told Ch' un-yü that he was not satisfied with the state of affairs in the south of his area, that the present ruler was old and ineffective, and that he would be pleased if he would proceed thither. Ch' un-yü acquiesced the King's commands, and inwardly congratulated himself that such good fortune should have befallen a rover like him. He was supplied with a superb attire, and goodbye entertainments were given in his honour.

Right before leaving he acknowledged to the King that he had no great self-confidence in his own powers, and suggested that he should be allowed to take with him Chou-pien and Tzŭ-hua as commissioners of justice and finance. The King gave his consent, and issued the required guidelines. The day of departure having actually shown up, both the King and the Queen came to see Ch' un-yü and his marriage partner off, and to Ch' un-yü the King said: "The province of Nan-k' o is wealthy and fertile; and the residents are brave and prosperous; it is by generosity that you should rule them." To her daughter the Queen said: "Your husband is violent and keen on wine. The duty of a partner is to be kind and submissive. Act well toward him, and I will have no stress and anxiety. Nan-k' o, it is actually true, is not very far-- only one day's journey; still, in parting from you my tears will flow." Ch' un-yü and his bride waved a goodbye, and were whirled away toward their destination, reaching Nan-k' o the exact same evening.

Once settled in the spot, Ch' un-yü set himself to become completely familiarized with the good manners and customs of the people, and to ease distress. To Chou-pien and Tzŭ-hua he confided all questions of administration, and in the course of twenty years a great enhancement was to be observed in the affairs of the province. The people revealed their gratitude by setting up a monument to his honour, while the King conferred upon him an estate and the dignity of a title, and in acknowledgment of their services promoted Chou-pien and Tzŭ-hua to extremely high posts. Ch' un-yü's kids also shared their dad's rewards; the 2 sons were given office, while the two daughters were betrothed to members of the royal family. There remained nothing which could contribute to his fame and success.

He meets with Disasters

About this duration the state of T'an-lo made an attack on the province of Nan-k'o. The King at the same time commanded that Chou-pien ought to continue at the head of 30,000 men to drive away the opponent. Chou-pien, loaded with confidence, assaulted the foe, but sustained a devastating defeat, and, hardly leaving with his life, returned to the capital, leaving the intruders to ransack the nation and retire. Ch'un-yü tossed Chou-pien into prison, and asked the

King what penalty should be visited upon him. His Majesty given Chou-pien his pardon; but that same month he died of illness.

Several days later Ch'un-yü's spouse also fell ill and died, whereupon he begged permission to resign his post and return to Court with his marriage partner's remains. This demand was given, and Tzŭ-hua was appointed in his stead. As Ch'un-yü, sad and dejected, was leaving the city with the funeral cortège, he found the roadway lined with people giving loud expression to their grief, and nearly all set to stop his taking his departure.

He returns Home

As he neared the capital the King and Queen, dressed in mourning, were waiting for the bier in tears. The Princess, after a posthumous title had been conferred upon her, was buried with great splendor several miles to the east of the city, while Ch' un-yü stayed in the capital, living in such state, and gaining so much impact, that he delighted the King's enviousness; and when it was predicted, by ways of signs in the heavens, that destroy threatened the kingdom, that its inhabitants would be swept away, and that this would be the work of an alien, the prediction appeared to point to enthusiastic designs on the part of Ch' un-yü, and means were taken to keep him under restraint.

Ch' un-yü, conscious that he had consistently filled a high office for several years, felt considerably grieved by these calumnies-- a result which the King could not keep away from noticing. He accordingly sent out for Ch' un-yü, and said: "For more than twenty years we have been connexions, though my poor daughter, regrettably, has not been spared to be a buddy to you in old age. Her mother is now looking after her kids; your own home you have not seen for several years; return to see your good friends; your kids will be cared for, and in 3 years you will see them again." "Is not this my home? Whither else am I to go?" was Ch' un-yü's reply. "My good friend," the King said laughingly, "you are a human being; you do not come from this place." At these words Ch' un-yü appeared to fall into a deep swoon, and he remained unconscious for a long time, after which he began to recall some glances of the far-off past. With tears in his eyes he pled that he might be allowed to go back to his home, and, saying farewell, he departed.

Outside the palace he found the exact same two authorities in purple outfits who had led the way so many years ago. A conveyance was also there, but this time it was a simple bullock-cart, with no outriders. He took the same road as before, and observed the same hills and streams. The two authorities were by no means enforcing this time, and when he asked how far was his destination they went on to hum and whistle and disregarded him. At last they travelled through an opening, and he acknowledged his own town, exactly as he had left it. The 2 authorities desired him to get down and walk up the steps before him, where, much to his horror, he saw himself resting in the porch. He was too much bedazed with horror to advance, but the two authorities called out his name sometimes, and upon this he awoke. The servants were dynamic about the home, and his two companions were still cleaning their feet. Every little thing was as he had left it, and the lifetime he had lived in his dream had occupied just a couple of moment. Calling out to his two friends, he made them follow him to the locust-tree, and explained the opening through which he had started his journey in dream-land.

An axe was sent for, and the interior of the trunk thrown open, whereupon a series of galleries was laid bare. At the root of the tree a mound of earth was found, in shape like a city, and swarming with ants. This was the capital of the kingdom in which he had resided in his dream. A balcony surrounded by a guard of ants was the home of the King and Queen, two winged bugs with red heads. Twenty feet or so along another gallery was found an old tortoise-shell covered with a thick growth of moss; it was the Tortoise-back Hill of the dream. In another direction was found a little mound of earth round which was coiled a root fit like a dragon's tongue; it was the grave of the King's daughter, Ch' un-yü's partner in the vision. As he recalled each event of the dream he was much impacted at discovering its equivalent in this nest of ants, and he refused to allow his companions to disrupt it further. They changed every little thing as they had found it; but that night a storm of wind and rain came, and next early morning not a vestige of the ants was to be seen. They had all disappeared, and here was the fulfilment of the warning in the dream, that the kingdom would be swept away.

Ch' un-yü Regenerate

At this time Ch' un-yü had not seen Chou-pien and Tzŭ-hua for some ten days. He sent a messenger to make inquiries about them, and the news he revived was that Chou-pien was dead and Tzŭ-hua lying ill. The short lived nature of man's existence revealed itself to him as he recalled the achievement of these two guys in the ant-world. From that day he ended up being a reformed man; beverage and dissipation were put aside. After 3 years had expired he passed away, therefore giving influence to the pledge of the ant-king that he should see his kids once again at the end of 3 years.

Why the Jung People have Heads of Pet dogs

The wave of conquest which swept from north to south in the earliest periods of Chinese history1 left on its way, like small isles in the ocean, certain remnants of aboriginal tribes which survived and continued to exist despite the sustained hostile attitude of the flood of alien settlers around them. When stationed at Foochow I saw the settlements of among these people which resided in the mountainous nation not very many miles inland from that spot. They were those of the Jung tribe, the members of which wore on their heads a large and strange headgear constructed of bamboo splints resting on a peg inserted in the chignon at the back of the head, the weight of the structure in front being counterbalanced by a pad, serving as a weight, connected to the end of the splints, which forecasted as far down as the middle of the shoulders. This structure was covered by a mantilla of red cloth which, when not rolled up, hid the entire head and face, The following legend, associated to me on the area, clarifies the beginning of the unusual headdress.

2 Tribes at War

In early times the Chief of a Chinese people (another version says an Emperor of China) was at war with the Chief of another people who came to assault his territory from the west. The Western Chief so badly defeated the Chinese army that none of the generals or soldiers could be caused to renew hostilities and endeavour to drive the opponent back to his own country. This distressed the Chinese Chief very much. As a last resort he provided a pronouncement guaranteeing his daughter in marriage to anybody who would bring him the head of his enemy, the Chief of the West.

The Chief's Promise

The people in the palace talked much of this promise made by the Chief, and their conversation was listened to by a great big white pet dog belonging to one of the generals. This dog, having pondered the matter well, waited till midnight and after that took over to the camping tent of the opponent Chief. The latter, in addition to his guard, was asleep; or, if the guard was not, the pet dog succeeded in avoiding him in the darkness. Getting in the tent, the dog nibbled through the Chief's neck and carried his head off in his mouth. At dawn he put it at the Chinese Chief's feet, and waited for his reward. The Chief was soon able to verify the fact that his enemy had been slain, for the headless body had triggered so much consternation in the hostile army that it had already begun to pull away from Chinese area.

A Weird Agreement

The pet dog then reminded the Chief of his pledge, and requested his daughter's hand in marriage. "But how," said the Chief, "can I possibly wed my daughter to a dog?" "Well," responded the dog, "will you agree to her wedding me if I change myself into a guy?" This seemed a safe promise to make, and the Chief concurred. The dog then stipulated that he needs to be placed under a big bell and that nobody should move it or look into it for a space of 280 days.

The Chiefs Curiosity

This was done, and for 279 days the bell remained unmoved, but on the 280th day the Chief could limit his interest no longer, and tilting up the bell saw that the pet dog had changed into a guy all except his head, the last day being required to complete the change. Nevertheless, the spell was now broken, and the outcome was a guy with a dog's head. Since it was the Chief's fault that, through his over-inquisitiveness, the dog could not become entirely a man, he was obliged to keep his guarantee, and the wedding appropriately happened, the bridegroom's head being veiled for the celebration by a red mantilla.

The Origin of a Customized

Sadly the fruit of the union took more after their father than their mom, and though comely of limb had extremely ugly functions.2 They were for that reason required to continue to wear the head-covering adopted by their dad at the marriage ceremony, and this became so much an crucial part of the tribal costume that not only has it been used since by their descendants, but a change of headgear has ended up being synonymous with a modification of husbands or a divorce. One account says that at the original bridal event the bride-to-be wore the red mantilla to prevent her seeing her spouse's ugly features, and that is why the headdress is worn by the ladies and not by the guys, or more typically by the previous than the latter, though other ones say that it was originally used by the ugly kids of both sexes.

CPSIA information can be obtained
at www.ICGtesting.com
Printed in the USA
LVHW010735251122
733813LV00001B/33

9 781704 376578